The War *of the* Worlds

A Kaplan SAT Score-Raising Classic

By H. G. Wells

KAPLAN

PUBLISHING

New York • Chicago

Contributing Editors: Mark Ward, Annette Riffle, Brandon Jones
Editorial Director: Jennifer Farthing
Editor: Patrick Kennedy
Production Editor: Dave Shaw
Production Artist: Ellen Gurak
Cover Designer: Carly Schnur

Published by Kaplan Publishing, a division of Kaplan, Inc.
888 Seventh Ave.
New York, NY 10106

Printed in the United States of America

November 2006
06 07 08   10 9 8 7 6 5 4 3 2 1

ISBN 13: 978-1-4195-9328-4
ISBN 10: 1-4195-9328-5

How to Use This Book

H. G. Wells's stories are not only filled with action and adventure—they're also filled with SAT words! Now Kaplan makes it as easy as 1-2-3 for you to learn these vocabulary words as you read the stories.

On the right-hand pages you'll find the text of H. G. Wells's *The War of the Worlds* with words **bolded** throughout. These bolded words are frequently found on the SAT. On the left-hand pages, Kaplan defines these SAT words, and gives you the part of speech, pronunciation, and synonyms for each word—everything you need to know to improve your vocabulary and to ace the SAT.

Some of the most challenging vocabulary words found in *The War of the Worlds* aren't likely to appear on the SAT, but we thought you might want to learn those, too. That's why we've <u>underlined</u> them throughout the text and added their definitions to a glossary at the end of the book. After all—you never know where they might pop up next!

So what are you waiting for? Start reading!

TABLE OF CONTENTS

Book One
The Coming of the Martians

Book Two
The Earth under the Martians

But who shall dwell in these worlds if they be inhabited? . . . Are we or they Lords of the World? . . . And how are all things made for man?

—KEPLER
(quoted in *The Anatomy of Melancholy*)

BOOK ONE

THE COMING OF THE MARTIANS

keenly (<u>keen</u> lee) *adv.* with great sensitivity and intelligence Synonyms: perceptively, sharply, shrewdly

scrutinise or **scrutinize** (<u>scrooh</u> tihn ized) *v.* **-ing, -ed** to inspect carefully Synonyms: examine, inspect, critique

transient (<u>trahn</u> zee ihnt) *adj.* passing with time, present only briefly Synonyms: temporary, transitory, ephemeral, fleeting

complacency (kuhm <u>play</u> sehn see) *n.* a feeling of self-satisfaction Synonyms: contentment, amenity, comfort

serene (suh <u>reen</u>) *adj.* calm in the face of disturbance or difficulty Synonyms: unruffled, composed, self-possessed

terrestrial (tuh <u>rehs</u> stree uhl) *adj.* 1. of or relating to the earth Synonyms: earthbound, earthlike 2. prosaic, mundane Synonyms: worldly, common, profane

enterprise (<u>ehn</u> tuhr prize) *n.* an undertaking of some complexity and scope Synonyms: adventure, campaign, endeavor

CHAPTER ONE

THE EVE OF THE WAR

No one would have believed in the last years of the nineteenth century that this world was being watched **keenly** and closely by intelligences greater than man's and yet as mortal as his own; that as men busied themselves about their various concerns they were **scrutinised** and studied, perhaps almost as narrowly as a man with a microscope might scrutinise the **transient** creatures that swarm and multiply in a drop of water. With infinite **complacency** men went to and fro over this globe about their little affairs, **serene** in their assurance of their empire over matter. It is possible that the infusoria under the microscope do the same. No one gave a thought to the older worlds of space as sources of human danger, or thought of them only to dismiss the idea of life upon them as impossible or improbable. It is curious to recall some of the mental habits of those departed days. At most **terrestrial** men fancied there might be other men upon Mars, perhaps inferior to themselves and ready to welcome a missionary **enterprise**. Yet across the gulf of space, minds that are to our minds as ours are to those of the beasts that perish, intellects vast and cool and unsympathetic, regarded this earth with envious eyes, and slowly and surely drew their

disillusionment (dih suhl <u>loo</u> zhuhn mehnt) *n.* disappointment; freedom from illusion   Synonyms: chagrin, disenchantment, despondency

nebular (<u>neh</u> byoo luhr) *adj.* indistinct, resembling a gaseous cloud   Synonyms: amorphous, scattered

hypothesis (high <u>pah</u> thuh sihs) *n.* a theoretical explanation that will then be tested through experimentation   Synonyms: theory, assumption, premise, presupposition

molten (<u>mole</u> tehn) *adj.* made liquid through heating   Synonyms: melted, liquefied

animated (<u>ann</u> ihm ate ehd) *adj.* full of life   Synonyms: lively, vibrant, expressive

superficial (soo puhr <u>fih</u> shuhl) *adj.* 1. of or near the outermost layer   Synonyms: surface   2. concerned only with the obvious   Synonyms: shallow, depthless, cursory

secular (<u>seh</u> kyoo luhr) *adj.* 1. unrelated to religious matters   Synonyms: lay, unsacred, earthly   2. occurring once in an age or century

attenuate (uh <u>tehn</u> yoo ate ehd) *v.* -ing, -ed to reduce or cut, to make more fine or thin   Synonyms: thin, deflate, constrict, abate

periodically (peer ee <u>odd</u> ihk lee) *adj.* occurring at regular intervals   Synonyms: recurrently, intermittently

inundate (<u>ihn</u> uhn date) *v.* -ing, -ed   to overwhelm   Synonyms: flood, submerge, engulf

temperate (<u>tehm</u> pehr iht) *adj.* mild, moderate   Synonyms: restrained, fair, controlled plans against us. And early in the twentieth century came the great **disillusionment**.

The planet Mars, I scarcely need remind the reader, revolves about the sun at a mean distance of 140,000,000 miles, and the light and heat it receives from the sun is barely half of that received by this world. It must be, if the **nebular hypothesis** has any truth, older than our world; and long before this earth ceased to be **molten**, life upon its surface must have begun its course. The fact that it is scarcely one seventh of the volume of the earth must have accelerated its cooling to the temperature at which life could begin. It has air and water and all that is necessary for the support of **animated** existence.

Yet so vain is man, and so blinded by his vanity, that no writer, up to the very end of the nineteenth century, expressed any idea that intelligent life might have developed there far, or indeed at all, beyond its earthly level. Nor was it generally understood that since Mars is older than our earth, with scarcely a quarter of the **superficial** area and remoter from the sun, it necessarily follows that it is not only more distant from time's beginning but nearer its end.

The **secular** cooling that must someday overtake our planet has already gone far indeed with our neighbour. Its physical condition is still largely a mystery, but we know now that even in its equatorial region the midday temperature barely approaches that of our coldest winter. Its air is much more **attenuated** than ours, its oceans have shrunk until they cover but a third of its surface, and as its slow seasons change huge snowcaps gather and melt about either pole and **periodically inundate** its **temperate** zones. That last stage of exhaustion, which to us is still incredibly remote, has become a present-day problem for the inhabitants of Mars. The immediate pressure of necessity has brightened their intellects, enlarged their powers, and hardened their hearts. And looking across space with instruments, and intelligences such as we have

eloquent (<u>eh</u> loh kwent) *adj.*   well-spoken   Synonyms: articulate, expressive, fluent

fertility (fuhr <u>tihl</u> iht ee) *n.*   ability to produce or grow   Synonyms: fruitfulness, productiveness, richness

alien (<u>ale</u> lee ihn) *adj.*   strange, foreign   Synonyms: exotic, separate, unusual

incessant (ihn <u>sehss</u> ant) *adj.*   continuing without pause or interruption   Synonyms: constant, unceasing, interminable, eternal

inferior (ihn <u>fee</u> ree uhr) *adj.*   lower in quality or esteem   Synonyms: lesser, secondary, subordinate

unanimity (yoon nah <u>nihm</u> ih tee) *n.*   state of complete agreement   Synonyms: accord, harmony, congruence

fluctuate (<u>fluhk</u> shoo ate) *v.* **-ing, -ed**   to vary with irregularity   Synonyms: oscillate, waver, swing scarcely dreamed of, they see, at its nearest distance only 35,000,000 of miles sunward of them, a morning star of hope, our own warmer planet, green with vegetation and grey with water, with a cloudy atmosphere **eloquent** of **fertility**, with glimpses through its drifting cloud wisps of broad stretches of populous country and narrow, navy-crowded seas.

And we men, the creatures who inhabit this earth, must be to them at least as **alien** and lowly as are the monkeys and lemurs to us. The intellectual side of man already admits that life is an **incessant** struggle for existence, and it would seem that this too is the belief of the minds upon Mars. Their world is far gone in its cooling and this world is still crowded with life, but crowded only with what they regard as **inferior** animals. To carry warfare sunward is, indeed, their only escape from the destruction that, generation after generation, creeps upon them.

And before we judge of them too harshly we must remember what ruthless and utter destruction our own species has wrought, not only upon animals, such as the vanished bison and the dodo, but upon its inferior races. The Tasmanians, in spite of their human likeness, were entirely swept out of existence in a war of extermination waged by European immigrants, in the space of fifty years. Are we such apostles of mercy as to complain if the Martians warred in the same spirit?

The Martians seem to have calculated their descent with amazing subtlety—their mathematical learning is evidently far in excess of ours—and to have carried out their preparations with a well-nigh perfect **unanimity**. Had our instruments permitted it, we might have seen the gathering trouble far back in the nineteenth century. Men like Schiaparelli watched the red planet—it is odd, by-the-bye, that for countless centuries Mars has been the star of war—but failed to interpret the **fluctuating** appearances of the markings they mapped so well. All that time the Martians must have been getting ready.

illuminate (ih <u>loom</u> ihn ate) *v.* **-ing, -ed**   1. to make brighter with light   Synonyms: highlight, lighten, kindle   2. to clarify, explain   Synonyms: enlighten, elucidate, express, edify

peculiar (pih <u>kyoo</u> lee uhr) *adj.*   out of the ordinary, odd   Synonyms: abnormal, curious, singular, unconventional

palpitate (<u>pahl</u> pih tate) *v.* **-ing, -ed**   to quiver, tremble   Synonyms: flutter, pulsate

incandescent (ihn kahn <u>dehss</u> ihnt) *adj.*   emitting light, often through being heated   Synonyms: brilliant, effulgent, luminous, phosphorescent

colossal (kuh lah suhl) *adj.*   extremely large, immense   Synonyms: enormous, gargantuan, titanic

singularly (<u>sihn</u> gyoo luhr lee) *adj.*   in a unique or novel manner   Synonyms: curiously, conspicuously, peculiarly

vigil (<u>vih</u> juhl) *n.*   a watch, kept especially during sleeping hours   Synonyms: surveillance, stakeout, lookout

feeble (<u>fee</u> buhl) *adj.*   lacking in strength, weak   Synonyms: enervated, impotent, sapless

oblong (<u>ahb</u> long) *adj.*   elongated in one direction   Synonyms: rectangular, elliptical, ovaloid

profundity (proh fuhn dih tee) *n.*   depth of meaning   Synonyms: discernment, penetration, sagacity

CHAPTER 1—THE EVE OF THE WAR

During the opposition of 1894 a great light was seen on the **illuminated** part of the disk, first at the Lick Observatory, then by Perrotin of Nice, and then by other observers. English readers heard of it first in the issue of *Nature* dated August 2. I am inclined to think that this blaze may have been the casting of the huge gun, in the vast pit sunk into their planet, from which their shots were fired at us. **Peculiar** markings, as yet unexplained, were seen near the site of that outbreak during the next two oppositions.

The storm burst upon us six years ago now. As Mars approached opposition, Lavelle of Java set the wires of the astronomical exchange **palpitating** with the amazing intelligence of a huge outbreak of **incandescent** gas upon the planet. It had occurred towards midnight of the twelfth; and the spectroscope, to which he had at once resorted, indicated a mass of flaming gas, chiefly hydrogen, moving with an enormous velocity towards this earth. This jet of fire had become invisible about a quarter past twelve. He compared it to a **colossal** puff of flame suddenly and violently squirted out of the planet, "as flaming gases rushed out of a gun."

A **singularly** appropriate phrase it proved. Yet the next day there was nothing of this in the papers except a little note in the *Daily Telegraph*, and the world went in ignorance of one of the gravest dangers that ever threatened the human race. I might not have heard of the eruption at all had I not met Ogilvy, the well-known astronomer, at Ottershaw. He was immensely excited at the news, and in the excess of his feelings invited me up to take a turn with him that night in a scrutiny of the red planet.

In spite of all that has happened since, I still remember that **vigil** very distinctly: the black and silent observatory, the shadowed lantern throwing a **feeble** glow upon the floor in the corner, the steady ticking of the clockwork of the telescope, the little slit in the roof—an **oblong profundity** with the stardust streaked across it. Ogilvy moved

transverse (<u>trahnz</u> vuhrs) *adj.* positioned across, cross-wise Synonyms: crossways, diagonally, aslant

recede (ree <u>seed</u>) *v.* **-ing, -ed** to draw back, retreat Synonyms: abate, decline, diminish, subside

vacancy (<u>vay</u> can see) *n.* an unoccupied space or position Synonyms: gap, vacuity, void

unfathomable (uhn <u>fah</u> thuhm uh buhl) *adj.* impossible to understand or measure Synonyms: immeasurable, boundless

calamity (cah <u>lahm</u> uh tee) *n.* a disastrous event Synonyms: catastrophe, cataclysm

unerring (uhn <u>ehr</u> ring) *adj.* free of mistakes or errors Synonyms: exact, faultless, impeccable, unfailing

siphon (<u>sie</u> fuhn) *n.* a tube used to take in or expel water Synonyms: channel, pump, funnel about, invisible but audible. Looking through the telescope, one saw a circle of deep blue and the little round planet swimming in the field. It seemed such a little thing, so bright and small and still, faintly marked with **transverse** stripes, and slightly flattened from the perfect round. But so little it was, so silvery warm—a pin's-head of light! It was as if it quivered, but really this was the telescope vibrating with the activity of the clockwork that kept the planet in view.

As I watched, the planet seemed to grow larger and smaller and to advance and **recede**, but that was simply that my eye was tired. Forty millions of miles it was from us—more than forty millions of miles of void. Few people realise the immensity of **vacancy** in which the dust of the material universe swims.

Near it in the field, I remember, were three faint points of light, three telescopic stars infinitely remote, and all around it was the **unfathomable** darkness of empty space. You know how that blackness looks on a frosty starlight night. In a telescope it seems far profounder. And invisible to me because it was so remote and small, flying swiftly and steadily towards me across that incredible distance, drawing nearer every minute by so many thousands of miles, came the Thing they were sending us, the Thing that was to bring so much struggle and **calamity** and death to the earth. I never dreamed of it then as I watched; no one on earth dreamed of that **unerring** missile.

That night, too, there was another jetting out of gas from the distant planet. I saw it. A reddish flash at the edge, the slightest projection of the outline just as the chronometer struck midnight; and at that I told Ogilvy and he took my place. The night was warm and I was thirsty, and I went stretching my legs clumsily and feeling my way in the darkness, to the little table where the **siphon** stood, while Ogilvy exclaimed at the streamer of gas that came out towards us.

minute (mie <u>noot</u>) *adj.*   especially small, barely noticeable   Synonyms: miniscule, tiny, diminutive, infinitesimal

speculation (spehk yool <u>ay</u> shihn) *n.*   a conclusion or explanation reached by conjecture or approximation   Synonyms: guess, hypothesis, supposition

scoff (skahf) *v.* **-ing, -ed**   to express scorn or derision   Synonyms: belittle, disdain, flout, gibe, jeer, ridicule

vulgar (<u>vuhl</u> guhr) *adj.*   indecent, marked by lack of taste and manners   Synonyms: base, boorish, coarse, common, unrefined

adjacent (uhd <u>jae</u> sihnt) *adj.*   positioned next to, beside   Synonyms: adjoining, contiguous, bordering

fluctuate (<u>fluhk</u> shoo ate) *v.* **-ing, -ed**   to vary with irregularity   Synonyms: oscillate, waver, swing

periodical (peer ee <u>ahd</u> ihk uhl) *n.*   a publication issued with regularity   Synonyms: journal, magazine, newspaper, quarterly

CHAPTER 1—THE EVE OF THE WAR

That night another invisible missile started on its way to the earth from Mars, just a second or so under twenty-four hours after the first one. I remember how I sat on the table there in the blackness, with patches of green and crimson swimming before my eyes. I wished I had a light to smoke by, little suspecting the meaning of the **minute** gleam I had seen and all that it would presently bring me. Ogilvy watched till one, and then gave it up; and we lit the lantern and walked over to his house. Down below in the darkness were Ottershaw and Chertsey and all their hundreds of people, sleeping in peace.

He was full of **speculation** that night about the condition of Mars, and **scoffed** at the **vulgar** idea of its having inhabitants who were signalling us. His idea was that meteorites might be falling in a heavy shower upon the planet, or that a huge volcanic explosion was in progress. He pointed out to me how unlikely it was that organic evolution had taken the same direction in the two **adjacent** planets.

"The chances against anything manlike on Mars are a million to one," he said.

Hundreds of observers saw the flame that night and the night after about midnight, and again the night after; and so for ten nights, a flame each night. Why the shots ceased after the tenth no one on earth has attempted to explain. It may be the gases of the firing caused the Martians inconvenience. Dense clouds of smoke or dust, visible through a powerful telescope on earth as little grey, **fluctuating** patches, spread through the clearness of the planet's atmosphere and obscured its more familiar features.

Even the daily papers woke up to the disturbances at last, and popular notes appeared here, there, and everywhere concerning the volcanoes upon Mars. The seriocomic **periodical** *Punch*, I remember, made a happy use of it in the political cartoon. And, all unsuspected, those missiles the Martians had fired at us drew earthward, rushing now at a pace of many miles a second

swift *adj.* able to move with great speed Synonyms: fleet, prompt, quick, rapid

petty (<u>peh</u> tee) *adj.* concerned with unimportant or trivial matters Synonyms: frivolous, inconsequent, secondary, trifling

jubilant (<u>joo</u> bihl ehnt) *adj.* marked by joyfulness and exultation Synonyms: elated, euphoric, rejoicing, thrilled

excursionist (ehks <u>cuhr</u> zhuhnn ihst) *n.* an individual visiting sites of interest Synonyms: tourist, voyager, wayfarer

shunt *v.* **-ing, -ed** to switch to an alternate course, push aside Synonyms: deflect, deter, redirect

tranquil (<u>trank</u> wihl) *adj.* free of disturbance, conflict, or tension Synonyms: composed, placid, serene, calm, unruffled

through the empty gulf of space, hour by hour and day by day, nearer and nearer. It seems to me now almost incredibly wonderful that, with that **swift** fate hanging over us, men could go about their **petty** concerns as they did. I remember how **jubilant** Markham was at securing a new photograph of the planet for the illustrated paper he edited in those days. People in these latter times scarcely realise the abundance and enterprise of our nineteenth-century papers. For my own part, I was much occupied in learning to ride the bicycle, and busy upon a series of papers discussing the probable developments of moral ideas as civilisation progressed.

One night (the first missile then could scarcely have been 10,000,000 miles away) I went for a walk with my wife. It was starlight and I explained the Signs of the Zodiac to her, and pointed out Mars, a bright dot of light creeping zenithward, towards which so many telescopes were pointed. It was a warm night. Coming home, a party of **excursionists** from Chertsey or Isleworth passed us singing and playing music. There were lights in the upper windows of the houses as the people went to bed. From the railway station in the distance came the sound of **shunting** trains, ringing and rumbling, softened almost into melody by the distance. My wife pointed out to me the brightness of the red, green, and yellow signal lights hanging in a framework against the sky. It seemed so safe and **tranquil**.

CHAPTER TWO

THE FALLING STAR

Then came the night of the first falling star. It was seen early in the morning, rushing over Winchester eastward, a line of flame high in the atmosphere. Hundreds must have seen it, and taken it for an ordinary falling star. Albin described it as leaving a greenish streak behind it that glowed for some seconds. Denning, our greatest authority on meteorites, stated that the height of its first appearance was about ninety or one hundred miles. It seemed to him that it fell to earth about one hundred miles east of him.

I was at home at that hour and writing in my study; and although my French windows face towards Ottershaw and the blind was up (for I loved in those days to look up at the night sky), I saw nothing of it. Yet this strangest of all things that ever came to earth from outer space must have fallen while I was sitting there, visible to me had I only looked up as it passed. Some of those who saw its flight say it travelled with a hissing sound. I myself heard nothing of that. Many people in Berkshire, Surrey, and Middlesex must have seen the fall of it, and, at most, have thought that another meteorite had descended. No one seems to have troubled to look for the fallen mass that night.

projectile (proh <u>jehk</u> tile) *n.*   an object thrown, flung, or fired   Synonyms: discharge, trajectile

incrustation (ihn kruh <u>stay</u> shuhn) *n.*   an external coating or crust   Synonyms: caking, skin, film, layer

forbid (fihr <u>bihd</u>) *v.* **-ding, forbade**   to command against performing a particular action   Synonyms: prohibit, ban, disallow, interdict, proscribe

CHAPTER 2—THE FALLING STAR

But very early in the morning poor Ogilvy, who had seen the shooting star and who was persuaded that a meteorite lay somewhere on the common between Horsell, Ottershaw, and Woking, rose early with the idea of finding it. Find it he did, soon after dawn, and not far from the sand pits. An enormous hole had been made by the impact of the **projectile**, and the sand and gravel had been flung violently in every direction over the heath, forming heaps visible a mile and a half away. The heather was on fire eastward, and a thin blue smoke rose against the dawn.

The Thing itself lay almost entirely buried in sand, amidst the scattered splinters of a fir tree it had shivered to fragments in its descent. The uncovered part had the appearance of a huge cylinder, caked over and its outline softened by a thick scaly dun-coloured **incrustation**. It had a diameter of about thirty yards. He approached the mass, surprised at the size and more so at the shape, since most meteorites are rounded more or less completely. It was, however, still so hot from its flight through the air as to **forbid** his near approach. A stirring noise within its cylinder he ascribed to the unequal cooling of its surface; for at that time it had not occurred to him that it might be hollow.

He remained standing at the edge of the pit that the Thing had made for itself, staring at its strange appearance, astonished chiefly at its unusual shape and colour, and dimly perceiving even then some evidence of design in its arrival. The early morning was wonderfully still, and the sun, just clearing the pine trees towards Weybridge, was already warm. He did not remember hearing any birds that morning, there was certainly no breeze stirring, and the only sounds were the faint movements from within the cindery cylinder. He was all alone on the common.

Then suddenly he noticed with a start that some of the grey clinker, the ashy incrustation that covered the mete-

excessive (ehk <u>sehss</u> ihv) *adj.*   going beyond what is normal or reasonable   Synonyms: exorbitant, extravagant, extreme, undue

clamber (<u>klahm</u> buhr) *v.* **-ing, -ed**   to climb or crawl with difficulty and awkwardness   Synonyms: scramble, wriggle, jostle, scurry

confine (kuhn <u>fine</u>) *v.* **-ing, -ed**   to maintain within strict limits   Synonyms: constrain, imprison, enclose, restrict

dreadful (<u>drehd</u> full) *adj.*   inspiring great fear or revulsion   Synonyms: appalling, atrocious, distressing, frightening, ghastly

arrest (uh <u>rehst</u>) *v.* **-ing, -ed**   to stop and hold in place; to seize   Synonyms: block, check, halt, apprehend, catch, collar

irresolute (ih <u>rehz</u> oh loot) *adj.*   incabable of deciding how to act or proceed   Synonyms: hesitant, indecisive, faltering, doubtful orite, was falling off the circular edge of the end. It was dropping off in flakes and raining down upon the sand. A large piece suddenly came off and fell with a sharp noise that brought his heart into his mouth.

For a minute he scarcely realised what this meant, and, although the heat was **excessive**, he **clambered** down into the pit close to the bulk to see the Thing more clearly. He fancied even then that the cooling of the body might account for this, but what disturbed that idea was the fact that the ash was falling only from the end of the cylinder.

And then he perceived that, very slowly, the circular top of the cylinder was rotating on its body. It was such a gradual movement that he discovered it only through noticing that a black mark that had been near him five minutes ago was now at the other side of the circumference. Even then he scarcely understood what this indicated, until he heard a muffled grating sound and saw the black mark jerk forward an inch or so. Then the thing came upon him in a flash. The cylinder was artificial—hollow—with an end that screwed out! Something within the cylinder was unscrewing the top!

"Good heavens!" said Ogilvy. "There's a man in it—men in it! Half roasted to death! Trying to escape!"

At once, with a quick mental leap, he linked the Thing with the flash upon Mars.

The thought of the **confined** creature was so **dreadful** to him that he forgot the heat and went forward to the cylinder to help turn. But luckily the dull radiation **arrested** him before he could burn his hands on the still-glowing metal. At that he stood **irresolute** for a moment, then turned, scrambled out of the pit, and set off running wildly into Woking. The time then must have been somewhere about six o'clock. He met a waggoner and tried to make him understand, but the tale he told and his appearance were so wild—his hat had fallen off in the pit—that the man simply drove on. He was equally unsuccessful with the potman who was just unlocking the doors of the

insensible (ihn <u>sehn</u> sih buhl) *adj.* unconscious
Synonyms: unresponsive, languid, lifeless

consolation (kahn suh <u>lay</u> shuhn) *n.* the act of com-
forting or reassuring Synonyms: assuagement,
easement, succor, encouragement

public-house by Horsell Bridge. The fellow thought he was a lunatic at large and made an unsuccessful attempt to shut him into the taproom. That sobered him a little; and when he saw Henderson, the London journalist, in his garden, he called over the palings and made himself understood.

"Henderson," he called, "you saw that shooting star last night?"

"Well?" said Henderson.

"It's out on Horsell Common now."

"Good Lord!" said Henderson. "Fallen meteorite! That's good."

"But it's something more than a meteorite. It's a cylinder—an artificial cylinder, man! And there's something inside."

Henderson stood up with his spade in his hand.

"What's that?" he said. He was deaf in one ear.

Ogilvy told him all that he had seen. Henderson was a minute or so taking it in. Then he dropped his spade, snatched up his jacket, and came out into the road. The two men hurried back at once to the common, and found the cylinder still lying in the same position. But now the sounds inside had ceased, and a thin circle of bright metal showed between the top and the body of the cylinder. Air was either entering or escaping at the rim with a thin, sizzling sound.

They listened, rapped on the scaly burnt metal with a stick, and, meeting with no response, they both concluded the man or men inside must be **insensible** or dead.

Of course the two were quite unable to do anything. They shouted **consolation** and promises, and went off back to the town again to get help. One can imagine them, covered with sand, excited and disordered, running up the little street in the bright sunlight just as the shop folks were taking down their shutters and people were opening their bedroom windows. Henderson went into the railway station at once, in order to telegraph the news to London.

reception (ree <u>sehpt</u> shun) *n.*   the process of acceptance or approval   Synonyms: accession, reaction, salutation, response

The newspaper articles had prepared men's minds for the **reception** of the idea.

By eight o'clock a number of boys and unemployed men had already started for the common to see the "dead men from Mars." That was the form the story took. I heard of it first from my newspaper boy about a quarter to nine when I went out to get my *Daily Chronicle*. I was naturally startled, and lost no time in going out and across the Ottershaw bridge to the sand pits.

colossal (kuh lah suhl) *adj.*   extremely large, immense
Synonyms: enormous, gargantuan, titanic

embed (ehm <u>behd</u>) *v.* **-ding, -ded**   to fix or enclose
firmly in surrounding material   Synonyms: implant,
ingrain, insert, set

perceive (puhr <u>seev</u>) *v.* **-ing, -ed**   to gain awareness of,
to detect   Synonyms: apprehend, distinguish, identify,
sense

vague (vayg) *adj.*   without definite shape, form, or
expression   Synonyms: ambiguous, hazy, nebulous,
indefinite, tenebrous

Chapter Three

On Horsell Common

I found a little crowd of perhaps twenty people surrounding the huge hole in which the cylinder lay. I have already described the appearance of that **colossal** bulk, **embedded** in the ground. The turf and gravel about it seemed charred as if by a sudden explosion. No doubt its impact had caused a flash of fire. Henderson and Ogilvy were not there. I think they **perceived** that nothing was to be done for the present, and had gone away to breakfast at Henderson's house.

There were four or five boys sitting on the edge of the Pit, with their feet dangling, and amusing themselves—until I stopped them—by throwing stones at the giant mass. After I had spoken to them about it, they began playing at "touch" in and out of the group of bystanders.

Among these were a couple of cyclists, a jobbing gardener I employed sometimes, a girl carrying a baby, Gregg the butcher and his little boy, and two or three loafers and golf caddies who were accustomed to hang about the railway station. There was very little talking. Few of the common people in England had anything but the **vaguest** astronomical ideas in those days. Most of them were staring quietly at the big tablelike end of the cylinder, which

inanimate (ihn <u>ann</u> ih miht) *adj*.   1. lacking in energy
   or activity   Synonyms: dull, inert, inactive, quiescent
   2. nonliving   Synonyms: barren, defunct

clamber (<u>klahm</u> buhr) *v*. **-ing, -ed**   to climb or crawl
   with difficulty and awkwardness   Synonyms: scramble,
   wriggle, jostle, scurry

hue (hyoo) *n*.   a shade or tint of a particular color
   Synonyms: tinge, tone, chroma

improbable (ihm <u>prohb</u> uh buhl) *adj*.   unlikely to take
   place or to have taken place   Synonyms: doubtful, fan-
   ciful, implausible, unbelievable, inconceivable

abstract (<u>ahb</u> strahkt) *adj*.   without concrete form;
   theoretical   Synonyms: hypothetical, abstruse, ideal,
   intellectual

was still as Ogilvy and Henderson had left it. I fancy the popular expectation of a heap of charred corpses was disappointed at this **inanimate** bulk. Some went away while I was there, and other people came. I **clambered** into the pit and fancied I heard a faint movement under my feet. The top had certainly ceased to rotate.

It was only when I got thus close to it that the strangeness of this object was at all evident to me. At the first glance it was really no more exciting than an overturned carriage or a tree blown across the road. Not so much so, indeed. It looked like a rusty gas float. It required a certain amount of scientific education to perceive that the grey scale of the Thing was no common oxide, that the yellowish-white metal that gleamed in the crack between the lid and the cylinder had an unfamiliar **hue**. "Extra-terrestrial" had no meaning for most of the onlookers.

At that time it was quite clear in my own mind that the Thing had come from the planet Mars, but I judged it **improbable** that it contained any living creature. I thought the unscrewing might be automatic. In spite of Ogilvy, I still believed that there were men in Mars. My mind ran fancifully on the possibilities of its containing manuscript, on the difficulties in translation that might arise, whether we should find coins and models in it, and so forth. Yet it was a little too large for assurance on this idea. I felt an impatience to see it opened. About eleven, as nothing seemed happening, I walked back, full of such thought, to my home in Maybury. But I found it difficult to get to work upon my **abstract** investigations.

In the afternoon the appearance of the common had altered very much. The early editions of the evening papers had startled London with enormous headlines:

"A MESSAGE RECEIVED FROM MARS"

"REMARKABLE STORY FROM WOKING"

and so forth. In addition, Ogilvy's wire to the Astronomical Exchange had roused every observatory in the three kingdoms.

considerable (kuhn <u>sihd</u> ehr uh buhl) *adj.* of great degree, extent, or amount; significant Synonyms: appreciable, extensive, major, substantial

glaringly (<u>glare</u> ihng lee) *adv.* 1. shining with great intensity Synonyms: blazingly, intensely, extremely 2. performed in an extremely noticeable fashion Synonyms: conspicuously, markedly, obviously

extinguish (ehk <u>stihng</u> wish) *v.* **-ing, -ed** to put out, as in a fire; to terminate Synonyms: douse, smother, stifle, suffocate

wield (weeld) *v.* **-ing, -ed** to handle competently and effectively Synonyms: brandish, command, control, operate, utilize

embed (ehm <u>behd</u>) *v.* **-ding, -ded** to fix or enclose firmly in surrounding material Synonyms: implant, ingrain, insert, set

impediment (ihm pehd ih mehnt) *n.* an obstacle or hindrance Synonyms: obstruction, detriment, handicap, encumbrance, stricture

excavation (ehks cuh <u>vay</u> shuhn) *n.* the act of unearthing, digging up Synonyms: exhuming, unearthing, disinterring, mining

audible (<u>awe</u> dih buhl) *adj.* able to be heard Synonyms: aural, discernible, hearable, perceptible

afford (uh <u>ford</u>) *v.* **-ing, -ed** 1. to posses the means to bear the cost or burden of Synonyms: bear, incur, manage, sustain 2. to provide or make available Synonyms: furnish, render, yield, supply

There were half a dozen flies or more from the Woking station standing in the road by the sand pits, a basket-chaise from Chobham, and a rather lordly carriage. Besides that, there was quite a heap of bicycles. In addition, a large number of people must have walked, in spite of the heat of the day, from Woking and Chertsey, so that there was altogether quite a **considerable** crowd—one or two gaily dressed ladies among the others.

It was **glaringly** hot, not a cloud in the sky nor a breath of wind, and the only shadow was that of the few scattered pine trees. The burning heather had been **extinguished**, but the level ground towards Ottershaw was blackened as far as one could see, and still giving off vertical streamers of smoke. An enterprising sweet-stuff dealer in the Chobham Road had sent up his son with a barrow-load of green apples and ginger beer.

Going to the edge of the pit, I found it occupied by a group of about half a dozen men—Henderson, Ogilvy, and a tall, fair-haired man that I afterwards learned was Stent, the Astronomer Royal, with several workmen **wielding** spades and pickaxes. Stent was giving directions in a clear, high-pitched voice. He was standing on the cylinder, which was now evidently much cooler; his face was crimson and streaming with perspiration, and something seemed to have irritated him.

A large portion of the cylinder had been uncovered, though its lower end was still **embedded**. As soon as Ogilvy saw me among the staring crowd on the edge of the pit he called to me to come down, and asked me if I would mind going over to see Lord Hilton, the lord of the manor.

The growing crowd, he said, was becoming a serious **impediment** to their **excavations**, especially the boys. They wanted a light railing put up, and help to keep the people back. He told me that a faint stirring was occasionally still **audible** within the case, but that the workmen had failed to unscrew the top, as it **afforded** no grip to them. The case appeared to be enormously thick, and it was possible

tumult (<u>tuh</u> muhlt) *n.* commotion, disturbance, and noise, as of a crowd Synonyms: agitation, bedlam, uproar, clamor, row

contemplate (<u>kahn</u> tehm playt) *v.* **-ing, -ed** to consider carefully Synonyms: deliberate, percolate, ruminate, ponder

waylay (way lay) *v.* **-ing, waylaid** to ambush Synonyms: intercept, assail, surprise that the faint sounds we heard represented a noisy **tumult** in the interior.

I was very glad to do as he asked, and so become one of the privileged spectators within the **contemplated** enclosure. I failed to find Lord Hilton at his house, but I was told he was expected from London by the six o'clock train from Waterloo; and as it was then about a quarter past five, I went home, had some tea, and walked up to the station to **waylay** him.

jostle (<u>jah</u> suhl) *v.* **-ing, -ed**   to push and shove, especially in vying for a position or advantage   Synonyms: elbow, nudge, shoulder, vie

peculiar (peh <u>kyool</u> ee uhr) *adj.*   out of the ordinary, unexpected   Synonyms: eccentric, curious, unique, idiosyncratic

CHAPTER FOUR

THE CYLINDER OPENS

When I returned to the common the sun was setting. Scattered groups were hurrying from the direction of Woking, and one or two persons were returning. The crowd about the pit had increased, and stood out black against the lemon yellow of the sky—a couple of hundred people, perhaps. There were raised voices, and some sort of struggle appeared to be going on about the pit. Strange imaginings passed through my mind. As I drew nearer I heard Stent's voice:

"Keep back! Keep back!"

A boy came running towards me.

"It's a-movin'," he said to me as he passed; "a-screwin' and a-screwin' out. I don't like it. I'm a-goin' 'ome, I am."

I went on to the crowd. There were really, I should think, two or three hundred people elbowing and **jostling** one another, the one or two ladies there being by no means the least active.

"He's fallen in the pit!" cried some one.

"Keep back!" said several.

The crowd swayed a little, and I elbowed my way through. Every one seemed greatly excited. I heard a **peculiar** humming sound from the pit.

confound (cuhn <u>fowned</u>) *v.* **-ing, -ed**   to bring about confusion; to perplex   Synonyms: baffle, discomfit, flabbergast, nonplus, puzzle, rattle

blunder (<u>bluh</u> duhr) *v.* **-ing, -ed**   to make a mistake of significant magnitude   Synonyms: botch, err, fumble, stumble

concussion (kuhn <u>cuhsh</u> uhn) *n.*   a violent blow or collision; an injury so caused   Synonyms: blow, bump, crash, impact, trauma

billowy (<u>bihl</u> low ee) *adj.*   consisting of swells or surges   Synonyms: bulgy, distent, undulating, inflated

luminous (<u>loo</u> mihn uhs) *adj.*   1. emitting light; glowing   Synonyms: brilliant, lustrous, incandescent, refulgent   2. intelligent and easily understood   Synonyms: lucid, perspicacious, comprehensible

writhe (rieth) *v.* **-ing, -ed**   to twist and contort, especially when caused by pain or struggle   Synonyms: distort, thrash, wriggle, distort, wriggle

inarticulate (ihn are <u>tihk</u> yoo leht) *adj.*   unable to communicate with sufficient clarity or intelligence   Synonyms: incoherent, unintelligible

ungovernable (uhn <u>guh</u> vehr nuh buhl) *adj.*   impossible to control   Synonyms: disorderly, fractious, raucous, unruly

petrify (<u>peh</u> trihf eye) *v.* **-ing, -ed**   to paralyze with fear or shock   Synonyms: daze, startle, stupefy, benumb

CHAPTER 4—THE CYLINDER OPENS

"I say!" said Ogilvy; "help keep these idiots back. We don't know what's in the **confounded** thing, you know!"

I saw a young man, a shop assistant in Woking I believe he was, standing on the cylinder and trying to scramble out of the hole again. The crowd had pushed him in.

The end of the cylinder was being screwed out from within. Nearly two feet of shining screw projected. Somebody **blundered** against me, and I narrowly missed being pitched onto the top of the screw. I turned, and as I did so the screw must have come out, for the lid of the cylinder fell upon the gravel with a ringing **concussion**. I stuck my elbow into the person behind me, and turned my head towards the Thing again. For a moment that circular cavity seemed perfectly black. I had the sunset in my eyes.

I think everyone expected to see a man emerge—possibly something a little unlike us terrestrial men, but in all essentials a man. I know I did. But, looking, I presently saw something stirring within the shadow: greyish **billowy** movements, one above another, and then two **luminous** disks—like eyes. Then something resembling a little grey snake, about the thickness of a walking stick, coiled up out of the **writhing** middle, and wriggled in the air towards me—and then another.

A sudden chill came over me. There was a loud shriek from a woman behind. I half turned, keeping my eyes fixed upon the cylinder still, from which other tentacles were now projecting, and began pushing my way back from the edge of the pit. I saw astonishment giving place to horror on the faces of the people about me. I heard **inarticulate** exclamations on all sides. There was a general movement backwards. I saw the shopman struggling still on the edge of the pit. I found myself alone, and saw the people on the other side of the pit running off, Stent among them. I looked again at the cylinder, and **ungovernable** terror gripped me. I stood **petrified** and staring.

steadfastly (<u>stehd</u> fast lee) *adv.*   with great determination and resolve   Synonyms: adamantly, doggedly, purposefully, staunchly

pulsate (<u>puhl</u> sayt) *v.* **-ing, -ed**   expanding and contracting with regularity   Synonyms: quiver, vibrate, oscillate, throb

lank *adj.*   long, thin, and often limp   Synonyms: gangling, gaunt, lean

appendage (uh <u>pehn</u> dihj) *n.*   an attached and subordinate part, especially a limb   Synonyms: adjunct, accessory, attachment

peculiar (pih <u>kyoo</u> lee uhr) *adj.*   out of the ordinary, odd   Synonyms: abnormal, curious, singular, unconventional

incessant (ihn <u>sehss</u> ant) *adj.*   continuing without pause or interruption   Synonyms: constant, unceasing, interminable, eternal

tumultuous (tuh <u>muhlt</u> yoo uhs) *adj.*   characterized by confusion and disorder   Synonyms: clamorous, agitated, raucous, turbulent

deliberation (deh lih buhr <u>ay</u> shuhn) *n.*   careful consideration of all sides of an issue   Synonyms: circumspection, prudence, forethought

tedious (<u>tee</u> dee uhs) *adj.*   so tiresome as to cause weariness; boring   Synonyms: banal, drab, laborious, monotonous, soporific

avert (uh <u>vurt</u>) *v.* **-ing, -ed**   1. to turn away, especially one's eyes   2. to prevent   Synonyms: avoid, deter, foil, preclude

CHAPTER 4—THE CYLINDER OPENS

A big greyish rounded bulk, the size, perhaps, of a bear, was rising slowly and painfully out of the cylinder. As it bulged up and caught the light, it glistened like wet leather.

Two large dark-coloured eyes were regarding me **steadfastly**. The mass that framed them, the head of the thing, was rounded, and had, one might say, a face. There was a mouth under the eyes, the lipless brim of which quivered and panted, and dropped saliva. The whole creature heaved and **pulsated** convulsively. A **lank** tentacular **appendage** gripped the edge of the cylinder, another swayed in the air.

Those who have never seen a living Martian can scarcely imagine the strange horror of its appearance. The **peculiar** V-shaped mouth with its pointed upper lip, the absence of brow ridges, the absence of a chin beneath the wedge-like lower lip, the **incessant** quivering of this mouth, the Gorgon groups of tentacles, the **tumultuous** breathing of the lungs in a strange atmosphere, the evident heaviness and painfulness of movement due to the greater gravitational energy of the earth—above all, the extraordinary intensity of the immense eyes—were at once vital, intense, inhuman, crippled and monstrous. There was something <u>fungoid</u> in the oily brown skin, something in the clumsy **deliberation** of the **tedious** movements unspeakably nasty. Even at this first encounter, this first glimpse, I was overcome with disgust and dread.

Suddenly the monster vanished. It had toppled over the brim of the cylinder and fallen into the pit, with a thud like the fall of a great mass of leather. I heard it give a peculiar thick cry, and <u>forthwith</u> another of these creatures appeared darkly in the deep shadow of the aperture.

I turned and, running madly, made for the first group of trees, perhaps a hundred yards away; but I ran slantingly and stumbling, for I could not **avert** my face from these things.

dwindle (<u>dwihn</u> duhl) *v.* **-ing, -ed**   to lessen in amount or intensity   Synonyms: diminish, ebb, fade, subside, wane

multitude (<u>muhl</u> tih tood) *n.*   a great quantity   Synonyms: drove, horde, host, mass, throng

derelict (<u>deh</u> ruh lihkt) *adj.*   worn out; abandoned   Synonyms: dilapidated, desolate, forsaken, neglected

CHAPTER 4—THE CYLINDER OPENS

There, among some young pine trees and furze bushes, I stopped, panting, and waited further developments. The common round the sand pits was dotted with people, standing like myself in a half-fascinated terror, staring at these creatures, or rather at the heaped gravel at the edge of the pit in which they lay. And then, with a renewed horror, I saw a round, black object bobbing up and down on the edge of the pit. It was the head of the shopman who had fallen in, but showing as a little black object against the hot western sun. Now he got his shoulder and knee up, and again he seemed to slip back until only his head was visible. Suddenly he vanished, and I could have fancied a faint shriek had reached me. I had a momentary impulse to go back and help him that my fears overruled.

Everything was then quite invisible, hidden by the deep pit and the heap of sand that the fall of the cylinder had made. Anyone coming along the road from Chobham or Woking would have been amazed at the sight—a **dwindling multitude** of perhaps a hundred people or more standing in a great irregular circle, in ditches, behind bushes, behind gates and hedges, saying little to one another and that in short, excited shouts, and staring, staring hard at a few heaps of sand. The barrow of ginger beer stood, a queer **derelict**, black against the burning sky, and in the sand pits was a row of deserted vehicles with their horses feeding out of nosebags or pawing the ground.

vantage (<u>van</u> tihj) *n.* a position likely to provide advantage or opportunity Synonyms: viewpoint, perspective

apex (<u>ay</u> pehks) *n.* the highest point, especially of a triangular shape Synonyms: acme, crest, crown, summit, vertex

accost (uh <u>cahst</u>) *v.* **-ing, -ed** to address with boldness and aggression Synonyms: harass, confront, provoke

articulate (ahr <u>tihk</u> yoo leht) *adj.* capable of expressing oneself clearly and eloquently Synonyms: eloquent, fluent, lucid

CHAPTER FIVE

THE HEAT-RAY

After the glimpse I had had of the Martians emerging from the cylinder in which they had come to the earth from their planet, a kind of fascination paralysed my actions. I remained standing knee-deep in the heather, staring at the mound that hid them. I was a battleground of fear and curiosity.

I did not dare to go back towards the pit, but I felt a passionate longing to peer into it. I began walking, therefore, in a big curve, seeking some point of **vantage** and continually looking at the sand heaps that hid these newcomers to our earth. Once a leash of thin black whips, like the arms of an octopus, flashed across the sunset and was immediately withdrawn, and afterwards a thin rod rose up, joint by joint, bearing at its **apex** a circular disk that spun with a wobbling motion. What could be going on there?

Most of the spectators had gathered in one or two groups—one a little crowd towards Woking, the other a knot of people in the direction of Chobham. Evidently they shared my mental conflict. There were few near me. One man I approached—he was, I perceived, a neighbour of mine, though I did not know his name—and **accosted**. But it was scarcely a time for **articulate** conversation.

derive (duhr <u>iev</u>) *v.* **-ing, -ed**   to originate or obtain from a particular source   Synonyms: acquire, arrive, evolve, procure

knoll (nohl) *n.*   a small mound or hill   Synonyms: hill, hillcock, hummock

intimation (ihn tih <u>may</u> shuhn) *n.*   a subtle, indirect suggestion   Synonyms: allusion, insinuation, innuendo, hint, implication

intermittent (ihn tuhr <u>mih</u> tehnt) *adj.*   occurring at irregular intervals   Synonyms: periodic, punctuated, fitful

consultation (kahn suhl <u>tay</u> shuhn) *n.*   an exchange of views and advice   Synonyms: deliberation, conference, council, discussion

"What ugly *brutes*!" he said. "Good God! What ugly brutes!" He repeated this over and over again.

"Did you see a man in the pit?" I said; but he made no answer to that. We became silent, and stood watching for a time side by side, **deriving**, I fancy, a certain comfort in one another's company. Then I shifted my position to a little **knoll** that gave me the advantage of a yard or more of elevation and when I looked for him presently he was walking towards Woking.

The sunset faded to twilight before anything further happened. The crowd far away on the left, towards Woking, seemed to grow, and I heard now a faint murmur from it. The little knot of people towards Chobham dispersed. There was scarcely an **intimation** of movement from the pit.

It was this, as much as anything, that gave people courage, and I suppose the new arrivals from Woking also helped to restore confidence. At any rate, as the dusk came on a slow, **intermittent** movement upon the sand pits began, a movement that seemed to gather force as the stillness of the evening about the cylinder remained unbroken. Vertical black figures in twos and threes would advance, stop, watch, and advance again, spreading out as they did so in a thin irregular crescent that promised to enclose the pit in its attenuated horns. I, too, on my side began to move towards the pit.

Then I saw some cabmen and others had walked boldly into the sand pits, and heard the clatter of hoofs and the <u>gride</u> of wheels. I saw a lad trundling off the barrow of apples. And then, within thirty yards of the pit, advancing from the direction of Horsell, I noted a little black knot of men, the foremost of whom was waving a white flag.

This was the Deputation. There had been a hasty **consultation**, and since the Martians were evidently, in spite of their repulsive forms, intelligent creatures, it had been

discreet (dihs <u>kreet</u>) *adj.* marked by wisdom and prudence in speech and action Synonyms: circumspect, prudent, judicious, tactful

luminous (<u>loo</u> mihn uhs) *adj.* 1. emitting light; glowing Synonyms: brilliant, lustrous, incandescent, refulgent 2. intelligent and easily understood Synonyms: lucid, perspicacious, comprehensible

abruptly (uh <u>bruhpt</u> lee) *adv.* without warning Synonyms: unexpectedly, suddenly, unpredictably

dispersal (dihs <u>puhrs</u> uhl) *n.* the act or process of distribution Synonyms: dissemination, circulation, scattering

apex (<u>ay</u> pehks) *n.* the highest point, especially of a triangular shape Synonyms: acme, crest, crown, summit, vertex

arrest (uh <u>rehst</u>) *v.* **-ing, -ed** to stop and hold in place; to seize Synonyms: block, check, halt, apprehend, catch, collar

pallid (<u>paa</u> lihd) *adj.* exceedingly pale; lacking in vitality Synonyms: wan, ashen, anemic

impinge (ihm <u>pihnj</u>) *v.* **-ing, -ed** to encroach upon; to collide with Synonyms: intrude, meddle, violate, invade resolved to show them, by approaching them with signals, that we too were intelligent.

Flutter, flutter, went the flag, first to the right, then to the left. It was too far for me to recognise anyone there, but afterwards I learned that Ogilvy, Stent, and Henderson were with others in this attempt at communication. This little group had in its advance dragged inward, so to speak, the circumference of the now almost complete circle of people, and a number of dim black figures followed it at **discreet** distances.

Suddenly there was a flash of light, and a quantity of **luminous** greenish smoke came out of the pit in three distinct puffs, which drove up, one after the other, straight into the still air.

This smoke (or flame, perhaps, would be the better word for it) was so bright that the deep blue sky overhead and the hazy stretches of brown common towards Chertsey, set with black pine trees, seemed to darken **abruptly** as these puffs arose, and to remain the darker after their **dispersal**. At the same time a faint hissing sound became audible.

Beyond the pit stood the little wedge of people with the white flag at its **apex**, **arrested** by these phenomena, a little knot of small vertical black shapes upon the black ground. As the green smoke arose, their faces flashed out **pallid** green, and faded again as it vanished. Then slowly the hissing passed into a humming, into a long, loud, droning noise. Slowly a humped shape rose out of the pit, and the ghost of a beam of light seemed to flicker out from it.

Forthwith flashes of actual flame, a bright glare leaping from one to another, sprang from the scattered group of men. It was as if some invisible jet **impinged** upon them and flashed into white flame. It was as if each man were suddenly and momentarily turned to fire.

inevitable (ihn <u>eh</u> viht uh buhl) *adj.*   impossible to avoid; certain to occur   Synonyms: destined, inescapable, obligatory, ordained

astound (uhs <u>townd</u>) *v.* **-ing, -ed**   to affect with wonder and amazement   Synonyms: confound, astonish

stupefy (stoo pih fie) *v.* **-ing, -ied**   to bring about dullness or insensitivity   Synonyms: stagger, startle, daze

dumbfound (<u>duhm</u> fownd) *v.* **-ing, -ed**   to perplex, to bring about astonishment and incredulity   Synonyms: bewilder, boggle, nonplus, overwhelm

undulate (<u>uhn</u> joo layt) *v.* **-ing, -ed**   to move in the manner of waves   Synonyms: ripple, quaver, palpitate, slither

void (voyd) *adj.*   empty; lacking in substantial content   Synonyms: abandoned, barren, vacant, vacuous

Then, by the light of their own destruction, I saw them staggering and falling, and their supporters turning to run.

I stood staring, not as yet realising that this was death leaping from man to man in that little distant crowd. All I felt was that it was something very strange. An almost noiseless and blinding flash of light, and a man fell head-long and lay still; and as the unseen shaft of heat passed over them, pine trees burst into fire, and every dry furze bush became with one dull thud a mass of flames. And far away towards Knaphill I saw the flashes of trees and hedges and wooden buildings suddenly set alight.

It was sweeping round swiftly and steadily, this flaming death, this invisible, **inevitable** sword of heat. I perceived it coming towards me by the flashing bushes it touched, and was too **astounded** and **stupefied** to stir. I heard the crackle of fire in the sand pits and the sudden squeal of a horse that was as suddenly stilled. Then it was as if an invisible yet intensely heated finger were drawn through the heather between me and the Martians, and all along a curving line beyond the sand pits the dark ground smoked and crackled. Something fell with a crash far away to the left where the road from Woking station opens out on the common. Forth-with the hissing and humming ceased, and the black, dome-like object sank slowly out of sight into the pit.

All this had happened with such swiftness that I had stood motionless, **dumbfounded** and dazzled by the flashes of light. Had that death swept through a full circle, it must inevitably have slain me in my surprise. But it passed and spared me, and left the night about me suddenly dark and unfamiliar.

The **undulating** common seemed now dark almost to blackness, except where its roadways lay grey and pale under the deep blue sky of the early night. It was dark, and suddenly **void** of men. Overhead the stars were mustering, and in the west the sky was still a pale, bright,

unman (uhn <u>maan</u>) *v.* **-ning, -ned**   to bring about the loss of spirit or courage   Synonyms: unnerve, demoralize, daunt, disconcert

persuasion (puhr <u>sway</u> zhuhn) *n.*   a belief firmly held; a conviction   Synonyms: certitude, opinion, partiality, predilection

verge (vuhrj) *n.*   the border or limit; threshold   Synonyms: boundary, brink, margin almost greenish blue. The tops of the pine trees and the roofs of Horsell came out sharp and black against the western afterglow. The Martians and their appliances were altogether invisible, save for that thin mast upon which their restless mirror wobbled. Patches of bush and isolated trees here and there smoked and glowed still, and the houses towards Woking station were sending up spires of flame into the stillness of the evening air.

Nothing was changed save for that and a terrible astonishment. The little group of black specks with the flag of white had been swept out of existence, and the stillness of the evening, so it seemed to me, had scarcely been broken.

It came to me that I was upon this dark common, helpless, unprotected, and alone. Suddenly, like a thing falling upon me from without, came—fear.

With an effort I turned and began a stumbling run through the heather.

The fear I felt was no rational fear, but a panic terror not only of the Martians, but of the dusk and stillness all about me. Such an extraordinary effect in **unmanning** me it had that I ran weeping silently as a child might do. Once I had turned, I did not dare to look back.

I remember I felt an extraordinary **persuasion** that I was being played with, that presently, when I was upon the very **verge** of safety, this mysterious death—as swift as the passage of light—would leap after me from the pit about the cylinder and strike me down.

essence (<u>ehs</u> ehns) *n.*   the most important, character-
istic properties   Synonyms: crux, fundamentals, core,
marrow

combustible (kuhm <u>buhst</u> ih buhl) *adj.*   able to be
burned or set aflame   Synonyms: explosive, flammable,
volatile, incendiary

distort (dihs <u>tort</u>) *v.* **-ing, -ed**   to bend or twist out of
shape or proportion   Synonyms: contort, deform,
warp

Chapter Six

The Heat-Ray in the Chobham Road

It is still a matter of wonder how the Martians are able to slay men so swiftly and so silently. Many think that in some way they are able to generate an intense heat in a chamber of practically absolute non-conductivity. This intense heat they project in a parallel beam against any object they choose, by means of a polished parabolic mirror of unknown composition, much as the parabolic mirror of a lighthouse projects a beam of light. But no one has absolutely proved these details. However it is done, it is certain that a beam of heat is the **essence** of the matter. Heat, and invisible, instead of visible, light. Whatever is **combustible** flashes into flame at its touch, lead runs like water, it softens iron, cracks and melts glass, and when it falls upon water, incontinently that explodes into steam.

That night nearly forty people lay under the starlight about the pit, charred and **distorted** beyond recognition, and all night long the common from Horsell to Maybury was deserted and brightly ablaze.

trivial (<u>trih</u> vee uhl) *adj.*   of little importance or value
Synonyms: frivolous, immaterial, minute, negligible

deter (dee <u>tuhr</u>) *v.* **-ring, -red**   to prevent a course of
action through instilling fear or uncertainty   Syn-
onyms: inhibit, daunt, dissuade, intimidate

CHAPTER 6—THE HEAT-RAY IN THE CHOBHAM ROAD

The news of the massacre probably reached Chobham, Woking, and Ottershaw about the same time. In Woking the shops had closed when the tragedy happened, and a number of people, shop people and so forth, attracted by the stories they had heard, were walking over the Horsell Bridge and along the road between the hedges that runs out at last upon the common. You may imagine the young people brushed up after the labours of the day, and making this novelty, as they would make any novelty, the excuse for walking together and enjoying a **trivial** flirtation. You may figure to yourself the hum of voices along the road in the <u>gloaming</u>. . . .

As yet, of course, few people in Woking even knew that the cylinder had opened, though poor Henderson had sent a messenger on a bicycle to the post office with a special wire to an evening paper.

As these folks came out by twos and threes upon the open, they found little knots of people talking excitedly and peering at the spinning mirror over the sand pits, and the newcomers were, no doubt, soon infected by the excitement of the occasion.

By half past eight, when the Deputation was destroyed, there may have been a crowd of three hundred people or more at this place, besides those who had left the road to approach the Martians nearer. There were three policemen too, one of whom was mounted, doing their best, under instructions from Stent, to keep the people back and **deter** them from approaching the cylinder. There was some booing from those more thoughtless and excitable souls to whom a crowd is always an occasion for noise and horse-play.

Stent and Ogilvy, anticipating some possibilities of a collision, had telegraphed from Horsell to the barracks as soon as the Martians emerged, for the help of a company of soldiers to protect these strange creatures from violence. After that they returned to lead that ill-fated advance. The description of their death, as it was seen by

intercept (ihn tuhr <u>sehpt</u>) *v.* **-ing, -ed** to deflect, block, or interrupt an intended course of action Synonyms: deflect, hinder, interlope, obstruct

drone (jrohn) *v.* **-ing, -ed** to emit a monotonous sound Synonyms: intone, chant, whirr

ignite (ihg <u>niet</u>) *v.* **-ing, -ed** to set fire to Synonyms: burn, enkindle, inflame the crowd, <u>tallies</u> very closely with my own impressions: the three puffs of green smoke, the deep humming note, and the flashes of flame.

But that crowd of people had a far narrower escape than mine. Only the fact that a hummock of heathery sand **intercepted** the lower part of the Heat-Ray saved them. Had the elevation of the parabolic mirror been a few yards higher, none could have lived to tell the tale. They saw the flashes and the men falling and an invisible hand, as it were, lit the bushes as it hurried towards them through the twilight. Then, with a whistling note that rose above the **droning** of the pit, the beam swung close over their heads, lighting the tops of the beech trees that line the road, and splitting the bricks, smashing the windows, firing the window frames, and bringing down in crumbling ruin a portion of the gable of the house nearest the corner.

In the sudden thud, hiss, and glare of the **igniting** trees, the panic-stricken crowd seems to have swayed hesitatingly for some moments. Sparks and burning twigs began to fall into the road, and single leaves like puffs of flame. Hats and dresses caught fire. Then came a crying from the common. There were shrieks and shouts, and suddenly a mounted policeman came galloping through the confusion with his hands clasped over his head, screaming.

"They're coming!" a woman shrieked, and incontinently everyone was turning and pushing at those behind, in order to clear their way to Woking again. They must have <u>bolted</u> as blindly as a flock of sheep. Where the road grows narrow and black between the high banks the crowd jammed, and a desperate struggle occurred. All that crowd did not escape; three persons at least, two women and a little boy, were crushed and trampled there, and left to die amid the terror and the darkness.

blunder (<u>bluhn</u> duhr) *v.* **-ing, -ed**   to make a mistake of significant magnitude   Synonyms: botch, err, fumble, stumble

pitiless (<u>piht</u> ee lehs) *adj.*   without mercy or remorse   Synonyms: callous, obdurate, unrelenting, inexorable

flourish (<u>fluhr</u> ihsh) *v.* **-ing, -ed**   to grow abundantly; thrive   Synonyms: blossom, burgeon, prosper

anguish (<u>aan</u> gwihsh) *n.*   extreme pain and suffering   Synonyms: affliction, agony, misery, torment, throe

abruptly (uh <u>bruhpt</u> lee) *adv.*   without warning   Synonyms: unexpectedly, suddenly, unpredictably

CHAPTER SEVEN

HOW I REACHED HOME

For my own part, I remember nothing of my flight except the stress of **blundering** against trees and stumbling through the heather. All about me gathered the invisible terrors of the Martians; that **pitiless** sword of heat seemed whirling to and fro, **flourishing** overhead before it descended and smote me out of life. I came into the road between the crossroads and Horsell, and ran along this to the crossroads.

At last I could go no further; I was exhausted with the violence of my emotion and of my flight, and I staggered and fell by the wayside. That was near the bridge that crosses the canal by the gasworks. I fell and lay still.

I must have remained there some time.

I sat up, strangely perplexed. For a moment, perhaps, I could not clearly understand how I came there. My terror had fallen from me like a garment. My hat had gone, and my collar had burst away from its fastener. A few minutes before, there had only been three real things before me—the immensity of the night and space and nature, my own feebleness and **anguish**, and the near approach of death. Now it was as if something turned over, and the point of view altered **abruptly**. There was no sensible transition

incline (<u>ihn</u> klien) *n.*   an angled surface; a slope   Synonyms: grade, gradient, inclination, ramp, rise

tumult (<u>tuh</u> muhlt) *n.*   commotion, disturbance, and noise, as of a crowd   Synonyms: agitation, bedlam, uproar, clamor, row

frantic (<u>fraan</u> tihk) *adj.*   excessively emotional; uncontrollably anxious   Synonyms: agitated, distraught, frenetic

exceptional (ehk <u>sehpt</u> shuhn uhl) *adj.*   deviating from the norm, especially in greatness of ability or intellect   Synonyms: extraordinary, noteworthy, remarkable, singular

incongruity (ihn kuhn <u>groo</u> iht ee) *n.*   the quality of disagreement or inconsistency   Synonyms: deviation, aberration, irregularity

serenity (suh <u>rehn</u> ih tee) *n.*   an absence of worry or stress; calmness   Synonyms: composure, placidity, tranquility from one state of mind to the other. I was immediately the self of every day again—a decent, ordinary citizen. The silent common, the impulse of my flight, the starting flames, were as if they had been in a dream. I asked myself had these latter things indeed happened? I could not credit it.

I rose and walked unsteadily up the steep **incline** of the bridge. My mind was blank wonder. My muscles and nerves seemed drained of their strength. I dare say I staggered drunkenly. A head rose over the arch, and the figure of a workman carrying a basket appeared. Beside him ran a little boy. He passed me, wishing me good night. I was minded to speak to him, but did not. I answered his greeting with a meaningless mumble and went on over the bridge.

Over the Maybury arch a train, a billowing **tumult** of white, firelit smoke, and a long caterpillar of lighted windows, went flying south—clatter, clatter, clap, rap, and it had gone. A dim group of people talked in the gate of one of the houses in the pretty little row of gables that was called Oriental Terrace. It was all so real and so familiar. And that behind me! It was **frantic**, fantastic! Such things, I told myself, could not be.

Perhaps I am a man of **exceptional** moods. I do not know how far my experience is common. At times I suffer from the strangest sense of detachment from myself and the world about me; I seem to watch it all from the outside, from somewhere inconceivably remote, out of time, out of space, out of the stress and tragedy of it all. This feeling was very strong upon me that night. Here was another side to my dream.

But the trouble was the blank **incongruity** of this **serenity** and the swift death flying yonder, not two miles away. There was a noise of business from the gasworks, and the electric lamps were all alight. I stopped at the group of people.

"What news from the common?" said I.

haggard (<u>haa</u> guhrd) *adj.*   worn and wearied in appearance   Synonyms: ashen, pallid, exhausted, fatigued

sufficiently (suh <u>fihsh</u> ehnt lee) *adv.*   to the degree necessary; adequately   Synonyms: sufficiently, suitably, fittingly, acceptably

neglect (nuh <u>glehkt</u>) *v.* **-ing, -ed**   to fail to provide proper care; to disregard   Synonyms: ignore, overlook, discount

allay (uh <u>lay</u>) *v.* **-ing, -ed**   to make bearable; relieve   Synonyms: alleviate, mitigate, abate, assuage, mollify

abruptly (uh <u>bruhpt</u> lee) *adv.*   without warning   Synonyms: unexpectedly, suddenly, unpredictably

CHAPTER 7—HOW I REACHED HOME

There were two men and a woman at the gate.

"Eh?" said one of the men, turning.

"What news from the common?" I said.

"'Ain't yer just *been* there?" asked the men.

"People seem fair silly about the common," said the woman over the gate. "What's it all abart?"

"Haven't you heard of the men from Mars?" said I; "the creatures from Mars?"

"Quite enough," said the woman over the gate. "Thenks"; and all three of them laughed.

I felt foolish and angry. I tried and found I could not tell them what I had seen. They laughed again at my broken sentences.

"You'll hear more yet," I said, and went on to my home.

I startled my wife at the doorway, so **haggard** was I. I went into the dining room, sat down, drank some wine, and so soon as I could collect myself **sufficiently** I told her the things I had seen. The dinner, which was a cold one, had already been served, and remained **neglected** on the table while I told my story.

"There is one thing," I said, to **allay** the fears I had aroused; "they are the most sluggish things I ever saw crawl. They may keep the pit and kill people who come near them, but they cannot get out of it. . . . But the horror of them!"

"Don't, dear!" said my wife, knitting her brows and putting her hand on mine.

"Poor Ogilvy!" I said. "To think he may be lying dead there!"

My wife at least did not find my experience incredible. When I saw how deadly white her face was, I ceased **abruptly**.

"They may come here," she said again and again.

I pressed her to take wine, and tried to reassure her.

"They can scarcely move," I said.

invigorate (ihn <u>vih</u> goh rayt) *v.* **-ing, -ed**   to energize; to fill with strength   Synonyms: animate, enliven, inspirit, vitalize

dispense (dih <u>spehns</u>) *v.* **-ing, -ed**   1. to administer; distribute   Synonyms: allot, allocate, disburse, supply 2. to absolve of an obligation or custom   Synonyms: exempt, excuse, release

exertion (ehg <u>zuhr</u> shuhn) *n.*   the use of substantial reserves of strength or energy   Synonyms: work, industry, effort, labor

insensible (ihn <u>sehn</u> sih buhl) *adj.*   unconscious Synonyms: unresponsive, languid, lifeless

anxious (<u>aank</u> shuhs) *adj.*   worried   Synonyms: apprehensive, disquieted, distressed, nervous

I began to comfort her and myself by repeating all that Ogilvy had told me of the impossibility of the Martians establishing themselves on the earth. In particular I laid stress on the gravitational difficulty. On the surface of the earth the force of gravity is three times what it is on the surface of Mars. A Martian, therefore, would weigh three times more than on Mars, albeit his muscular strength would be the same. His own body would be a <u>cope</u> of lead to him. That, indeed, was the general opinion. Both *The Times* and the *Daily Telegraph*, for instance, insisted on it the next morning, and both overlooked, just as I did, two obvious modifying influences.

The atmosphere of the earth, we now know, contains far more oxygen or far less argon (whichever way one likes to put it) than does Mars. The **invigorating** influences of this excess of oxygen upon the Martians indisputably did much to counterbalance the increased weight of their bodies. And, in the second place, we all overlooked the fact that such mechanical intelligence as the Martian possessed was quite able to **dispense** with muscular **exertion** at a pinch.

But I did not consider these points at the time, and so my reasoning was dead against the chances of the invaders. With wine and food, the confidence of my own table, and the necessity of reassuring my wife, I grew by **insensible** degrees courageous and secure.

"They have done a foolish thing," said I, fingering my wineglass. "They are dangerous because, no doubt, they are mad with terror. Perhaps they expected to find no living things—certainly no intelligent living things."

"A shell in the pit" said I, "if the worst comes to the worst will kill them all."

The intense excitement of the events had no doubt left my perceptive powers in a state of <u>erethism</u>. I remember that dinner table with extraordinary vividness even now. My dear wife's sweet **anxious** face peering at me from under the pink lamp shade, the white cloth with its silver and

denounce (dee <u>nownce</u>) *v.* **-ing, -ed**   to openly condemn or reject   Synonyms: condemn, castigate, censure, excoriate

timidity (tih <u>mihd</u> uh tee) *adj.*   fearfulness and hesitation, especially with respect to the unfamiliar or unknown   Synonyms: inhibition, bashfulness, shyness, reserve

pitiless (<u>piht</u> ee lehs) *adj.*   without mercy or remorse   Synonyms: callous, obdurate, unrelenting, inexorable

CHAPTER 7—HOW I REACHED HOME

glass table furniture—for in those days even philosophical writers had many little luxuries—the crimson-purple wine in my glass, are photographically distinct. At the end of it I sat, tempering nuts with a cigarette, regretting Ogilvy's rashness, and **denouncing** the shortsighted **timidity** of the Martians.

So some respectable dodo in the Mauritius might have lorded it in his nest, and discussed the arrival of that shipful of **pitiless** sailors in want of animal food. "We will peck them to death tomorrow, my dear."

I did not know it, but that was the last civilised dinner I was to eat for very many strange and terrible days.

dovetail (<u>duhv</u> tayl) *v.* **-ing, -ed** to bring into a tight fit Synonyms: coincide, conjoin, accord, link

ultimatum (uhl tihm <u>ay</u> tuhm) *n.* a statement of final demands or terms, the refusal of which brings penalty Synonyms: offer, demand, decree, stipulation

canard (kuh <u>nahrd</u>) *n.* a misleading or falsified account or claim Synonyms: fabrication, lie, fallacy, yarn

authentication (aw thehn tihk <u>ay</u> shuhn) *n.* the confirmation of credentials, origin, or truthfulness Synonyms: authorization, certification, guarantee, endorsement

inert (ihn <u>uhrt</u>) *adj.* incapable of or lethargic in movement or activity Synonyms: lifeless, languid, torpid, indolent

CHAPTER EIGHT

FRIDAY NIGHT

The most extraordinary thing to my mind, of all the strange and wonderful things that happened upon that Friday, was the **dovetailing** of the commonplace habits of our social order with the first beginnings of the series of events that was to topple that social order <u>headlong</u>. If on Friday night you had taken a pair of compasses and drawn a circle with a radius of five miles round the Woking sand pits, I doubt if you would have had one human being outside it, unless it were some relation of Stent or of the three or four cyclists or London people lying dead on the common, whose emotions or habits were at all affected by the new-comers. Many people had heard of the cylinder, of course, and talked about it in their leisure, but it certainly did not make the sensation that an **ultimatum** to Germany would have done.

In London that night poor Henderson's telegram describing the gradual unscrewing of the shot was judged to be a **canard**, and his evening paper, after wiring for **authentication** from him and receiving no reply—the man was killed—decided not to print a special edition.

Even within the five-mile circle the great majority of people were **inert**. I have already described the behaviour

novel (<u>nah</u> vuhl) *adj.*   markedly different, original, or unique   Synonyms: fresh, innovative, neoteric, singular

shunt *v.* **-ing, -ed**   to switch to an alternate course, push aside   Synonyms: deflect, deter, redirect

monopoly (muh <u>nah</u> puh lee) *n.*   complete control over a particular commodity or market   Synonyms: syndicate, cartel

perceptible (puhr <u>sehpt</u> ih buhl) *adj.*   able to be sensed or detected   Synonyms: noticeable, discernible, observable, palpable, tangible

linger (<u>lihn</u> guhr) *v.* **-ing, -ed**   to remain, especially out of reluctance   Synonyms: dally, dawdle, tarry, loll of the men and women to whom I spoke. All over the district people were dining and supping; working men were gardening after the labours of the day, children were being put to bed, young people were wandering through the lanes love-making, students sat over their books.

Maybe there was a murmur in the village streets, a **novel** and dominant topic in the public-houses, and here and there a messenger, or even an eye-witness of the later occurrences, caused a whirl of excitement, a shouting, and a running to and fro; but for the most part the daily routine of working, eating, drinking, sleeping, went on as it had done for countless years—as though no planet Mars existed in the sky. Even at Woking station and Horsell and Chobham that was the case.

In Woking junction, until a late hour, trains were stopping and going on, others were **shunting** on the sidings, passengers were <u>alighting</u> and waiting, and everything was proceeding in the most ordinary way. A boy from the town, trenching on Smith's **monopoly**, was selling papers with the afternoon's news. The ringing impact of trucks, the sharp whistle of the engines from the junction, mingled with their shouts of "Men from Mars!" Excited men came into the station about nine o'clock with incredible <u>tidings</u>, and caused no more disturbance than drunkards might have done. People rattling Londonwards peered into the darkness outside the carriage windows, and saw only a rare, flickering, vanishing spark dance up from the direction of Horsell, a red glow and a thin veil of smoke driving across the stars, and thought that nothing more serious than a heath fire was happening. It was only round the edge of the common that any disturbance was **perceptible**. There were half a dozen villas burning on the Woking border. There were lights in all the houses on the common side of the three villages, and the people there kept awake till dawn.

A curious crowd **lingered** restlessly, people coming and going but the crowd remaining, both on the Chobham

contort (kuhn <u>tort</u>) *v.* **-ing, -ed**   to bend out of shape
Synonyms: distort, convolute, gnarl, misshape, warp

inflammation (ihn fluh <u>may</u> shuhn) *n.*   1. a bodily area
of swelling, pain, and irritation   Synonyms: affection,
contusion, hemhorrage   2. an area literally aflame
Synonyms: conflagration, fire, blaze

immemorial (ih meh <u>mor</u> ree uhl) *adj.*   past the limit of
memory or history; extremely old   Synonyms: ancient,
primeval, prehistoric

indefatigable (ihn dih <u>faa</u> tihg uh buhl) *adj.*   exhibiting
great and seemingly boundless energy; incapable of
exhaustion   Synonyms: tireless, dogged, unflagging,
relentless, unwearying

deploy (dee <u>ploy</u>) *v.* **-ing, -ed**   to distribute or position
to achieve a strategic purpose   Synonyms: position,
utilize

and Horsell bridges. One or two adventurous souls, it was afterwards found, went into the darkness and crawled quite near the Martians; but they never returned, for now and again a light-ray, like the beam of a warship's searchlight swept the common, and the Heat-Ray was ready to follow. Save for such, that big area of common was silent and desolate, and the charred bodies lay about on it all night under the stars, and all the next day. A noise of hammering from the pit was heard by many people.

So you have the state of things on Friday night. In the centre, sticking into the skin of our old planet Earth like a poisoned dart, was this cylinder. But the poison was scarcely working yet. Around it was a patch of silent common, <u>smouldering</u> in places, and with a few dark, dimly seen objects lying in **contorted** attitudes here and there. Here and there was a burning bush or tree. Beyond was a fringe of excitement, and farther than that fringe the **inflammation** had not crept as yet. In the rest of the world the stream of life still flowed as it had flowed for **immemorial** years. The fever of war that would presently clog vein and artery, deaden nerve and destroy brain, had still to develop.

All night long the Martians were hammering and stirring, sleepless, **indefatigable**, at work upon the machines they were making ready, and ever and again a puff of greenish-white smoke whirled up to the starlit sky.

About eleven a company of soldiers came through Horsell, and **deployed** along the edge of the common to form a <u>cordon</u>. Later a second company marched through Chobham to deploy on the north side of the common. Several officers from the Inkerman barracks had been on the common earlier in the day, and one, Major Eden, was reported to be missing. The colonel of the regiment came to the Chobham bridge and was busy questioning the crowd at midnight. The military authorities were certainly alive to the seriousness of the business. About eleven, the next morning's papers were able to say, a <u>squadron</u> of

THE WAR OF THE WORLDS

hussars, two <u>Maxims,</u> and about four hundred men of the Cardigan regiment started from Aldershot.

A few seconds after midnight the crowd in the Chertsey road, Woking, saw a star fall from heaven into the pine woods to the northwest. It had a greenish colour, and caused a silent brightness like summer lightning. This was the second cylinder.

lassitude (<u>laa</u> sih tood) *n.*   a state of significantly diminished energy or concern   Synonyms: torpor, lethargy, apathy, listlessness

fluctuate (<u>fluhk</u> shoo ate) *v.* **-ing, -ed**   to vary with irregularity   Synonyms: oscillate, waver, swing

CHAPTER NINE

THE FIGHTING BEGINS

Saturday lives in my memory as a day of suspense. It was a day of **lassitude** too, hot and close, with, I am told, a rapidly **fluctuating** barometer. I had slept but little, though my wife had succeeded in sleeping, and I rose early. I went into my garden before breakfast and stood listening, but towards the common there was nothing stirring but a lark.

The milkman came as usual. I heard the rattle of his chariot and I went round to the side gate to ask the latest news. He told me that during the night the Martians had been surrounded by troops, and that guns were expected. Then—a familiar, reassuring note—I heard a train running towards Woking.

"They aren't to be killed," said the milkman, "if that can possibly be avoided."

I saw my neighbour gardening, chatted with him for a time, and then strolled in to breakfast. It was a most unexceptional morning. My neighbour was of opinion that the troops would be able to capture or to destroy the Martians during the day.

sentinel (<u>sehn</u> tihn ehl) *n.*   one who stands guard or
awaits a particular occurrence   Synonyms: sentry,
lookout, guardian

dispute (dihs <u>pyoot</u>) *n.*   an argument or debate
Synonyms: conflict, controversy, embroilment, dissension

peculiar (pih <u>kyoo</u> lee uhr) *adj.*   out of the ordinary, odd
Synonyms: abnormal, curious, singular, unconventional

"It's a pity they make themselves so unapproachable," he said. "It would be curious to know how they live on another planet; we might learn a thing or two."

He came up to the fence and extended a handful of strawberries, for his gardening was as generous as it was enthusiastic. At the same time he told me of the burning of the pine woods about the Byfleet Golf Links.

"They say," said he, "that there's another of those blessed things fallen there—number two. But one's enough, surely. This lot'll cost the insurance people a pretty penny before everything's settled." He laughed with an air of the greatest good humour as he said this. The woods, he said, were still burning, and pointed out a haze of smoke to me. "They will be hot under foot for days, on account of the thick soil of pine needles and turf," he said, and then grew serious over "poor Ogilvy."

After breakfast, instead of working, I decided to walk down towards the common. Under the railway bridge I found a group of soldiers—sappers, I think, men in small round caps, dirty red jackets unbuttoned, and showing their blue shirts, dark trousers, and boots coming to the calf. They told me no one was allowed over the canal, and, looking along the road towards the bridge, I saw one of the Cardigan men standing **sentinel** there. I talked with these soldiers for a time; I told them of my sight of the Martians on the previous evening. None of them had seen the Martians, and they had but the vaguest ideas of them, so that they plied me with questions. They said that they did not know who had authorised the movements of the troops; their idea was that a **dispute** had arisen at the Horse Guards. The ordinary sapper is a great deal better educated than the common soldier, and they discussed the **peculiar** conditions of the possible fight with some acuteness. I described the Heat-Ray to them, and they began to argue among themselves.

"Crawl up under cover and rush 'em, say I," said one.

contemplative (kuhn <u>tehm</u> pluh tihv) *adj.* tending to think deeply Synonyms: pensive, thoughtful, introspective, pondering, ruminative

"Get aht!" said another. "What's cover against this 'ere 'eat? Sticks to cook yer! What we got to do is to go as near as the ground'll let us, and then drive a trench."

"Blow yer trenches! You always want trenches; you ought to ha' been born a rabbit Snippy."

"'Ain't they got any necks, then?" said a third, abruptly —a little, **contemplative**, dark man, smoking a pipe.

I repeated my description.

"Octopuses," said he, "that's what I calls 'em. Talk about fishers of men—fighters of fish it is this time!"

"It ain't no murder killing beasts like that," said the first speaker.

"Why not shell the darned things strite off and finish 'em?" said the little dark man. "You carn tell what they might do."

"Where's your shells?" said the first speaker. "There ain't no time. Do it in a rush, that's my tip, and do it at once."

So they discussed it. After a while I left them, and went on to the railway station to get as many morning papers as I could.

But I will not weary the reader with a description of that long morning and of the longer afternoon. I did not succeed in getting a glimpse of the common, for even Horsell and Chobham church towers were in the hands of the military authorities. The soldiers I addressed didn't know anything; the officers were mysterious as well as busy. I found people in the town quite secure again in the presence of the military, and I heard for the first time from Marshall, the tobacconist, that his son was among the dead on the common. The soldiers had made the people on the outskirts of Horsell lock up and leave their houses.

I got back to lunch about two, very tired for, as I have said, the day was extremely hot and dull; and in order to refresh myself I took a cold bath in the afternoon. About half past four I went up to the railway station to

armament (<u>aar</u> muh mehnt) *n.* the weaponry and instruments used in warfare   Synonyms: ammunition, arms, ordnance, materiel

belligerent (buh lih juh rehnt) *adj.* eager to engage in conflict; hostile   Synonyms: bellicose, combative, contentious, militant

vigorously (<u>vih</u> goh ruhs lee) *adv.* with great energy and vitality   Synonyms: ardently, assiduously, diligently, vivaciously

detonation (deh tuh <u>nay</u> shuhn) *n.* a violent release of energy; an explosion   Synonyms: blast, eruption, rupture get an evening paper, for the morning papers had contained only a very inaccurate description of the killing of Stent, Henderson, Ogilvy, and the others. But there was little I didn't know. The Martians did not show an inch of themselves. They seemed busy in their pit, and there was a sound of hammering and an almost continuous streamer of smoke. Apparently they were busy getting ready for a struggle. "Fresh attempts have been made to signal, but without success," was the stereotyped formula of the papers. A sapper told me it was done by a man in a ditch with a flag on a long pole. The Martians took as much notice of such advances as we should of the lowing of a cow.

I must confess the sight of all this **armament**, all this preparation, greatly excited me. My imagination became **belligerent**, and defeated the invaders in a dozen striking ways; something of my schoolboy dreams of battle and heroism came back. It hardly seemed a fair fight to me at that time. They seemed very helpless in that pit of theirs.

About three o'clock there began the thud of a gun at measured intervals from Chertsey or Addlestone. I learned that the smouldering pine wood into which the second cylinder had fallen was being shelled, in the hope of destroying that object before it opened. It was only about five, however, that a field gun reached Chobham for use against the first body of Martians.

About six in the evening, as I sat at tea with my wife in the summerhouse talking **vigorously** about the battle that was lowering upon us, I heard a muffled **detonation** from the common, and immediately after a gust of firing. Close on the heels of that came a violent rattling crash, quite close to us, that shook the ground; and, starting out upon the lawn, I saw the tops of the trees about the Oriental College burst into smoky red flame, and the tower of the little church beside it slide down into ruin. The pinnacle of the mosque had vanished, and the roof line of the college itself looked as if a hundred-ton gun had been at

bevy (<u>beh</u> vee) *n.*   an assemblage or group   Synonyms: gathering, cluster, menagerie, troupe

lurid (<u>loo</u> rihd) *adj.*   1. sensational in detail; causing shock or horror   Synonyms: shocking, macabre, obscene, offensive   2. strangely pale   Synonyms: pallid, eerie, ashen work upon it. One of our chimneys cracked as if a shot had hit it, flew, and a piece of it came clattering down the tiles and made a heap of broken red fragments upon the flower bed by my study window.

I and my wife stood amazed. Then I realised that the crest of Maybury Hill must be within range of the Martians' Heat-Ray now that the college was cleared out of the way.

At that I gripped my wife's arm, and without ceremony ran her out into the road. Then I fetched out the servant, telling her I would go upstairs myself for the box she was clamouring for.

"We can't possibly stay here," I said; and as I spoke the firing reopened for a moment upon the common.

"But where are we to go?" said my wife in terror.

I thought perplexed. Then I remembered her cousins at Leatherhead.

"Leatherhead!" I shouted above the sudden noise.

She looked away from me downhill. The people were coming out of their houses, astonished.

"How are we to get to Leatherhead?" she said.

Down the hill I saw a **bevy** of <u>hussars</u> ride under the railway bridge; three galloped through the open gates of the Oriental College; two others dismounted, and began running from house to house. The sun, shining through the smoke that drove up from the tops of the trees, seemed blood red, and threw an unfamiliar **lurid** light upon everything.

"Stop here," said I; "you are safe here"; and I started off at once for the Spotted Dog, for I knew the landlord had a horse and dog cart. I ran, for I perceived that in a moment everyone upon this side of the hill would be moving. I found him in his bar, quite unaware of what was going on behind his house. A man stood with his back to me, talking to him.

"I must have a pound," said the landlord, "and I've no one to drive it."

CHAPTER 9—THE FIGHTING BEGINS

"I'll give you two," said I, over the stranger's shoulder.

"What for?"

"And I'll bring it back by midnight," I said.

"Lord!" said the landlord; "what's the hurry? I'm selling my bit of a pig. Two pounds, and you bring it back? What's going on now?"

I explained hastily that I had to leave my home, and so secured the dog cart. At the time it did not seem to me nearly so urgent that the landlord should leave his. I took care to have the cart there and then, drove it off down the road, and, leaving it in charge of my wife and servant, rushed into my house and packed a few valuables, such plate as we had, and so forth. The beech trees below the house were burning while I did this, and the palings up the road glowed red. While I was occupied in this way, one of the dismounted hussars came running up. He was going from house to house, warning people to leave. He was going on as I came out of my front door, lugging my treasures, done up in a tablecloth. I shouted after him:

"What news?"

He turned, stared, bawled something about "crawling out in a thing like a dish cover," and ran on to the gate of the house at the crest. A sudden whirl of black smoke driving across the road hid him for a moment. I ran to my neighbour's door and rapped to satisfy myself of what I already knew, that his wife had gone to London with him and had locked up their house. I went in again, according to my promise, to get my servant's box, lugged it out, clapped it beside her on the tail of the dog cart, and then caught the reins and jumped up into the driver's seat beside my wife. In another moment we were clear of the smoke and noise, and spanking down the opposite slope of Maybury Hill towards Old Woking.

In front was a quiet sunny landscape, a wheat field ahead on either side of the road, and the Maybury Inn with its swinging sign. I saw the doctor's cart ahead of me. At the bottom of the hill I turned my head to look

intermittent (ihn tuhr <u>mih</u> tehnt) *adj.*   occurring at
  irregular intervals   Synonyms: periodic, punctuated,
  fitful

tumult (<u>tuh</u> muhlt) *n.*   commotion, disturbance, and
  noise, as of a crowd   Synonyms: agitation, bedlam,
  uproar, clamor, row

at the hillside I was leaving. Thick streamers of black smoke shot with threads of red fire were driving up into the still air, and throwing dark shadows upon the green treetops eastward. The smoke already extended far away to the east and west—to the Byfleet pine woods eastward, and to Woking on the west. The road was dotted with people running towards us. And very faint now, but very distinct through the hot, quiet air, one heard the whirr of a machine-gun that was presently stilled, and an **intermittent** cracking of rifles. Apparently the Martians were setting fire to everything within range of their Heat-Ray.

I am not an expert driver, and I had immediately to turn my attention to the horse. When I looked back again the second hill had hidden the black smoke. I slashed the horse with the whip, and gave him a loose rein until Woking and Send lay between us and that quivering **tumult.** I overtook and passed the doctor between Woking and Send.

lush (luhsh) *adj.*   characterized by abundance or extravagance   Synonyms: opulent, verdant, profuse, voluptuous, extravagant

cease (sees) *v.* **-ing, -ed**   to stop performing or put an end to an activity or task   Synonyms: desist, discontinue, cessation, conclude, quit

abruptly (uh <u>bruhpt</u> lee) *adv.*   without warning   Synonyms: unexpectedly, suddenly, unpredictably

misadventure (<u>mihs</u> aad vehn chuhr) *n.*   an incident characterized by misfortune or injury   Synonyms: mishap, accident, blunder, debacle, cataclysm

commend (kuh <u>mehnd</u>) *v.* **-ing, -ed**   to approve of, to give over to   Synonyms: praise, acclaim, assign, entrust

oppress (uh <u>prehs</u>) *v.* **-ing, -ed**   to keep down through the use of excessive and unjust force   Synonyms: subdue, persecute, subjugate, tyrannize

foreboding (fuhr <u>boh</u> dihng) *n.*   a sense of the coming of evil or misfortune   Synonyms: augury, portent, omen, premonition

feverishly (<u>fee</u> vuh rihsh lee) *adv.*   in an intensely emotional or agitated manner   Synonyms: nervously, agitatedly, fervidly, vehemently

Chapter Ten

In the Storm

Leatherhead is about twelve miles from Maybury Hill. The scent of hay was in the air through the **lush** meadows beyond Pyrford, and the hedges on either side were sweet and gay with multitudes of dog-roses. The heavy firing that had broken out while we were driving down Maybury Hill **ceased** as **abruptly** as it began, leaving the evening very peaceful and still. We got to Leatherhead without **misadventure** about nine o'clock, and the horse had an hour's rest while I took supper with my cousins and **commended** my wife to their care.

My wife was curiously silent throughout the drive, and seemed **oppressed** with **forebodings** of evil. I talked to her reassuringly, pointing out that the Martians were tied to the Pit by sheer heaviness, and at the utmost could but crawl a little out of it; but she answered only in monosyllables. Had it not been for my promise to the innkeeper, she would, I think, have urged me to stay in Leatherhead that night. Would that I had! Her face, I remember, was very white as we parted.

For my own part, I had been **feverishly** excited all day. Something very like the war fever that occasionally runs through a civilised community had got into my blood, and

fusillade (<u>fyoo</u> sih lahd) *n.*   an outburst or barrage, as from firearms discharging in quick succession   Synonyms: bombardment, barrage, torrent, hail, shelling

extermination (ehks turhr mih <u>nay</u> shuhn) *n.*   the act of completely destroying   Synonyms: annihilation, obliteration, extinction, ruination

albeit (ahl <u>bee</u> iht) *conj.*   although, even though   Synonyms: despite, even if, notwithstanding, supposing

intimately (<u>ihn</u> tih miht lee) *adv.*   in an extremely close or private manner   Synonyms: privately, personally

contagion (cuhn <u>tay</u> juhn) *n.*   an agent that causes illness   Synonyms: taint, virus

revert (ree <u>vuhrt</u>) *v.* **-ing, -ed**   to return to a previous state or condition   Synonyms: backslide, inverse, retrograde, transpose

precipitate (pree <u>sihp</u> ih tayt) *v.* **-ing, -ed**   to bring about; cause   Synonyms: advance, expedite, hasten, trigger in my heart I was not so very sorry that I had to return to Maybury that night. I was even afraid that that last **fusillade** I had heard might mean the **extermination** of our invaders from Mars. I can best express my state of mind by saying that I wanted to be in at the death.

It was nearly eleven when I started to return. The night was unexpectedly dark; to me, walking out of the lighted passage of my cousins' house, it seemed indeed black, and it was as hot and close as the day. Overhead the clouds were driving fast, **albeit** not a breath stirred the shrubs about us. My cousins' man lit both lamps. Happily, I knew the road **intimately**. My wife stood in the light of the doorway, and watched me until I jumped up into the dog cart. Then abruptly she turned and went in, leaving my cousins side by side wishing me good hap.

I was a little depressed at first with the **contagion** of my wife's fears, but very soon my thoughts **reverted** to the Martians. At that time I was absolutely in the dark as to the course of the evening's fighting. I did not know even the circumstances that had **precipitated** the conflict. As I came through Ockham (for that was the way I returned, and not through Send and Old Woking) I saw along the western horizon a blood-red glow, which as I drew nearer, crept slowly up the sky. The driving clouds of the gathering thunderstorm mingled there with masses of black and red smoke.

Ripley Street was deserted, and except for a lighted window or so the village showed not a sign of life; but I narrowly escaped an accident at the corner of the road to Pyrford, where a knot of people stood with their backs to me. They said nothing to me as I passed. I do not know what they knew of the things happening beyond the hill, nor do I know if the silent houses I passed on my way were sleeping securely, or deserted and empty, or harassed and watching against the terror of the night.

From Ripley until I came through Pyrford I was in the valley of the Wey, and the red glare was hidden from

intimation (ihn tih <u>may</u> shuhn) *n.* a subtle, indirect suggestion Synonyms: allusion, insinuation, innuendo, hint, implication

peal (peel) *v.* **-ing, -ed** to ring out sonorously, especially to mark time or change Synonyms: chime, carillon, resounding

silhouette (sihl oh <u>weht</u>) *n.* an outline, especially of a human form Synonyms: contour, etching, shadow

behold (bee <u>hohld</u>) *v.* **-ing, -ed** to see, look at, or comprehend Synonyms: contemplate, discern, distinguish, perceive

lurid (<u>loo</u> rihd) *adj.* 1. sensational in detail; causing shock or horror Synonyms: shocking, macabre, obscene, offensive 2. strangely pale Synonyms: pallid, eerie, ashen

apparition (ah puh <u>rihsh</u> shuhn) *n.* a specter or ghost; an unexpected appearance Synonyms: chimera, haunt, phantom, visitant

accompaniment (uh <u>cuhm</u> puh nee mehnt) *n.* a subordinate part, often in music, which provides support Synonyms: adjunct, backing, accessory

detonate (<u>deh</u> tuh nayt) *v.* **-ing, -ed** to cause to explode Synonyms: set off, fulminate

reverberation (ree vuhrb eh ray shuhn) *n.* an echo; a sound's persistence Synonyms: ringing, repercussion

regard (ree <u>gahrd</u>) *v.* **-ing, -ed** to observe with great attention; to consider in a particular manner Synonyms: attend, contemplate, scrutinize, adjudge

abruptly (uh <u>bruhpt</u> lee) *adv.* without warning Synonyms: unexpectedly, suddenly, unpredictably

arrest (uh <u>rehst</u>) *v.* **-ing, -ed** to stop and hold in place; to seize Synonyms: block, check, halt, apprehend, catch, collar

elusive (ee <u>looh</u> sihv) *adj.* difficult to capture or define Synonyms: ambiguous, evanescent, intangible, shifty

bewilder (bee <u>wihl</u> duhr) *v.* **-ing, -ed** to bring about confusion or disorientation Synonyms: baffle, befuddle, confound, daze me. As I ascended the little hill beyond Pyrford Church the glare came into view again, and the trees about me shivered with the first **intimation** of the storm that was upon me. Then I heard midnight **pealing** out from Pyrford Church behind me, and then came the **silhouette** of Maybury Hill, with its tree-tops and roofs black and sharp against the red.

Even as I **beheld** this a **lurid** green glare lit the road about me and showed the distant woods towards Addlestone. I felt a tug at the reins. I saw that the driving clouds had been pierced as it were by a thread of green fire, suddenly lighting their confusion and falling into the field to my left. It was the third falling star!

Close on its **apparition**, and blindingly violet by contrast, danced out the first lightning of the gathering storm, and the thunder burst like a rocket overhead. The horse took the bit between his teeth and bolted.

A moderate incline runs towards the foot of Maybury Hill, and down this we clattered. Once the lightning had begun, it went on in as rapid a succession of flashes as I have ever seen. The thunderclaps, treading one on the heels of another and with a strange crackling **accompaniment**, sounded more like the working of a gigantic electric machine than the usual **detonating reverberations**. The flickering light was blinding and confusing, and a thin hail smote gustily at my face as I drove down the slope.

At first I **regarded** little but the road before me, and then **abruptly** my attention was **arrested** by something that was moving rapidly down the opposite slope of Maybury Hill. At first I took it for the wet roof of a house, but one flash following another showed it to be in swift rolling movement. It was an **elusive** vision—a moment of **bewildering** darkness, and then, in a flash like daylight, the red masses of the Orphanage near the crest of the hill, the green tops of the pine trees, and this problematical object came out clear and sharp and bright.

tumult (<u>tuh</u> muhlt) *n.* commotion, disturbance, and noise, as of a crowd Synonyms: agitation, bedlam, uproar, clamor, row

mingle (<u>mihn</u> guhl) *v.* **-ing, -ed** to bring together; to mix Synonyms: admix, interweave, commingle, meld

riot (<u>rie</u> uht) *n.* a public and often unrestrained disturbance created by a crowd Synonyms: uprising, commotion, ruckus, tumult

brittle (<u>brih</u> tuhl) *adj.* likely to break or crumble when exposed to pressure Synonyms: frail, delicate, fragile

silhouette (sihl ohw <u>eht</u>) *n.* an outline, especially of a human form Synonyms: contour, etching, shadow

colossal (kuh lah suhl) *adj.* extremely large, immense Synonyms: enormous, gargantuan, titanic

mechanism (<u>mehk</u> uh nihz uhm) *n.* a mechanical device; a relationship of parts resembling that of a machine Synonyms: system, apparatus, appliance

insensate (ihn <u>sehn</u> seht) *adj.* unfeeling; lacking in awareness or sensitivity Synonyms: callous, insensible, dull, unresponsive

CHAPTER 10—IN THE STORM

And this Thing I saw! How can I describe it? A monstrous tripod, higher than many houses, striding over the young pine trees, and smashing them aside in its career; a walking engine of glittering metal, striding now across the heather; articulate ropes of steel dangling from it, and the clattering tumult of its passage mingling with the riot of the thunder. A flash, and it came out vividly, heeling over one way with two feet in the air, to vanish and reappear almost instantly as it seemed, with the next flash, a hundred yards nearer. Can you imagine a milking stool tilted and bowled violently along the ground? That was the impression those instant flashes gave. But instead of a milking stool imagine it a great body of machinery on a tripod stand.

Then suddenly the trees in the pine wood ahead of me were parted, as brittle reeds are parted by a man thrusting through them; they were snapped off and driven headlong, and a second huge tripod appeared, rushing, as it seemed, headlong towards me. And I was galloping hard to meet it! At the sight of the second monster my nerve went altogether. Not stopping to look again, I wrenched the horse's head hard round to the right and in another moment the dog cart had heeled over upon the horse; the shafts smashed noisily, and I was flung sideways and fell heavily into a shallow pool of water.

I crawled out almost immediately, and crouched, my feet still in the water, under a clump of furze. The horse lay motionless (his neck was broken, poor brute!) and by the lightning flashes I saw the black bulk of the overturned dog cart and the silhouette of the wheel still spinning slowly. In another moment the colossal mechanism went striding by me, and passed uphill towards Pyrford.

Seen nearer, the Thing was incredibly strange, for it was no mere insensate machine driving on its way. Machine it was, with a ringing metallic pace, and long, flexible, glittering tentacles (one of which gripped a young pine tree) swinging and rattling about its strange body. It picked its

brazen (<u>bray</u> zehn) *adj.* 1. inappropriately bold; audacious   Synonyms: shameless, impertinent, tawdry
2. made of or resembling brass   Synonyms: brassy

surmount (suhr <u>mownt</u>) *v.* **-ing, -ed** 1. to overcome
Synonyms: best, conquer, defeat   2. to position on top
of   Synonyms: top, crown, crest

inevitable (ihn <u>eh</u> viht uh buhl) *adj.* impossible to
avoid; certain to occur   Synonyms: destined, inescapable, obligatory, ordained

exultant (ehks <u>uhl</u> tehnt) *adj.* marked by great joy,
especially as the result of a success or conquest
Synonyms: triumphant, ecstatic, elated, jubilant

intermittent (ihn tuhr <u>mih</u> tehnt) *adj.* occurring at
irregular intervals   Synonyms: periodic, punctuated,
fitful

astonishment (uh <u>stah</u> nihsh mehnt) *n.* a state of surprise, shock, or amazement   Synonyms: bewilderment,
awe, stupefaction, wonderment

imminent (<u>ih</u> muh nehnt) *adj.* occurring in the immediate future   Synonyms: expectant, forthcoming,
impending

peril (<u>peh</u> ruhl) *n.* the possibility of misfortune; the
state of danger and risk   Synonyms: jeopardy, hazard,
menace, endangerment

desist (dee <u>sihst</u>) *v.* **-ing, -ed** to cease; to stop performing an activity or task   Synonyms: forbear, abstain,
surcease, discontinue

avail (uh <u>vayl</u>) *v.* **-ing, -ed** to be useful to   Synonyms:
benefit, satisfy, suffice

road as it went striding along, and the **brazen** hood that **surmounted** it moved to and fro with the **inevitable** suggestion of a head looking about. Behind the main body was a huge mass of white metal like a gigantic fisherman's basket, and puffs of green smoke squirted out from the joints of the limbs as the monster swept by me. And in an instant it was gone.

So much I saw then, all vaguely for the flickering of the lightning, in blinding highlights and dense black shadows.

As it passed it set up an **exultant** deafening howl that drowned the thunder—"Aloo! Aloo!"—and in another minute it was with its companion, half a mile away, stooping over something in the field. I have no doubt this Thing in the field was the third of the ten cylinders they had fired at us from Mars.

For some minutes I lay there in the rain and darkness watching, by the **intermittent** light, these monstrous beings of metal moving about in the distance over the hedge tops. A thin hail was now beginning, and as it came and went their figures grew misty and then flashed into clearness again. Now and then came a gap in the lightning, and the night swallowed them up.

I was soaked with hail above and puddle water below. It was some time before my blank **astonishment** would let me struggle up the bank to a drier position, or think at all of my **imminent peril**.

Not far from me was a little one-roomed squatter's hut of wood, surrounded by a patch of potato garden. I struggled to my feet at last, and, crouching and making use of every chance of cover, I made a run for this. I hammered at the door, but I could not make the people hear (if there were any people inside), and after a time I **desisted**, and, **availing** myself of a ditch for the greater part of the way, succeeded in crawling, unobserved by these monstrous machines, into the pine woods towards Maybury.

torrent (<u>toh</u> rehnt) *n.*   a great outpouring; a flood
Synonyms: flow, cascade, shower, spate

foliage (<u>foh</u> lee ihj) *n.*   a group of plant leaves
Synonyms: umbrage, vegetation, verdure

wretchedness (<u>rehtch</u> ihd nehs) *n.*   state of misery,
misfortune, or inferiority   Synonyms: rue, suffering,
torment, throe

motive (<u>moh</u> tihv) *n.*   an impulse to action   Synonyms: basis, incentive, inspiration, stimulus

reel *v.* **-ing, -ed**   to fall, stagger, or sway as the result of
imbalance   Synonyms: wobble, falter, careen

CHAPTER 10—IN THE STORM

Under cover of this I pushed on, wet and shivering now, towards my own house. I walked among the trees trying to find the footpath. It was very dark indeed in the wood, for the lightning was now becoming infrequent, and the hail, which was pouring down in a **torrent**, fell in columns through the gaps in the heavy **foliage**.

If I had fully realised the meaning of all the things I had seen I should have immediately worked my way round through Byfleet to Street Cobham, and so gone back to rejoin my wife at Leatherhead. But that night the strangeness of things about me, and my physical **wretchedness**, prevented me, for I was bruised, weary, wet to the skin, deafened and blinded by the storm.

I had a vague idea of going on to my own house, and that was as much **motive** as I had. I staggered through the trees, fell into a ditch and bruised my knees against a plank, and finally splashed out into the lane that ran down from the College Arms. I say splashed, for the storm water was sweeping the sand down the hill in a muddy torrent. There in the darkness a man blundered into me and sent me **reeling** back.

He gave a cry of terror, sprang sideways, and rushed on before I could gather my wits sufficiently to speak to him. So heavy was the stress of the storm just at this place that I had the hardest task to win my way up the hill. I went close up to the fence on the left and worked my way along its palings.

Near the top I stumbled upon something soft, and, by a flash of lightning, saw between my feet a heap of black broadcloth and a pair of boots. Before I could distinguish clearly how the man lay, the flicker of light had passed. I stood over him waiting for the next flash. When it came, I saw that he was a sturdy man, cheaply but not shabbily dressed; his head was bent under his body, and he lay crumpled up close to the fence, as though he had been flung violently against it.

repugnance (ree <u>puhg</u> nahns) *n.* intense dislike; aversion Synonyms: anathema, abhorrence, loathing, detestation

conveyance (kun <u>vay</u> ehns) *n.* the act of transferring or transporting property, title, or material Synonyms: carriage, transference, bond, charter

gingerly (<u>jihn</u> juhr lee) *adv.* with great caution; carefully Synonyms: circumspectly, delicately, discreetly

tumult (<u>tuh</u> muhlt) *n.* commotion, disturbance, and noise, as of a crowd Synonyms: agitation, bedlam, uproar, clamor, row

ruddy (<u>ruh</u> dee) *adj.* having a healthy, flushed coloration Synonyms: rosy, flushed, glowing

CHAPTER 10—IN THE STORM

Overcoming the **repugnance** natural to one who had never before touched a dead body, I stooped and turned him over to feel for his heart. He was quite dead. Apparently his neck had been broken. The lightning flashed for a third time, and his face leaped upon me. I sprang to my feet. It was the landlord of the Spotted Dog, whose **conveyance** I had taken.

I stepped over him **gingerly** and pushed on up the hill. I made my way by the police station and the College Arms towards my own house. Nothing was burning on the hillside, though from the common there still came a red glare and a rolling **tumult** of **ruddy** smoke beating up against the drenching hail. So far as I could see by the flashes, the houses about me were mostly uninjured. By the College Arms a dark heap lay in the road.

Down the road towards Maybury Bridge there were voices and the sound of feet, but I had not the courage to shout or to go to them. I let myself in with my latchkey, closed, locked and bolted the door, staggered to the foot of the staircase, and sat down. My imagination was full of those striding metallic monsters, and of the dead body smashed against the fence.

I crouched at the foot of the staircase with my back to the wall, shivering violently.

impenetrably (ihm <u>pehn</u> uh truh blee) *adv.* in a manner impossible to understand, penetrate, or enter
Synonyms: impassably, hermetically, impermeably

vivid (<u>vih</u> vihd) *adj.* fresh, bright, and distinct Synonyms: animated, brilliant, dynamic, lively, resplendent

grotesque (groh <u>tehsk</u>) *adj.* severely distorted or hideous in appearance Synonyms: deformed, bizarre, outlandish, aberrant, malformed

minute (mie <u>noot</u>) *adj.* especially small, barely noticeable
Synonyms: miniscule, tiny, diminutive, infinitesimal

writhe (rieth) *v.* **-ing, -ed** to twist and contort, especially when caused by pain or struggle Synonyms: distort, thrash, wriggle

CHAPTER ELEVEN

AT THE WINDOW

I have already said that my storms of emotion have a trick of exhausting themselves. After a time I discovered that I was cold and wet, and with little pools of water about me on the stair carpet. I got up almost mechanically, went into the dining room and drank some whiskey, and then I was moved to change my clothes.

After I had done that I went upstairs to my study, but why I did so I do not know. The window of my study looks over the trees and the railway towards Horsell Common. In the hurry of our departure this window had been left open. The passage was dark, and, by contrast with the picture the window frame enclosed, the side of the room seemed **impenetrably** dark. I stopped short in the door-way.

The thunderstorm had passed. The towers of the Oriental College and the pine trees about it had gone, and very far away, lit by a **vivid** red glare, the common about the sand pits was visible. Across the light huge black shapes, **grotesque** and strange, moved busily to and fro.

It seemed indeed as if the whole country in that direction was on fire—a broad hillside set with **minute** tongues of flame, swaying and **writhing** with the gusts of the dying

conflagration (kahn fluh <u>gray</u> shuhn) *n.* a large, often uncontrolled fire Synonyms: wildfire, inferno, blaze

resinous (<u>reh</u> zihn uhs) *adj.* similar in characteristics to pitch, tar, or any of a number of sticky, viscous substances secreted by plants Synonyms: glutinous, gummy, mucilaginous, viscid

tang (taang) *n.* a particularly sharp or piquant flavor or essence Synonyms: zest, relish, bite, pungency

char (chahr) *v.* **-ing, -ed** to burn on the surface; to blacken through heat or fire Synonyms: scorch, sear, singe, cauterize

oblong (<u>ahb</u> long) *adj.* elongated in one direction Synonyms: rectangular, elliptical, ovaloid

interval (<u>ihn</u> tuhr vuhl) *n.* the space, distance, or time between two units, demarcations, or instants Synonyms: gap, interim, period, interregnum

spectacle (<u>spehk</u> tuh kuhl) *n.* a notable, unusual, or unfortunate sight, often a public display Synonyms: exhibition, marvel, wonder

expanse (ehk <u>spaans</u>) *n.* a large, open area Synonyms: breadth, spread, wilderness, tract

distinguish (dih <u>stihng</u> wihsh) *v.* **-ing, -ed** to perceive as distinct or different from others Synonyms: characterize, ascertain, categorize, identify, individuate

chaos (<u>kay</u> ahs) *n.* great confusion or disorder Synonyms: anarchy, disarray, pandemonium, tumult

disgorge (dihs <u>gohrj</u>) *v.* **-ing, -ed** to spew forth, often violently Synonyms: discharge, eructate, erupt storm, and throwing a red reflection upon the cloud-scud above. Every now and then a haze of smoke from some nearer **conflagration** drove across the window and hid the Martian shapes. I could not see what they were doing, nor the clear form of them, nor recognise the black objects they were busied upon. Neither could I see the nearer fire, though the reflections of it danced on the wall and ceiling of the study. A sharp, **resinous tang** of burning was in the air.

I closed the door noiselessly and crept towards the window. As I did so, the view opened out until, on the one hand, it reached to the houses about Woking station, and on the other to the **charred** and blackened pine woods of Byfleet. There was a light down below the hill, on the railway, near the arch, and several of the houses along the Maybury road and the streets near the station were glowing ruins. The light upon the railway puzzled me at first; there were a black heap and a vivid glare, and to the right of that a row of yellow **oblongs**. Then I perceived this was a wrecked train, the fore part smashed and on fire, the hinder carriages still upon the rails.

Between these three main centres of light—the houses, the train, and the burning county towards Chobham—stretched irregular patches of dark country, broken here and there by **intervals** of dimly glowing and smoking ground. It was the strangest **spectacle**, that black **expanse** set with fire. It reminded me, more than anything else, of the Potteries at night. At first I could **distinguish** no people at all, though I peered intently for them. Later I saw against the light of Woking station a number of black figures hurrying one after the other across the line.

And this was the little world in which I had been living securely for years, this fiery **chaos**! What had happened in the last seven hours I still did not know; nor did I know, though I was beginning to guess, the relation between these mechanical colossi and the sluggish lumps I had seen **disgorged** from the cylinder. With a queer feeling of

impersonal (ihm <u>puhr</u> suh nuhl) *adj.* emotionless;
lacking response to or awareness of human contact
Synonyms: cold, detached, indifferent,
unpassioned

mechanism (<u>mehk</u> uh nihz uhm) *n.* a mechanical
device; a relationship of parts resembling that of a
machine Synonyms: system, apparatus, appliance

rouse (raawz) *v.* **-ing, -ed** to inspire to action Synonyms: provoke, vivify, animate, innervate, exhilarate

lethargy (<u>leh</u> thuhr jee) *n.* a state of lifelessness, torpor, or apathy Synonyms: indolence, sloth, listlessness

clamber (<u>klahm</u> buhr) *v.* **-ing, -ed** to climb or crawl
with difficulty and awkwardness Synonyms: scramble,
wriggle, jostle, scurry

torpor (<u>tohr</u> puhr) *n.* a state of inactivity and mental
insensibility Synonyms: lethargy, stupor, ennui, funk

astride (uh <u>stried</u>) *adv.* with a leg to either side
Synonyms: astraddle, straddling

impersonal interest I turned my desk chair to the window, sat down, and stared at the blackened country, and particularly at the three gigantic black things that were going to and fro in the glare about the sand pits.

They seemed amazingly busy. I began to ask myself what they could be. Were they intelligent **mechanisms**? Such a thing I felt was impossible. Or did a Martian sit within each, ruling, directing, using, much as a man's brain sits and rules in his body? I began to compare the things to human machines, to ask myself for the first time in my life how an ironclad or a steam engine would seem to an intelligent lower animal.

The storm had left the sky clear, and over the smoke of the burning land the little fading pinpoint of Mars was dropping into the west, when a soldier came into my garden. I heard a slight scraping at the fence, and **rousing** myself from the **lethargy** that had fallen upon me, I looked down and saw him dimly, **clambering** over the palings. At the sight of another human being my **torpor** passed, and I leaned out of the window eagerly.

"Hist!" said I, in a whisper.

He stopped **astride** of the fence in doubt. Then he came over and across the lawn to the corner of the house. He bent down and stepped softly.

"Who's there?" he said, also whispering, standing under the window and peering up.

"Where are you going?" I asked.

"God knows."

"Are you trying to hide?"

"That's it."

"Come into the house," I said.

I went down, unfastened the door, and let him in, and locked the door again. I could not see his face. He was hatless, and his coat was unbuttoned.

"My God!" he said, as I drew him in.

"What has happened?" I asked.

obscurity (uhb <u>skyoor</u> ih tee) *n.*   the state of being unknown or difficult to perceive or understand   Synonyms: ambiguity, uncertainty, equivocality

gesture (<u>jehst</u> choor) *n.*   the movement of the body to articulate or emphasize a thought or feeling   Synonyms: expression, genuflection, salute, pantomime

despair (dih <u>spehr</u>) *n.*   a state in which hope has been lost   Synonyms: dejection, despondency, tribulation, melancholy

dose (dohs) *n.*   a measured amount, especially of a medicine   Synonyms: portion, dram, prescription

abruptly (uh <u>bruhpt</u> lee) *adv.*   without warning   Synonyms: unexpectedly, suddenly, unpredictably

precipitate (pree <u>sihp</u> ih tayt) *v.* **-ing, -ed**   to bring about; cause   Synonyms: advance, expedite, hasten, trigger

depression (dee <u>preh</u> shuhn) *n.*   1. a state of complete hopelessness   Synonyms: despair, despondency, dejection, melancholy   2. a hollowed-out or sunken area   Synonyms: dent, crater, cavity, hollow, impression

ammunition (ah myoo <u>nih</u> shuhn) *n.*   objects that can be fired for purposes of combat   Synonyms: projectiles, armament, munitions, ordnance

"What hasn't?" In the **obscurity** I could see he made a **gesture** of **despair**. "They wiped us out—simply wiped us out," he repeated again and again.

He followed me, almost mechanically, into the dining room.

"Take some whiskey," I said, pouring out a stiff **dose**.

He drank it. Then **abruptly** he sat down before the table, put his head on his arms, and began to sob and weep like a little boy, in a perfect passion of emotion, while I, with a curious forgetfulness of my own recent despair, stood beside him, wondering.

It was a long time before he could steady his nerves to answer my questions, and then he answered perplexingly and brokenly. He was a driver in the artillery, and had only come into action about seven. At that time firing was going on across the common, and it was said the first party of Martians were crawling slowly towards their second cylinder under cover of a metal shield.

Later this shield staggered up on tripod legs and became the first of the fighting-machines I had seen. The gun he drove had been unlimbered near Horsell, in order to command the sand pits, and its arrival it was that had **precipitated** the action. As the limber gunners went to the rear, his horse trod in a rabbit hole and came down, throwing him into a **depression** of the ground. At the same moment the gun exploded behind him, the **ammunition** blew up, there was fire all about him, and he found himself lying under a heap of charred dead men and dead horses.

"I lay still," he said, "scared out of my wits, with the fore quarter of a horse atop of me. We'd been wiped out. And the smell—good God! Like burnt meat! I was hurt across the back by the fall of the horse, and there I had to lie until I felt better. Just like parade it had been a minute before—then stumble, bang, swish!"

"Wiped out!" he said.

furtively (<u>fuhr</u> tihv lee) *adv.*   stealthily; with ulterior motives   Synonyms: secretly, shiftily, shadily

fugitive (<u>fyoo</u> jih tihv) *n.*   an individual on the run, often being pursued in connection with a crime   Synonyms: outlaw, criminal, refugee

scintillate (<u>sihn</u> tihl ayt) *v.* **-ing, -ed**   to emit or reflect light; to sparkle   Synonyms: beam, shimmer, shine, flash

ejaculatory (ee <u>jaak</u> yoo luh toh ree) *adj.*   uttered suddenly and with great animation   Synonym: exclamatory

impassable (ihm <u>pahs</u> ih buhl) *adj.*   incapable of being crossed or overcome   Synonyms: impenetrable, unpierceable, impervious, inviolable

scald (skahld) *v.* **-ing, -ed**   to burn, especially with liquid or steam   Synonyms: burn, broil, scorch

scorch (skohrch) *v.* **-ing, -ed**   to burn, especially with the result of discoloring the outer layer   Synonyms: singe, sear, blacken

tentacle (<u>tehn</u> tih kuhl) *n.*   a long and unsegmented appendage with the ability to grasp

He had hid under the dead horse for a long time, peeping out **furtively** across the common. The Cardigan men had tried a rush, in skirmishing order, at the pit, simply to be swept out of existence. Then the monster had risen to its feet and had begun to walk leisurely to and fro across the common among the few **fugitives**, with its headlike hood turning about exactly like the head of a cowled human being. A kind of arm carried a complicated metallic case, about which green flashes **scintillated,** and out of the funnel of this there smoked the Heat-Ray.

In a few minutes there was, so far as the soldier could see, not a living thing left upon the common, and every bush and tree upon it that was not already a blackened skeleton was burning. The hussars had been on the road beyond the curvature of the ground, and he saw nothing of them. He heard the Martians rattle for a time and then become still. The giant saved Woking station and its cluster of houses until the last; then in a moment the Heat-Ray was brought to bear, and the town became a heap of fiery ruins. Then the Thing shut off the Heat-Ray, and turning its back upon the artilleryman, began to waddle away towards the <u>smouldering</u> pine woods that sheltered the second cylinder. As it did so a second glittering Titan built itself up out of the pit.

The second monster followed the first, and at that the artilleryman began to crawl very cautiously across the hot heather ash towards Horsell. He managed to get alive into the ditch by the side of the road, and so escaped to Woking. There his story became **ejaculatory**. The place was **impassable**. It seems there were a few people alive there, frantic for the most part and many burned and **scalded**. He was turned aside by the fire, and hid among some almost **scorching** heaps of broken wall as one of the Martian giants returned. He saw this one pursue a man, catch him up in one of its steely **tentacles**, and knock his head against the trunk of a pine tree. At last, after night-

embankment (ehm <u>baank</u> mehnt) *n.* a mound of earth or stone used as a barrier or as protection Synonyms: bulwark, barrier, rampart

skulk (skuhlk) *v.* **-ing, -ed** to move about with stealth; to evade Synonyms: slink, lurk, sneak

gaunt (gawnt) *adj.* exceedingly thin Synonyms: emaciated, haggard, attenuated, cadaverous

pitiless (<u>piht</u> ee lehs) *adj.* without mercy or remorse Synonyms: callous, obdurate, unrelenting, inexorable

wreckage (<u>rehk</u> ihj) *n.* the remains of that which has been destroyed Synonyms: debris, detritus, refuse, rubbish

indiscriminate (ihn dih <u>skrihm</u> mihn eht) *adj.* incapable of making fine distinctions; haphazard Synonyms: random, sweeping, imperceptive, mingled, jumbled, unselective

universal (yoo nih vuhrs uhl) *adj.* inclusive of, pertaining to, or common to all members Synonyms: all-inclusive, broad, catholic, worldwide, ubiquitous

survey (<u>suhr</u> vay) *v.* **-ing, -ed** to examine carefully Synonyms: analysis, audit, overview, inquiry, examination, compendium

desolation (deh suh <u>lay</u> shuhn) *n.* the state of being completely destroyed, forsaken, or abandoned Synonyms: ruin, barrenness, extinction, dissolution fall, the artilleryman made a rush for it and got over the railway embankment.

Since then he had been skulking along towards Maybury, in the hope of getting out of danger Londonward. People were hiding in trenches and cellars, and many of the survivors had made off towards Woking village and Send. He had been consumed with thirst until he found one of the water mains near the railway arch smashed, and the water bubbling out like a spring upon the road.

That was the story I got from him, bit by bit. He grew calmer telling me and trying to make me see the things he had seen. He had eaten no food since midday, he told me early in his narrative, and I found some mutton and bread in the pantry and brought it into the room. We lit no lamp for fear of attracting the Martians, and ever and again our hands would touch upon bread or meat. As he talked, things about us came darkly out of the darkness, and the trampled bushes and broken rose trees outside the window grew distinct. It would seem that a number of men or animals had rushed across the lawn. I began to see his face, blackened and haggard, as no doubt mine was also.

When we had finished eating we went softly upstairs to my study, and I looked again out of the open window. In one night the valley had become a valley of ashes. The fires had dwindled now. Where flames had been there were now streamers of smoke; but the countless ruins of shattered and gutted houses and blasted and blackened trees that the night had hidden stood out now gaunt and terrible in the pitiless light of dawn. Yet here and there some object had had the luck to escape—a white railway signal here, the end of a greenhouse there, white and fresh amid the wreckage. Never before in the history of warfare had destruction been so indiscriminate and so universal. And shining with the growing light of the east, three of the metallic giants stood about the pit, their cowls rotating as though they were surveying the desolation they had made.

vivid (<u>vih</u> vihd) *adj.*   fresh, bright, and distinct   Synonyms: animated, brilliant, dynamic, lively, resplendent

vapour or **vapor** (<u>vay</u> puhr) *n.*   a mist or spray; the gaseous state of a particular material   Synonyms: gas, haze, miasma, fog

CHAPTER 11—AT THE WINDOW

It seemed to me that the pit had been enlarged, and ever and again puffs of **vivid** green **vapour** streamed up and out of it towards the brightening dawn—streamed up, whirled, broke, and vanished.

Beyond were the pillars of fire about Chobham. They became pillars of bloodshot smoke at the first touch of day.

inevitably (ihn <u>eh</u> viht uh blee) *adv.*   in such a manner
as is unable to be avoided   Synonyms: certainly, inescapably, necessarily

CHAPTER TWELVE

WHAT I SAW OF THE DESTRUCTION OF WEYBRIDGE AND SHEPPERTON

As the dawn grew brighter we withdrew from the window from which we had watched the Martians, and went very quietly downstairs.

The artilleryman agreed with me that the house was no place to stay in. He proposed, he said, to make his way Londonward, and thence rejoin his battery—No. 12, of the Horse Artillery. My plan was to return at once to Leatherhead; and so greatly had the strength of the Martians impressed me that I had determined to take my wife to Newhaven, and go with her out of the country forthwith. For I already perceived clearly that the country about London must **inevitably** be the scene of a disastrous struggle before such creatures as these could be destroyed.

Between us and Leatherhead, however, lay the third cylinder, with its guarding giants. Had I been alone, I think I should have taken my chance and struck across country.

dissuade (dihs <u>wayd</u>) *v.* **-ing, -ed**   to convince against a certain course of action   Synonyms: deter, derail, disincline, exhort, remonstrate

detour (<u>dee</u> tohr) *n.*   a more roundabout route than is customarily necessary, usually utilized when the main route is unavailable   Synonyms: deviation, diversion, shunpike, circumvention

ransack (<u>raan</u> sahk) *v.* **-ing, -ed**   to search thoroughly, as for valuables; to pillage   Synonyms: appropriate, plunder, scour, purloin, raid

char (chahr) *v.* **-ing, -ed**   to burn on the surface; to blacken through heat or fire   Synonyms: scorch, sear, singe, cauterize

debris (dih <u>bree</u>) *n.*   the remnants of something that has been destroyed   Synonyms: litter, detritus, rubble, wreckage

sodden (<u>sah</u> dihn) *adj.*   soaked through   Synonyms: saturated, drenched, waterlogged

dismal (<u>dihz</u> muhl) *adj.*   bringing about despair; exceedingly poor in quality   Synonyms: disheartening, inauspicious, tedious, depressing, lugubrious

foliage (<u>foh</u> lee ihj) *n.*   a group of plant leaves   Synonyms: umbrage, vegetation, verdure

But the artilleryman **dissuaded** me: "It's no kindness to the right sort of wife," he said, "to make her a widow"; and in the end I agreed to go with him, under cover of the woods, northward as far as Street Cobham before I parted with him. Thence I would make a big **detour** by Epsom to reach Leatherhead.

I should have started at once, but my companion had been in active service and he knew better than that. He made me **ransack** the house for a flask, which he filled with whiskey; and we lined every available pocket with packets of biscuits and slices of meat. Then we crept out of the house, and ran as quickly as we could down the ill-made road by which I had come overnight. The houses seemed deserted. In the road lay a group of three **charred** bodies close together, struck dead by the Heat-Ray; and here and there were things that people had dropped—a clock, a slipper, a silver spoon, and the like poor valuables. At the corner turning up towards the post office a little cart, filled with boxes and furniture, and horseless, heeled over on a broken wheel. A cash box had been hastily smashed open and thrown under the **debris**.

Except the lodge at the Orphanage, which was still on fire, none of the houses had suffered very greatly here. The Heat-Ray had shaved the chimney tops and passed. Yet, save ourselves, there did not seem to be a living soul on Maybury Hill. The majority of the inhabitants had escaped, I suppose, by way of the Old Woking road—the road I had taken when I drove to Leatherhead—or they had hidden.

We went down the lane, by the body of the man in black, **sodden** now from the overnight hail, and broke into the woods at the foot of the hill. We pushed through these towards the railway without meeting a soul. The woods across the line were but the scarred and blackened ruins of woods; for the most part the trees had fallen, but a certain proportion still stood, **dismal** grey stems, with dark brown **foliage** instead of green.

scorch (skohrch) *v.* **-ing, -ed**   to burn, especially with the result of discoloring the outer layer   Synonyms: singe, sear, blacken

hail (hayl) *v.* **-ing, -ed**   to greet or catch the attention of   Synonyms: salute, call, address, accost

halt (hawlt) *v.* **-ing, -ed**   to cause to stop or cease, especially temporarily   Synonyms: arrest, adjourn, intermit, impede, suspend

confound (cuhn <u>fowned</u>) *v.* **-ing, -ed**   to bring about confusion; to perplex   Synonyms: baffle, discomfit, flabbergast, nonplus, puzzle, rattle

vivid (<u>vih</u> vihd) *adj.*   fresh, bright, and distinct   Synonyms: animated, brilliant, dynamic, lively, resplendent

CHAPTER 12—WHAT I SAW OF THE DESTRUCTION

On our side the fire had done no more than **scorch** the nearer trees; it had failed to secure its footing. In one place the woodmen had been at work on Saturday; trees, felled and freshly trimmed, lay in a clearing, with heaps of sawdust by the sawing-machine and its engine. Hard by was a temporary hut, deserted. There was not a breath of wind this morning, and everything was strangely still. Even the birds were hushed, and as we hurried along I and the artilleryman talked in whispers and looked now and again over our shoulders. Once or twice we stopped to listen.

After a time we drew near the road, and as we did so we heard the clatter of hoofs and saw through the tree stems three cavalry soldiers riding slowly towards Woking. We **hailed** them, and they **halted** while we hurried towards them. It was a lieutenant and a couple of privates of the 8th Hussars, with a stand like a theodolite, which the artilleryman told me was a <u>heliograph</u>.

"You are the first men I've seen coming this way this morning," said the lieutenant. "What's brewing?"

His voice and face were eager. The men behind him stared curiously. The artilleryman jumped down the bank into the road and saluted.

"Gun destroyed last night, sir. Have been hiding. Trying to rejoin battery, sir. You'll come in sight of the Martians, I expect, about half a mile along this road."

"What the dickens are they like?" asked the lieutenant.

"Giants in armour, sir. Hundred feet high. Three legs and a body like 'luminium, with a mighty great head in a hood, sir."

"Get out!" said the lieutenant. "What **confounded** nonsense!"

"You'll see, sir. They carry a kind of box, sir, that shoots fire and strikes you dead."

"What d'ye mean—a gun?"

"No, sir," and the artilleryman began a **vivid** account of the Heat-Ray. Halfway through, the lieutenant inter-

shabby (<u>shaa</u> bee) *adj.*   worn out; in poor condition due to overuse   Synonyms: dingy, desolate, threadbare, ragged, meager, tattered

assiduously (uh <u>sihd</u> yoo uhs lee) *adv.*   with great attention and care   Synonyms: diligently, thoroughly, attentively, carefully

engage (ihn <u>gayj</u>) *v.* **-ing, -ed**   to become thoroughly involved with; to pledge, as in a service or contract   Synonyms: appoint, commission, lease, enlist, enthrall, captivate rupted him and looked up at me. I was still standing on the bank by the side of the road.

"It's perfectly true," I said.

"Well," said the lieutenant, "I suppose it's my business to see it too. Look here"—to the artilleryman—"we're detailed here clearing people out of their houses. You'd better go along and report yourself to Brigadier-General Marvin, and tell him all you know. He's at Weybridge. Know the way?"

"I do," I said; and he turned his horse southward again.

"Half a mile, you say?" said he.

"At most," I answered, and pointed over the treetops southward. He thanked me and rode on, and we saw them no more.

Farther along we came upon a group of three women and two children in the road, busy clearing out a labourer's cottage. They had got hold of a little hand truck, and were piling it up with unclean-looking bundles and shabby furniture. They were all too assiduously engaged to talk to us as we passed.

By Byfleet station we emerged from the pine trees, and found the country calm and peaceful under the morning sunlight. We were far beyond the range of the Heat-Ray there, and had it not been for the silent desertion of some of the houses, the stirring movement of packing in others, and the knot of soldiers standing on the bridge over the railway and staring down the line towards Woking, the day would have seemed very like any other Sunday.

Several farm waggons and carts were moving creakily along the road to Addlestone, and suddenly through the gate of a field we saw, across a stretch of flat meadow, six twelve-pounders standing neatly at equal distances pointing towards Woking. The gunners stood by the guns waiting, and the ammunition waggons were at a business-like distance. The men stood almost as if under inspection.

hesitate (<u>hehz</u> ih tayt) *v.* **-ing, -ed**   to pause as if unwilling or unsure   Synonyms: dally, flounder, linger, tergiversate, vacillate, demur

rampart (<u>raam</u> pahrt) *n.*   a border built for defensive purposes   Synonyms: embankment, bulwark, barricade, stronghold

engage (ihn <u>gayj</u>) *v.* **-ing, -ed**   to become thoroughly involved with; to pledge, as in a service or contract   Synonyms: appoint, commission, lease, enlist, enthrall, captivate

tumult (<u>tuh</u> muhlt) *n.*   commotion, disturbance, and noise, as of a crowd   Synonyms: agitation, bedlam, uproar, clamor, row

sabbatical (suh <u>baa</u> tihk uhl) *n.*   a period of leave from an endeavor or occupation   Synonyms: furlough, leave of absence

assume (uh <u>soom</u>) *v.* **-ing, -ed**   1. to suppose; to take for granted   Synonyms: presume, estimate, hypothesize, infer   2. to put on, as in an article of clothing   Synonyms: don

expostulate (ehks <u>pahs</u> choo layt) *v.* **-ing, -ed**   to attempt to dissuade through reasoning   Synonyms: protest, debate, remonstrate

"That's good!" said I. "They will get one fair shot, at any rate."

The artilleryman **hesitated** at the gate.

"I shall go on," he said.

Farther on towards Weybridge, just over the bridge, there were a number of men in white fatigue jackets throwing up a long **rampart**, and more guns behind.

"It's bows and arrows against the lightning, anyhow," said the artilleryman. "They 'aven't seen that fire-beam yet."

The officers who were not actively **engaged** stood and stared over the treetops southwestward, and the men digging would stop every now and again to stare in the same direction.

Byfleet was in a **tumult**; people packing, and a score of hussars, some of them dismounted, some on horseback, were hunting them about. Three or four black government waggons, with crosses in white circles, and an old omnibus, among other vehicles, were being loaded in the village street. There were scores of people, most of them sufficiently **sabbatical** to have **assumed** their best clothes. The soldiers were having the greatest difficulty in making them realise the gravity of their position. We saw one shrivelled old fellow with a huge box and a score or more of flower pots containing orchids, angrily **expostulating** with the corporal who would leave them behind. I stopped and gripped his arm.

"Do you know what's over there?" I said, pointing at the pine tops that hid the Martians.

"Eh?" said he, turning. "I was explainin' these is vallyble."

"Death!" I shouted. "Death is coming! Death!" and leaving him to digest that if he could, I hurried on after the artillery-man. At the corner I looked back. The soldier had left him, and he was still standing by his box, with the pots of orchids on the lid of it, and staring vaguely over the trees.

miscellany (<u>mih</u> suh lay nee) *n.*   an assortment of a great variety of items   Synonyms: collection, melee, mélange, compilation, assortment

conveyance (kun <u>vay</u> ehns) *n.*   the act of transferring or transporting property, title, or material   Synonyms: carriage, transference, bond, charter

vicar (<u>vie</u> kuhr) *n.*   a priest or cleric who acts on behalf of a higher-ranking clergyman   Synonyms: delegate, consul, proxy

refuge (<u>reh</u> fyooj) *n.*   shelter or protection; a place providing shelter or protection   Synonyms: asylum, preserve, sanctuary, stronghold

savage (<u>saa</u> vihj) *adj.*   ferocious; vicious   Synonyms: fierce, atrocious, unrelenting, pitiless

treble (<u>treh</u> buhl) *adj.*   high in pitch   Synonyms: shrill, sharp

fugitive (<u>fyoo</u> jih tihv) *n.*   an individual on the run, often being pursued in connection with a crime   Synonyms: outlaw, criminal, refugee

128

No one in Weybridge could tell us where the headquarters were established; the whole place was in such confusion as I had never seen in any town before. Carts, carriages everywhere, the most astonishing **miscellany** of **conveyances** and horseflesh. The respectable inhabitants of the place, men in golf and boating costumes, wives prettily dressed, were packing, river-side loafers energetically helping, children excited, and, for the most part, highly delighted at this astonishing variation of their Sunday experiences. In the midst of it all the worthy **vicar** was very pluckily holding an early celebration, and his bell was jangling out above the excitement.

I and the artilleryman, seated on the step of the drinking fountain, made a very passable meal upon what we had brought with us. Patrols of soldiers—here no longer hussars, but grenadiers in white—were warning people to move now or to take **refuge** in their cellars as soon as the firing began. We saw as we crossed the railway bridge that a growing crowd of people had assembled in and about the railway station, and the swarming platform was piled with boxes and packages. The ordinary traffic had been stopped, I believe, in order to allow of the passage of troops and guns to Chertsey, and I have heard since that a **savage** struggle occurred for places in the special trains that were put on at a later hour.

We remained at Weybridge until midday, and at that hour we found ourselves at the place near Shepperton Lock where the Wey and Thames join. Part of the time we spent helping two old women to pack a little cart. The Wey has a **treble** mouth, and at this point boats are to be hired, and there was a ferry across the river. On the Shepperton side was an inn with a lawn, and beyond that the tower of Shepperton Church—it has been replaced by a spire—rose above the trees.

Here we found an excited and noisy crowd of **fugitives**. As yet the flight had not grown to a panic, but there were already far more people than all the boats going to

jest (jehst) *v.* **-ing, -ed**   to joke or act playfully   Synonyms: joke, kid, banter, gibe, tease, spoof

formidable (<u>fohr</u> mihd uh buhl) *adj.*   causing fear, dread, wonder, or astonishment   Synonyms: appalling, daunting, redoubtable, awesome, tremendous

vivid (<u>vih</u> vihd) *adj.*   fresh, bright, and distinct   Synonyms: animated, brilliant, dynamic, lively, resplendent

prohibit (proh <u>hih</u> biht) *v.* **-ing, -ed**   to disallow; to ban   Synonyms: constrain, enjoin, outlaw, restrict, veto

arrest (uh <u>rehst</u>) *v.* **-ing, -ed**   to stop and hold in place; to seize   Synonyms: block, check, halt, apprehend, catch, collar

unconcernedly (uhn kuhn <u>suhr</u> nihd lee) *adv.*   without trepidation or worry; casually   Synonyms: coolly, composedly, comfortably

CHAPTER 12—WHAT I SAW OF THE DESTRUCTION

and fro could enable to cross. People came panting along under heavy burdens; one husband and wife were even carrying a small outhouse door between them, with some of their household goods piled thereon. One man told us he meant to try to get away from Shepperton station.

There was a lot of shouting, and one man was even **jesting**. The idea people seemed to have here was that the Martians were simply **formidable** human beings, who might attack and sack the town, to be certainly destroyed in the end. Every now and then people would glance nervously across the Wey, at the meadows towards Chertsey, but everything over there was still.

Across the Thames, except just where the boats landed, everything was quiet, in **vivid** contrast with the Surrey side. The people who landed there from the boats went tramping off down the lane. The big ferryboat had just made a journey. Three or four soldiers stood on the lawn of the inn, staring and jesting at the fugitives, without offering to help. The inn was closed, as it was now within **prohibited** hours.

"What's that?" cried a boatman, and "Shut up, you fool!" said a man near me to a yelping dog. Then the sound came again, this time from the direction of Chertsey, a muffled thud—the sound of a gun.

The fighting was beginning. Almost immediately unseen batteries across the river to our right, unseen because of the trees, took up the chorus, firing heavily one after the other. A woman screamed. Everyone stood **arrested** by the sudden stir of battle, near us and yet invisible to us. Nothing was to be seen save flat meadows, cows feeding **unconcernedly** for the most part, and silvery pollard willows motionless in the warm sunlight.

"The sojers'll stop 'em," said a woman beside me, doubtfully. A haziness rose over the treetops.

Then suddenly we saw a rush of smoke far away up the river, a puff of smoke that jerked up into the air and hung; and forthwith the ground heaved under foot and a

astonish (uh <u>stah</u> nihsh) *v.* **-ing, -ed**   to fill with delight, amazement, or disbelief   Synonyms: astound, bewilder, flabbergast, dumbfound

obliquely (oh <u>bleek</u> lee) *adv.*   indirectly; at an angle
Synonyms: sideways, angled, crosswise

flourish (flohr ihsh) *v.* **-ing, -ed**   1. to prosper; to fare well   Synonyms: blossom, burgeon, thrive   2. to wield with great showmanship   Synonyms: brandish, flaunt, wag

smite (smiet) *v.* **smiting, smote**   to strike heavily in order to damage or destroy   Synonyms: strike, harrow, beset, afflict

hoarse (hohrs) *adj.*   harsh in sound   Synonyms: throaty, raspy, husky, ragged

unheeded (uhn <u>heed</u> ehd) *adj.*   ignored or disregarded
Synonyms: neglected, unconsidered

heavy explosion shook the air, smashing two or three windows in the houses near, and leaving us **astonished**.

"Here they are!" shouted a man in a blue jersey. "Yonder! D'yer see them? Yonder!"

Quickly, one after the other, one, two, three, four of the armoured Martians appeared, far away over the little trees, across the flat meadows that stretched towards Chertsey, and striding hurriedly towards the river. Little cowled figures they seemed at first, going with a rolling motion and as fast as flying birds.

Then, advancing **obliquely** towards us, came a fifth. Their armoured bodies glittered in the sun as they swept swiftly forward upon the guns, growing rapidly larger as they drew nearer. One on the extreme left, the remotest that is, **flourished** a huge case high in the air, and the ghostly, terrible Heat-Ray I had already seen on Friday night **smote** towards Chertsey, and struck the town.

At sight of these strange, swift, and terrible creatures the crowd near the water's edge seemed to me to be for a moment horror-struck. There was no screaming or shouting, but a silence. Then a **hoarse** murmur and a movement of feet—a splashing from the water. A man, too frightened to drop the <u>portmanteau</u> he carried on his shoulder, swung round and sent me staggering with a blow from the corner of his burden. A woman thrust at me with her hand and rushed past me. I turned with the rush of the people, but I was not too terrified for thought. The terrible Heat-Ray was in my mind. To get under water! That was it!

"Get under water!" I shouted, **unheeded**.

I faced about again, and rushed towards the approaching Martian, rushed right down the gravelly beach and headlong into the water. Others did the same. A boatload of people putting back came leaping out as I rushed past. The stones under my feet were muddy and slippery, and the river was so low that I ran perhaps twenty feet scarcely waist-deep. Then, as the Martian towered overhead

suffocate (<u>suh</u> fuh kayt) *v.* **-ing, -ed**   to harm, kill, or be so harmed through blocking the intake of oxygen Synonyms: choke, asphyxiate, smother, stifle

generator (<u>jehn</u> uh ray tuhr) *n.*   a machine that produces energy, especially electrical energy   Synonyms: engine, producer

wade (wayd) *v.* **-ing, -ed**   to move with difficulty or great effort, especially through water   Synonyms: plod, bathe, drudge, stumble

rivet (<u>rih</u> veht) *v.* **-ing, -ed**   1. to fasten with a rivet 2. to completely capture the attention of   Synonyms: captivate, enthrall, engross

exultation (ehg zuhl <u>tay</u> shuhn) *n.*   a triumphant or blissful state   Synonyms: celebration, elation, jubilation, reveling scarcely a couple of hundred yards away, I flung myself forward under the surface. The splashes of the people in the boats leaping into the river sounded like thunderclaps in my ears. People were landing hastily on both sides of the river.

But the Martian machine took no more notice for the moment of the people running this way and that than a man would of the confusion of ants in a nest against which his foot has kicked. When, half **suffocated**, I raised my head above water, the Martian's hood pointed at the batteries that were still firing across the river, and as it advanced it swung loose what must have been the **generator** of the Heat-Ray.

In another moment it was on the bank, and in a stride **wading** halfway across. The knees of its foremost legs bent at the farther bank, and in another moment it had raised itself to its full height again, close to the village of Shepperton. Forthwith the six guns which, unknown to anyone on the right bank, had been hidden behind the outskirts of that village, fired simultaneously. The sudden near concussion, the last close upon the first, made my heart jump. The monster was already raising the case generating the Heat-Ray as the first shell burst six yards above the hood.

I gave a cry of astonishment. I saw and thought nothing of the other four Martian monsters; my attention was **riveted** upon the nearer incident. Simultaneously two other shells burst in the air near the body as the hood twisted round in time to receive, but not in time to dodge, the fourth shell.

The shell burst clean in the face of the Thing. The hood bulged, flashed, was whirled off in a dozen tattered fragments of red flesh and glittering metal.

"Hit!" shouted I, with something between a scream and a cheer.

I heard answering shouts from the people in the water about me. I could have leaped out of the water with that momentary **exultation**.

decapitate (dee <u>kahp</u> ih tay tehd) *v.* **-ing, -ed**   to behead

colossus (kuh <u>lah</u> suhs) *n.*   an extremely large and powerful object or individual   Synonyms: behemoth, giant, goliath, titan

reel *v.* **-ing, -ed**   to fall, stagger, or sway as the result of imbalance   Synonyms: wobble, falter, careen

slay (slay) *v.* **-ing, slain**   to kill, often with great violence   Synonyms: assassinate, murder, exterminate, destroy, liquidate

intricate (<u>ihn</u> trih keht) *adj.*   extremely complex in composition   Synonyms: complicated, baroque, labyrinthine, abstruse, daedal

incapable (ihn <u>kay</u> puh buhl) *adj.*   lacking in a particular ability; unable   Synonyms: disqualified, inept, impotent, unfit

blunder (<u>bluhn</u> duhr) *v.* **-ing, -ed**   to make a mistake of significant magnitude   Synonyms: botch, err, fumble, stumble

seethe (seeth) *v.* **-ing, -ed**   to be in an excited or angry state; to literally boil   Synonyms: churn, foam, storm, flare, bristle

patent (<u>paa</u> tehnt) *adj.*   obvious; apparent   Synonyms: conspicuous, plain, gross, downright, straightforward

tumultuous (tuh <u>muhlt</u> yoo uhs) *adj.*   characterized by confusion and disorder   Synonyms: clamorous, agitated, raucous, turbulent

submerge (suhb <u>muhrj</u>) *v.* **-ing, -ed**   to immerse in liquid   Synonyms: dunk, sink, engulf, douse, drench

intermittent (ihn tuhr mih <u>mih</u> tehnt) *adj.*   occurring at irregular intervals   Synonyms: periodic, punctuated, fitful

froth (frawth) *n.*   foam; bubbles formed from the agitation of a liquid   Synonyms: effervescence, fizz, suds, ebullition

amid (uh <u>mihd</u>) *prep.*   among; surrounded by   Synonyms: amongst, between, during, throughout

CHAPTER 12—WHAT I SAW OF THE DESTRUCTION

The **decapitated colossus reeled** like a drunken giant; but it did not fall over. It recovered its balance by a miracle, and, no longer heeding its steps and with the camera that fired the Heat-Ray now rigidly upheld, it reeled swiftly upon Shepperton. The living intelligence, the Martian within the hood, was **slain** and splashed to the four winds of heaven, and the Thing was now but a mere **intricate** device of metal whirling to destruction. It drove along in a straight line, **incapable** of guidance. It struck the tower of Shepperton Church, smashing it down as the impact of a battering ram might have done, swerved aside, **blundered** on and collapsed with tremendous force into the river out of my sight.

A violent explosion shook the air, and a spout of water, steam, mud, and shattered metal shot far up into the sky. As the camera of the Heat-Ray hit the water, the latter had immediately flashed into steam. In another moment a huge wave, like a muddy tidal bore but almost scaldingly hot, came sweeping round the bend upstream. I saw people struggling shorewards, and heard their screaming and shouting faintly above the **seething** and roar of the Martian's collapse.

For a moment I heeded nothing of the heat, forgot the **patent** need of self-preservation. I splashed through the **tumultuous** water, pushing aside a man in black to do so, until I could see round the bend. Half a dozen deserted boats pitched aimlessly upon the confusion of the waves. The fallen Martian came into sight downstream, lying across the river, and for the most part **submerged.**

Thick clouds of steam were pouring off the wreckage, and through the tumultuously whirling wisps I could see, **intermittently** and vaguely, the gigantic limbs churning the water and flinging a splash and spray of mud and **froth** into the air. The tentacles swayed and struck like living arms, and, save for the helpless purposelessness of these movements, it was as if some wounded thing were struggling for its life **amid** the waves. Enormous quantities of

ruddy (<u>ruh</u> dee) *adj.* having a healthy, flushed coloration   Synonyms: rosy, flushed, glowing

flurry (<u>fluh</u> ree) *n.* a sudden burst of activity   Synonyms: bustle, turmoil, whirlwind, furor, ferment

inaudibly (ihn <u>aw</u> dih blee) *adv.* in a manner impossible to hear or detect   Synonyms: silently, softly

unavailingly (uhn uh <u>vayl</u> ihng lee) *adv.* done without achieving a stated purpose   Synonyms: ineffectually, ineffectively

blunder (<u>bluhn</u> duhr) *v.* **-ing, -ed** to make a mistake of significant magnitude   Synonyms: botch, err, fumble, stumble

magnify (<u>maag</u> nih fie) *v.* **-ing, magnified** to enlarge in appearance; to cause to appear more significant   Synonyms: exalt, aggrandize, intensify, inflate, redouble

clangorous (<u>claan</u> guhr uhs) *adj.* characterized by forceful metallic sound   Synonyms: clattery, resonant, ringing, stentorian

din (dihn) *n.* a collection of loud, often harsh, sounds   Synonyms: clangor, racket, row, tumult, uproar

incandescent (ihn kahn <u>dehss</u> ihnt) *adj.* emitting light, often through being heated   Synonyms: brilliant, effulgent, luminous, phosphorescent

lurid (<u>loo</u> rihd) *adj.* 1. sensational in detail; causing shock or horror   Synonyms: shocking, macabre, obscene, offensive   2. strangely pale   Synonyms: pallid, eerie, ashen

intact (ihn <u>taakt</u>) *adj.* maintaining soundness and completeness in construction   Synonyms: uninjured, unimpaired, whole, sound

pallid (<u>paa</u> lihd) *adj.* exceedingly pale; lacking in vitality   Synonyms: wan, ashen, anemic

dumbfound (<u>duhm</u> fownd) *v.* **-ing, -ed** to perplex, to bring about astonishment and incredulity   Synonyms: bewilder, boggle, nonplus, overwhelm a **ruddy**-brown fluid were spurting up in noisy jets out of the machine.

My attention was diverted from this death **flurry** by a furious yelling, like that of the thing called a siren in our manufacturing towns. A man, knee-deep near the towing path, shouted **inaudibly** to me and pointed. Looking back, I saw the other Martians advancing with gigantic strides down the riverbank from the direction of Chertsey. The Shepperton guns spoke this time **unavailingly**.

At that I ducked at once under water, and, holding my breath until movement was an agony, **blundered** painfully ahead under the surface as long as I could. The water was in a tumult about me, and rapidly growing hotter.

When for a moment I raised my head to take breath and throw the hair and water from my eyes, the steam was rising in a whirling white fog that at first hid the Martians altogether. The noise was deafening. Then I saw them dimly, colossal figures of grey, **magnified** by the mist. They had passed by me, and two were stooping over the frothing, tumultuous ruins of their comrade.

The third and fourth stood beside him in the water, one perhaps two hundred yards from me, the other towards Laleham. The generators of the Heat-Rays waved high, and the hissing beams smote down this way and that.

The air was full of sound, a deafening and confusing conflict of noises—the **clangorous din** of the Martians, the crash of falling houses, the thud of trees, fences, sheds flashing into flame, and the crackling and roaring of fire. Dense black smoke was leaping up to mingle with the steam from the river, and as the Heat-Ray went to and fro over Weybridge its impact was marked by flashes of **incandescent** white, that gave place at once to a smoky dance of **lurid** flames. The nearer houses still stood **intact**, awaiting their fate, shadowy, faint and **pallid** in the steam, with the fire behind them going to and fro.

For a moment perhaps I stood there, breast-high in the almost boiling water, **dumbfounded** at my position, hope-

reek *n.*   a thick fog; a steam or vapor   Synonyms: fume, smog, haze

dismay (dihs <u>may</u>) *n.*   a loss of resolve, as in the face of danger or intimidation   Synonyms: consternation, apprehension, disillusionment

dissolve (dih <u>sahlv</u>) *v.* **-ing, -ed**   to melt into a solution; to dismiss   Synonyms: diffuse, liquefy, adjourn, sever, terminate

crest (crehst) *v.* **-ing, -ed**   to reach the top of; to decorate with a ridge or other ornament   Synonyms: cap, culminate

debris (dih <u>bree</u>) *n.*   the remnants of something that has been destroyed   Synonyms: litter, detritus, rubble, wreckage

recede (ree <u>seed</u>) *v.* **-ing, -ed**   to draw back, retreat   Synonyms: abate, decline, diminish, subside

interminably (ihn tuhr mihn uh blee) *adj.*   unceasingly; without apparent end   Synonyms: continuously, endlessly, perpetually, relentlessly less of escape. Through the **reek** I could see the people who had been with me in the river scrambling out of the water through the reeds, like little frogs hurrying through grass from the advance of a man, or running to and fro in utter **dismay** on the towing path.

Then suddenly the white flashes of the Heat-Ray came leaping towards me. The houses caved in as they **dissolved** at its touch, and darted out flames; the trees changed to fire with a roar. The Ray flickered up and down the towing path, licking off the people who ran this way and that, and came down to the water's edge not fifty yards from where I stood. It swept across the river to Shepperton, and the water in its track rose in a boiling <u>weal</u> **crested** with steam. I turned shoreward.

In another moment the huge wave, well-nigh at the boiling-point had rushed upon me. I screamed aloud, and scalded, half blinded, agonised, I staggered through the leaping, hissing water towards the shore. Had my foot stumbled, it would have been the end. I fell helplessly, in full sight of the Martians, upon the broad, bare gravelly spit that runs down to mark the angle of the Wey and Thames. I expected nothing but death.

I have a dim memory of the foot of a Martian coming down within a score of yards of my head, driving straight into the loose gravel, whirling it this way and that and lifting again; of a long suspense, and then of the four carrying the **debris** of their comrade between them, now clear and then presently faint through a veil of smoke, **receding interminably**, as it seemed to me, across a vast space of river and meadow. And then, very slowly, I realised that by a miracle I had escaped.

terrestrial (tuh <u>rehs</u> stree uhl) *adj.* 1. of or relating to the earth Synonyms: earthbound, earthlike 2. prosaic, mundane Synonyms: worldly, common, profane

encumber (ihn <u>cuhm</u> buhr) *v.* **-ing, -ed** to burden, as with weight or obligation Synonyms: burden, oppress, saddle, trammel, impede

stray *adj.* having so moved away from an established route, group, or norm Synonyms: erratic, vagrant, abandoned

negligible (<u>nehg</u> lih juh buhl) *adj.* of little relevance or importance Synonyms: insignificant, inconsequential, remote, trifling, trivial

advent (<u>aad</u> vehnt) *n.* an arrival of great importance; a beginning Synonyms: onset, visitation, inception, approach, coming

antagonist (aan <u>taa</u> guh nihst) *n.* one who opposes, especially with respect to the main character of a drama or narrative Synonyms: adversary, opponent, rival, competitor

furious (<u>fyoo</u> ree uhs) *adj.* full of anger Synonyms: enraged, fierce, wrathful, livid, rabid

CHAPTER THIRTEEN

HOW I FELL IN WITH
THE CURATE

After getting this sudden lesson in the power of **terrestrial** weapons, the Martians retreated to their original position upon Horsell Common; and in their haste, and **encumbered** with the debris of their smashed companion, they no doubt overlooked many such a **stray** and **negligible** victim as myself. Had they left their comrade and pushed on forthwith, there was nothing at that time between them and London but batteries of twelve-pounder guns, and they would certainly have reached the capital in advance of the <u>tidings</u> of their approach; as sudden, dreadful, and destructive their **advent** would have been as the earthquake that destroyed Lisbon a century ago.

But they were in no hurry. Cylinder followed cylinder on its interplanetary flight; every twenty-four hours brought them reinforcement. And meanwhile the military and naval authorities, now fully alive to the tremendous power of their **antagonists**, worked with **furious** energy. Every minute a fresh gun came into position until, before twilight, every copse, every row of suburban villas on

expectant (ehk <u>spehk</u> tehnt) *adj.* in a state of anticipation Synonyms: apprehensive, awaiting, vigilant, pregnant, gravid

encampment (ehn <u>caamp</u> mehnt) *n.* the site on which temporary residences are erected Synonyms: barracks, dormitory, garrison, quarters

proximity (prahk <u>sihm</u> ih tee) *n.* the condition of being close to Synonyms: nearness, juxtaposition, closeness, adjacency

venture (<u>vehn</u> chuhr) *n.* an undertaking, often involving significant risk Synonyms: gamble, enterprise, endeavor, investment, speculation

sentinel (<u>sehn</u> tihn ehl) *n.* one who stands guard or awaits a particular occurrence Synonyms: sentry, lookout, guardian

sodden (<u>sah</u> dihn) *adj.* soaked through Synonyms: saturated, drenched, waterlogged

contrive (kuhn <u>triev</u>) *v.* -ing, -ed to formulate a plan; to invent Synonyms: concoct, manufacture, scheme, engineer

tedious (<u>tee</u> dee uhs) *adj.* so tiresome as to cause weariness; boring Synonyms: banal, drab, laborious, monotonous, soporific the hilly slopes about Kingston and Richmond, masked an **expectant** black muzzle. And through the charred and desolated area—perhaps twenty square miles altogether—that encircled the Martian **encampment** on Horsell Common, through charred and ruined villages among the green trees, through the blackened and smoking arcades that had been but a day ago pine spinneys, crawled the devoted scouts with the <u>heliographs</u> that were presently to warn the gunners of the Martian approach. But the Martians now understood our command of artillery and the danger of human **proximity**, and not a man **ventured** within a mile of either cylinder, save at the price of his life.

It would seem that these giants spent the earlier part of the afternoon in going to and fro, transferring everything from the second and third cylinders—the second in Addlestone Golf Links and the third at Pyrford—to their original pit on Horsell Common. Over that, above the blackened heather and ruined buildings that stretched far and wide, stood one as **sentinel**, while the rest abandoned their vast fighting-machines and descended into the pit. They were hard at work there far into the night, and the towering pillar of dense green smoke that rose therefrom could be seen from the hills about Merrow, and even, it is said, from Banstead and Epsom Downs.

And while the Martians behind me were thus preparing for their next <u>sally</u>, and in front of me Humanity gathered for the battle, I made my way with infinite pains and labour from the fire and smoke of burning Weybridge towards London.

I saw an abandoned boat, very small and remote, drifting down-stream; and throwing off the most of my **sodden** clothes, I went after it, gained it, and so escaped out of that destruction. There were no oars in the boat, but I **contrived** to paddle, as well as my parboiled hands would allow, down the river towards Halliford and Walton, going very **tediously** and continually looking behind me,

tranquil (<u>trank</u> wihl) *adj.*   free of disturbance, conflict, or tension   Synonyms: composed, placid, serene, calm, unruffled

desolate (<u>deh</u> suh liht) *adj.*   uninhabited; unfit for habitation   Synonyms: barren, unfrequented, barren, vacant, waste

obstructive (uhb <u>stuhk</u> tihv) *adj.*   blocking a passage; standing in the way   Synonyms: hindering, impeding, opposing

scorch (skohrch) *v.* **-ing, -ed**   to burn, especially with the result of discoloring the outer layer   Synonyms: singe, sear, blacken

impotent (<u>ihm</u> puh tehnt) *adj.*   lacking in strength, power, or effectiveness   Synonyms: enervated, infirm, ineffectual, weak as you may well understand. I followed the river, because I considered that the water gave me my best chance of escape should these giants return.

The hot water from the Martian's overthrow drifted downstream with me, so that for the best part of a mile I could see little of either bank. Once, however, I made out a string of black figures hurrying across the meadows from the direction of Weybridge. Halliford, it seemed, was deserted, and several of the houses facing the river were on fire. It was strange to see the place quite **tranquil**, quite **desolate** under the hot blue sky, with the smoke and little threads of flame going straight up into the heat of the afternoon. Never before had I seen houses burning without the accompaniment of an **obstructive** crowd. A little farther on the dry reeds up the bank were smoking and glowing, and a line of fire inland was marching steadily across a late field of hay.

For a long time I drifted, so painful and weary was I after the violence I had been through, and so intense the heat upon the water. Then my fears got the better of me again, and I resumed my paddling. The sun **scorched** my bare back. At last, as the bridge at Walton was coming into sight round the bend, my fever and faintness overcame my fears, and I landed on the Middlesex bank and lay down, deadly sick, amid the long grass. I suppose the time was then about four or five o'clock. I got up presently, walked perhaps half a mile without meeting a soul, and then lay down again in the shadow of a hedge. I seem to remember talking, wanderingly, to myself during that last spurt. I was also very thirsty, and bitterly regretful I had drunk no more water. It is a curious thing that I felt angry with my wife; I cannot account for it, but my **impotent** desire to reach Leatherhead worried me excessively.

I do not clearly remember the arrival of the curate, so that probably I dozed. I became aware of him as a seated figure in soot-smudged shirt sleeves, and with his upturned, clean-shaven face staring at a faint flickering

THE WAR OF THE WORLDS

scald (scahld) *v.* **-ing, -ed** to burn, especially with liquid or steam Synonyms: burn, broil, scorch

retreat (ree <u>treet</u>) *v.* **-ing, -ed** to draw back, especially from a position gained Synonyms: evacuate, withdraw, depart, retire

vacantly (<u>vay</u> kihnt lee) *adv.* without energy and focus; apathetically Synonyms: emptily, listlessly, lifelessly

relapse (<u>ree</u> laaps) *v.* **-ing, -ed** to revert; to return to an earlier state or condition Synonyms: backslide, regress, worsen

148

that danced over the sky. The sky was what is called a mackerel sky—rows and rows of faint down-plumes of cloud, just tinted with the midsummer sunset.

I sat up, and at the rustle of my motion he looked at me quickly.

"Have you any water?" I asked abruptly.

He shook his head.

"You have been asking for water for the last hour," he said.

For a moment we were silent, taking stock of each other. I dare say he found me a strange enough figure, naked, save for my water-soaked trousers and socks, **scalded**, and my face and shoulders blackened by the smoke. His face was a fair weakness, his chin **retreated**, and his hair lay in crisp, almost flaxen curls on his low forehead; his eyes were rather large, pale blue, and blankly staring. He spoke abruptly, looking **vacantly** away from me.

"What does it mean?" he said. "What do these things mean?"

I stared at him and made no answer.

He extended a thin white hand and spoke in almost a complaining tone.

"Why are these things permitted? What sins have we done? The morning service was over, I was walking through the roads to clear my brain for the afternoon, and then—fire, earthquake, death! As if it were Sodom and Gomorrah! All our work undone, all the work—— What are these Martians?"

"What are we?" I answered, clearing my throat.

He gripped his knees and turned to look at me again. For half a minute, perhaps, he stared silently.

"I was walking through the roads to clear my brain," he said. "And suddenly—fire, earthquake, death!"

He **relapsed** into silence, with his chin now sunken almost to his knees.

Presently he began waving his hand.

demented (dih <u>mehn</u> tehd) *adj.*   insane   Synonyms:
lunatic, mad, crazy, deranged

evident (<u>eh</u> vih dehnt) *adj.*   apparent; easy to understand
Synonyms: obvious, logical, indisputable, distinct

verge (vuhrj) *n.*   the border or limit; threshold   Synonyms: boundary, brink, margin

officiate (uh <u>fih</u> shee ayt) *v.* **-ing, -ed**   to referee; to
assume a position of authority and arbitration   Syn-
onyms: manage, preside, umpire, command, direct

dawn *v.* **-ing, -ed**   to emerge; to begin to be understood
Synonyms: appear, unfold, develop

regard (ree <u>gahrd</u>) *v.* **-ing, -ed**   to observe with great
attention; to consider in a particular manner   Syn-
onyms: attend, contemplate, scrutinize, adjudge

laboured or **labored** (<u>lay</u> buhrd) *adj.*   requiring great
and often unpleasant effort   Synonyms: arduous, difficult, strained, toilsome

"All the work—all the Sunday schools—What have we done—what has Weybridge done? Everything gone—everything destroyed. The church! We rebuilt it only three years ago. Gone! Swept out of existence! Why?"

Another pause, and he broke out again like one **demented**.

"The smoke of her burning goeth up for ever and ever!" he shouted.

His eyes flamed, and he pointed a lean finger in the direction of Weybridge.

By this time I was beginning to take his measure. The tremendous tragedy in which he had been involved—it was **evident** he was a fugitive from Weybridge—had driven him to the very **verge** of his reason.

"Are we far from Sunbury?" I said, in a matter-of-fact tone.

"What are we to do?" he asked. "Are these creatures everywhere? Has the earth been given over to them?"

"Are we far from Sunbury?"

"Only this morning I **officiated** at early celebration—"

"Things have changed," I said, quietly. "You must keep your head. There is still hope."

"Hope!"

"Yes. Plentiful hope—for all this destruction!"

I began to explain my view of our position. He listened at first, but as I went on the interest **dawning** in his eyes gave place to their former stare, and his **regard** wandered from me.

"This must be the beginning of the end," he said, interrupting me. "The end! The great and terrible day of the Lord! When men shall call upon the mountains and the rocks to fall upon them and hide them—hide them from the face of Him that sitteth upon the throne!"

I began to understand the position. I ceased my **laboured** reasoning, struggled to my feet, and, standing over him, laid my hand on his shoulder.

calamity (cah <u>lahm</u> uh tee) *n.*   a disastrous event
Synonyms: catastrophe, cataclysm

invulnerable (ihn <u>vuhl</u> nuhr uh buhl) *adj.*   unable to be
attacked or harmed   Synonyms: impregnable, invin-
cible, impervious

pitiless (<u>piht</u> ee lehs) *adj.*   without mercy or remorse
Synonyms: callous, obdurate, unrelenting, inexorable

resonance (<u>rehz</u> uh nihns) *n.*   the quality of richness,
depth, and vibration   Synonyms: euphony, reverberation

remote (ree <u>moht</u>) *adj.*   located at a distance in space
or time   Synonyms: alien, obscure, far-flung, secluded

splendour or **splendor** (<u>splehn</u> duhr) *n.*   the state of being
filled with light; magnificence   Synonyms: brilliance,
dazzle, luster, radiance, pomp

CHAPTER 13—HOW I FELL IN WITH THE CURATE

"Be a man!" said I. "You are scared out of your wits! What good is religion if it collapses under **calamity**? Think of what earthquakes and floods, wars and volcanoes, have done before to men! Did you think God had exempted Weybridge? He is not an insurance agent."

For a time he sat in blank silence.

"But how can we escape?" he asked, suddenly. "They are **invulnerable**, they are **pitiless**."

"Neither the one nor, perhaps, the other," I answered. "And the mightier they are the more sane and wary should we be. One of them was killed yonder not three hours ago."

"Killed!" he said, staring about him. "How can God's ministers be killed?"

"I saw it happen." I proceeded to tell him. "We have chanced to come in for the thick of it," said I, "and that is all."

"What is that flicker in the sky?" he asked abruptly.

I told him it was the heliograph signalling—that it was the sign of human help and effort in the sky.

"We are in the midst of it," I said, "quiet as it is. That flicker in the sky tells of the gathering storm. Yonder, I take it are the Martians, and Londonward, where those hills rise about Richmond and Kingston and the trees give cover, earthworks are being thrown up and guns are being placed. Presently the Martians will be coming this way again."

And even as I spoke he sprang to his feet and stopped me by a gesture.

"Listen!" he said.

From beyond the low hills across the water came the dull **resonance** of distant guns and a **remote** weird crying. Then everything was still. A cockchafer came droning over the hedge and past us. High in the west the crescent moon hung faint and pale above the smoke of Weybridge and Shepperton and the hot, still **splendour** of the sunset.

"We had better follow this path," I said, "northward."

imminent (<u>ih</u> muh nehnt) *adj.*   occurring in the immediate future   Synonyms: expectant, forthcoming,
impending

brevity (<u>breh</u> vih tee) *n.*   the quality of being of short
duration   Synonyms: terseness, concision, curtness,
economy

formidable (<u>fohr</u> mihd uh buhl) *adj.*   causing fear, dread,
wonder, or astonishment   Synonyms: appalling,
daunting, redoubtable, awesome, tremendous

incapable (ihn <u>kay</u> puh buhl) *adj.*   lacking in a particular
ability; unable   Synonyms: disqualified, inept, impo-
tent, unfit

CHAPTER FOURTEEN

IN LONDON

My younger brother was in London when the Martians fell at Woking. He was a medical student working for an **imminent** examination, and he heard nothing of the arrival until Saturday morning. The morning papers on Saturday contained, in addition to lengthy special articles on the planet Mars, on life in the planets, and so forth, a brief and vaguely worded telegram, all the more striking for its **brevity**.

The Martians, alarmed by the approach of a crowd, had killed a number of people with a quick-firing gun, so the story ran. The telegram concluded with the words: "**Formidable** as they seem to be, the Martians have not moved from the pit into which they have fallen, and, indeed, seem **incapable** of doing so. Probably this is due to the relative strength of the earth's gravitational energy." On that last text their leader-writer expanded very comfortingly.

Of course all the students in the crammer's biology class, to which my brother went that day, were intensely interested, but there were no signs of any unusual excitement in the streets. The afternoon papers puffed scraps of news under big headlines. They had nothing to tell beyond the

anxiety (aang <u>zie</u> ih tee) *n.*   a state of intense apprehension, worry, uncertainty, and fear, especially in anticipation of some future occurrence.   Synonyms: angst, disquiet, dread, foreboding, uneasiness

dispatch (<u>dihs</u> paatch) *v.* **-ing, -ed**   to send off to perform a specific function   Synonyms: consign, hasten, quicken, transmit

ascertain (aa suhr tayn) *v.* **-ing, -ed**   to determine with certainty, especially after careful observation or experimentation   Synonyms: ensure, divine, verify, discover

nocturnal (nahk <u>tuhr</u> nuhl) *adj.*   active at night and at rest during the day

waylay (way lay) *v.* **-ing, waylaid**   to ambush   Synonyms: intercept, assail, surprise movements of troops about the common, and the burning of the pine woods between Woking and Weybridge, until eight. Then the *St. James's Gazette*, in an extra-special edition, announced the bare fact of the interruption of telegraphic communication. This was thought to be due to the falling of burning pine trees across the line. Nothing more of the fighting was known that night, the night of my drive to Leatherhead and back.

My brother felt no **anxiety** about us, as he knew from the description in the papers that the cylinder was a good two miles from my house. He made up his mind to run down that night to me, in order, as he says, to see the Things before they were killed. He **dispatched** a telegram, which never reached me, about four o'clock, and spent the evening at a music hall.

In London, also, on Saturday night there was a thunderstorm, and my brother reached Waterloo in a cab. On the platform from which the midnight train usually starts he learned, after some waiting, that an accident prevented trains from reaching Woking that night. The nature of the accident he could not **ascertain**; indeed, the railway authorities did not clearly know at that time. There was very little excitement in the station, as the officials, failing to realise that anything further than a breakdown between Byfleet and Woking junction had occurred, were running the theatre trains which usually passed through Woking round by Virginia Water or Guildford. They were busy making the necessary arrangements to alter the route of the Southampton and Portsmouth Sunday League excursions. A **nocturnal** newspaper reporter, mistaking my brother for the traffic manager, to whom he bears a slight resemblance, **waylaid** and tried to interview him. Few people, excepting the railway officials, connected the breakdown with the Martians.

I have read, in another account of these events, that on Sunday morning "all London was electrified by the news from Woking." As a matter of fact, there was nothing to

justify (<u>juhs</u> tih fie) *v.* **-ing, -justified**   to show to be appropriate, reasonable, or warranted · Synonyms: legitimize, condone, countenance, substantiate, confirm

extravagant (ehk <u>straa</u> vih gehnt) *adj.*   excessively lush, showy, or expensive   Synonyms: ostentatious, immoderate, garish, gaudy, pretentious

tremor (<u>treh</u> muhr) *n.*   a vibration, especially of the earth   Synonyms: wobble, quaking, flutter, agitation

adjacent (uhd <u>jae</u> sihnt) *adj.*   positioned next to, beside   Synonyms: adjoining, contiguous, bordering

menagerie (muh <u>nah</u> zheh ree) *n.*   a collection of markedly diverse individuals   Synonyms: hodgepodge, collection, band

default (dee <u>fawlt</u>) *n.*   the failure to fulfill a required obligation   Synonyms: delinquency, dereliction, neglect, privation

justify that very **extravagant** phrase. Plenty of Londoners did not hear of the Martians until the panic of Monday morning. Those who did took some time to realise all that the hastily worded telegrams in the Sunday papers conveyed. The majority of people in London do not read Sunday papers.

The habit of personal security, moreover, is so deeply fixed in the Londoner's mind, and startling intelligence so much a matter of course in the papers, that they could read without any personal **tremors**: "About seven o'clock last night the Martians came out of the cylinder, and, moving about under an armour of metallic shields, have completely wrecked Woking station with the **adjacent** houses, and massacred an entire battalion of the Cardigan Regiment. No details are known. Maxims have been absolutely useless against their armour; the field guns have been disabled by them. Flying hussars have been galloping into Chertsey. The Martians appear to be moving slowly towards Chertsey or Windsor. Great anxiety prevails in West Surrey, and earthworks are being thrown up to check the advance Londonward." That was how the Sunday *Sun* put it, and a clever and remarkably prompt "handbook" article in the *Referee* compared the affair to a **menagerie** suddenly let loose in a village.

No one in London knew positively of the nature of the armoured Martians, and there was still a fixed idea that these monsters must be sluggish: "crawling," "creeping painfully"—such expressions occurred in almost all the earlier reports. None of the telegrams could have been written by an eyewitness of their advance. The Sunday papers printed separate editions as further news came to hand, some even in **default** of it. But there was practically nothing more to tell people until late in the afternoon, when the authorities gave the press agencies the news in their possession. It was stated that the people of Walton and Weybridge, and all the district were pouring along the roads Londonward, and that was all. My brother

allusion (ah <u>loo</u> zhuhn) *n.* an indirect reference; a suggestion of Synonyms: hint, implication, insinuation, innuendo, intimation

innumerable (ih <u>noo</u> muhr uh buhl) *adj.* too great in quantity to be counted Synonyms: countless, numerous, incalculable, infinite

disseminate (dih <u>seh</u> mih nayt) *v.* **-ing, -ed** to scatter about; to distribute Synonyms: circulate, diffuse, promulgate, propagate, strew

abruptly (uh <u>bruhpt</u> lee) *adv.* without warning Synonyms: unexpectedly, suddenly, unpredictably

cease (sees) *v.* **-ing, -ed** to stop or put an end to an activity or task Synonyms: desist, discontinue, cessation, conclude, quit went to church at the Foundling Hospital in the morning, still in ignorance of what had happened on the previous night. There he heard **allusions** made to the invasion, and a special prayer for peace. Coming out, he bought a *Referee*. He became alarmed at the news in this, and went again to Waterloo station to find out if communication were restored. The omnibuses, carriages, cyclists, and **innumerable** people walking in their best clothes seemed scarcely affected by the strange intelligence that the news venders were **disseminating**. People were interested, or, if alarmed, alarmed only on account of the local residents. At the station he heard for the first time that the Windsor and Chertsey lines were now interrupted. The porters told him that several remarkable telegrams had been received in the morning from Byfleet and Chertsey stations, but that these had **abruptly ceased**.

My brother could get very little precise detail out of them.

"There's fighting going on about Weybridge" was the extent of their information.

The train service was now very much disorganised. Quite a number of people who had been expecting friends from places on the South-Western network were standing about the station. One grey-headed old gentleman came and abused the South-Western Company bitterly to my brother. "It wants showing up," he said.

One or two trains came in from Richmond, Putney, and Kingston, containing people who had gone out for a day's boating and found the locks closed and a feeling of panic in the air. A man in a blue and white blazer addressed my brother, full of strange tidings.

"There's hosts of people driving into Kingston in traps and carts and things, with boxes of valuables and all that," he said. "They come from Molesey and Weybridge and Walton, and they say there's been guns heard at Chertsey, heavy firing, and that mounted soldiers have told them to get off at once because the Martians are coming. *We* heard

excursionist (ehks <u>cuhr</u> zhuhnn ihst) *n.* an individual visiting sites of interest   Synonyms: tourist, voyager, wayfarer

hearsay (<u>heer</u> say) *n.* uncorroborated information passed from person to person   Synonyms: buzz, rumor, gossip, talk, wire

terminus (<u>tuhr</u> mihn uhs) *n.* the end point, especially in reference to a transportation system

invariably (ihn <u>vehr</u> ree uh blee) *adv.* in an unchanging manner   Synonyms: inevitably, eternally, without exception, ever

pleasantry (<u>pleh</u> zuhn tree) *n.* a polite or good-natured remark   Synonyms: nicety, quip, repartee

loafer (<u>loh</u> fuhr) *n.* an individual characterized by laziness   Synonyms: idler, lounger, malingerer, wastrel

transverse (<u>trahnz</u> vuhrs) *adj.* positioned across, crosswise   Synonyms: crossways, diagonally, aslant guns firing at Hampton Court station, but we thought it was thunder. What the dickens does it all mean? The Martians can't get out of their pit, can they?"

My brother could not tell him.

Afterwards he found that the vague feeling of alarm had spread to the clients of the underground railway, and that the Sunday **excursionists** began to return from all over the South-Western "lung"—Barnes, Wimbledon, Richmond Park, Kew, and so forth—at unnaturally early hours; but not a soul had anything more than vague **hearsay** to tell of. Everyone connected with the **terminus** seemed ill-tempered.

About five o'clock the gathering crowd in the station was immensely excited by the opening of the line of communication, which is almost **invariably** closed, between the South-Eastern and the South-Western stations, and the passage of carriage trucks bearing huge guns and carriages crammed with soldiers. These were the guns that were brought up from Woolwich and Chatham to cover Kingston. There was an exchange of **pleasantries**: "You'll get eaten!" "We're the beast-tamers!" and so forth. A little while after that a squad of police came into the station and began to clear the public off the platforms, and my brother went out into the street again.

The church bells were ringing for evensong, and a squad of Salvation Army lassies came singing down Waterloo Road. On the bridge a number of **loafers** were watching a curious brown scum that came drifting down the stream in patches. The sun was just setting, and the Clock Tower and the Houses of Parliament rose against one of the most peaceful skies it is possible to imagine, a sky of gold, barred with long **transverse** stripes of reddish-purple cloud. There was talk of a floating body. One of the men there, a reservist he said he was, told my brother he had seen the heliograph flickering in the west.

In Wellington Street my brother met a couple of sturdy roughs who had just been rushed out of Fleet Street with

placard (<u>plaa</u> kuhrd) *n.* a small sign or notice for public display of information   Synonyms: notice, ad, display, poster, ad

catastrophe (kaa <u>taa</u> struh fee) *n.* an incident that results in overwhelming loss, often occurring suddenly   Synonyms: debacle, fiasco, calamity, devastation, cataclysm

repulse (ree <u>puhls</u>) *v.* **-ing, -ed** to drive out; to push or keep away   Synonyms: check, stave off, rebut, reject, fend off

smite (smiet) *v.* **smiting, smote** to strike heavily in order to damage or destroy   Synonyms: strike, harrow, beset, afflict

annihilate (uh <u>nie</u> ihl ayt) *v.* **-ing, -ed** to destroy completely   Synonyms: decimate, abrogate, slaughter, liquidate, massacre

dispatch (<u>dihs</u> paatch) *v.* **-ing, -ed** to send off to perform a specific function   Synonyms: consign, hasten, quicken, transmit

invulnerable (ihn <u>vuhl</u> nuhr uh buhl) *adj.* unable to be attacked or harmed   Synonyms: impregnable, invincible, impervious

transit (<u>traan</u> ziht) *n.* the state of passing through; the movement of goods or people   Synonyms: conveyance, carriage, transportation, progression still-wet newspapers and staring **placards**. "Dreadful **catastrophe!**" they bawled one to the other down Wellington Street. "Fighting at Weybridge! Full description! **Repulse** of the Martians! London in Danger!" He had to give threepence for a copy of that paper.

Then it was, and then only, that he realised something of the full power and terror of these monsters. He learned that they were not merely a handful of small sluggish creatures, but that they were minds swaying vast mechanical bodies; and that they could move swiftly and **smite** with such power that even the mightiest guns could not stand against them.

They were described as "vast spiderlike machines, nearly a hundred feet high, capable of the speed of an express train, and able to shoot out a beam of intense heat." Masked batteries, chiefly of field guns, had been planted in the country about Horsell Common, and especially between the Woking district and London. Five of the machines had been seen moving towards the Thames, and one, by a happy chance, had been destroyed.

In the other cases the shells had missed, and the batteries had been at once **annihilated** by the Heat-Rays. Heavy losses of soldiers were mentioned, but the tone of the **dispatch** was optimistic.

The Martians had been repulsed; they were not **invulnerable**. They had retreated to their triangle of cylinders again, in the circle about Woking. Signallers with heliographs were pushing forward upon them from all sides. Guns were in rapid **transit** from Windsor, Portsmouth, Aldershot, Woolwich—even from the north; among others, long wire-guns of ninety-five tons from Woolwich. Altogether one hundred and sixteen were in position or being hastily placed, chiefly covering London. Never before in England had there been such a vast or rapid concentration of military material.

Any further cylinders that fell, it was hoped, could be destroyed at once by high explosives, which were being

grave (grayv) *adj.* fraught with difficulty, seriousness, or solemnity   Synonyms: sober, leaden, solelemn, somber, staid

exhort (ehg <u>zohrt</u>) *v.* **-ing, -ed**   to strongly urge; to adamantly appeal   Synonyms: admonish, beseech, enjoin, goad, incite

dispose (dihs <u>pohz</u>) *v.* **-ing, -ed**   to transfer possession of; to throw away or cast off   Synonyms: bestow, discard, jettison, relinquish, unload

elaborate (ee <u>laab</u> uh riht) *adj.*   complex and rich in detail   Synonyms: intricant, labarynthine, extravagant, embellished

reiterate (ree <u>ih</u> tuhr ayt) *v.* **-ing, -ed**   to do again, especially for purposes of reinforcement or emphasis   Synonyms: echo, iterate, recapitulate, rehash, reprise

assurance (uh <u>shoor</u> ehns) *n.*   an appeal meant to restore or bolster confidence   Synonyms: affirmation, pledge, profession, support

proclamation (prahk luh <u>may</u> shuhn) *n.*   a formal, often public, announcement   Synonyms: declaration, pronouncement, decree, edict

apathy (<u>aa</u> puh thee) *n.*   a state of indifference or lack of interest in matters of significant import   Synonyms: detachment, lassitude, insouciance, insensibility, aloofness, disinterest

raiment (<u>ray</u> mehnt) *n.*   clothing, especially of a decorative type   Synonyms: apparel, accoutrement, outfit, vestment rapidly manufactured and distributed. No doubt, ran the report, the situation was of the strangest and **gravest** description, but the public was **exhorted** to avoid and discourage panic. No doubt the Martians were strange and terrible in the extreme, but at the outside there could not be more than twenty of them against our millions.

The authorities had reason to suppose, from the size of the cylinders, that at the outside there could not be more than five in each cylinder—fifteen altogether. And one at least was **disposed** of—perhaps more. The public would be fairly warned of the approach of danger, and **elaborate** measures were being taken for the protection of the people in the threatened southwestern suburbs. And so, with **reiterated assurances** of the safety of London and the ability of the authorities to cope with the difficulty, this quasi-**proclamation** closed.

This was printed in enormous type on paper so fresh that it was still wet, and there had been no time to add a word of comment. It was curious, my brother said, to see how ruthlessly the usual contents of the paper had been hacked and taken out to give this place.

All down Wellington Street people could be seen fluttering out the pink sheets and reading, and the Strand was suddenly noisy with the voices of an army of hawkers following these pioneers. Men came scrambling off buses to secure copies. Certainly this news excited people intensely, whatever their previous **apathy**. The shutters of a map shop in the Strand were being taken down, my brother said, and a man in his Sunday **raiment**, lemon-yellow gloves even, was visible inside the window hastily fastening maps of Surrey to the glass.

Going on along the Strand to Trafalgar Square, the paper in his hand, my brother saw some of the fugitives from West Surrey. There was a man with his wife and two boys and some articles of furniture in a cart such as greengrocers use. He was driving from the direction of Westminster Bridge; and close behind him came a hay

haggard (<u>haa</u> guhrd) *adj.*   worn and wearied in appearance   Synonyms: ashen, pallid, exhausted, fatigued

conspicuously (kuhn <u>spihk</u> yoo uhs lee) *adv.*   in a particularly noticeable or obvious fashion   Synonyms: apparently, manifestly, palpably, patently, transparently

refugee (<u>reh</u> fyoo jee) *n.*   one displaced and in search of refuge, especially during a calamity   Synonyms: escapee, evacuee, expatriate, pariah, renegade, fugitive

profess (pruh <u>fehs</u>) *v.* **-ing, -ed**   to claim openly, as in a belief or doctrine   Synonyms: affirm, maintain, predicate, proclaim

animate (<u>ah</u> nih mayt) *v.* **-ing, -ed**   to fill with energy and liveliness   Synonyms: inspire, activate, embolden, arouse, vitalize waggon with five or six respectable-looking people in it, and some boxes and bundles. The faces of these people were **haggard**, and their entire appearance contrasted **conspicuously** with the Sabbath-best appearance of the people on the omnibuses. People in fashionable clothing peeped at them out of cabs. They stopped at the Square as if undecided which way to take, and finally turned eastward along the Strand. Some way behind these came a man in workday clothes, riding one of those old-fashioned tricycles with a small front wheel. He was dirty and white in the face.

My brother turned down towards Victoria, and met a number of such people. He had a vague idea that he might see something of me. He noticed an unusual number of police regulating the traffic. Some of the **refugees** were exchanging news with the people on the omnibuses. One was **professing** to have seen the Martians. "Boilers on stilts, I tell you, striding along like men." Most of them were excited and **animated** by their strange experience.

Beyond Victoria the public-houses were doing a lively trade with these arrivals. At all the street corners groups of people were reading papers, talking excitedly, or staring at these unusual Sunday visitors. They seemed to increase as night drew on, until at last the roads, my brother said, were like Epsom High Street on a Derby Day. My brother addressed several of these fugitives and got unsatisfactory answers from most.

None of them could tell him any news of Woking except one man, who assured him that Woking had been entirely destroyed on the previous night.

"I come from Byfleet," he said; "man on a bicycle came through the place in the early morning, and ran from door to door warning us to come away. Then came soldiers. We went out to look, and there were clouds of smoke to the south—nothing but smoke, and not a soul coming that way. Then we heard the guns at Chertsey, and folks com-

incapacity (ihn kuh <u>paa</u> sih tee) *n.* the lack of a particular ability, often in reference to basic strength and functionality Synonyms: incapability, handicap, impotency, incompetence

dispose (dihs <u>pohz</u>) *v.* **-ing, -ed** to transfer possession of; to throw away or cast off Synonyms: bestow, discard, jettison, relinquish, unload

distinguish (dih <u>stihng</u> wihsh) *v.* **-ing, -ed** to perceive as distinct or different from others Synonyms: characterize, ascertain, categorize, identify, individuate

anxious (<u>aank</u> shihs) *adj.* extremely worried or uneasy about a particular matter Synonyms: apprehensive, disquieted, distressed, overwrought

magnitude (<u>maag</u> nih tood) *n.* greatness in importance, authority, position, or size Synonyms: consequence, greatness, import, eminence

incline (ihn <u>klien</u>) *v.* **-ing, -ed** to hold a particular preference or opinion Synonyms: favor, bias, prefer, predispose

nomadic (noh <u>maad</u> ihk) *adj.* roaming about; having no fixed place of residence Synonyms: itinerant, migrant, perambulant, peripatetic

oppressive (uh <u>preh</u> sihv) *adj.* difficult to endure, especially in reference to injustice Synonyms: overwhelming, dismal, burdensome, onerous, overbearing

intermittently (ihn tuhr <u>miht</u> tehnt lee) *adv.* at irregular intervals; erratically Synonyms: occasionally, spasmodically, irregularly, unpredictably

prowl *v.* **-ing, -ed** to move with stealth, especially in search of prey Synonyms: slink, stalk, tramp, patrol

lurid (<u>loo</u> rihd) *adj.* 1. sensational in detail; causing shock or horror Synonyms: shocking, macabre, obscene, offensive 2. strangely pale Synonyms: pallid, eerie, ashen

clamour or **clamor** (<u>klah</u> muhr) *n.* 1. a jumble of sound and activity, often discordant Synonyms: bustle, babel, commotion, pandemonium 2. an outcry meant as an expression of discontent or objection Synonyms: complaint, lament, tumult ing from Weybridge. So I've locked up my house and come on."

At the time there was a strong feeling in the streets that the authorities were to blame for their **incapacity** to **dispose** of the invaders without all this inconvenience.

About eight o'clock a noise of heavy firing was distinctly audible all over the south of London. My brother could not hear it for the traffic in the main thoroughfares, but by striking through the quiet back streets to the river he was able to **distinguish** it quite plainly.

He walked from Westminster to his apartments near Regent's Park, about two. He was now very **anxious** on my account, and disturbed at the evident **magnitude** of the trouble. His mind was **inclined** to run, even as mine had run on Saturday, on military details. He thought of all those silent, expectant guns, of the suddenly **nomadic** countryside; he tried to imagine "boilers on stilts" a hundred feet high.

There were one or two cartloads of refugees passing along Oxford Street, and several in the Marylebone Road, but so slowly was the news spreading that Regent Street and Portland Place were full of their usual Sunday-night promenaders, albeit they talked in groups, and along the edge of Regent's Park there were as many silent couples "walking out" together under the scattered gas lamps as ever there had been. The night was warm and still, and a little **oppressive**; the sound of guns continued **intermittently**, and after midnight there seemed to be sheet lightning in the south.

He read and re-read the paper, fearing the worst had happened to me. He was restless, and after supper **prowled** out again aimlessly. He returned and tried in vain to divert his attention to his examination notes. He went to bed a little after midnight, and was awakened from **lurid** dreams in the small hours of Monday by the sound of door knockers, feet running in the street, distant drumming, and a **clamour** of bells. Red reflections danced on

disarray (dihs uh <u>ray</u>) *n.*   a state of great confusion or disorder   Synonyms: chaos, disharmony, disorganization, clutter

enquiry (<u>ehn</u> kwih ree) *n.*   the act of examination or questioning a particular affair   Synonyms: audit, interrogation, investigation, fishing, disquisition

vehement (<u>vee</u> eh mehnt) *adj.*   marked by emotional intensity and assertiveness of expression   Synonyms: passionate, ardent, fervent, inflamed, frantic

illumination (ih loom ih <u>nay</u> shun) *n.*   the act of filling with light, clarity, or understanding   Synonyms: light, radiance, brilliance, enlightenment

abruptly (uh <u>bruhpt</u> lee) *adv.*   without warning   Synonyms: unexpectedly, suddenly, unpredictably

forerunner (<u>fohr</u> ruhn uhr) *n.*   one who comes before   Synonyms: ancestor, forbear, predecessor, harbinger

procession (proh <u>sehs</u> shuhn) *n.*   an orderly movement forward   Synonyms: parade, succession, series, march, course, consecution

gradient (<u>gray</u> dee ihnt) *n.*   a part that ascends or descends   Synonyms: slope, pitch, rise, angle, incline, declivity

incomprehensible (ihn kahm pree <u>hehn</u> sih buhl) *adj.* impossible to understand or make sense of   Synonyms: baffling, inscrutable, opaque, unintelligible, unfathomable

crane (krayn) *v.* **-ing, -ed**   to move into an uncomfortable position, especially for the purposes of a better view   Synonyms: extend, crook, protract the ceiling. For a moment he lay astonished, wondering whether day had come or the world gone mad. Then he jumped out of bed and ran to the window.

His room was an attic and as he thrust his head out, up and down the street there were a dozen echoes to the noise of his window sash, and heads in every kind of night **disarray** appeared. **Enquiries** were being shouted. "They are coming!" bawled a policeman, hammering at the door; "the Martians are coming!" and hurried to the next door.

The sound of drumming and trumpeting came from the Albany Street Barracks, and every church within earshot was hard at work killing sleep with a **vehement** disorderly tocsin. There was a noise of doors opening, and window after window in the houses opposite flashed from darkness into yellow **illumination**.

Up the street came galloping a closed carriage, bursting **abruptly** into noise at the corner, rising to a clattering climax under the window, and dying away slowly in the distance. Close on the rear of this came a couple of cabs, the **forerunners** of a long **procession** of flying vehicles, going for the most part to Chalk Farm station, where the North-Western special trains were loading up, instead of coming down the **gradient** into Euston.

For a long time my brother stared out of the window in blank astonishment, watching the policemen hammering at door after door, and delivering their **incomprehensible** message. Then the door behind him opened, and the man who lodged across the landing came in, dressed only in shirt, trousers, and slippers, his braces loose about his waist, his hair disordered from his pillow.

"What the devil is it?" he asked. "A fire? What a devil of a row!"

They both **craned** their heads out of the window, straining to hear what the policemen were shouting. People were coming out of the side streets, and standing in groups at the corners talking.

bawl *v.* **-ing, -ed**   to wail, cry, or shout with great force
Synonyms: bark, clamor, howl, shriek

suffocation (suh fuh <u>kay</u> shuhn) *n.*   the act of blocking the intake of oxygen to kill or harm   Synonyms:
asphyxiation, smothering, stifling

inert (ihn <u>uhrt</u>) *adj.*   incapable of or lethargic in movement or activity   Synonyms: lifeless, languid, torpid,
indolent

contagion (cuhn <u>tay</u> juhn) *n.*   an agent that causes illness
Synonyms: taint, virus

unanimous (yoo <u>naa</u> nih muhs) *adj.*   characterized by
complete agreement by all parties   Synonyms: accor-
dant, concerted, consonant, homogenous, assenting

"What the devil is it all about?" said my brother's fellow lodger.

My brother answered him vaguely and began to dress, running with each garment to the window in order to miss nothing of the growing excitement. And presently men selling unnaturally early newspapers came bawling into the street:

"London in danger of suffocation! The Kingston and Richmond defences forced! Fearful massacres in the Thames Valley!"

And all about him—in the rooms below, in the houses on each side and across the road, and behind in the Park Terraces and in the hundred other streets of that part of Marylebone, and the Westbourne Park district and St. Pancras, and westward and northward in Kilburn and St. John's Wood and Hampstead, and eastward in Shoreditch and Highbury and Haggerston and Hoxton, and, indeed, through all the vastness of London from Ealing to East Ham—people were rubbing their eyes, and opening windows to stare out and ask aimless questions, dressing hastily as the first breath of the coming storm of Fear blew through the streets. It was the dawn of the great panic. London, which had gone to bed on Sunday night oblivious and inert, was awakened, in the small hours of Monday morning, to a vivid sense of danger.

Unable from his window to learn what was happening, my brother went down and out into the street, just as the sky between the parapets of the houses grew pink with the early dawn. The flying people on foot and in vehicles grew more numerous every moment. "Black Smoke!" he heard people crying, and again "Black Smoke!" The contagion of such a unanimous fear was inevitable. As my brother hesitated on the door-step, he saw another news vender approaching, and got a paper forthwith. The man was running away with the rest, and selling his papers for a shilling each as he ran—a grotesque mingling of profit and panic.

dispatch (<u>dihs</u> paatch) *v.* **-ing, -ed** to send off to perform a specific function Synonyms: consign, hasten, quicken, transmit

tumult (<u>tuh</u> muhlt) *n.* commotion, disturbance, and noise, as of a crowd Synonyms: agitation, bedlam, uproar, clamor, row

flaunt (flawnt) *v.* **-ing, -ed** to put shamelessly on display Synonyms: exhibit, advertise, display, broadcast, parade

And from this paper my brother read that catastrophic **dispatch** of the Commander-in-Chief:

"The Martians are able to discharge enormous clouds of a black and poisonous vapour by means of rockets. They have smothered our batteries, destroyed Richmond, Kingston, and Wimbledon, and are advancing slowly towards London, destroying everything on the way. It is impossible to stop them. There is no safety from the Black Smoke but in instant flight."

That was all, but it was enough. The whole population of the great six-million city was stirring, slipping, running; presently it would be pouring _en masse_ northward.

"Black Smoke!" the voices cried. "Fire!"

The bells of the neighbouring church made a jangling **tumult**, a cart carelessly driven smashed, amid shrieks and curses, against the water trough up the street. Sickly yellow lights went to and fro in the houses, and some of the passing cabs **flaunted** unextinguished lamps. And overhead the dawn was growing brighter, clear and steady and calm.

He heard footsteps running to and fro in the rooms, and up and down stairs behind him. His landlady came to the door, loosely wrapped in dressing gown and shawl; her husband followed ejaculating.

As my brother began to realise the import of all these things, he turned hastily to his own room, put all his available money—some ten pounds altogether—into his pockets, and went out again into the streets.

fugitive (<u>fyoo</u> jih tihv) *n.*   an individual on the run, often being pursued in connection with a crime   Synonyms: outlaw, criminal, refugee

ascertain (aa suhr tayn) *v.* **-ing, -ed**   to determine with certainty, especially after careful observation or experimentation   Synonyms: ensure, divine, verify, discover

expectant (ehk <u>spehk</u> tehnt) *adj.*   in a state of anticipation   Synonyms: apprehensive, awaiting, vigilant, pregnant, gravid

Chapter Fifteen

What Had Happened in Surrey

It was while the curate had sat and talked so wildly to me under the hedge in the flat meadows near Halliford, and while my brother was watching the **fugitives** stream over Westminster Bridge, that the Martians had resumed the offensive. So far as one can **ascertain** from the conflicting accounts that have been put forth, the majority of them remained busied with preparations in the Horsell pit until nine that night, hurrying on some operation that disengaged huge volumes of green smoke.

But three certainly came out about eight o'clock and, advancing slowly and cautiously, made their way through Byfleet and Pyrford towards Ripley and Weybridge, and so came in sight of the **expectant** batteries against the setting sun. These Martians did not advance in a body, but in a line, each perhaps a mile and a half from his nearest fellow. They communicated with one another by means of sirenlike howls, running up and down the scale from one note to another.

ineffectual (ihn uh <u>fehk</u> choo uhl) *adj.*   incapable of
producing a desired outcome   Synonyms: failed, ineffective, unavailing, worthless

serenely (suh <u>reen</u> lee) *adv.*   with calmness and composure   Synonyms: peacefully, composedly, limpidly,
sedately

gingerly (<u>jihn</u> juhr lee) *adv.*   with great caution; carefully
Synonyms: circumspectly, delicately, discreetly

mettle (meh tuhl) *n.*   courageousness; the quality of one's
character   Synonyms: backbone, bravery, resolve,
spirit, resolution, fortitude

frantic (<u>fraan</u> tihk) *adj.*   excessively emotional; uncontrollably anxious   Synonyms: agitated, distraught,
frenetic

tediously (<u>tee</u> dee uhs lee) *adv.*   in a manner so tiresome,
especially by reason of dullness, as to cause weariness
Synonyms: dully, lifelessly, insipidly, drudgingly

blight (bliet) *n.*   any of a number of diseases that infect
and damage plants, especially crops   Synonyms: bane,
canker, pestilence, withering, rot

apparently (uh <u>paa</u> rehnt lee) *adv.*   unmistakably;
detectably by sight   Synonyms: ostensibly, obviously,
patently, plainly

CHAPTER 15—WHAT HAD HAPPENED IN SURREY

It was this howling and firing of the guns at Ripley and St. George's Hill that we had heard at Upper Halliford. The Ripley gunners, unseasoned artillery volunteers who ought never to have been placed in such a position, fired one wild, premature, ineffectual volley, and bolted on horse and foot through the deserted village, while the Martian, without using his Heat-Ray, walked serenely over their guns, stepped gingerly among them, passed in front of them, and so came unexpectedly upon the guns in Painshill Park, which he destroyed.

The St. George's Hill men, however, were better led or of a better mettle. Hidden by a pine wood as they were, they seem to have been quite unsuspected by the Martian nearest to them. They laid their guns as deliberately as if they had been on parade, and fired at about a thousand yards' range.

The shells flashed all round him, and he was seen to advance a few paces, stagger, and go down. Everybody yelled together, and the guns were reloaded in frantic haste. The overthrown Martian set up a prolonged ululation, and immediately a second glittering giant, answering him, appeared over the trees to the south. It would seem that a leg of the tripod had been smashed by one of the shells. The whole of the second volley flew wide of the Martian on the ground, and, simultaneously, both his companions brought their Heat-Rays to bear on the battery. The ammunition blew up, the pine trees all about the guns flashed into fire, and only one or two of the men who were already running over the crest of the hill escaped.

After this it would seem that the three took counsel together and halted, and the scouts who were watching them report that they remained absolutely stationary for the next half hour. The Martian who had been overthrown crawled tediously out of his hood, a small brown figure, oddly suggestive from that distance of a speck of blight, and apparently engaged in the repair of his sup-

sentinel (<u>sehn</u> tihn ehl) *n.*   one who stands guard or awaits a particular occurrence   Synonyms: sentry, lookout, guardian

devise (dih <u>viez</u>) *v.* **-ing, -ed**   to formulate or design, especially with respect to a scheme or plan   Synonyms: conceive, machinate, invent, craft, concoct port. About nine he had finished, for his <u>cowl</u> was then seen above the trees again.

It was a few minutes past nine that night when these three **sentinels** were joined by four other Martians, each carrying a thick black tube. A similar tube was handed to each of the three, and the seven proceeded to distribute themselves at equal distances along a curved line between St. George's Hill, Weybridge, and the village of Send, southwest of Ripley.

A dozen rockets sprang out of the hills before them so soon as they began to move, and warned the waiting <u>batteries</u> about Ditton and Esher. At the same time four of their fighting machines, similarly armed with tubes, crossed the river, and two of them, black against the western sky, came into sight of myself and the curate as we hurried wearily and painfully along the road that runs northward out of Halliford. They moved, as it seemed to us, upon a cloud, for a milky mist covered the fields and rose to a third of their height.

At this sight the curate cried faintly in his throat, and began running; but I knew it was no good running from a Martian, and I turned aside and crawled through dewy nettles and brambles into the broad ditch by the side of the road. He looked back, saw what I was doing, and turned to join me.

The two halted, the nearer to us standing and facing Sunbury, the remoter being a grey indistinctness towards the evening star, away towards Staines.

The occasional howling of the Martians had ceased; they took up their positions in the huge crescent about their cylinders in absolute silence. It was a crescent with twelve miles between its horns. Never since the **devising** of gunpowder was the beginning of a battle so still. To us and to an observer about Ripley it would have had precisely the same effect—the Martians seemed in solitary possession of the <u>darkling</u> night, lit only as it was by the slender moon, the stars, the <u>afterglow</u> of the daylight, and

ruddy (<u>ruh</u> dee) *adj.*   having a healthy, flushed coloration
Synonyms: rosy, flushed, glowing

vigilant (<u>vih</u> jihl ihnt) *adj.*   carefully attentive; on the
alert   Synonyms: watchful, alert, acute, keen, sharp

encampment (ehn <u>caamp</u> mehnt) *n.*   the site on which
temporary residences are erected   Synonyms: barracks,
dormitory, garrison, quarters

unanimity (yoon nah <u>nihm</u> ih tee) *n.*   state of complete
agreement   Synonyms: accord, harmony, congruence

onslaught (<u>ahn</u> slawt) *n.*   an overwhelming assault
Synonyms: barrage, attack, assailment, onrush, offensive, incursion

sentinel (<u>sehn</u> tihn ehl) *n.*   one who stands guard or
awaits a particular occurrence   Synonyms: sentry,
lookout, guardian

interminable (ihn <u>tuhr</u> mihn uh buhl) *adj.*   without or
seemingly without end   Synonyms: infinite, boring,
incessant, eternal, perpetual

concussion (kuhn <u>cuhsh</u> uhn) *n.*   a violent blow or collision; an injury so caused   Synonyms: blow, bump, crash,
impact, trauma

the **ruddy** glare from St. George's Hill and the woods of Painshill.

But facing that crescent everywhere—at Staines, Hounslow, Ditton, Esher, Ockham, behind hills and woods south of the river, and across the flat grass meadows to the north of it, wherever a cluster of trees or village houses gave sufficient cover—the guns were waiting. The signal rockets burst and rained their sparks through the night and vanished, and the spirit of all those watching batteries rose to a tense expectation. The Martians had but to advance into the line of fire, and instantly those motionless black forms of men, those guns glittering so darkly in the early night, would explode into a thunderous fury of battle.

No doubt the thought that was uppermost in a thousand of those **vigilant** minds, even as it was uppermost in mine, was the riddle—how much they understood of us. Did they grasp that we in our millions were organized, disciplined, working together? Or did they interpret our spurts of fire, the sudden stinging of our shells, our steady investment of their **encampment**, as we should the furious **unanimity** of **onslaught** in a disturbed hive of bees? Did they dream they might exterminate us? (At that time no one knew what food they needed.) A hundred such questions struggled together in my mind as I watched that vast **sentinel** shape. And in the back of my mind was the sense of all the huge unknown and hidden forces Londonward. Had they prepared pitfalls? Were the powder mills at Hounslow ready as a snare? Would the Londoners have the heart and courage to make a greater Moscow of their mighty province of houses?

Then, after an **interminable** time, as it seemed to us, crouching and peering through the hedge, came a sound like the distant **concussion** of a gun. Another nearer, and then another. And then the Martian beside us raised his tube on high and discharged it, gunwise, with a heavy report that made the ground heave. The one towards

detonation (deh tuh <u>nay</u> shuhn) *n.*   a violent release of energy; an explosion   Synonyms: blast, eruption, rupture

scald (scahld) *v.* **-ing, -ed**   to burn, especially with liquid or steam   Synonyms: burn, broil, scorch

clamber (<u>klahm</u> buhr) *v.* **-ing, -ed**   to climb or crawl with difficulty and awkwardness   Synonyms: scramble, wriggle, jostle, scurry

tumult (<u>tuh</u> muhlt) *n.*   commotion, disturbance, and noise, as of a crowd   Synonyms: agitation, bedlam, uproar, clamor, row

recede (ree <u>seed</u>) *v.* **-ing, -ed**   to draw back, retreat   Synonyms: abate, decline, diminish, subside

clamber (<u>klahm</u> buhr) *v.* **-ing, -ed**   to climb or crawl with difficulty and awkwardness   Synonyms: scramble, wriggle, jostle, scurry

summit (suh miht) *n.*   the apex; the highest point or level   Synonyms: acme, apogee, culmination, climax

CHAPTER 15—WHAT HAD HAPPENED IN SURREY

Staines answered him. There was no flash, no smoke, simply that loaded **detonation**.

I was so excited by these heavy minute-guns following one another that I so far forgot my personal safety and my **scalded** hands as to **clamber** up into the hedge and stare towards Sunbury. As I did so a second report followed, and a big projectile hurtled overhead towards Hounslow. I expected at least to see smoke or fire, or some such evidence of its work. But all I saw was the deep blue sky above, with one solitary star, and the white mist spreading wide and low beneath. And there had been no crash, no answering explosion. The silence was restored; the minute lengthened to three.

"What has happened?" said the curate, standing up beside me.

"Heaven knows!" said I.

A bat flickered by and vanished. A distant **tumult** of shouting began and ceased. I looked again at the Martian, and saw he was now moving eastward along the river-bank, with a swift, rolling motion.

Every moment I expected the fire of some hidden battery to spring upon him; but the evening calm was unbroken. The figure of the Martian grew smaller as he **receded**, and presently the mist and the gathering night had swallowed him up. By a common impulse we **clambered** higher. Towards Sunbury was a dark appearance, as though a conical hill had suddenly come into being there, hiding our view of the farther country; and then, remoter across the river, over Walton, we saw another such **summit**. These hill-like forms grew lower and broader even as we stared.

Moved by a sudden thought, I looked northward, and there I perceived a third of these cloudy black <u>kopjes</u> had risen.

Everything had suddenly become very still. Far away to the southeast, marking the quiet, we heard the Martians hooting to one another, and then the air quivered again

187

ominous (ah mihn uhs) *adj.* indicative of a threat or an impending misfortune Synonyms: menacing, threatening, baleful, sinister, inauspicious

pungent (<u>puhn</u> jehnt) *adj.* sharp and penetrating in odor or flavor Synonyms: poignant, piquant, acrid, bitter

tumultuous (tuh <u>muhlt</u> yoo uhs) *adj.* characterized by confusion and disorder Synonyms: clamorous, agitated, raucous, turbulent

insoluble (ihn <u>sohl</u> yoo buhl) *adj.* incapable of being dissolved

diffuse (dih fyooz) *v.* **-ing, -ed** to distribute and cause to spread rapidly Synonyms: scatter, strew, disseminate

reluctantly (ree luhk tehnt lee) *adv.* with resistance or unwillingness Synonyms: hesitantly, warily, cautiously, guardedly with the distant thud of their guns. But the earthly artillery made no reply.

Now at the time we could not understand these things, but later I was to learn the meaning of these **ominous** kopjes that gathered in the twilight. Each of the Martians, standing in the great crescent I have described, had discharged, by means of the gunlike tube he carried, a huge canister over whatever hill, copse, cluster of houses, or other possible cover for guns, chanced to be in front of him. Some fired only one of these, some two—as in the case of the one we had seen; the one at Ripley is said to have discharged no fewer than five at that time. These canisters smashed on striking the ground—they did not explode—and incontinently disengaged an enormous volume of heavy, inky vapour, coiling and pouring upward in a huge and ebony cumulus cloud, a gaseous hill that sank and spread itself slowly over the surrounding country. And the touch of that vapour, the inhaling of its **pungent** wisps, was death to all that breathes.

It was heavy, this vapour, heavier than the densest smoke, so that, after the first **tumultuous** uprush and outflow of its impact, it sank down through the air and poured over the ground in a manner rather liquid than gaseous, abandoning the hills, and streaming into the valleys and ditches and watercourses even as I have heard the carbonic-acid gas that pours from volcanic clefts is wont to do. And where it came upon water some chemical action occurred, and the surface would be instantly covered with a powdery scum that sank slowly and made way for more. The scum was absolutely **insoluble**, and it is a strange thing, seeing the instant effect of the gas, that one could drink without hurt the water from which it had been strained. The vapour did not **diffuse** as a true gas would do. It hung together in banks, flowing sluggishly down the slope of the land and driving **reluctantly** before the wind, and very slowly it combined with the mist and moisture of the air, and sank to the earth in the form of

spectrum (spehk truhm) *n.*   a representation of energy, light, or color distribution   Synonyms: range, scope, scale

tumultuous (tuh <u>muhlt</u> yoo uhs) *adj.*   characterized by confusion and disorder   Synonyms: clamorous, agitated, raucous, turbulent

dispersion (dihs <u>puhr</u> zhuhn) *n.*   the process of spreading or scattering widely   Synonyms: diffusion, circulation, dissipation, distribution

precipitation (pree sihp ih <u>tay</u> shuhn) *n.*   a hasty fall or surge, as of water in a rainstorm

accord (uh <u>kohrd</u>) *n.*   a state of agreement   Synonyms: unanimity, concert, agreement, harmony

intermittently (ihn tuhr <u>miht</u> tehnt lee) *adv.*   at irregular intervals; erratically   Synonyms: occasionally, spasmodically, irregularly, unpredictably dust. Save that an unknown element giving a group of four lines in the blue of the **spectrum** is concerned, we are still entirely ignorant of the nature of this substance.

Once the **tumultuous** upheaval of its **dispersion** was over, the black smoke clung so closely to the ground, even before its **precipitation**, that fifty feet up in the air, on the roofs and upper stories of high houses and on great trees, there was a chance of escaping its poison altogether, as was proved even that night at Street Cobham and Ditton.

The man who escaped at the former place tells a wonderful story of the strangeness of its coiling flow, and how he looked down from the church spire and saw the houses of the village rising like ghosts out of its inky nothingness. For a day and a half he remained there, weary, starving and sun-scorched, the earth under the blue sky and against the prospect of the distant hills a velvet-black expanse, with red roofs, green trees, and, later, black-veiled shrubs and gates, barns, outhouses, and walls, rising here and there into the sunlight.

But that was at Street Cobham, where the black vapour was allowed to remain until it sank of its own **accord** into the ground. As a rule the Martians, when it had served its purpose, cleared the air of it again by wading into it and directing a jet of steam upon it.

This they did with the vapour banks near us, as we saw in the starlight from the window of a deserted house at Upper Halliford, whither we had returned. From there we could see the searchlights on Richmond Hill and Kingston Hill going to and fro, and about eleven the windows rattled, and we heard the sound of the huge siege guns that had been put in position there. These continued **intermittently** for the space of a quarter of an hour, sending chance shots at the invisible Martians at Hampton and Ditton, and then the pale beams of the electric light vanished, and were replaced by a bright red glow.

Then the fourth cylinder fell—a brilliant green meteor—as I learned afterwards, in Bushey Park. Before

haphazard (haap <u>haa</u> zuhrd) *adj.*   dependent on or the result of chance circumstances   Synonyms: accidental, spontaneous, designless, unplanned

enterprise (<u>ehn</u> tuhr prize) *n.*   an undertaking of some complexity and scope   Synonyms: adventure, campaign, endeavor

mutiny (<u>myoo</u> tih nee) *v.* **-ing, mutinied**   to rebel against the supervising authority, especially in the case of sailors against their captain.   Synonyms: riot, revolt, rebel, insurrect

spasmodic (spaaz <u>mahd</u> ihk) *adj.*   occurring convulsively or at irregular intervals   Synonyms: twitching, spastic, sporadic, spurtive, desultory the guns on the Richmond and Kingston line of hills began, there was a fitful <u>cannonade</u> far away in the south-west, due, I believe, to guns being fired **haphazard** before the black vapour could overwhelm the gunners.

So, setting about it as methodically as men might smoke out a wasps' nest, the Martians spread this strange stifling vapour over the Londonward country. The horns of the crescent slowly moved apart, until at last they formed a line from Hanwell to Coombe and Malden. All night through their destructive tubes advanced. Never once, after the Martian at St. George's Hill was brought down, did they give the artillery the ghost of a chance against them. Wherever there was a possibility of guns being laid for them unseen, a fresh canister of the black vapour was discharged, and where the guns were openly displayed the Heat-Ray was brought to bear.

By midnight the blazing trees along the slopes of Richmond Park and the glare of Kingston Hill threw their light upon a network of black smoke, blotting out the whole valley of the Thames and extending as far as the eye could reach. And through this two Martians slowly waded, and turned their hissing steam jets this way and that.

They were sparing of the Heat-Ray that night, either because they had but a limited supply of material for its production or because they did not wish to destroy the country but only to crush and overawe the opposition they had aroused. In the latter aim they certainly succeeded. Sunday night was the end of the organised opposition to their movements. After that no body of men would stand against them, so hopeless was the **enterprise**. Even the crews of the torpedo-boats and destroyers that had brought their quick-firers up the Thames refused to stop, **mutinied**, and went down again. The only offensive operation men ventured upon after that night was the preparation of mines and pitfalls, and even in that their energies were frantic and **spasmodic**.

limber (<u>lihm</u> buhr) *adj.*   easily able to bend; flexible
Synonyms: supple, lissome, elastic, lithe

resonance (<u>rehz</u> uh nihns) *n.*   the quality of richness,
depth, and vibration   Synonyms: euphony, reverberation

projectile (proh <u>jehk</u> tile) *n.*   an object thrown, flung, or
fired   Synonyms: discharge, trajectile

palpable (<u>paal</u> puh buhl) *adj.*   detectable by touch;
perceptible   Synonyms: tangible, apparent, concrete,
substantial

antagonist (aan <u>taa</u> guh nihst) *n.*   one who opposes,
especially with respect to the main character of a
drama or narrative   Synonyms: adversary, opponent,
rival, competitor

writhe (rieth) *v.* **-ing, -ed**   to twist and contort, especially when caused by pain or struggle   Synonyms:
distort, thrash, wriggle, distort, wriggle

opaque (oh <u>payk</u>) *adj.*   impossible to penetrate with
light   Synonyms: nontranslucent, obfuscated, turbid,
nontransparent, impenetrable

One has to imagine, as well as one may, the fate of those <u>batteries</u> towards Esher, waiting so tensely in the twilight. Survivors there were none. One may picture the orderly expectation, the officers alert and watchful, the gunners ready, the ammunition piled to hand, the **limber** gunners with their horses and waggons, the groups of civilian spectators standing as near as they were permitted, the evening stillness, the ambulances and hospital tents with the burned and wounded from Weybridge; then the dull **resonance** of the shots the Martians fired, and the clumsy **projectile** whirling over the trees and houses and smashing amid the neighbouring fields.

One may picture, too, the sudden shifting of the attention, the swiftly spreading coils and bellyings of that blackness advancing headlong, towering heavenward, turning the twilight to a **palpable** darkness, a strange and horrible **antagonist** of vapour striding upon its victims, men and horses near it seen dimly, running, shrieking, falling headlong, shouts of dismay, the guns suddenly abandoned, men choking and **writhing** on the ground, and the swift broadening-out of the **opaque** cone of smoke. And then night and extinction—nothing but a silent mass of impenetrable vapour hiding its dead.

Before dawn the black vapour was pouring through the streets of Richmond, and the disintegrating organism of government was, with a last expiring effort, rousing the population of London to the necessity of flight.

torrent (<u>toh</u> rehnt) *n.*   a great outpouring; a flood
Synonyms: flow, cascade, shower, spate

tumult (<u>tuh</u> muhlt) *n.*   commotion, disturbance, and
noise, as of a crowd   Synonyms: agitation, bedlam,
uproar, clamor, row

coherency (koh <u>hee</u> rehn see) *n.*   speaking clearly and
logically

infuriate (ihn <u>fyoo</u> ree ayt) *v.*   to make extremely angry
Synonyms: incense, rile, enrage

CHAPTER SIXTEEN

THE EXODUS FROM LONDON

So you understand the roaring wave of fear that swept through the greatest city in the world just as Monday was dawning—the stream of flight rising swiftly to a **torrent**, lashing in a foaming **tumult** round the railway stations, banked up into a horrible struggle about the shipping in the Thames, and hurrying by every available channel northward and eastward. By ten o'clock the police organisation, and by midday even the railway organisations, were losing **coherency**, losing shape and efficiency, guttering, softening, running at last in that swift liquefaction of the social body.

All the railway lines north of the Thames and the South-Eastern people at Cannon Street had been warned by midnight on Sunday, and trains were being filled. People were fighting savagely for standing-room in the carriages even at two o'clock. By three, people were being trampled and crushed even in Bishopsgate Street, a couple of hundred yards or more from Liverpool Street station; revolvers were fired, people stabbed, and the policemen who had been sent to direct the traffic, exhausted and **infuriated**, were breaking the heads of the people they were called out to protect.

stalwart (<u>stahl</u> wuhrt) *adj.*   physically strong; committed completely to a cause or principle   Synonyms: brave, hefty, indomitable, intrepid, undaunted, valiant

foremost (<u>fohr</u> mohst) *adj.*   in the first position, either physically or in terms of importance   Synonyms: headmost, champion, primary, principal, premier

CHAPTER 16—THE EXODUS FROM LONDON

And as the day advanced and the engine drivers and stokers refused to return to London, the pressure of the flight drove the people in an ever-thickening multitude away from the stations and along the northward-running roads. By midday a Martian had been seen at Barnes, and a cloud of slowly sinking black vapour drove along the Thames and across the flats of Lambeth, cutting off all escape over the bridges in its sluggish advance. Another bank drove over Ealing, and surrounded a little island of survivors on Castle Hill, alive, but unable to escape.

After a fruitless struggle to get aboard a North-Western train at Chalk Farm—the engines of the trains that had loaded in the goods yard there *ploughed* through shrieking people, and a dozen **stalwart** men fought to keep the crowd from crushing the driver against his furnace—my brother emerged upon the Chalk Farm road, dodged across through a hurrying swarm of vehicles, and had the luck to be **foremost** in the sack of a cycle shop. The front tire of the machine he got was punctured in dragging it through the window, but he got up and off, notwithstanding, with no further injury than a cut wrist. The steep foot of Haverstock Hill was impassable owing to several overturned horses, and my brother struck into Belsize Road.

So he got out of the fury of the panic, and, skirting the Edgware Road, reached Edgware about seven, fasting and wearied, but well ahead of the crowd. Along the road people were standing in the roadway, curious, wondering. He was passed by a number of cyclists, some horsemen, and two motor cars. A mile from Edgware the rim of the wheel broke, and the machine became unridable. He left it by the roadside and trudged through the village. There were shops half opened in the main street of the place, and people crowded on the pavement and in the doorways and windows, staring astonished at this extraordinary procession of fugitives that was beginning. He succeeded in getting some food at an inn.

loiter (<u>loy</u> tuhr) *v.* **-ing, -ed**   to stay purposelessly or aimlessly in place; to proceed haltingly and without apparent direction or objective   Synonyms: idle, dawdle, dillydally

congest (kuhn <u>jehst</u>) *v.* **-ing, -ed**   to fill past capacity; to overcrowd

vague (vayg) *adj.*   without definite shape, form, or expression   Synonyms: ambiguous, hazy, nebulous, indefinite, tenebrous

induce (ihn <u>doos</u>) *v.*   to bring about a particular occurrence; to persuade   Synonyms: cause, actuate, motivate, prompt

desist (dee <u>sihst</u>) *v.* **-ing, -ed**   to cease; to stop performing an activity or task   Synonyms: forbear, abstain, surcease, discontinue

antagonist (aan <u>taa</u> guh nihst) *n.*   one who opposes, especially with respect to the main character of a drama or narrative   Synonyms: adversary, opponent, rival, competitor

chivalry (<u>shih</u> vuhl ree) *n.*   the qualities associated with knighthood, especially in terms of decorum   Synonyms: valor, courtesy, gallantry, politeness

CHAPTER 16—THE EXODUS FROM LONDON

For a time he remained in Edgware not knowing what next to do. The flying people increased in number. Many of them, like my brother, seemed inclined to **loiter** in the place. There was no fresh news of the invaders from Mars.

At that time the road was crowded, but as yet far from **congested**. Most of the fugitives at that hour were mounted on cycles, but there were soon motor cars, <u>hansom</u> cabs, and carriages hurrying along, and the dust hung in heavy clouds along the road to St. Albans.

It was perhaps a **vague** idea of making his way to Chelmsford, where some friends of his lived, that at last **induced** my brother to strike into a quiet lane running eastward. Presently he came upon a <u>stile</u>, and, crossing it, followed a footpath northeastward. He passed near several farmhouses and some little places whose names he did not learn. He saw few fugitives until, in a grass lane towards High Barnet, he happened upon two ladies who became his fellow travellers. He came upon them just in time to save them.

He heard their screams, and, hurrying round the corner, saw a couple of men struggling to drag them out of the little pony-<u>chaise</u> in which they had been driving, while a third with difficulty held the frightened pony's head. One of the ladies, a short woman dressed in white, was simply screaming; the other, a dark, slender figure, slashed at the man who gripped her arm with a whip she held in her disengaged hand.

My brother immediately grasped the situation, shouted, and hurried towards the struggle. One of the men **desisted** and turned towards him, and my brother, realising from his **antagonist's** face that a fight was unavoidable, and being an expert boxer, went into him <u>forthwith</u> and sent him down against the wheel of the chaise.

It was no time for <u>pugilistic</u> **chivalry** and my brother laid him quiet with a kick, and gripped the collar of the man who pulled at the slender lady's arm. He heard the

antagonist (aan <u>taa</u> guh nihst) *n.* one who opposes, especially with respect to the main character of a drama or narrative Synonyms: adversary, opponent, rival, competitor

recede (ree <u>seed</u>) *v.* **-ing, -ed** to draw back, retreat Synonyms: abate, decline, diminish, subside

pluckily (<u>pluhk</u> ih lee) *adv.* with courage, especially in exceedingly difficult circumstances

insensible (ihn <u>sehn</u> sih buhl) *adj.* unconscious Synonyms: unresponsive, languid, lifeless clatter of hoofs, the whip stung across his face, a third **antagonist** struck him between the eyes, and the man he held wrenched himself free and made off down the lane in the direction from which he had come.

Partly stunned, he found himself facing the man who had held the horse's head, and became aware of the <u>chaise</u> **receding** from him down the lane, swaying from side to side, and with the women in it looking back. The man before him, a burly rough, tried to close, and he stopped him with a blow in the face. Then, realising that he was deserted, he dodged round and made off down the lane after the chaise, with the sturdy man close behind him, and the fugitive, who had turned now, following remotely.

Suddenly he stumbled and fell; his immediate pursuer went <u>headlong</u>, and he rose to his feet to find himself with a couple of antagonists again. He would have had little chance against them had not the slender lady very **pluckily** pulled up and returned to his help. It seems she had had a revolver all this time, but it had been under the seat when she and her companion were attacked. She fired at six yards' distance, narrowly missing my brother. The less courageous of the robbers made off, and his companion followed him, cursing his cowardice. They both stopped in sight down the lane, where the third man lay **insensible**.

"Take this!" said the slender lady, and she gave my brother her revolver.

"Go back to the chaise," said my brother, wiping the blood from his split lip.

She turned without a word—they were both panting—and they went back to where the lady in white struggled to hold back the frightened pony.

The robbers had evidently had enough of it. When my brother looked again they were retreating.

"I'll sit here," said my brother, "if I may"; and he got upon the empty front seat. The lady looked over her shoulder.

rouse (raawz) *v.* **-ing, -ed** to inspire to action Synonyms: provoke, vivify, animate, innervate, exhilarate

encampment (ehn <u>caamp</u> mehnt) *n.* the site on which temporary residences are erected Synonyms: barracks, dormitory, garrison, quarters

"Give me the reins," she said, and laid the whip along the pony's side. In another moment a bend in the road hid the three men from my brother's eyes.

So, quite unexpectedly, my brother found himself, panting, with a cut mouth, a bruised jaw, and bloodstained knuckles, driving along an unknown lane with these two women.

He learned they were the wife and the younger sister of a surgeon living at Stanmore, who had come in the small hours from a dangerous case at Pinner, and heard at some railway station on his way of the Martian advance. He had hurried home, **roused** the women—their servant had left them two days before—packed some provisions, put his revolver under the seat—luckily for my brother—and told them to drive on to Edgware, with the idea of getting a train there. He stopped behind to tell the neighbours. He would <u>overtake</u> them, he said, at about half past four in the morning, and now it was nearly nine and they had seen nothing of him. They could not stop in Edgware because of the growing traffic through the place, and so they had come into this side lane.

That was the story they told my brother in fragments when <u>presently</u> they stopped again, nearer to New Barnet. He promised to stay with them, at least until they could determine what to do, or until the missing man arrived, and professed to be an expert shot with the revolver—a weapon strange to him—in order to give them confidence.

They made a sort of **encampment** by the <u>wayside</u>, and the pony became happy in the hedge. He told them of his own escape out of London, and all that he knew of these Martians and their ways. The sun crept higher in the sky, and after a time their talk died out and gave place to an uneasy state of anticipation. Several <u>wayfarers</u> came along the lane, and of these my brother gathered such news as he could. Every broken answer he had deepened his impression of the great disaster that had come

persuasion (puhr <u>sway</u> zhuhn) *n.* a belief firmly held; a conviction Synonyms: certitude, opinion, partiality, predilection

broach (brohch) *v.* to bring up a topic for discussion Synonyms: approach, interject, introduce, raise, touch on

tumultuous (tuh <u>muhlt</u> yoo uhs) *adj.* characterized by confusion and disorder Synonyms: clamorous, agitated, raucous, turbulent

jaded (<u>jay</u> dehd) world-wearied; worn out by disappointment or difficulty Synonyms: indifferent, fatigued, dulled, spent, surfeited

haggard (<u>haa</u> guhrd) *adj.* worn and wearied in appearance Synonyms: ashen, pallid, exhausted, fatigued

on humanity, deepened his **persuasion** of the immediate necessity for prosecuting this flight. He urged the matter upon them.

"We have money," said the slender woman, and hesitated.

Her eyes met my brother's, and her hesitation ended.

"So have I," said my brother.

She explained that they had as much as thirty pounds in gold, besides a five-pound note, and suggested that with that they might get upon a train at St. Albans or New Barnet. My brother thought that was hopeless, seeing the fury of the Londoners to crowd upon the trains, and **broached** his own idea of striking across Essex towards Harwich and thence escaping from the country altogether.

Mrs. Elphinstone—that was the name of the woman in white—would listen to no reasoning, and kept calling upon "George"; but her sister-in-law was astonishingly quiet and deliberate, and at last agreed to my brother's suggestion. So, designing to cross the Great North Road, they went on towards Barnet, my brother leading the pony to save it as much as possible.

As the sun crept up the sky the day became excessively hot, and under foot a thick, whitish sand grew burning and blinding, so that they travelled only very slowly. The hedges were grey with dust. And as they advanced towards Barnet a **tumultuous** murmuring grew stronger.

They began to meet more people. For the most part these were staring before them, murmuring indistinct questions, **jaded**, **haggard**, unclean. One man in evening dress passed them on foot, his eyes on the ground. They heard his voice, and, looking back at him, saw one hand clutched in his hair and the other beating invisible things. His paroxysm of rage over, he went on his way without once looking back.

As my brother's party went on towards the crossroads to the south of Barnet they saw a woman approaching the

confluence (<u>kahn</u> floo ens) *n.*   a coming together at a particular point   Synonyms: concourse, concurrence, meeting, junction

sallow (<u>saa</u> loh) *adj.*   possessing a complexion that suggests sickliness   Synonyms: anemic, ashen, pasty, wan, jaundiced

façade (fuh <u>sahd</u>) *n.*   1. the face or front of something, especially a building   2. a false front; a representation designed to mislead   Synonyms: appearance, show, veneer, semblance, mask

tumultuous (tuh <u>muhlt</u> yoo uhs) *adj.*   characterized by confusion and disorder   Synonyms: clamorous, agitated, raucous, turbulent

torrent (<u>toh</u> rehnt) *n.*   a great outpouring; a flood   Synonyms: flow, cascade, shower, spate

luminous (<u>loo</u> mihn uhs) *adj.*   emitting light; glowing   Synonyms: brilliant, lustrous, incandescent, refulgent   2. intelligent and easily understood   Synonyms: lucid, perspicacious, comprehensible

perpetually (puhr <u>peht</u> choo uh lee) *adv.*   without end or seeming to be without end   Synonyms: interminably, continually, everlastingly road across some fields on their left, carrying a child and with two other children; and then passed a man in dirty black, with a thick stick in one hand and a small port-manteau in the other. Then round the corner of the lane, from between the villas that guarded it at its **confluence** with the high road, came a little cart drawn by a sweating black pony and driven by a **sallow** youth in a bowler hat, grey with dust. There were three girls, East End factory girls, and a couple of little children crowded in the cart.

"This'll tike us rahnd Edgware?" asked the driver, wild-eyed, white-faced; and when my brother told him it would if he turned to the left, he whipped up at once without the formality of thanks.

My brother noticed a pale grey smoke or haze rising among the houses in front of them, and veiling the white **façade** of a terrace beyond the road that appeared between the backs of the villas. Mrs. Elphinstone suddenly cried out at a number of tongues of smoky red flame leaping up above the houses in front of them against the hot, blue sky. The **tumultuous** noise resolved itself now into the disorderly mingling of many voices, the gride of many wheels, the creaking of waggons, and the staccato of hoofs. The lane came round sharply not fifty yards from the crossroads.

"Good heavens!" cried Mrs. Elphinstone. "What is this you are driving us into?"

My brother stopped.

For the main road was a boiling stream of people, a **torrent** of human beings rushing northward, one pressing on another. A great bank of dust, white and **luminous** in the blaze of the sun, made everything within twenty feet of the ground grey and indistinct and was **perpetually** renewed by the hurrying feet of a dense crowd of horses and of men and women on foot, and by the wheels of vehicles of every description.

"Way!" my brother heard voices crying. "Make way!"

pungent (<u>puhn</u> jehnt) *adj.*   sharp and penetrating in odor or flavor   Synonyms: poignant, piquant, acrid, bitter

tumultuous (tuh <u>muhlt</u> yoo uhs) *adj.*   characterized by confusion and disorder   Synonyms: clamorous, agitated, raucous, turbulent

recede (ree <u>seed</u>) *v.* **-ing, -ed**   to draw back, retreat   Synonyms: abate, decline, diminish, subside

multitude (<u>muhl</u> tih tood) *n.*   a great quantity   Synonyms: drove, horde, host, mass, throng

tumult (<u>tuh</u> muhlt) *n.*   commotion, disturbance, and noise, as of a crowd   Synonyms: agitation, bedlam, uproar, clamor, row

recede (ree <u>seed</u>) *v.* **-ing, -ed**   to draw back, retreat   Synonyms: abate, decline, diminish, subside

blunder (<u>bluhn</u> duhr) *v.* **-ing, -ed**   to make a mistake of significant magnitude   Synonyms: botch, err, fumble, stumble

CHAPTER 16—THE EXODUS FROM LONDON

It was like riding into the smoke of a fire to approach the meeting point of the lane and road; the crowd roared like a fire, and the dust was hot and **pungent**. And, indeed, a little way up the road a villa was burning and sending rolling masses of black smoke across the road to add to the confusion.

Two men came past them. Then a dirty woman, carrying a heavy bundle and weeping. A lost retriever dog, with hanging tongue, circled dubiously round them, scared and wretched, and fled at my brother's threat.

So much as they could see of the road Londonward between the houses to the right was a **tumultuous** stream of dirty, hurrying people, pent in between the villas on either side; the black heads, the crowded forms, grew into distinctness as they rushed towards the corner, hurried past, and merged their individuality again in a **receding multitude** that was swallowed up at last in a cloud of dust.

"Go on! Go on!" cried the voices. "Way! Way!"

One man's hands pressed on the back of another. My brother stood at the pony's head. Irresistibly attracted, he advanced slowly, pace by pace, down the lane.

Edgware had been a scene of confusion, Chalk Farm a riotous **tumult**, but this was a whole population in movement. It is hard to imagine that host. It had no character of its own. The figures poured out past the corner, and **receded** with their backs to the group in the lane. Along the margin came those who were on foot threatened by the wheels, stumbling in the ditches, **blundering** into one another.

The carts and carriages crowded close upon one another, making little way for those swifter and more impatient vehicles that darted forward every now and then when an opportunity showed itself of doing so, sending the people scattering against the fences and gates of the villas.

"Push on!" was the cry. "Push on! They are coming!"

gesticulate (jehs <u>tihck</u> yoo layt) *v.* **-ing, -ed** to move the body, especially the hands and arms, for purposes of communication Synonyms: sign, mime, gesture

bawl *v.* **-ing, -ed** to wail, cry, or shout with great force Synonyms: bark, clamor, howl, shriek

conveyance (kun <u>vay</u> ehns) *n.* the act of transferring or transporting property, title, or material Synonyms: carriage, transference, bond, charter

haggard (<u>haa</u> guhrd) *adj.* worn and wearied in appearance Synonyms: ashen, pallid, exhausted, fatigued

tumult (<u>tuh</u> muhlt) *n.* commotion, disturbance, and noise, as of a crowd Synonyms: agitation, bedlam, uproar, clamor, row

In one cart stood a blind man in the uniform of the Salvation Army, **gesticulating** with his crooked fingers and **bawling**, "Eternity! Eternity!" His voice was hoarse and very loud so that my brother could hear him long after he was lost to sight in the dust. Some of the people who crowded in the carts whipped stupidly at their horses and quarrelled with other drivers; some sat motionless, staring at nothing with miserable eyes; some gnawed their hands with thirst, or lay prostrate in the bottoms of their **conveyances**. The horses' bits were covered with foam, their eyes bloodshot.

There were cabs, carriages, shop cars, waggons, beyond counting; a mail cart, a road-cleaner's cart marked "Vestry of St. Pancras," a huge timber waggon crowded with roughs. A brewer's dray rumbled by with its two near wheels splashed with fresh blood.

"Clear the way!" cried the voices. "Clear the way!"

"Eter-nity! Eter-nity!" came echoing down the road.

There were sad, **haggard** women tramping by, well dressed, with children that cried and stumbled, their dainty clothes smothered in dust, their weary faces smeared with tears. With many of these came men, sometimes helpful, sometimes lowering and savage. Fighting side by side with them pushed some weary street outcast in faded black rags, wide-eyed, loud-voiced, and foul-mouthed. There were sturdy workmen thrusting their way along, wretched, unkempt men, clothed like clerks or shopmen, struggling spasmodically; a wounded soldier my brother noticed, men dressed in the clothes of railway porters, one wretched creature in a nightshirt with a coat thrown over it.

But varied as its composition was, certain things all that host had in common. There were fear and pain on their faces, and fear behind them. A **tumult** up the road, a quarrel for a place in a waggon, sent the whole host of them quickening their pace; even a man so scared and broken that his knees bent under him was galvanised for

213

reproach (ree <u>prohch</u>) *v.* **-ing, -ed** to communicate disapproval or disappointment; to blame or accuse Synonyms: admonishment, criticism, reprimand, opprobrium

torpor (<u>tohr</u> puhr) *n.* a state of inactivity and mental insensibility Synonyms: lethargy, stupor, ennui, funk

bawl *v.* **-ing, -ed** to wail, cry, or shout with great force Synonyms: bark, clamor, howl, shriek a moment into renewed activity. The heat and dust had already been at work upon this multitude. Their skins were dry, their lips black and cracked. They were all thirsty, weary, and footsore. And amid the various cries one heard disputes, **reproaches**, groans of weariness and fatigue; the voices of most of them were hoarse and weak. Through it all ran a refrain:

"Way! Way! The Martians are coming!"

Few stopped and came aside from that flood. The lane opened slantingly into the main road with a narrow opening, and had a delusive appearance of coming from the direction of London. Yet a kind of <u>eddy</u> of people drove into its mouth; weaklings elbowed out of the stream, who for the most part rested but a moment before plunging into it again. A little way down the lane, with two friends bending over him, lay a man with a bare leg, wrapped about with bloody rags. He was a lucky man to have friends.

A little old man, with a grey military moustache and a filthy black frock coat, limped out and sat down beside the trap, removed his boot—his sock was blood-stained— shook out a pebble, and hobbled on again; and then a little girl of eight or nine, all alone, threw herself under the hedge close by my brother, weeping.

"I can't go on! I can't go on!"

My brother woke from his **torpor** of astonishment and lifted her up, speaking gently to her, and carried her to Miss Elphinstone. So soon as my brother touched her she became quite still, as if frightened.

"Ellen!" shrieked a woman in the crowd, with tears in her voice—"Ellen!" And the child suddenly darted away from my brother, crying "Mother!"

"They are coming," said a man on horseback, riding past along the lane.

"Out of the way, there!" **bawled** a coachman, towering high; and my brother saw a closed carriage turning into the lane.

disgorge (dihs <u>gohrj</u>) *v.* **-ing, -ed**   to spew forth, often violently   Synonyms: discharge, eructate, erupt

reel *v.* **-ing, -ed**   to fall, stagger, or sway as the result of imbalance   Synonyms: wobble, falter, careen

CHAPTER 16—THE EXODUS FROM LONDON

The people crushed back on one another to avoid the horse. My brother pushed the pony and <u>chaise</u> back into the hedge, and the man drove by and stopped at the turn of the way. It·was a carriage, with a pole for a pair of horses, but only one was in the traces. My brother saw dimly through the dust that two men lifted out something on a white stretcher and put it gently on the grass beneath the <u>privet</u> hedge.

One of the men came running to my brother.

"Where is there any water?" he said. "He is dying fast, and very thirsty. It is Lord Garrick."

"Lord Garrick!" said my brother; "the Chief Justice?"

"The water?" he said.

"There may be a tap," said my brother, "in some of the houses. We have no water. I dare not leave my people."

The man pushed against the crowd towards the gate of the corner house.

"Go on!" said the people, thrusting at him. "They are coming! Go on!"

Then my brother's attention was distracted by a bearded, eagle-faced man lugging a small handbag, which split even as my brother's eyes rested on it and **disgorged** a mass of <u>sovereigns</u> that seemed to break up into separate coins as it struck the ground. They rolled <u>hither and thither</u> among the struggling feet of men and horses. The man stopped and looked stupidly at the heap, and the shaft of a cab struck his shoulder and sent him **reeling**. He gave a shriek and dodged back, and a cartwheel shaved him narrowly.

"Way!" cried the men all about him. "Make way!"

So soon as the cab had passed, he flung himself, with both hands open, upon the heap of coins, and began thrusting handfuls in his pocket. A horse rose close upon him, and in another moment, half rising, he had been borne down under the horse's hoofs.

"Stop!" screamed my brother, and pushing a woman out of his way, tried to clutch the bit of the horse.

multitudinous (muhl tih <u>tood</u> ih nuhs) *adj.*   existing in great quantity; consisting of numerous individuals Synonyms: abounding, abundant, profuse, myriad, multifarious, teeming

writhe (rieth) *v.* **-ing, -ed**   to twist and contort, especially when caused by pain or struggle   Synonyms: distort, thrash, wriggle

concussion (kuhn <u>cuhsh</u> uhn) *n.*   a violent blow or collision; an injury so caused   Synonyms: blow, bump, crash, impact, trauma

torrent (<u>toh</u> rehnt) *n.*   a great outpouring; a flood Synonyms: flow, cascade, shower, spate

dilate (<u>die</u> layt) *v.* **-ing, -ed**   to cause to enlarge, expand, or widen   Synonyms: augment, distend, protract, inflate

Before he could get to it, he heard a scream under the wheels, and saw through the dust the rim passing over the poor wretch's back. The driver of the cart slashed his whip at my brother, who ran round behind the cart. The **multitudinous** shouting confused his ears. The man was **writhing** in the dust among his scattered money, unable to rise, for the wheel had broken his back, and his lower limbs lay limp and dead. My brother stood up and yelled at the next driver, and a man on a black horse came to his assistance.

"Get him out of the road," said he; and, clutching the man's collar with his free hand, my brother lugged him sideways. But he still clutched after his money, and regarded my brother fiercely, hammering at his arm with a handful of gold. "Go on! Go on!" shouted angry voices behind.

"Way! Way!"

There was a smash as the pole of a carriage crashed into the cart that the man on horseback stopped. My brother looked up, and the man with the gold twisted his head round and bit the wrist that held his collar. There was a **concussion**, and the black horse came staggering sideways, and the carthorse pushed beside it. A hoof missed my brother's foot by a hair's breadth. He released his grip on the fallen man and jumped back. He saw anger change to terror on the face of the poor wretch on the ground, and in a moment he was hidden and my brother was borne backward and carried past the entrance of the lane, and had to fight hard in the **torrent** to recover it.

He saw Miss Elphinstone covering her eyes, and a little child, with all a child's want of sympathetic imagination, staring with **dilated** eyes at a dusty something that lay black and still, ground and crushed under the rolling wheels. "Let us go back!" he shouted, and began turning the pony round. "We cannot cross this—hell," he said and they went back a hundred yards the way they had come, until the fighting crowd was hidden. As they passed the

219

perplex (puhr <u>plehks</u>) *v.* **-ing, -ed** to bring about confusion, uncertainty, or doubt Synonyms: baffle, befuddle, nonplus, perturb, stump

resolute (<u>rehz</u> oh loot) *adj.* characterized by determination in action or belief Synonyms: adamant, persevering, firm, uncompromising, steadfast

torrent (<u>toh</u> rehnt) *n.* a great outpouring; a flood Synonyms: flow, cascade, shower, spate

volition (voh <u>lih</u> shihn) *n.* the ability to make a conscious choice Synonyms: free will, accord, willingness, choosing

rout (rowt) *n.* a complete defeat Synonyms: beating, drubbing, vanquishment, thrashing

din (dihn) *n.* a collection of loud, often harsh, sounds Synonyms: clangor, racket, row, tumult, uproar bend in the lane my brother saw the face of the dying man in the ditch under the <u>privet</u>, deadly white and drawn, and shining with perspiration. The two women sat silent, crouching in their seat and shivering.

Then beyond the bend my brother stopped again. Miss Elphinstone was white and pale, and her sister-in-law sat weeping, too wretched even to call upon "George." My brother was horrified and **perplexed**. So soon as they had retreated he realised how urgent and unavoidable it was to attempt this crossing. He turned to Miss Elphinstone, suddenly **resolute**.

"We must go that way," he said, and led the pony round again.

For the second time that day this girl proved her quality. To force their way into the **torrent** of people, my brother plunged into the traffic and held back a cab horse, while she drove the pony across its head. A waggon locked wheels for a moment and ripped a long splinter from the <u>chaise</u>. In another moment they were caught and swept forward by the stream. My brother, with the cabman's whip marks red across his face and hands, scrambled into the chaise and took the reins from her.

"Point the revolver at the man behind," he said, giving it to her, "if he presses us too hard. No!—point it at his horse."

Then he began to look out for a chance of edging to the right across the road. But once in the stream he seemed to lose **volition**, to become a part of that dusty **rout**. They swept through Chipping Barnet with the torrent; they were nearly a mile beyond the centre of the town before they had fought across to the opposite side of the way. It was **din** and confusion indescribable; but in and beyond the town the road forks repeatedly, and this to some extent relieved the stress.

They struck eastward through Hadley, and there on either side of the road, and at another place farther on they came upon a great multitude of people drinking

halt (hawlt) *v.* **-ing, -ed**   to cause to stop or cease,
especially temporarily   Synonyms: arrest, adjourn,
intermit, impede, suspend

at the stream, some fighting to come at the water. And farther on, from a lull near East Barnet, they saw two trains running slowly one after the other without signal or order—trains swarming with people, with men even among the coals behind the engines—going northward along the Great Northern Railway. My brother supposes they must have filled outside London, for at that time the furious terror of the people had rendered the central termini impossible.

Near this place they **halted** for the rest of the afternoon, for the violence of the day had already utterly exhausted all three of them. They began to suffer the beginnings of hunger; the night was cold, and none of them dared to sleep. And in the evening many people came hurrying along the road nearby their stopping place, fleeing from unknown dangers before them, and going in the direction from which my brother had come.

annihilate (uh <u>nie</u> ihl ayt) *v.* **-ing, -ed**   to destroy completely   Synonyms: decimate, abrogate, slaughter, liquidate, massacre

frantic (<u>fraan</u> tihk) *adj.*   excessively emotional; uncontrollably anxious   Synonyms: agitated, distraught, frenetic

rout (rowt) *n.*   a complete defeat   Synonyms: beating, drubbing, vanquishment, thrashing

stippled (<u>stih</u> puhld) *adj.*   marked in short swatches or dots   Synonyms: dotted, speckled

THE "THUNDER CHILD"

Had the Martians aimed only at destruction, they might on Monday have **annihilated** the entire population of London, as it spread itself slowly through the home counties. Not only along the road through Barnet, but also through Edgware and Waltham Abbey, and along the roads eastward to Southend and Shoeburyness, and south of the Thames to Deal and Broadstairs, poured the same **frantic rout**. If one could have hung that June morning in a balloon in the blazing blue above London every northward and eastward road running out of the tangled maze of streets would have seemed **stippled** black with the streaming fugitives, each dot a human agony of terror and physical distress. I have set forth at length in the last chapter my brother's account of the road through Chipping Barnet, in order that my readers may realise how that swarming of black dots appeared to one of those concerned. Never before in the history of the world had such a mass of human beings moved and suffered together. The legendary hosts of Goths and Huns, the hugest armies Asia has ever seen, would have been but a drop in that current. And this was no disciplined march; it was a stampede—a stampede gigantic and terrible—without order

rout (rowt) *n.*   a complete defeat   Synonyms: beating, drubbing, vanquishment, thrashing

derelict (<u>deh</u> ruh lihkt) *adj.*   worn out; abandoned   Synonyms: dilapidated, desolate, forsaken, neglected

incessantly (ihn <u>sehss</u> ant lee) *adv.*   without pause or interruption   Synonyms: constantly, unceasingly, interminably, eternally

ramification (raa mih fih <u>kay</u> shuhn) *n.*   that which grows out of or is caused by a particular problem or situation   Synonyms: consequence, extension, upshot and without a goal, six million people unarmed and unprovisioned, driving <u>headlong</u>. It was the beginning of the **rout** of civilisation, of the massacre of mankind.

Directly below him the balloonist would have seen the network of streets far and wide, houses, churches, squares, crescents, gardens—already **derelict**—spread out like a huge map, and in the southward blotted. Over Ealing, Richmond, Wimbledon, it would have seemed as if some monstrous pen had flung ink upon the chart. Steadily, **incessantly**, each black splash grew and spread, shooting out **ramifications** this way and that, now banking itself against rising ground, now pouring swiftly over a crest into a new-found valley, exactly as a gout of ink would spread itself upon blotting paper.

And beyond, over the blue hills that rise southward of the river, the glittering Martians went to and fro, calmly and methodically spreading their poison cloud over this patch of country and then over that, laying it again with their steam jets when it had served its purpose, and taking possession of the conquered country. They do not seem to have aimed at extermination so much as at complete demoralisation and the destruction of any opposition. They exploded any stores of powder they came upon, cut every telegraph, and wrecked the railways here and there. They were <u>hamstringing</u> mankind. They seemed in no hurry to extend the field of their operations, and did not come beyond the central part of London all that day. It is possible that a very considerable number of people in London stuck to their houses through Monday morning. Certain it is that many died at home suffocated by the Black Smoke.

Until about midday the Pool of London was an astonishing scene. Steamboats and shipping of all sorts lay there, tempted by the enormous sums of money offered by fugitives, and it is said that many who swam out to these vessels were thrust off with boathooks and drowned. About one o'clock in the afternoon the thinning remnant

clamber (<u>klahm</u> buhr) *v.* **-ing, -ed** to climb or crawl with difficulty and awkwardness   Synonyms: scramble, wriggle, jostle, scurry

hearsay (<u>heer</u> say) *n.* uncorroborated information passed from person to person   Synonyms: buzz, rumor, gossip, talk, wire of a cloud of the black vapour appeared between the arches of Blackfriars Bridge. At that the Pool became a scene of mad confusion, fighting, and collision, and for some time a multitude of boats and barges jammed in the northern arch of the Tower Bridge, and the sailors and lightermen had to fight savagely against the people who swarmed upon them from the riverfront. People were actually **clambering** down the piers of the bridge from above.

When, an hour later, a Martian appeared beyond the Clock Tower and waded down the river, nothing but wreckage floated above Limehouse.

Of the falling of the fifth cylinder I have presently to tell. The sixth star fell at Wimbledon. My brother, keeping watch beside the women in the chaise in a meadow, saw the green flash of it far beyond the hills. On Tuesday the little party, still set upon getting across the sea, made its way through the swarming country towards Colchester. The news that the Martians were now in possession of the whole of London was confirmed. They had been seen at Highgate, and even, it was said, at Neasden. But they did not come into my brother's view until the morrow.

That day the scattered multitudes began to realise the urgent need of provisions. As they grew hungry the rights of property ceased to be regarded. Farmers were out to defend their cattle-sheds, granaries, and ripening root crops with arms in their hands. A number of people now, like my brother, had their faces eastward, and there were some desperate souls even going back towards London to get food. These were chiefly people from the northern suburbs, whose knowledge of the Black Smoke came by **hearsay**. He heard that about half the members of the government had gathered at Birmingham, and that enormous quantities of high explosives were being prepared to be used in automatic mines across the Midland counties.

He was also told that the Midland Railway Company had replaced the desertions of the first day's panic, had

placard (<u>plaa</u> kuhrd) *n.* a small sign or notice for public display of information   Synonyms: notice, ad, display, poster

deter (dee <u>tuhr</u>) *v.* **-ring, -red**   to prevent a course of action through instilling fear or uncertainty   Synonyms: inhibit, daunt, dissuade, intimidate

vain (vayn) *adj.*   ineffective in achieving a desired purpose   Synonyms: unsuccessful, fruitless, worthless, futile

furtive (<u>fuhr</u> tihv) *adj.*   done in secret; performed with ulterior motives   Synonyms: secretive, artful, guileful, stealthy, skulking resumed traffic, and was running northward trains from St. Albans to relieve the congestion of the home counties. There was also a **placard** in Chipping Ongar announcing that large stores of flour were available in the northern towns and that within twenty-four hours bread would be distributed among the starving people in the neighbourhood. But this intelligence did not **deter** him from the plan of escape he had formed, and the three pressed eastward all day, and heard no more of the bread distribution than this promise. Nor, as a matter of fact, did anyone else hear more of it. That night fell the seventh star, falling upon Primrose Hill. It fell while Miss Elphinstone was watching, for she took that duty alternately with my brother. She saw it.

On Wednesday the three fugitives—they had passed the night in a field of unripe wheat—reached Chelmsford, and there a body of the inhabitants, calling itself the Committee of Public Supply, seized the pony as provisions, and would give nothing in exchange for it but the promise of a share in it the next day. Here there were rumours of Martians at Epping, and news of the destruction of Waltham Abbey Powder Mills in a **vain** attempt to blow up one of the invaders.

People were watching for Martians here from the church towers. My brother, very luckily for him as it chanced, preferred to push on at once to the coast rather than wait for food, although all three of them were very hungry. By midday they passed through Tillingham, which, strangely enough, seemed to be quite silent and deserted, save for a few **furtive** plunderers hunting for food. Near Tillingham they suddenly came in sight of the sea, and the most amazing crowd of shipping of all sorts that it is possible to imagine.

For after the sailors could no longer come up the Thames, they came on to the Essex coast, to Harwich and Walton and Clacton, and afterwards to Foulness and Shoebury, to bring off the people. They lay in a huge sickle-

vigilant (<u>vih</u> jihl ihnt) *adj.* carefully attentive; on the alert   Synonyms: watchful, alert, acute, keen, sharp

shaped curve that vanished into mist at last towards the
Naze. Close inshore was a multitude of fishing smacks—
English, Scotch, French, Dutch, and Swedish; steam
launches from the Thames, yachts, electric boats; and
beyond were ships of large burden, a multitude of filthy
<u>colliers</u>, trim merchantmen, cattle ships, passenger boats,
petroleum tanks, ocean <u>tramps</u>, an old white transport
even, neat white and grey liners from Southampton and
Hamburg; and along the blue coast across the Blackwater
my brother could make out dimly a dense swarm of boats
chaffering with the people on the beach, a swarm which
also extended up the Blackwater almost to Maldon.

About a couple of miles out lay an ironclad, very low
in the water, almost, to my brother's perception, like a
water-logged ship. This was the ram *Thunder Child*. It was
the only warship in sight, but far away to the right over
the smooth surface of the sea—for that day there was a
dead calm—lay a serpent of black smoke to mark the
next ironclads of the Channel Fleet, which hovered in an
extended line, steam up and ready for action, across the
Thames <u>estuary</u> during the course of the Martian conquest, **vigilant** and yet powerless to prevent it.

At the sight of the sea, Mrs. Elphinstone, in spite of
the assurances of her sister-in-law, gave way to panic. She
had never been out of England before, she would rather
die than trust herself friendless in a foreign country, and
so forth. She seemed, poor woman, to imagine that the
French and the Martians might prove very similar. She
had been growing increasingly hysterical, fearful, and
depressed during the two days' journeyings. Her great
idea was to return to Stanmore. Things had been always
well and safe at Stanmore. They would find George at
Stanmore.

It was with the greatest difficulty they could get her
down to the beach, where <u>presently</u> my brother succeeded
in attracting the attention of some men on a paddle
steamer from the Thames. They sent a boat and drove a

albeit (ahl <u>bee</u> iht) *conj.* although, even though Synonyms: despite, even if, notwithstanding, supposing

exorbitant (ehg <u>zohr</u> bih tehnt) *adj.* well beyond the norms of decency or reason Synonyms: extravagant, extortinate, excessive, overboard, preposterous

revert (ree <u>vuhrt</u>) *v.* **-ing, -ed** to return to a previous state or condition Synonyms: backslide, inverse, retrograde, transpose

parody (<u>pah</u> ruh dee) *n.* a work that ridicules a particular style, convention, artist, or practice Synonyms: caricature, spoof, raillery, lampoon

234

bargain for thirty-six pounds for the three. The steamer was going, these men said, to Ostend.

It was about two o'clock when my brother, having paid their fares at the gangway, found himself safely aboard the steamboat with his charges. There was food aboard, **albeit** at **exorbitant** prices, and the three of them contrived to eat a meal on one of the seats forward.

There were already a couple of score of passengers aboard, some of whom had expended their last money in securing a passage, but the captain lay off the Blackwater until five in the afternoon, picking up passengers until the seated decks were even dangerously crowded. He would probably have remained longer had it not been for the sound of guns that began about that hour in the south. As if in answer, the ironclad seaward fired a small gun and hoisted a string of flags. A jet of smoke sprang out of her funnels.

Some of the passengers were of opinion that this firing came from Shoeburyness, until it was noticed that it was growing louder. At the same time, far away in the southeast the masts and upperworks of three ironclads rose one after the other out of the sea, beneath clouds of black smoke. But my brother's attention speedily **reverted** to the distant firing in the south. He fancied he saw a column of smoke rising out of the distant grey haze.

The little steamer was already flapping her way eastward of the big crescent of shipping, and the low Essex coast was growing blue and hazy, when a Martian appeared, small and faint in the remote distance, advancing along the muddy coast from the direction of Foulness. At that the captain on the bridge swore at the top of his voice with fear and anger at his own delay, and the paddles seemed infected with his terror. Every soul aboard stood at the <u>bulwarks</u> or on the seats of the steamer and stared at that distant shape, higher than the trees or church towers inland, and advancing with a leisurely **parody** of a human stride.

intercept (ihn tuhr <u>sehpt</u>) *v.* **-ing, -ed**   to deflect, block, or interrupt an intended course of action   Synonyms: deflect, hinder, interlope, obstruct

multitudinous (muhl tih <u>tood</u> ih nuhs) *adj.*   existing in great quantity; consisting of numerous individuals   Synonyms: abounding, abundant, profuse, myriad, multifarious, teeming

exertion (ehg <u>zuhr</u> shuhn) *n.*   the use of substantial reserves of strength or energy   Synonyms: work, industry, effort, labor

recede (ree <u>seed</u>) *v.* **-ing, -ed**   to draw back, retreat   Synonyms: abate, decline, diminish, subside

ominous (ah mihn uhs) *adj.*   indicative of a threat or an impending misfortune   Synonyms: menacing, threatening, baleful, sinister, inauspicious

writhe (rieth) *v.* **-ing, -ed**   to twist and contort, especially when caused by pain or struggle   Synonyms: distort, thrash, wriggle

CHAPTER 17—THE "THUNDER CHILD"

It was the first Martian my brother had seen, and he stood, more amazed than terrified, watching this Titan advancing deliberately towards the shipping, wading farther and farther into the water as the coast fell away. Then, far away beyond the Crouch, came another, striding over some stunted trees, and then yet another, still farther off, wading deeply through a shiny mudflat that seemed to hang halfway up between sea and sky. They were all stalking seaward, as if to **intercept** the escape of the **multitudinous** vessels that were crowded between Foulness and the Naze. In spite of the throbbing **exertions** of the engines of the little paddle-boat, and the pouring foam that her wheels flung behind her, she **receded** with terrifying slowness from this **ominous** advance.

Glancing northwestward, my brother saw the large crescent of shipping already **writhing** with the approaching terror; one ship passing behind another, another coming round from broadside to end on, steamships whistling and giving off volumes of steam, sails being let out, launches rushing hither and thither. He was so fascinated by this and by the creeping danger away to the left that he had no eyes for anything seaward. And then a swift movement of the steamboat (she had suddenly come round to avoid being run down) flung him headlong from the seat upon which he was standing. There was a shouting all about him, a trampling of feet, and a cheer that seemed to be answered faintly. The steamboat lurched and rolled him over upon his hands.

He sprang to his feet and saw to starboard, and not a hundred yards from their heeling, pitching boat, a vast iron bulk like the blade of a plough tearing through the water, tossing it on either side in huge waves of foam that leaped towards the steamer, flinging her paddles helplessly in the air, and then sucking her deck down almost to the waterline.

A douche of spray blinded my brother for a moment. When his eyes were clear again he saw the monster had

237

formidable (<u>fohr</u> mihd uh buhl) *adj.*   causing fear, dread, wonder, or astonishment   Synonyms: appalling, daunting, redoubtable, awesome, tremendous

antagonist (aan <u>taa</u> guh nihst) *n.*   one who opposes, especially with respect to the main character of a drama or narrative   Synonyms: adversary, opponent, rival, competitor

recede (ree <u>seed</u>) *v.* **-ing, -ed**   to draw back, retreat   Synonyms: abate, decline, diminish, subside

torrent (<u>toh</u> rehnt) *n.*   a great outpouring; a flood   Synonyms: flow, cascade, shower, spate

gaunt (gawnt) *adj.*   exceedingly thin   Synonyms: emaciated, haggard, attenuated, cadaverous

retreat (ree <u>treet</u>) *v.* **-ing, -ed**   to draw back, especially from a position gained   Synonyms: evacuate, withdraw, depart, retire passed and was rushing landward. Big iron upperworks rose out of this <u>headlong</u> structure, and from that twin funnels projected and spat a smoking blast shot with fire. It was the torpedo ram, *Thunder Child*, steaming headlong, coming to the rescue of the threatened shipping.

Keeping his footing on the heaving deck by clutching the <u>bulwarks</u>, my brother looked past this charging leviathan at the Martians again, and he saw the three of them now close together, and standing so far out to sea that their tripod supports were almost entirely submerged. Thus sunken, and seen in remote perspective, they appeared far less **formidable** than the huge iron bulk in whose wake the steamer was pitching so helplessly. It would seem they were regarding this new **antagonist** with astonishment. To their intelligence, it may be, the giant was even such another as themselves. The *Thunder Child* fired no gun, but simply drove full speed towards them. It was probably her not firing that enabled her to get so near the enemy as she did. They did not know what to make of her. One shell, and they would have sent her to the bottom <u>forthwith</u> with the Heat-Ray.

She was steaming at such a pace that in a minute she seemed halfway between the steamboat and the Martians—a diminishing black bulk against the **receding** horizontal expanse of the Essex coast.

Suddenly the foremost Martian lowered his tube and discharged a canister of the black gas at the ironclad. It hit her larboard side and glanced off in an inky jet that rolled away to seaward, an unfolding **torrent** of Black Smoke, from which the ironclad drove clear. To the watchers from the steamer, low in the water and with the sun in their eyes, it seemed as though she were already among the Martians.

They saw the **gaunt** figures separating and rising out of the water as they **retreated** shoreward, and one of them raised the camera-like generator of the Heat-Ray. He held it pointing obliquely downward, and a bank of steam

inarticulate (ihn are <u>tihk</u> yoo leht) *adj.*   unable to communicate with sufficient clarity or intelligence Synonyms: incoherent, unintelligible

tumult (<u>tuh</u> muhlt) *n.*   commotion, disturbance, and noise, as of a crowd   Synonyms: agitation, bedlam, uproar, clamor, row

impetus (ihm peh tuhs) *n.*   that which inspires or provides energy for a particular action   Synonyms: catalyst, stimulus, incentive, motivation, incitation sprang from the water at its touch. It must have driven through the iron of the ship's side like a white-hot iron rod through paper.

A flicker of flame went up through the rising steam, and then the Martian reeled and staggered. In another moment he was cut down, and a great body of water and steam shot high in the air. The guns of the *Thunder Child* sounded through the reek, going off one after the other, and one shot splashed the water high close by the steamer, ricocheted towards the other flying ships to the north, and smashed a smack to matchwood.

But no one heeded that very much. At the sight of the Martian's collapse the captain on the bridge yelled **inarticulately**, and all the crowding passengers on the steamer's stern shouted together. And then they yelled again. For, surging out beyond the white **tumult**, drove something long and black, the flames streaming from its middle parts, its ventilators and funnels spouting fire.

She was alive still; the steering gear, it seems, was intact and her engines working. She headed straight for a second Martian, and was within a hundred yards of him when the Heat-Ray came to bear. Then with a violent thud, a blinding flash, her decks, her funnels, leaped upward. The Martian staggered with the violence of her explosion, and in another moment the flaming wreckage, still driving forward with the **impetus** of its pace, had struck him and crumpled him up like a thing of cardboard. My brother shouted involuntarily. A boiling tumult of steam hid everything again.

"Two!" yelled the captain.

Everyone was shouting. The whole steamer from end to end rang with frantic cheering that was taken up first by one and then by all in the crowding multitude of ships and boats that was driving out to sea.

The steam hung upon the water for many minutes, hiding the third Martian and the coast altogether. And all this time the boat was paddling steadily out to sea and away

recede (ree <u>seed</u>) *v.* **-ing, -ed**   to draw back, retreat
  Synonyms: abate, decline, diminish, subside

abruptly (uh <u>bruhpt</u> lee) *adv.*   without warning
  Synonyms: unexpectedly, suddenly, unpredictably

interminable (ihn <u>tuhr</u> mihn uh buhl) *adj.*   without or
  seemingly without end   Synonyms: infinite, boring,
  incessant, eternal, perpetual

luminous (<u>loo</u> mihn uhs) *adj.*   1. emitting light; glowing
  Synonyms: brilliant, lustrous, incandescent, refulgent   2. intelligent and easily understood   Synonyms:
  lucid, perspicacious, comprehensible

from the fight; and when at last the confusion cleared, the drifting bank of black vapour intervened, and nothing of the *Thunder Child* could be made out, nor could the third Martian be seen. But the ironclads to seaward were now quite close and standing in towards shore past the steamboat.

The little vessel continued to beat its way seaward, and the ironclads **receded** slowly towards the coast, which was hidden still by a marbled bank of vapour, part steam, part black gas, <u>eddying</u> and combining in the strangest way. The fleet of refugees was scattering to the northeast; several smacks were sailing between the ironclads and the steamboat. After a time, and before they reached the sinking cloud bank, the warships turned northward, and then **abruptly** went about and passed into the thickening haze of evening southward. The coast grew faint, and at last indistinguishable amid the low banks of clouds that were gathering about the sinking sun.

Then suddenly out of the golden haze of the sunset came the vibration of guns, and a form of black shadows moving. Everyone struggled to the rail of the steamer and peered into the blinding furnace of the west, but nothing was to be distinguished clearly. A mass of smoke rose slanting and barred the face of the sun. The steamboat throbbed on its way through an **interminable** suspense.

The sun sank into grey clouds, the sky flushed and darkened, the evening star trembled into sight. It was deep twilight when the captain cried out and pointed. My brother strained his eyes. Something rushed up into the sky out of the greyness—rushed slantingly upward and very swiftly into the **luminous** clearness above the clouds in the western sky; something flat and broad, and very large, that swept round in a vast curve, grew smaller, sank slowly, and vanished again into the grey mystery of the night. And as it flew it rained down darkness upon the land.

Book Two

THE EARTH UNDER
THE MARTIANS

anxiety (aang <u>zie</u> ih tee) *n.* a state of intense apprehension, worry, uncertainty, and fear, especially in
anticipation of some future occurrence. Synonyms:
angst, disquiet, dread, foreboding, uneasiness

circumspection (suhr kuhm <u>spehk</u> shuhn) *n.* the act of
behaving with care and appropriateness Synonyms:
deliberation, forethought, discretion, prudence

consolation (kahn suh <u>lay</u> shuhn) *n.* the act of com-
forting or reassuring Synonyms: assuagement,
easement, succor, encouragement

perpetual (puhr <u>peht</u> choo uhl) *adj.* without end or
seemingly without end Synonyms: interminable, con-
tinual, everlasting

CHAPTER ONE

UNDER FOOT

In the first book I have wandered so much from my own adventures to tell of the experiences of my brother that all through the last two chapters I and the curate have been lurking in the empty house at Halliford <u>whither</u> we fled to escape the Black Smoke. There I will resume. We stopped there all Sunday night and all the next day—the day of the panic—in a little island of daylight, cut off by the Black Smoke from the rest of the world. We could do nothing but wait in aching inactivity during those two weary days.

My mind was occupied by **anxiety** for my wife. I figured her at Leatherhead, terrified, in danger, mourning me already as a dead man. I paced the rooms and cried aloud when I thought of how I was cut off from her, of all that might happen to her in my absence. My cousin I knew was brave enough for any emergency, but he was not the sort of man to realise danger quickly, to rise promptly. What was needed now was not bravery, but **circumspection**. My only **consolation** was to believe that the Martians were moving London-ward and away from her. Such vague anxieties keep the mind sensitive and painful. I grew very weary and irritable with the curate's **perpetual** ejaculations; I tired of the sight of his selfish despair.

ineffectual (ihn uh <u>fehk</u> choo uhl) *adj.*   incapable of producing a desired outcome   Synonyms: failed, ineffective, unavailing, worthless

remonstrance (ree <u>mahn</u> struhns) *n.*   an expression, especially formal, of complaint or protest   Synonyms: assertion, remonstration, argument, accusation

scald (scahld) *v.* **-ing, -ed**   to burn, especially with liquid or steam   Synonyms: burn, broil, scorch

lethargic (luh <u>thahr</u> jihk) *adj.*   lacking in vitality or activity   Synonyms: lazy, laggard, languid, phlegmatic, idle

CHAPTER 1—UNDER FOOT

After some **ineffectual remonstrance** I kept away from him, staying in a room—evidently a children's schoolroom—containing globes, forms, and copybooks. When he followed me thither, I went to a box room at the top of the house and, in order to be alone with my aching miseries, locked myself in.

We were hopelessly hemmed in by the Black Smoke all that day and the morning of the next. There were signs of people in the next house on Sunday evening—a face at a window and moving lights, and later the slamming of a door. But I do not know who these people were, nor what became of them. We saw nothing of them next day. The Black Smoke drifted slowly riverward all through Monday morning, creeping nearer and nearer to us, driving at last along the roadway outside the house that hid us.

A Martian came across the fields about midday, laying the stuff with a jet of superheated steam that hissed against the walls, smashed all the windows it touched, and **scalded** the curate's hand as he fled out of the front room. When at last we crept across the sodden rooms and looked out again, the country northward was as though a black snowstorm had passed over it. Looking towards the river, we were astonished to see an unaccountable redness mingling with the black of the scorched meadows.

For a time we did not see how this change affected our position, save that we were relieved of our fear of the Black Smoke. But later I perceived that we were no longer hemmed in, that now we might get away. So soon as I realised that the way of escape was open, my dream of action returned. But the curate was **lethargic**, unreasonable.

"We are safe here," he repeated; "safe here."

I resolved to leave him—would that I had! Wiser now for the artilleryman's teaching, I sought out food and drink. I had found oil and rags for my burns, and I also took a hat and a flannel shirt that I found in one of the bedrooms. When it was clear to him that I meant to go

THE WAR OF THE WORLDS

reconcile (<u>reh</u> kuhn siel) *v.* **-ing, -ed**   to accept a given circumstance; to settle or resolve a dispute   Synonyms: make peace, placate, resolve, conciliate, harmonize, mediate

contort (kuhn <u>tort</u>) *v.* **-ing, -ed**   to bend out of shape   Synonyms: distort, convolute, gnarl, misshape, warp

misadventure (<u>mihs</u> aad vehn chuhr) *n.*   an incident characterized by misfortune or injury   Synonyms: mishap, accident, blunder, debacle, cataclysm

rout (rowt) *n.*   a complete defeat   Synonyms: beating, drubbing, vanquishment, thrashing

scrutiny (<u>scroo</u> tih nee) *n.*   close and careful examination, observation, or study   Synonyms: analysis, inquiry, perlustration, inspection alone—had **reconciled** myself to going alone—he suddenly roused himself to come. And all being quiet throughout the afternoon, we started about five o'clock, as I should judge, along the blackened road to Sunbury.

In Sunbury, and at intervals along the road, were dead bodies lying in **contorted** attitudes, horses as well as men, overturned carts and luggage, all covered thickly with black dust. That pall of cindery powder made me think of what I had read of the destruction of Pompeii. We got to Hampton Court without **misadventure**, our minds full of strange and unfamiliar appearances, and at Hampton Court our eyes were relieved to find a patch of green that had escaped the suffocating drift. We went through Bushey Park, with its deer going to and fro under the chestnuts, and some men and women hurrying in the distance towards Hampton, and so we came to Twickenham. These were the first people we saw.

Away across the road the woods beyond Ham and Petersham were still afire. Twickenham was uninjured by either Heat-Ray or Black Smoke, and there were more people about here, though none could give us news. For the most part they were like ourselves, taking advantage of a lull to shift their quarters. I have an impression that many of the houses here were still occupied by scared inhabitants, too frightened even for flight. Here too the evidence of a hasty **rout** was abundant along the road. I remember most vividly three smashed bicycles in a heap, pounded into the road by the wheels of subsequent carts. We crossed Richmond Bridge about half past eight. We hurried across the exposed bridge, of course, but I noticed floating down the stream a number of red masses, some many feet across. I did not know what these were—there was no time for **scrutiny**—and I put a more horrible interpretation on them than they deserved. Here again on the Surrey side were black dust that had once been smoke, and dead bodies—a heap near the approach to the sta-

aghast (uh <u>gaast</u>) *adj.* marked by a state of fear, dread, or apprehension Synonyms: appalled, horrified, confounded, dumbfounded, agape

foolhardy (<u>fool</u> hahr dee) *adj.* reckless; heedless of potential consequences Synonyms: rash, impetuous, audacious, imprudent, headstrong tion; but we had no glimpse of the Martians until we were some way towards Barnes.

We saw in the blackened distance a group of three people running down a side street towards the river, but otherwise it seemed deserted. Up the hill Richmond town was burning briskly; outside the town of Richmond there was no trace of the Black Smoke.

Then suddenly, as we approached Kew, came a number of people running, and the upperworks of a Martian fighting-machine loomed in sight over the housetops, not a hundred yards away from us. We stood **aghast** at our danger, and had the Martian looked down we must immediately have perished. We were so terrified that we dared not go on, but turned aside and hid in a shed in a garden. There the curate crouched, weeping silently, and refusing to stir again.

But my fixed idea of reaching Leatherhead would not let me rest, and in the twilight I ventured out again. I went through a shrubbery, and along a passage beside a big house standing in its own grounds, and so emerged upon the road towards Kew. The curate I left in the shed, but he came hurrying after me.

That second start was the most **foolhardy** thing I ever did. For it was manifest the Martians were about us. No sooner had the curate overtaken me than we saw either the fighting-machine we had seen before or another, far away across the meadows in the direction of Kew Lodge. Four or five little black figures hurried before it across the green-grey of the field, and in a moment it was evident this Martian pursued them. In three strides he was among them, and they ran radiating from his feet in all directions. He used no Heat-Ray to destroy them, but picked them up one by one. Apparently he tossed them into the great metallic carrier which projected behind him, much as a workman's basket hangs over his shoulder.

It was the first time I realised that the Martians might have any other purpose than destruction with defeated

petrify (<u>peh</u> trihf eye) *v.* **-ing, -ed**   to paralyze with fear or shock   Synonyms: daze, startle, stupefy, benumb

venture (<u>vehn</u> chuhr) *n.*   an undertaking, often involving significant risk   Synonyms: gamble, enterprise, endeavor, investment, speculation

blunder (<u>bluhn</u> duhr) *v.* **-ing, -ed**   to make a mistake of significant magnitude   Synonyms: botch, err, fumble, stumble

scorch (skohrch) *v.* **-ing, -ed**   to burn, especially with the result of discoloring the outer layer   Synonyms: singe, sear, blacken

ashen (<u>aa</u> shehn) *adj.*   excessively pale, as due to grief, sickness, or fright   Synonyms: anemic, pallid, sallow, wan

intact (ihn <u>taakt</u>) *adj.*   maintaining soundness and completeness in construction   Synonyms: uninjured, unimpaired, whole, sound humanity. We stood for a moment **petrified**, then turned and fled through a gate behind us into a walled garden, fell into, rather than found, a fortunate ditch, and lay there, scarce daring to whisper to each other until the stars were out.

I suppose it was nearly eleven o'clock before we gathered courage to start again, no longer **venturing** into the road, but sneaking along hedgerows and through plantations, and watching keenly through the darkness, he on the right and I on the left, for the Martians, who seemed to be all about us. In one place we **blundered** upon a **scorched** and blackened area, now cooling and **ashen**, and a number of scattered dead bodies of men, burned horribly about the heads and trunks but with their legs and boots mostly **intact**; and of dead horses, fifty feet, perhaps, behind a line of four ripped guns and smashed gun carriages.

Sheen, it seemed, had escaped destruction, but the place was silent and deserted. Here we happened on no dead, though the night was too dark for us to see into the side roads of the place. In Sheen my companion suddenly complained of faintness and thirst, and we decided to try one of the houses.

The first house we entered, after a little difficulty with the window, was a small semi-detached villa, and I found nothing eatable left in the place but some mouldy cheese. There was, however, water to drink; and I took a hatchet, which promised to be useful in our next house-breaking.

We then crossed to a place where the road turns towards Mortlake. Here there stood a white house within a walled garden, and in the pantry of this domicile we found a store of food—two loaves of bread in a pan, an uncooked steak, and the half of a ham. I give this catalogue so precisely because, as it happened, we were destined to subsist upon this store for the next fortnight. Bottled beer stood under a shelf, and there were two bags of haricot beans and some limp lettuces. This pantry opened into a kind

adjacent (uhd <u>jae</u> sihnt) *adj.*   positioned next to, beside
  Synonyms: adjoining, contiguous, bordering

timorous (<u>tih</u> muh ruhs) *adj.*   characterized by excessive
  anxiety   Synonyms: timid, anxious, nervous, fearful,
  petrified

concussion (kuhn <u>cuhsh</u> uhn) *n.*   a violent blow or collision; an injury so caused   Synonyms: blow, bump,
  crash, impact, trauma

multitude (<u>muhl</u> tih tood) *n.*   a great quantity
  Synonyms: drove, horde, host, mass, throng

insensible (ihn <u>sehn</u> sih buhl) *adj.*   unconscious
  Synonyms: unresponsive, languid, lifeless

of wash-up kitchen, and in this was firewood; there was also a cupboard, in which we found nearly a dozen of burgundy, tinned soups and salmon, and two tins of biscuits.

We sat in the **adjacent** kitchen in the dark—for we dared not strike a light—and ate bread and ham, and drank beer out of the same bottle. The curate, who was still **timorous** and restless, was now, oddly enough, for pushing on, and I was urging him to keep up his strength by eating when the thing happened that was to imprison us.

"It can't be midnight yet," I said, and then came a blinding glare of vivid green light. Everything in the kitchen leaped out, clearly visible in green and black, and vanished again. And then followed such a **concussion** as I have never heard before or since. So close on the heels of this as to seem instantaneous came a thud behind me, a clash of glass, a crash and rattle of falling masonry all about us, and the plaster of the ceiling came down upon us, smashing into a **multitude** of fragments upon our heads. I was knocked <u>headlong</u> across the floor against the oven handle and stunned. I was **insensible** for a long time, the curate told me, and when I came to we were in darkness again, and he, with a face wet, as I found afterwards, with blood from a cut forehead, was dabbing water over me.

For some time I could not recollect what had happened. Then things came to me slowly. A bruise on my temple asserted itself.

"Are you better?" asked the curate in a whisper.

At last I answered him. I sat up.

"Don't move," he said. "The floor is covered with smashed crockery from the dresser. You can't possibly move without making a noise, and I fancy *they* are outside."

We both sat quite silent, so that we could scarcely hear each other breathing. Everything seemed deadly still, but once something near us, some plaster or broken brick-

intermittent (ihn tuhr <u>mih</u> tehnt) *adj.* occurring at irregular intervals Synonyms: periodic, punctuated, fitful

incomprehensible (ihn kahm pree <u>hehn</u> sih buhl) *adj.* impossible to understand or make sense of Synonyms: baffling, inscrutable, opaque, unintelligible, unfathomable

aperture (aa puhr choor) *n.* an opening, especially through which light passes Synonyms: breach, fissure, gap, rift, vent

sentinel (<u>sehn</u> tihn ehl) *n.* one who stands guard or awaits a particular occurrence Synonyms: sentry, lookout, guardian

circumspectly (<u>suhr</u> kuhms spehkt lee) *adv.* with great caution, care, and mindfulness Synonyms: discretely, prudently work, slid down with a rumbling sound. Outside and very near was an **intermittent**, metallic rattle.

"That!" said the curate, when presently it happened again.

"Yes," I said. "But what is it?"

"A Martian!" said the curate.

I listened again.

"It was not like the Heat-Ray," I said, and for a time I was inclined to think one of the great fighting-machines had stumbled against the house, as I had seen one stumble against the tower of Shepperton Church.

Our situation was so strange and **incomprehensible** that for three or four hours, until the dawn came, we scarcely moved. And then the light filtered in, not through the window, which remained black, but through a triangular **aperture** between a beam and a heap of broken bricks in the wall behind us. The interior of the kitchen we now saw greyly for the first time.

The window had been burst in by a mass of garden mould, which flowed over the table upon which we had been sitting and lay about our feet. Outside, the soil was banked high against the house. At the top of the window frame we could see an uprooted drainpipe. The floor was littered with smashed hardware; the end of the kitchen towards the house was broken into, and since the daylight shone in there, it was evident the greater part of the house had collapsed. Contrasting vividly with this ruin was the neat dresser, stained in the fashion, pale green, and with a number of copper and tin vessels below it, the wallpaper imitating blue and white tiles, and a couple of coloured supplements fluttering from the walls above the kitchen range.

As the dawn grew clearer, we saw through the gap in the wall the body of a Martian, standing **sentinel**, I suppose, over the still glowing cylinder. At the sight of that we crawled as **circumspectly** as possible out of the twilight of the kitchen into the darkness of the scullery.

abruptly (uh <u>bruhpt</u> lee) *adv.* without warning Synonyms: unexpectedly, suddenly, unpredictably

intermittently (ihn tuhr <u>miht</u> tehnt lee) *adv.* at irregular intervals; erratically Synonyms: occasionally, spasmodically, irregularly, unpredictably

incline (<u>ihn</u> klien) *v.* **-ing, -ed** to hold a particular preference or opinion Synonyms: favor, bias, prefer, predispose

CHAPTER 1—UNDER FOOT

Abruptly the right interpretation dawned upon my mind.

"The fifth cylinder," I whispered, "the fifth shot from Mars, has struck this house and buried us under the ruins!"

For a time the curate was silent, and then he whispered:

"God have mercy upon us!"

I heard him presently whimpering to himself.

Save for that sound we lay quite still in the scullery; I for my part scarce dared breathe, and sat with my eyes fixed on the faint light of the kitchen door. I could just see the curate's face, a dim, oval shape, and his collar and cuffs. Outside there began a metallic hammering, then a violent hooting, and then again, after a quiet interval, a hissing like the hissing of an engine. These noises, for the most part problematical, continued **intermittently**, and seemed if anything to increase in number as time wore on. Presently a measured thudding and a vibration that made everything about us quiver and the vessels in the pantry ring and shift, began and continued. Once the light was eclipsed, and the ghostly kitchen doorway became absolutely dark. For many hours we must have crouched there, silent and shivering, until our tired attention failed. . . .

At last I found myself awake and very hungry. I am **inclined** to believe we must have spent the greater portion of a day before that awakening. My hunger was at a stride so insistent that it moved me to action. I told the curate I was going to seek food, and felt my way towards the pantry. He made me no answer, but so soon as I began eating the faint noise I made stirred him up and I heard him crawling after me.

aperture (aa puhr choor) *n.* an opening, especially through which light passes Synonyms: breach, fissure, gap, rift, vent

tranquil (<u>trank</u> wihl) *adj.* free of disturbance, conflict, or tension Synonyms: composed, placid, serene, calm, unruffled

CHAPTER TWO

WHAT WE SAW FROM THE RUINED HOUSE

After eating we crept back to the scullery, and there I must have dozed again, for when presently I looked round I was alone. The thudding vibration continued with wearisome persistence. I whispered for the curate several times, and at last felt my way to the door of the kitchen. It was still daylight, and I perceived him across the room, lying against the triangular hole that looked out upon the Martians. His shoulders were hunched, so that his head was hidden from me.

I could hear a number of noises almost like those in an engine shed; and the place rocked with that beating thud. Through the **aperture** in the wall I could see the top of a tree touched with gold and the warm blue of a **tranquil** evening sky. For a minute or so I remained watching the curate, and then I advanced, crouching and stepping with extreme care amid the broken crockery that littered the floor.

I touched the curate's leg, and he started so violently that a mass of plaster went sliding down outside and fell

rampart (<u>raam</u> pahrt) *n.* a border built for defensive purposes Synonyms: embankment, bulwark, barricade, stronghold

debris (dih <u>bree</u>) *n.* the remnants of something that has been destroyed Synonyms: litter, detritus, rubble, wreckage

adjacent (uhd <u>jae</u> sihnt) *adj.* positioned next to, beside Synonyms: adjoining, contiguous, bordering

excavation (ehks cuh <u>vay</u> shuhn) *n.* the act of unearthing, digging up Synonyms: exhuming, unearthing, disinterring, mining with a loud impact. I gripped his arm, fearing he might cry out, and for a long time we crouched motionless. Then I turned to see how much of our **rampart** remained. The detachment of the plaster had left a vertical slit open in the **debris**, and by raising myself cautiously across a beam I was able to see out of this gap into what had been overnight a quiet suburban roadway. Vast, indeed, was the change that we beheld.

The fifth cylinder must have fallen right into the midst of the house we had first visited. The building had vanished, completely smashed, pulverised, and dispersed by the blow. The cylinder lay now far beneath the original foundations—deep in a hole, already vastly larger than the pit I had looked into at Woking. The earth all round it had splashed under that tremendous impact—"splashed" is the only word—and lay in heaped piles that hid the masses of the **adjacent** houses. It had behaved exactly like mud under the violent blow of a hammer. Our house had collapsed backward; the front portion, even on the ground floor, had been destroyed completely; by a chance the kitchen and scullery had escaped, and stood buried now under soil and ruins, closed in by tons of earth on every side save towards the cylinder. Over that aspect we hung now on the very edge of the great circular pit the Martians were engaged in making. The heavy beating sound was evidently just behind us, and ever and again a bright green vapour drove up like a veil across our peep-hole.

The cylinder was already opened in the centre of the pit, and on the farther edge of the pit, amid the smashed and gravel-heaped shrubbery, one of the great fighting-machines, deserted by its occupant, stood stiff and tall against the evening sky. At first I scarcely noticed the pit and the cylinder, although it has been convenient to describe them first, on account of the extraordinary glittering mechanism I saw busy in the **excavation**, and on

impetus (ihm peh tuhs) *n.*   that which inspires or provides energy for a particular action   Synonyms: catalyst, stimulus, incentive, motivation, incitation

agile (<u>aa</u> juhl) *adj.*   well-coordinated; nimble   Synonyms: deft, dexterous, sportive, spry, supple

retract (ree <u>traakt</u>) *v.* **-ing, -ed**   to take back or draw in   Synonyms: abjure, disclaim, disown, renege, recant

animate (<u>ah</u> nih mayt) *v.* **-ing, -ed**   to fill with energy and liveliness   Synonyms: inspire, activate, embolden, arouse, vitalize

monotony (muh <u>nah</u> tuh nee) *n.*   a complete lack of variation, often to the point of tediousness   Synonyms: sameness, tedium, repetitiousness, invariability

vogue (vohg) *n.*   that which is currently in fashion or popular acceptance   Synonyms: custom, practice, mode, prevalence, trend account of the strange creatures that were crawling slowly and painfully across the heaped mould near it.

The mechanism it certainly was that held my attention first. It was one of those complicated fabrics that have since been called handling-machines, and the study of which has already given such an enormous **impetus** to terrestrial invention. As it dawned upon me first, it presented a sort of metallic spider with five jointed, **agile** legs, and with an extraordinary number of jointed levers, bars, and reaching and clutching tentacles about its body. Most of its arms were **retracted**, but with three long tentacles it was fishing out a number of rods, plates, and bars which lined the covering and apparently strengthened the walls of the cylinder. These, as it extracted them, were lifted out and deposited upon a level surface of earth behind it.

Its motion was so swift, complex, and perfect that at first I did not see it as a machine, in spite of its metallic glitter. The fighting-machines were coordinated and **animated** to an extraordinary pitch, but nothing to compare with this. People who have never seen these structures, and have only the ill-imagined efforts of artists or the imperfect descriptions of such eye-witnesses as myself to go upon, scarcely realise that living quality.

I recall particularly the illustration of one of the first pamphlets to give a consecutive account of the war. The artist had evidently made a hasty study of one of the fighting-machines, and there his knowledge ended. He presented them as tilted, stiff tripods, without either flexibility or subtlety, and with an altogether misleading **monotony** of effect. The pamphlet containing these renderings had a considerable **vogue**, and I mention them here simply to warn the reader against the impression they may have created. They were no more like the Martians I saw in action than a Dutch doll is like a human being. To my mind, the pamphlet would have been much better without them.

cerebral (suh <u>ree</u> bruhl) *adj.*   relating to or requiring the use of the higher intellectual faculties   Synonyms: scholarly, intellectual, learned

dexterous (<u>dehk</u> stehr uhs) *adj.*   characterized by skillfulness in the use of the hands   Synonyms: proficient, adroit, expert, handy, savvy

transient (<u>trahn</u> zee ihnt) *adj.*   passing with time, present only briefly   Synonyms: temporary, transitory, ephemeral, fleeting

tactile (taak tiel) *adj.*   of or related to the sense of touch; able to be perceived by the sense of touch   Synonyms: palpable, material, tangible

At first, I say, the handling-machine did not impress me as a machine, but as a crablike creature with a glittering integument, the controlling Martian whose delicate tentacles actuated its movements seeming to be simply the equivalent of the crab's **cerebral** portion. But then I perceived the resemblance of its grey-brown, shiny, leathery integument to that of the other sprawling bodies beyond, and the true nature of this **dexterous** workman dawned upon me. With that realisation my interest shifted to those other creatures, the real Martians. Already I had had a **transient** impression of these, and the first nausea no longer obscured my observation. Moreover, I was concealed and motionless, and under no urgency of action.

They were, I now saw, the most unearthly creatures it is possible to conceive. They were huge round bodies—or, rather, heads—about four feet in diameter, each body having in front of it a face. This face had no nostrils—indeed, the Martians do not seem to have had any sense of smell, but it had a pair of very large dark-coloured eyes, and just beneath this a kind of fleshy beak. In the back of this head or body—I scarcely know how to speak of it—was the single tight tympanic surface, since known to be anatomically an ear, though it must have been almost useless in our dense air. In a group round the mouth were sixteen slender, almost whiplike tentacles, arranged in two bunches of eight each. These bunches have since been named rather aptly, by that distinguished anatomist, Professor Howes, the *hands*. Even as I saw these Martians for the first time they seemed to be endeavouring to raise themselves on these hands, but of course, with the increased weight of terrestrial conditions, this was impossible. There is reason to suppose that on Mars they may have progressed upon them with some facility.

The internal anatomy, I may remark here, as dissection has since shown, was almost equally simple. The greater part of the structure was the brain, sending enormous nerves to the eyes, ear, and **tactile** tentacles. Besides this

pulmonary (<u>puhl</u> mihn eh ree) *adj.*　of or related to the lungs

carnivorous (cahr <u>nih</u> voh ruhs) *adj.*　meat-eating

heterogeneous (heh tehr oh <u>jee</u> nee uhs) *adj.*　composed of unlike or dissimilar parts　Synonyms: miscellaneous, composite, multifarious, disparate were the bulky lungs, into which the mouth opened, and the heart and its vessels. The **pulmonary** distress caused by the denser atmosphere and greater gravitational attraction was only too evident in the convulsive movements of the outer skin.

And this was the sum of the Martian organs. Strange as it may seem to a human being, all the complex apparatus of digestion, which makes up the bulk of our bodies, did not exist in the Martians. They were heads—merely heads. Entrails they had none. They did not eat, much less digest. Instead, they took the fresh, living blood of other creatures, and *injected* it into their own veins. I have myself seen this being done, as I shall mention in its place. But, squeamish as I may seem, I cannot bring myself to describe what I could not endure even to continue watching. Let it suffice to say, blood obtained from a still living animal, in most cases from a human being, was run directly by means of a little pipette into the recipient canal. . . .

The bare idea of this is no doubt horribly repulsive to us, but at the same time I think that we should remember how repulsive our **carnivorous** habits would seem to an intelligent rabbit.

The physiological advantages of the practice of injection are undeniable, if one thinks of the tremendous waste of human time and energy occasioned by eating and the digestive process. Our bodies are half made up of glands and tubes and organs, occupied in turning **heterogeneous** food into blood. The digestive processes and their reaction upon the nervous system sap our strength and colour our minds. Men go happy or miserable as they have healthy or unhealthy livers, or sound gastric glands. But the Martians were lifted above all these organic fluctuations of mood and emotion.

Their undeniable preference for men as their source of nourishment is partly explained by the nature of the remains of the victims they had brought with them as

feeble (<u>fee</u> buhl) *adj.*   lacking in strength, weak   Synonyms: enervated, impotent, sapless

physiology (fihz ee <u>ah</u> luh jee) *n.*   the study of living organisms and their interrelated parts

periodical (peer ee <u>ahd</u> ihk uhl) *n.*   a publication issued with regularity   Synonyms: journal, magazine, newspaper, quarterly

tumultuous (tuh <u>muhlt</u> yoo uhs) *adj.*   characterized by confusion and disorder   Synonyms: clamorous, agitated, raucous, turbulent

terrestrial (tuh <u>rehs</u> stree uhl) *adj.*   1. of or relating to the earth   Synonyms: earthbound, earthlike   2. prosaic, mundane   Synonyms: worldly, common, profane provisions from Mars. These creatures, to judge from the shrivelled remains that have fallen into human hands, were bipeds with flimsy, silicious skeletons (almost like those of the silicious sponges) and **feeble** musculature, standing about six feet high and having round, erect heads, and large eyes in flinty sockets. Two or three of these seem to have been brought in each cylinder, and all were killed before earth was reached. It was just as well for them, for the mere attempt to stand upright upon our planet would have broken every bone in their bodies.

And while I am engaged in this description, I may add in this place certain further details which, although they were not all evident to us at the time, will enable the reader who is unacquainted with them to form a clearer picture of these offensive creatures.

In three other points their **physiology** differed strangely from ours. Their organisms did not sleep, any more than the heart of man sleeps. Since they had no extensive muscular mechanism to recuperate, that **periodical** extinction was unknown to them. They had little or no sense of fatigue, it would seem. On earth they could never have moved without effort, yet even to the last they kept in action. In twenty-four hours they did twenty-four hours of work, as even on earth is perhaps the case with the ants.

In the next place, wonderful as it seems in a sexual world, the Martians were absolutely without sex, and therefore without any of the **tumultuous** emotions that arise from that difference among men. A young Martian, there can now be no dispute, was really born upon earth during the war, and it was found attached to its parent, partially *budded* off, just as young lilybulbs bud off, or like the young animals in the fresh-water polyp.

In man, in all the higher **terrestrial** animals, such a method of increase has disappeared; but even on this earth it was certainly the primitive method. Among the lower animals, up even to those first cousins of the ver-

supersede (soo puhr <u>seed</u>) *v.* **-ing, -ed** to take precedence over; to replace Synonyms: override, overrule, displace, oust, usurp, succeed

speculative (<u>spehk</u> yoo lah tihv) *adj.* based upon conjecture Synonyms: conjectural, theoretical, hypothetical, notional

repute (rih <u>pyoot</u>) *n.* reputation Synonyms: character, credit, esteem, standing

defunct (dih <u>fuhnkt</u>) *adj.* no longer relevant or functional Synonyms: extinct, obsolete, inoperative, exanimate, expired

caricature (<u>kaa</u> rih kaa choor) *n.* an exaggerated likeness, often for humorous or insulting effect Synonyms: cartoon, distortion, parody, lampoon

facetious (fuh <u>see</u> shihs) *adj.* in a joking manner Synonyms: kidding, jocular, farcical, droll, sportive, playful

salient (say lee ihnt) *adj.* of greatest prominence or conspicuousness Synonyms: arrestive, notable, protruding, significant, pronounced

trivial (trih vee uhl) *adj.* of little importance or relevance Synonyms: unimportant, negligible, inappreciable, frivolous, nonessential tebrated animals, the Tunicates, the two processes occur side by side, but finally the sexual method **superseded** its competitor altogether. On Mars, however, just the reverse has apparently been the case.

It is worthy of remark that a certain **speculative** writer of quasi-scientific **repute**, writing long before the Martian invasion, did forecast for man a final structure not unlike the actual Martian condition. His prophecy, I remember, appeared in November or December, 1893, in a long-**defunct** publication, the *Pall Mall Budget*, and I recall a **caricature** of it in a pre-Martian periodical called *Punch*. He pointed out—writing in a foolish, **facetious** tone—that the perfection of mechanical appliances must ultimately supersede limbs; the perfection of chemical devices, digestion; that such organs as hair, external nose, teeth, ears, and chin were no longer essential parts of the human being, and that the tendency of natural selection would lie in the direction of their steady diminution through the coming ages. The brain alone remained a cardinal necessity. Only one other part of the body had a strong case for survival, and that was the hand, "teacher and agent of the brain." While the rest of the body dwindled, the hands would grow larger.

There is many a true word written in jest, and here in the Martians we have beyond dispute the actual accomplishment of such a suppression of the animal side of the organism by the intelligence. To me it is quite credible that the Martians may be descended from beings not unlike ourselves, by a gradual development of brain and hands (the latter giving rise to the two bunches of delicate tentacles at last) at the expense of the rest of the body. Without the body the brain would, of course, become a mere selfish intelligence, without any of the emotional substratum of the human being.

The last **salient** point in which the systems of these creatures differed from ours was in what one might have thought a very **trivial** particular. Micro-organisms, which

contagion (cuhn <u>tay</u> juhn) *n.*   an agent that causes
illness   Synonyms: taint, virus

terrestrial (tuh <u>rehs</u> stree uhl) *adj.*   1. of or relating to
the earth   Synonyms: earthbound, earthlike   2. pro-
saic, mundane   Synonyms: worldly, common, profane

cause so much disease and pain on earth, have either never appeared upon Mars or Martian sanitary science eliminated them ages ago. A hundred diseases, all the fevers and **contagions** of human life, consumption, cancers, tumours and such morbidities, never enter the scheme of their life. And speaking of the differences between the life on Mars and **terrestrial** life, I may allude here to the curious suggestions of the red weed.

Apparently the vegetable kingdom in Mars, instead of having green for a dominant colour, is of a vivid blood-red tint. At any rate, the seeds which the Martians (intentionally or accidentally) brought with them gave rise in all cases to red-coloured growths. Only that known popularly as the red weed, however, gained any footing in competition with terrestrial forms. The red creeper was quite a transitory growth, and few people have seen it growing. For a time, however, the red weed grew with astonishing vigour and luxuriance. It spread up the sides of the pit by the third or fourth day of our imprisonment, and its cactus-like branches formed a carmine fringe to the edges of our triangular window. And afterwards I found it broadcast throughout the country, and especially wherever there was a stream of water.

The Martians had what appears to have been an auditory organ, a single round drum at the back of the head-body, and eyes with a visual range not very different from ours except that, according to Philips, blue and violet were as black to them. It is commonly supposed that they communicated by sounds and tentacular gesticulations; this is asserted, for instance, in the able but hastily compiled pamphlet (written evidently by someone not an eye-witness of Martian actions) to which I have already alluded, and which, so far, has been the chief source of information concerning them. Now no surviving human being saw so much of the Martians in action as I did. I take no credit to myself for an accident, but the fact is so. And I assert that I watched them closely time after time,

peculiar (pih <u>kyoo</u> lee uhr) *adj.* out of the ordinary, odd   Synonyms: abnormal, curious, singular, unconventional

preconception (pree kuhn <u>sehpt</u> shuhn) *n.* an idea formulated without basis in adequate information Synonyms: assumption, bias, prejudice, presupposition

vehemence (<u>vee</u> uh mehns) *n.* intensity of emotion or expression   Synonyms: ardor, passion, gusto, enthusiasm, fervor

decorum (dih <u>kohr</u> uhm) *n.* appropriateness in manners and conduct   Synonyms: propriety, civility, gentility, politesse, etiquette and that I have seen four, five, and (once) six of them sluggishly performing the most elaborately complicated operations together without either sound or gesture. Their **peculiar** hooting invariably preceded feeding; it had no modulation, and was, I believe, in no sense a signal, but merely the expiration of air preparatory to the suctional operation. I have a certain claim to at least an elementary knowledge of psychology, and in this matter I am convinced—as firmly as I am convinced of anything—that the Martians interchanged thoughts without any physical intermediation. And I have been convinced of this in spite of strong **preconceptions**. Before the Martian invasion, as an occasional reader here or there may remember, I had written with some little **vehemence** against the telepathic theory.

The Martians wore no clothing. Their conceptions of ornament and **decorum** were necessarily different from ours; and not only were they evidently much less sensible of changes of temperature than we are, but changes of pressure do not seem to have affected their health at all seriously. Yet though they wore no clothing, it was in the other artificial additions to their bodily resources that their great superiority over man lay. We men, with our bicycles and road-skates, our Lilienthal soaring-machines, our guns and sticks and so forth, are just in the beginning of the evolution that the Martians have worked out. They have become practically mere brains, wearing different bodies according to their needs just as men wear suits of clothes and take a bicycle in a hurry or an umbrella in the wet. And of their appliances, perhaps nothing is more wonderful to a man than the curious fact that what is the dominant feature of almost all human devices in mechanism is absent—the *wheel* is absent; among all the things they brought to earth there is no trace or suggestion of their use of wheels. One would have at least expected it in locomotion. And in this connection it is curious to remark that even on this earth Nature has never hit upon

expedient (ehk <u>spee</u> dee ehnt) *n.* a means to a desired end Synonyms: resource, device, contrivance, resort, stratagem

abstain (aab <u>stayn</u>) *v.* to refrain from a particular action or practice, especially out of self-discipline or self-denial Synonyms: abjure, forbear, forgo, pass, eschew

ineffectual (ihn uh <u>fehk</u> choo uhl) *adj.* incapable of producing a desired outcome Synonyms: failed, ineffective, unavailing, worthless

eloquent (<u>eh</u> loh kwent) *adj.* well-spoken Synonyms: articulate, expressive, fluent the wheel, or has preferred other **expedients** to its development. And not only did the Martians either not know of (which is incredible), or **abstain** from, the wheel, but in their apparatus singularly little use is made of the fixed pivot or relatively fixed pivot, with circular motions thereabout confined to one plane. Almost all the joints of the machinery present a complicated system of sliding parts moving over small but beautifully curved friction bearings. And while upon this matter of detail, it is remarkable that the long leverages of their machines are in most cases actuated by a sort of sham musculature of the disks in an elastic sheath; these disks become polarised and drawn closely and powerfully together when traversed by a current of electricity. In this way the curious parallelism to animal motions, which was so striking and disturbing to the human beholder, was attained. Such quasi-muscles abounded in the crablike handling-machine which, on my first peeping out of the slit, I watched unpacking the cylinder. It seemed infinitely more alive than the actual Martians lying beyond it in the sunset light, panting, stirring **ineffectual** tentacles, and moving feebly after their vast journey across space.

While I was still watching their sluggish motions in the sunlight, and noting each strange detail of their form, the curate reminded me of his presence by pulling violently at my arm. I turned to a scowling face, and silent, **eloquent** lips. He wanted the slit, which permitted only one of us to peep through; and so I had to forego watching them for a time while he enjoyed that privilege.

When I looked again, the busy handling-machine had already put together several of the pieces of apparatus it had taken out of the cylinder into a shape having an unmistakable likeness to its own; and down on the left a busy little digging mechanism had come into view, emitting jets of green vapour and working its way round the pit, excavating and embanking in a methodical and discriminating manner. This it was which had caused the

refuge (<u>reh</u> fyooj) *n.*   shelter or protection; a place providing shelter or protection   Synonyms: asylum, preserve, sanctuary, stronghold regular beating noise, and the rhythmic shocks that had kept our ruinous **refuge** quivering. It piped and whistled as it worked. So far as I could see, the thing was without a directing Martian at all.

refuge (<u>reh</u> fyooj) *n.* shelter or protection; a place providing shelter or protection   Synonyms: asylum, preserve, sanctuary, stronghold

incur (ihn <u>kuhr</u>) *v.* **-ing, -ed**   to become subject or liable to, often through a particular action   Synonyms: contract, draw, provoke, arouse

grotesque (groh <u>tehsk</u>) *adj.*   severely distorted or hideous in appearance   Synonyms: deformed, bizarre, outlandish, aberrant, malformed

disposition (dihs poh <u>zih</u> shuhn) *n.*   one's usual mood or temperament   Synonyms: character, constitution, nature, proclivity, propensity

vitiate (vih tee ayt) *v.* **-ing, -ed**   to make imperfect, irrelevant, or impure   Synonyms: abrogate, annul, debase, negate, corrupt

Chapter Three

The Days of Imprisonment

The arrival of a second fighting-machine drove us from our peephole into the scullery, for we feared that from his elevation the Martian might see down upon us behind our barrier. At a later date we began to feel less in danger of their eyes, for to an eye in the dazzle of the sunlight outside our **refuge** must have been blank blackness, but at first the slightest suggestion of approach drove us into the scullery in heart-throbbing retreat. Yet terrible as was the danger we **incurred**, the attraction of peeping was for both of us irresistible. And I recall now with a sort of wonder that, in spite of the infinite danger in which we were between starvation and a still more terrible death, we could yet struggle bitterly for that horrible privilege of sight. We would race across the kitchen in a **grotesque** way between eagerness and the dread of making a noise, and strike each other, and thrust and kick, within a few inches of exposure.

The fact is that we had absolutely incompatible **dispositions** and habits of thought and action, and our danger and isolation only accentuated the incompatibility. At Halliford I had already come to hate the curate's trick of helpless exclamation, his stupid rigidity of mind. His endless muttering monologue **vitiated** every effort I made to

efficacious (eh fih <u>kay</u> shuhs) *adj.* capable of bringing about a desired result Synonyms: capable, puissant, operative, efficient, competent

importunity (ihm pohr <u>too</u> nih tee) *n.* a request marked by insistence and desperation, often to an inappropriate degree Synonyms: entreaty, overture, petition, plea, proposition

timorous (<u>tih</u> muh ruhs) *adj.* characterized by excessive anxiety Synonyms: timid, anxious, nervous, fearful, petrified

pitiless (<u>piht</u> ee lehs) *adj.* without mercy or remorse Synonyms: callous, obdurate, unrelenting, inexorable

venture (<u>vehn</u> chuhr) *n.* an undertaking, often involving significant risk Synonyms: gamble, enterprise, endeavor, investment, speculation think out a line of action, and drove me at times, thus pent up and intensified, almost to the verge of craziness. He was as lacking in restraint as a silly woman. He would weep for hours together, and I verily believe that to the very end this spoiled child of life thought his weak tears in some way **efficacious**. And I would sit in the darkness unable to keep my mind off him by reason of his **importunities**. He ate more than I did, and it was in vain I pointed out that our only chance of life was to stop in the house until the Martians had done with their pit, that in that long patience a time might presently come when we should need food. He ate and drank impulsively in heavy meals at long intervals. He slept little.

As the days wore on, his utter carelessness of any consideration so intensified our distress and danger that I had, much as I loathed doing it, to resort to threats, and at last to blows. That brought him to reason for a time. But he was one of those weak creatures, void of pride, **timorous**, anaemic, hateful souls, full of shifty cunning, who face neither God nor man, who face not even themselves.

It is disagreeable for me to recall and write these things, but I set them down that my story may lack nothing. Those who have escaped the dark and terrible aspects of life will find my brutality, my flash of rage in our final tragedy, easy enough to blame; for they know what is wrong as well as any, but not what is possible to tortured men. But those who have been under the shadow, who have gone down at last to elemental things, will have a wider charity.

And while within we fought out our dark, dim contest of whispers, snatched food and drink, and gripping hands and blows, without, in the **pitiless** sunlight of that terrible June, was the strange wonder, the unfamiliar routine of the Martians in the pit. Let me return to those first new experiences of mine. After a long time I **ventured** back to the peephole, to find that the new-comers had been reinforced

novel (<u>nah</u> vuhl) *adj.* markedly different, original, or unique   Synonyms: fresh, innovative, neoteric, singular

periodically (peer ee <u>odd</u> ihk lee) *adj.* occurring at regular intervals   Synonyms: recurrently, intermittently

dexterous (<u>dehk</u> stehr uhs) *adj.* characterized by skillfulness in the use of the hands   Synonyms: proficient, adroit, expert, handy, savvy

inert (ihn <u>uhrt</u>) *adj.* incapable of or lethargic in movement or activity   Synonyms: lifeless, languid, torpid, indolent

acute (uh <u>kyoot</u>) *adj.* 1. particularly sharp or severe   Synonyms: acuminous, pointed, fierce, keen
2. particularly perceptive or insightful   Synonyms: astute, perspicacious, canny, clever, perceptive

by the occupants of no fewer than three of the fighting-machines. These last had brought with them certain fresh appliances that stood in an orderly manner about the cylinder. The second handling-machine was now completed, and was busied in serving one of the **novel** contrivances the big machine had brought. This was a body resembling a milk can in its general form, above which oscillated a pear-shaped receptacle, and from which a stream of white powder flowed into a circular basin below.

The oscillatory motion was imparted to this by one tentacle of the handling-machine. With two spatulate hands the handling-machine was digging out and flinging masses of clay into the pear-shaped receptacle above, while with another arm it **periodically** opened a door and removed rusty and blackened clinkers from the middle part of the machine. Another steely tentacle directed the powder from the basin along a ribbed channel towards some receiver that was hidden from me by the mound of bluish dust. From this unseen receiver a little thread of green smoke rose vertically into the quiet air. As I looked, the handling-machine, with a faint and musical clinking, extended, telescopic fashion, a tentacle that had been a moment before a mere blunt projection, until its end was hidden behind the mound of clay. In another second it had lifted a bar of white aluminium into sight, untarnished as yet, and shining dazzlingly, and deposited it in a growing stack of bars that stood at the side of the pit. Between sunset and starlight this **dexterous** machine must have made more than a hundred such bars out of the crude clay, and the mound of bluish dust rose steadily until it topped the side of the pit.

The contrast between the swift and complex movements of these contrivances and the **inert** panting clumsiness of their masters was **acute**, and for days I had to tell myself repeatedly that these latter were indeed the living of the two things.

inarticulate (ihn are <u>tihk</u> yoo leht) *adj.*   unable to communicate with sufficient clarity or intelligence Synonyms: incoherent, unintelligible

gesticulate (jehs <u>tihck</u> yoo layt) *v.* **-ing, -ed**   to move the body, especially the hands and arms, for purposes of communication   Synonyms: sign, mime, gesture

clamber (<u>klahm</u> buhr) *v.* **-ing, -ed**   to climb or crawl with difficulty and awkwardness   Synonyms: scramble, wriggle, jostle, scurry

frantic (<u>fraan</u> tihk) *adj.*   excessively emotional; uncontrollably anxious   Synonyms: agitated, distraught, frenetic

integument (ihn <u>tehg</u> yoo mihnt) *n.*   the outer layer or covering, especially with respect to a living body

enigma (ee <u>nihg</u> muh) *n.*   something that perplexes or cannot be explained   Synonyms: riddle, mystery, puzzlement

ruddy (<u>ruh</u> dee) *adj.*   having a healthy, flushed coloration   Synonyms: rosy, flushed, glowing

CHAPTER 3—THE DAYS OF IMPRISONMENT

The curate had possession of the slit when the first men were brought to the pit. I was sitting below, huddled up, listening with all my ears. He made a sudden movement backward, and I, fearful that we were observed, crouched in a spasm of terror. He came sliding down the rubbish and crept beside me in the darkness, **inarticulate**, **gesticulating**, and for a moment I shared his panic. His gesture suggested a resignation of the slit, and after a little while my curiosity gave me courage, and I rose up, stepped across him, and **clambered** up to it. At first I could see no reason for his **frantic** behaviour. The twilight had now come, the stars were little and faint, but the pit was illuminated by the flickering green fire that came from the aluminium-making. The whole picture was a flickering scheme of green gleams and shifting rusty black shadows, strangely trying to the eyes. Over and through it all went the bats, heeding it not at all. The sprawling Martians were no longer to be seen, the mound of blue-green powder had risen to cover them from sight, and a fighting-machine, with its legs contracted, crumpled, and abbreviated, stood across the corner of the pit. And then, amid the clangour of the machinery, came a drifting suspicion of human voices, that I entertained at first only to dismiss.

I crouched, watching this fighting-machine closely, satisfying myself now for the first time that the hood did indeed contain a Martian. As the green flames lifted I could see the oily gleam of his **integument** and the brightness of his eyes. And suddenly I heard a yell, and saw a long tentacle reaching over the shoulder of the machine to the little cage that hunched upon its back. Then something—something struggling violently—was lifted high against the sky, a black, vague **enigma** against the starlight; and as this black object came down again, I saw by the green brightness that it was a man. For an instant he was clearly visible. He was a stout, **ruddy**, middle-aged man, well dressed; three days before, he must have been walking the world, a man of considerable consequence. I

vain (vayn) *adj.*   ineffective in achieving a desired purpose   Synonyms: unsuccessful, fruitless, worthless, futile

incapable (ihn <u>kay</u> puh buhl) *adj.*   lacking in a particular ability; unable   Synonyms: disqualified, inept, impotent, unfit

culminate (<u>kuhl</u> mih nayt) *v.* **-ing, -ed**   to come to an end or reach the point of climax   Synonyms: conclude, crown, terminate, finish, climax

vestige (<u>veh</u> stihj) *n.*   a visible trace of that which is no longer present, especially in the case of an obsolete part, organ, or system   Synonyms: sign, token, trace, residue, remnant

encampment (ehn <u>caamp</u> mehnt) *n.*   the site on which temporary residences are erected   Synonyms: barracks, dormitory, garrison, quarters could see his staring eyes and gleams of light on his studs and watch chain. He vanished behind the mound, and for a moment there was silence. And then began a shrieking and a sustained and cheerful hooting from the Martians.

I slid down the rubbish, struggled to my feet, clapped my hands over my ears, and bolted into the scullery. The curate, who had been crouching silently with his arms over his head, looked up as I passed, cried out quite loudly at my desertion of him, and came running after me.

That night, as we lurked in the scullery, balanced between our horror and the terrible fascination this peeping had, although I felt an urgent need of action I tried in **vain** to conceive some plan of escape; but afterwards, during the second day, I was able to consider our position with great clearness. The curate, I found, was quite **incapable** of discussion; this new and **culminating** atrocity had robbed him of all **vestiges** of reason or forethought. Practically he had already sunk to the level of an animal. But as the saying goes, I gripped myself with both hands. It grew upon my mind, once I could face the facts, that terrible as our position was, there was as yet no justification for absolute despair. Our chief chance lay in the possibility of the Martians making the pit nothing more than a temporary **encampment**. Or even if they kept it permanently, they might not consider it necessary to guard it, and a chance of escape might be afforded us. I also weighed very carefully the possibility of our digging a way out in a direction away from the pit, but the chances of our emerging within sight of some sentinel fighting-machine seemed at first too great. And I should have had to do all the digging myself. The curate would certainly have failed me.

It was on the third day, if my memory serves me right, that I saw the lad killed. It was the only occasion on which I actually saw the Martians feed. After that experience I avoided the hole in the wall for the better part of a day. I went into the scullery, removed the door, and spent some

excavation (ehks cuh <u>vay</u> shuhn) *n.*   the act of unearthing, digging up   Synonyms: exhuming, unearthing,
disinterring, mining

serenity (suh <u>rehn</u> ih tee) *n.*   an absence of worry or
stress; calmness   Synonyms: composure, placidity,
tranquility

hours digging with my hatchet as silently as possible; but when I had made a hole about a couple of feet deep the loose earth collapsed noisily, and I did not dare continue. I lost heart, and lay down on the scullery floor for a long time, having no spirit even to move. And after that I abandoned altogether the idea of escaping by **excavation**.

It says much for the impression the Martians had made upon me that at first I entertained little or no hope of our escape being brought about by their overthrow through any human effort. But on the fourth or fifth night I heard a sound like heavy guns.

It was very late in the night, and the moon was shining brightly. The Martians had taken away the excavating-machine, and, save for a fighting-machine that stood in the remoter bank of the pit and a handling-machine that was buried out of my sight in a corner of the pit immediately beneath my peephole, the place was deserted by them. Except for the pale glow from the handling-machine and the bars and patches of white moonlight the pit was in darkness, and, except for the clinking of the handling-machine, quite still. That night was a beautiful **serenity**; save for one planet, the moon seemed to have the sky to herself. I heard a dog howling, and that familiar sound it was that made me listen. Then I heard quite distinctly a booming exactly like the sound of great guns. Six distinct reports I counted, and after a long interval six again. And that was all.

desist (dee <u>sihst</u>) *v.* **-ing, -ed**   to cease; to stop performing an activity or task   Synonyms: forbear, abstain, surcease, discontinue

feeble (<u>fee</u> buhl) *adj.*   lacking in strength, weak   Synonyms: enervated, impotent, sapless

interminable (ihn <u>tuhr</u> mihn uh buhl) *adj.*   without or seemingly without end   Synonyms: infinite, boring, incessant, eternal, perpetual

THE DEATH OF THE CURATE

It was on the sixth day of our imprisonment that I peeped for the last time, and <u>presently</u> found myself alone. Instead of keeping close to me and trying to oust me from the slit, the curate had gone back into the scullery. I was struck by a sudden thought. I went back quickly and quietly into the scullery. In the darkness I heard the curate drinking. I snatched in the darkness, and my fingers caught a bottle of burgundy.

For a few minutes there was a tussle. The bottle struck the floor and broke, and I **desisted** and rose. We stood panting and threatening each other. In the end I planted myself between him and the food, and told him of my determination to begin a discipline. I divided the food in the pantry, into rations to last us ten days. I would not let him eat any more that day. In the afternoon he made a **feeble** effort to get at the food. I had been dozing, but in an instant I was awake. All day and all night we sat face to face, I weary but resolute, and he weeping and complaining of his immediate hunger. It was, I know, a night and a day, but to me it seemed—it seems now—an **interminable** length of time.

cajole (kuh <u>johl</u>) *v.* **-ing, -ed**   to influence through gentle urging or flattery   Synonyms: entice, induce, wheedle, coax

avail (uh <u>vayl</u>) *v.* **-ing, -ed**   to be useful to   Synonyms: benefit, satisfy, suffice

desist (dee <u>sihst</u>) *v.* **-ing, -ed**   to cease; to stop performing an activity or task   Synonyms: forbear, abstain, surcease, discontinue

paradoxical (paa ruh <u>dahks</u> ih kuhl) *adj.*   true despite an apparent contradiction in terms   Synonyms: incongruent, discrepant, disconsonant

revert (ree <u>vuhrt</u>) *v.* **-ing, -ed**   to return to a previous state or condition   Synonyms: backslide, inverse, retrograde, transpose

CHAPTER 4—THE DEATH OF THE CURATE

And so our widened incompatibility ended at last in open conflict. For two vast days we struggled in undertones and wrestling contests. There were times when I beat and kicked him madly, times when I **cajoled** and persuaded him, and once I tried to bribe him with the last bottle of burgundy, for there was a rain-water pump from which I could get water. But neither force nor kindness **availed**; he was indeed beyond reason. He would neither **desist** from his attacks on the food nor from his noisy babbling to himself. The rudimentary precautions to keep our imprisonment endurable he would not observe. Slowly I began to realise the complete overthrow of his intelligence, to perceive that my sole companion in this close and sickly darkness was a man insane.

From certain vague memories I am inclined to think my own mind wandered at times. I had strange and hideous dreams whenever I slept. It sounds **paradoxical**, but I am inclined to think that the weakness and insanity of the curate warned me, braced me, and kept me a sane man.

On the eighth day he began to talk aloud instead of whispering, and nothing I could do would moderate his speech.

"It is just, O God!" he would say, over and over again. "It is just. On me and mine be the punishment laid. We have sinned, we have fallen short. There was poverty, sorrow; the poor were trodden in the dust, and I held my peace. I preached acceptable folly—my God, what folly!—when I should have stood up, though I died for it, and called upon them to repent—repent! . . . Oppressors of the poor and needy . . . ! The wine press of God!"

Then he would suddenly **revert** to the matter of the food I withheld from him, praying, begging, weeping, at last threatening. He began to raise his voice—I prayed him not to. He perceived a hold on me—he threatened he would shout and bring the Martians upon us. For a time that scared me; but any concession would have shortened our chance of escape beyond estimating. I defied him,

299

torrent (<u>toh</u> rehnt) *n.* a great outpouring; a flood
  Synonyms: flow, cascade, shower, spate

implore (ihm <u>plohr</u>) *v.* **-ing, -ed** to make a desperate
  appeal Synonyms: entreat, beseech, beg, supplicate

aperture (aa puhr choor) *n.* an opening, especially
  through which light passes Synonyms: breach, fissure,
  gap, rift, vent

debris (dih <u>bree</u>) *n.* the remnants of something that
  has been destroyed Synonyms: litter, detritus, rubble,
  wreckage

CHAPTER 4—THE DEATH OF THE CURATE

although I felt no assurance that he might not do this thing. But that day, at any rate, he did not. He talked with his voice rising slowly, through the greater part of the eighth and ninth days—threats, entreaties, mingled with a **torrent** of half-sane and always frothy repentance for his vacant sham of God's service, such as made me pity him. Then he slept awhile, and began again with renewed strength, so loudly that I must needs make him desist.

"Be still!" I **implored**.

He rose to his knees, for he had been sitting in the darkness near the copper.

"I have been still too long," he said, in a tone that must have reached the pit, "and now I must bear my witness. Woe unto this unfaithful city! Woe! Woe! Woe! Woe! Woe! To the inhabitants of the earth by reason of the other voices of the trumpet—"

"Shut up!" I said, rising to my feet, and in a terror lest the Martians should hear us. "For God's sake—"

"Nay," shouted the curate, at the top of his voice, standing likewise and extending his arms. "Speak! The word of the Lord is upon me!"

In three strides he was at the door leading into the kitchen.

"I must bear my witness! I go! It has already been too long delayed."

I put out my hand and felt the meat chopper hanging to the wall. In a flash I was after him. I was fierce with fear. Before he was halfway across the kitchen I had overtaken him. With one last touch of humanity I turned the blade back and struck him with the butt. He went headlong forward and lay stretched on the ground. I stumbled over him and stood panting. He lay still.

Suddenly I heard a noise without, the run and smash of slipping plaster, and the triangular **aperture** in the wall was darkened. I looked up and saw the lower surface of a handling-machine coming slowly across the hole. One of its gripping limbs curled amid the **debris**; another limb

petrify (<u>peh</u> trihf eye) *v.* **-ing, -ed**   to paralyze with fear or shock   Synonyms: daze, startle, stupefy, benumb

scrutinise or **scrutinize** (<u>scrooh</u> tihn ized) *v.* **-ing, -ed**   to inspect carefully   Synonyms: examine, inspect, critique

CHAPTER 4—THE DEATH OF THE CURATE

appeared, feeling its way over the fallen beams. I stood **petrified**, staring. Then I saw through a sort of glass plate near the edge of the body the face, as we may call it, and the large dark eyes of a Martian, peering, and then a long metallic snake of tentacle came feeling slowly through the hole.

I turned by an effort, stumbled over the curate, and stopped at the scullery door. The tentacle was now some way, two yards or more, in the room, and twisting and turning, with queer sudden movements, this way and that. For a while I stood fascinated by that slow, fitful advance. Then, with a faint, hoarse cry, I forced myself across the scullery. I trembled violently; I could scarcely stand upright. I opened the door of the coal cellar, and stood there in the darkness staring at the faintly lit doorway into the kitchen, and listening. Had the Martian seen me? What was it doing now?

Something was moving to and fro there, very quietly; every now and then it tapped against the wall, or started on its movements with a faint metallic ringing, like the movements of keys on a split-ring. Then a heavy body—I knew too well what—was dragged across the floor of the kitchen towards the opening. Irresistibly attracted, I crept to the door and peeped into the kitchen. In the triangle of bright outer sunlight I saw the Martian, in its Briareus of a handling-machine, **scrutinizing** the curate's head. I thought at once that it would infer my presence from the mark of the blow I had given him.

I crept back to the coal cellar, shut the door, and began to cover myself up as much as I could, and as noiselessly as possible in the darkness, among the firewood and coal therein. Every now and then I paused, rigid, to hear if the Martian had thrust its tentacles through the opening again.

Then the faint metallic jingle returned. I traced it slowly feeling over the kitchen. Presently I heard it nearer—in the scullery, as I judged. I thought that its length might

copious (<u>koh</u> pee uhs) *adj.* present or existing in great quantity Synonyms: abundant, profuse, ample, bounteous

intolerable (ihn <u>tah</u> luhr uh buhl) *adj.* impossible to bear or accept Synonyms: insufferable, excruciating, unbearable, unacceptable, unendurable

infinity (ihn <u>fihn</u> ih tee) *n.* the concept of unending time or number Synonyms: endlessness, eternity, forever be insufficient to reach me. I prayed **copiously**. It passed, scraping faintly across the cellar door. An age of almost **intolerable** suspense intervened; then I heard it fumbling at the latch! It had found the door! The Martians understood doors!

It worried at the catch for a minute, perhaps, and then the door opened.

In the darkness I could just see the thing—like an elephant's trunk more than anything else—waving towards me and touching and examining the wall, coals, wood and ceiling. It was like a black worm swaying its blind head to and fro.

Once, even, it touched the heel of my boot. I was on the verge of screaming; I bit my hand. For a time the tentacle was silent. I could have fancied it had been withdrawn. Presently, with an abrupt click, it gripped something—I thought it had me!—and seemed to go out of the cellar again. For a minute I was not sure. Apparently it had taken a lump of coal to examine.

I seized the opportunity of slightly shifting my position, which had become cramped, and then listened. I whispered passionate prayers for safety.

Then I heard the slow, deliberate sound creeping towards me again. Slowly, slowly it drew near, scratching against the walls and tapping the furniture.

While I was still doubtful, it rapped smartly against the cellar door and closed it. I heard it go into the pantry, and the biscuit-tins rattled and a bottle smashed, and then came a heavy bump against the cellar door. Then silence that passed into an **infinity** of suspense.

Had it gone?

At last I decided that it had.

It came into the scullery no more; but I lay all the tenth day in the close darkness, buried among coals and firewood, not daring even to crawl out for the drink for which I craved. It was the eleventh day before I ventured so far from my security.

ebb (ehb) *v.* **-ing, -ed**   a reduction, often gradual, in number, amount, or strength   Synonyms: abatement, decline, dwindling, lessening

despondent (dih <u>spahn</u> dehnt) *adj.*   characterized by extreme despair or hopelessness   Synonyms: depressed, downcast, glum, dispirited, forlorn

accustom (uh <u>cuhst</u> uhm) *v.* **-ing, -ed**   to make or grow familiar with through repetition, use, or habit   Synonyms: acclimate, season, habituate, adapt

embolden (ehm <u>bohld</u> ehn) *v.* **-ing, -ed**   to make courageous and daring; to motivate   Synonyms: activate, arouse, quicken, enliven, hearten

THE STILLNESS

My first act before I went into the pantry was to fasten the door between the kitchen and the scullery. But the pantry was empty; every scrap of food had gone. Apparently, the Martian had taken it all on the previous day. At that discovery I despaired for the first time. I took no food, or no drink either, on the eleventh or the twelfth day.

At first my mouth and throat were parched, and my strength **ebbed** sensibly. I sat about in the darkness of the scullery, in a state of **despondent** wretchedness. My mind ran on eating. I thought I had become deaf, for the noises of movement I had been **accustomed** to hear from the pit had ceased absolutely. I did not feel strong enough to crawl noiselessly to the peephole, or I would have gone there.

On the twelfth day my throat was so painful that, taking the chance of alarming the Martians, I attacked the creaking rain-water pump that stood by the sink, and got a couple of glassfuls of blackened and tainted rain water. I was greatly refreshed by this, and **emboldened** by the fact that no enquiring tentacle followed the noise of my pumping.

sumptuous (<u>suhmp</u> choo uhs) *adj.* of excessively high quality or price; lush and luxuriant Synonyms: extravagant, lavish, opulent, grand, elegant

keen (keen) *adj.* marked by great sensitivity and intelligence Synonyms: perceptive, sharp, shrewd

obscurity (uhb <u>skyoor</u> ih tee) *n.* the state of being unknown or difficult to perceive or understand Synonyms: ambiguity, uncertainty, equivocality

CHAPTER 5—THE STILLNESS

During these days, in a rambling, inconclusive way, I thought much of the curate and of the manner of his death.

On the thirteenth day I drank some more water, and dozed and thought disjointedly of eating and of vague impossible plans of escape. Whenever I dozed I dreamt of horrible phantasms, of the death of the curate, or of **sumptuous** dinners; but, asleep or awake, I felt a **keen** pain that urged me to drink again and again. The light that came into the scullery was no longer grey, but red. To my disordered imagination it seemed the colour of blood.

On the fourteenth day I went into the kitchen, and I was surprised to find that the fronds of the red weed had grown right across the hole in the wall, turning the half-light of the place into a crimson-coloured **obscurity**.

It was early on the fifteenth day that I heard a curious, familiar sequence of sounds in the kitchen, and, listening, identified it as the snuffing and scratching of a dog. Going into the kitchen, I saw a dog's nose peering in through a break among the ruddy fronds. This greatly surprised me. At the scent of me he barked shortly.

I thought if I could induce him to come into the place quietly I should be able, perhaps, to kill and eat him; and in any case, it would be advisable to kill him, lest his actions attracted the attention of the Martians.

I crept forward, saying "Good dog!" very softly; but he suddenly withdrew his head and disappeared.

I listened—I was not deaf—but certainly the pit was still. I heard a sound like the flutter of a bird's wings, and a hoarse croaking, but that was all.

For a long while I lay close to the peephole, but not daring to move aside the red plants that obscured it. Once or twice I heard a faint pitter-patter like the feet of the dog going hither and thither on the sand far below me, and there were more birdlike sounds, but that was all. At length, encouraged by the silence, I looked out.

multitude (<u>muhl</u> tih tood) *n.* a great quantity
Synonyms: drove, horde, host, mass, throng

afford (uh <u>ford</u>) *v.* **-ing, -ed** 1. to posses the means
to bear the cost or burden of Synonyms: bear, incur,
manage, sustain 2. to provide or make available Synonyms: furnish, render, yield, supply

practicable (<u>prahk</u> tihk uh buhl) *adj.* employable to a
specific end; of particular usefulness Synonyms: fea-
sible, utile, viable, workable

intersperse (ihn tuhr <u>spuhrs</u>) *v.* **-ing, -ed** to place or
distribute among other items at intervals Synonyms:
scatter, sprinkle, infuse, pepper, intermix

terrestrial (tuh <u>rehs</u> stree uhl) *adj.* 1. of or relating to
the earth Synonyms: earthbound, earthlike 2. pro-
saic, mundane Synonyms: worldly, common, profane

Except in the corner, where a **multitude** of crows hopped and fought over the skeletons of the dead the Martians had consumed, there was not a living thing in the pit.

I stared about me, scarcely believing my eyes. All the machinery had gone. Save for the big mound of greyish-blue powder in one corner, certain bars of aluminium in another, the black birds, and the skeletons of the killed, the place was merely an empty circular pit in the sand.

Slowly I thrust myself out through the red weed, and stood upon the mound of rubble. I could see in any direction save behind me, to the north, and neither Martians nor sign of Martians were to be seen. The pit dropped sheerly from my feet, but a little way along the rubbish **afforded** a **practicable** slope to the summit of the ruins. My chance of escape had come. I began to tremble.

I hesitated for some time, and then, in a gust of desperate resolution, and with a heart that throbbed violently, I scrambled to the top of the mound in which I had been buried so long.

I looked about again. To the northward, too, no Martian was visible.

When I had last seen this part of Sheen in the daylight it had been a straggling street of comfortable white and red houses, **interspersed** with abundant shady trees. Now I stood on a mound of smashed brickwork, clay, and gravel, over which spread a multitude of red cactus-shaped plants, knee-high, without a solitary **terrestrial** growth to dispute their footing. The trees near me were dead and brown, but further a network of red thread scaled the still living stems.

The neighbouring houses had all been wrecked, but none had been burned; their walls stood, sometimes to the second story, with smashed windows and shattered doors. The red weed grew tumultuously in their roofless rooms. Below me was the great pit, with the crows struggling for its refuse. A number of other birds hopped about among

gaunt (gawnt) *adj.*   exceedingly thin   Synonyms: emaciated, haggard, attenuated, cadaverous

the ruins. Far away I saw a **gaunt** cat slink crouchingly along a wall, but traces of men there were none.

The day seemed, by contrast with my recent confinement, dazzlingly bright, the sky a glowing blue. A gentle breeze kept the red weed that covered every scrap of unoccupied ground gently swaying. And oh! the sweetness of the air!

noisome (<u>noy</u> suhm) *adj.*   so repulsive as to cause physical sickness; reprehensible   Synonyms: repugnant, putrid, nauseating, loathsome

lurid (<u>loo</u> rihd) *adj.*   1. sensational in detail; causing shock or horror   Synonyms: shocking, macabre, obscene, offensive   2. strangely pale   Synonyms: pallid, eerie, ashen

oppress (uh <u>prehs</u>) *v.* **-ing, -ed**   to keep down through the use of excessive and unjust force   Synonyms: subdue, persecute, subjugate, tyrannize

persuasion (puhr <u>sway</u> zhuhn) *n.*   a belief firmly held; a conviction   Synonyms: certitude, opinion, partiality, predilection

CHAPTER SIX

THE WORK OF FIFTEEN DAYS

For some time I stood tottering on the mound regardless of my safety. Within that **noisome** den from which I had emerged I had thought with a narrow intensity only of our immediate security. I had not realised what had been happening to the world, had not anticipated this startling vision of unfamiliar things. I had expected to see Sheen in ruins—I found about me the landscape, weird and **lurid,** of another planet.

For that moment I touched an emotion beyond the common range of men, yet one that the poor brutes we dominate know only too well. I felt as a rabbit might feel returning to his burrow and suddenly confronted by the work of a dozen busy navvies digging the foundations of a house. I felt the first inkling of a thing that presently grew quite clear in my mind, that **oppressed** me for many days, a sense of dethronement, a **persuasion** that I was no longer a master, but an animal among the animals, under the Martian heel. With us it would be as with them, to lurk and watch, to run and hide; the fear and empire of man had passed away.

motive (<u>moh</u> tihv) *n.*   an impulse to action
  Synonyms: basis, incentive, inspiration, stimulus

dismal (<u>dihz</u> muhl) *adj.*   bringing about despair;
  exceedingly poor in quality   Synonyms: disheartening,
  inauspicious, tedious, depressing, lugubrious

clamber (<u>klahm</u> buhr) *v.* **-ing, -ed**   to climb or crawl
  with difficulty and awkwardness   Synonyms: scramble,
  wriggle, jostle, scurry

whet (weht) *v.* **-ting, -ted**   to arouse or stimulate
  Synonyms: animate, awaken, quicken, rouse, stir

fecundity (fih <u>kuhn</u> dih tee) *n.*   the ability to create and
  produce, as in offspring or creative work   Synonyms:
  fertility, prolificity, productivity, fruitfulness, feracity,
  virility

CHAPTER 6—THE WORK OF FIFTEEN DAYS

But so soon as this strangeness had been realised it passed, and my dominant **motive** became the hunger of my long and **dismal** fast. In the direction away from the pit I saw, beyond a red-covered wall, a patch of garden ground unburied. This gave me a hint, and I went knee-deep, and sometimes neck-deep, in the red weed. The density of the weed gave me a reassuring sense of hiding. The wall was some six feet high, and when I attempted to **clamber** it I found I could not lift my feet to the crest. So I went along by the side of it, and came to a corner and a rockwork that enabled me to get to the top, and tumble into the garden I coveted. Here I found some young onions, a couple of gladiolus bulbs, and a quantity of immature carrots, all of which I secured, and, scrambling over a ruined wall, went on my way through scarlet and crimson trees towards Kew—it was like walking through an avenue of gigantic blood drops—possessed with two ideas: to get more food, and to limp, as soon and as far as my strength permitted, out of this accursed unearthly region of the pit.

Some way farther, in a grassy place, was a group of mushrooms which also I devoured, and then I came upon a brown sheet of flowing shallow water, where meadows used to be. These fragments of nourishment served only to **whet** my hunger. At first I was surprised at this flood in a hot, dry summer, but afterwards I discovered that it was caused by the tropical exuberance of the red weed. Directly this extraordinary growth encountered water it straightway became gigantic and of unparalleled **fecundity**. Its seeds were simply poured down into the water of the Wey and Thames, and its swiftly growing and Titanic water fronds speedily choked both those rivers.

At Putney, as I afterwards saw, the bridge was almost lost in a tangle of this weed, and at Richmond, too, the Thames water poured in a broad and shallow stream across the meadows of Hampton and Twickenham. As the water spread the weed followed them, until the ruined

317

desolation (deh suh <u>lay</u> shuhn) *n.* the state of being completely destroyed, forsaken, or abandoned   Synonyms: ruin, barrenness, extinction, dissolution

succumb (suh <u>kuhm</u>) *v.* **-ing, -ed**   to give in or over to a superior force   Synonyms: accede, surrender, capitulate, buckle

terrestrial (tuh <u>rehs</u> stree uhl) *adj.*   1. of or relating to the earth   Synonyms: earthbound, earthlike   2. prosaic, mundane   Synonyms: worldly, common, profane

brittle (<u>brih</u> tuhl) *adj.*   likely to break or crumble when exposed to pressure   Synonyms: frail, delicate, fragile

vestige (<u>veh</u> stihj) *n.*   a visible trace of that which is no longer present, especially in the case of an obsolete part, organ, or system   Synonyms: sign, token, trace, residue, remnant

slake (slayk) *v.* **-ing, -ed**   to satisfy   Synonyms: quench, relieve, mitigate

spate (spayt) *n.*   a sudden abundance or excess   Synonyms: outpouring, flood, salvo, burst, gush

ransack (<u>raan</u> sahk) *v.* **-ing, -ed**   to search thoroughly, as for valuables; to pillage   Synonyms: appropriate, plunder, scour, purloin, raid villas of the Thames valley were for a time lost in this red swamp, whose margin I explored, and much of the **desolation** the Martians had caused was concealed.

In the end the red weed **succumbed** almost as quickly as it had spread. A cankering disease, due, it is believed, to the action of certain bacteria, presently seized upon it. Now by the action of natural selection, all **terrestrial** plants have acquired a resisting power against bacterial diseases—they never succumb without a severe struggle, but the red weed rotted like a thing already dead. The fronds became bleached, and then shrivelled and **brittle**. They broke off at the least touch, and the waters that had stimulated their early growth carried their last **vestiges** out to sea.

My first act on coming to this water was, of course, to **slake** my thirst. I drank a great deal of it and, moved by an impulse, gnawed some fronds of red weed; but they were watery, and had a sickly, metallic taste. I found the water was sufficiently shallow for me to wade securely, although the red weed impeded my feet a little; but the flood evidently got deeper towards the river, and I turned back to Mortlake. I managed to make out the road by means of occasional ruins of its villas and fences and lamps, and so presently I got out of this **spate** and made my way to the hill going up towards Roehampton and came out on Putney Common.

Here the scenery changed from the strange and unfamiliar to the wreckage of the familiar: patches of ground exhibited the devastation of a cyclone, and in a few score yards I would come upon perfectly undisturbed spaces, houses with their blinds trimly drawn and doors closed, as if they had been left for a day by the owners, or as if their inhabitants slept within. The red weed was less abundant; the tall trees along the lane were free from the red creeper. I hunted for food among the trees, finding nothing, and I also raided a couple of silent houses, but they had already been broken into and **ransacked**. I rested for the remain-

circuitously (suhr <u>kyoo</u> iht uhs lee) *adv.* in a round-about, excessively indirect manner Synonyms: circularly, obliquely, tortuously

desolate (<u>deh</u> suh liht) *adj.* uninhabited; unfit for habitation Synonyms: barren, unfrequented, barren, vacant, waste der of the daylight in a shrubbery, being, in my enfeebled condition, too fatigued to push on.

All this time I saw no human beings, and no signs of the Martians. I encountered a couple of hungry-looking dogs, but both hurried **circuitously** away from the advances I made them. Near Roehampton I had seen two human skeletons—not bodies, but skeletons, picked clean—and in the wood by me I found the crushed and scattered bones of several cats and rabbits and the skull of a sheep. But though I gnawed parts of these in my mouth, there was nothing to be got from them.

After sunset I struggled on along the road towards Putney, where I think the Heat-Ray must have been used for some reason. And in the garden beyond Roehampton I got a quantity of immature potatoes, sufficient to stay my hunger. From this garden one looked down upon Putney and the river. The aspect of the place in the dusk was singularly **desolate**: blackened trees, blackened, desolate ruins, and down the hill the sheets of the flooded river, red-tinged with the weed. And over all—silence. It filled me with indescribable terror to think how swiftly that desolating change had come.

For a time I believed that mankind had been swept out of existence, and that I stood there alone, the last man left alive. Hard by the top of Putney Hill I came upon another skeleton, with the arms dislocated and removed several yards from the rest of the body. As I proceeded I became more and more convinced that the extermination of mankind was, save for such stragglers as myself, already accomplished in this part of the world. The Martians, I thought, had gone on and left the country desolated, seeking food elsewhere. Perhaps even now they were destroying Berlin or Paris, or it might be they had gone northward.

ransack (<u>raan</u> sahk) *v.* **-ing, -ed**   to search thoroughly, as for valuables; to pillage   Synonyms: appropriate, plunder, scour, purloin, raid

verge (vuhrj) *n.*   the border or limit; threshold   Synonyms: boundary, brink, margin

succession (suhk <u>seh</u> shuhn) *n.*   a number of things that share a specific character and follow each other

vague (vayg) *adj.*   without definite shape, form, or expression   Synonyms: ambiguous, hazy, nebulous, indefinite, tenebrous

CHAPTER SEVEN

THE MAN ON PUTNEY HILL

I spent that night in the inn that stands at the top of Putney Hill, sleeping in a made bed for the first time since my flight to Leatherhead. I will not tell the needless trouble I had breaking into that house—afterwards I found the front door was on the latch—nor how I **ransacked** every room for food, until just on the **verge** of despair, in what seemed to me to be a servant's bedroom, I found a rat-gnawed crust and two tins of pineapple. The place had been already searched and emptied. In the bar I afterwards found some biscuits and sandwiches that had been overlooked. The latter I could not eat, they were too rotten, but the former not only stayed my hunger, but filled my pockets. I lit no lamps, fearing some Martian might come beating that part of London for food in the night. Before I went to bed I had an interval of restlessness, and prowled from window to window, peering out for some sign of these monsters. I slept little. As I lay in bed I found myself thinking consecutively—a thing I do not remember to have done since my last argument with the curate. During all the intervening time my mental condition had been a hurrying **succession** of **vague** emotional states or

receptivity (ree sehp <u>tihv</u> ih tee) *n.*   the quality or state of being open to, aware of, or accepting   Synonyms: responsiveness, open-mindedness, acceptivity

remorse (ree mohrs) *n.*   suffering inflicted by ethical regret   Synonyms: guilt, rue, contrition

inevitably (ihn <u>eh</u> viht uh blee) *adv.*   in such a manner as is unable to be avoided   Synonyms: certainly, inescapably, necessarily

static (<u>stah</u> tihk) *adj.*   characterized by stillness or lack of change   Synonyms: changeless, fixed, rigid, unvarying, stationary a sort of stupid **receptivity**. But in the night my brain, reinforced, I suppose, by the food I had eaten, grew clear again, and I thought.

Three things struggled for possession of my mind: the killing of the curate, the whereabouts of the Martians, and the possible fate of my wife. The former gave me no sensation of horror or **remorse** to recall; I saw it simply as a thing done, a memory infinitely disagreeable but quite without the quality of remorse. I saw myself then as I see myself now, driven step by step towards that hasty blow, the creature of a sequence of accidents leading **inevitably** to that. I felt no condemnation; yet the memory, **static**, unprogressive, haunted me. In the silence of the night, with that sense of the nearness of God that sometimes comes into the stillness and the darkness, I stood my trial, my only trial, for that moment of wrath and fear. I retraced every step of our conversation from the moment when I had found him crouching beside me, heedless of my thirst, and pointing to the fire and smoke that streamed up from the ruins of Weybridge. We had been incapable of co-operation—grim chance had taken no heed of that. Had I foreseen, I should have left him at Halliford. But I did not foresee; and crime is to foresee and do. And I set this down as I have set all this story down, as it was. There were no witnesses—all these things I might have concealed. But I set it down, and the reader must form his judgment as he will.

And when, by an effort, I had set aside that picture of a prostrate body, I faced the problem of the Martians and the fate of my wife. For the former I had no data; I could imagine a hundred things, and so, unhappily, I could for the latter. And suddenly that night became terrible. I found myself sitting up in bed, staring at the dark. I found myself praying that the Heat-Ray might have suddenly and painlessly struck her out of being. Since the night of my return from Leatherhead I had not prayed. I had uttered prayers, fetish prayers, had prayed as hea-

extremity (ehk <u>streh</u> muh tee) *n.* the furthest point or furthest limit of something

steadfastly (<u>stehd</u> fast lee) *adv.* with great determination and resolve Synonyms: adamantly, doggedly, purposefully, staunchly

dominion (doh <u>mihn</u> yuhn) *n.* the area over which one exercises power or control Synonyms: authority, commission, realm, turf, territory

vestige (<u>veh</u> stihj) *n.* a visible trace of that which is no longer present, especially in the case of an obsolete part, organ, or system Synonyms: sign, token, trace, residue, remnant

torrent (<u>toh</u> rehnt) *n.* a great outpouring; a flood Synonyms: flow, cascade, shower, spate

inscribe (ihn <u>skrieb</u>) *v.* **-ing, -ed** to engrave, write on, or otherwise mark a surface Synonyms: etch, impress, indite, scribe, imprint

languid (<u>laan</u> gwihd) *adj.* characterized by lifelessness and lack of energy Synonyms: enervated, dull, phlegmatic, torpid, languorous

vague (vayg) *adj.* without definite shape, form, or expression Synonyms: ambiguous, hazy, nebulous, indefinite, tenebrous

expanse (ehk <u>spaans</u>) *n.* an open, unspoiled area, often particularly large Synonyms: space, scope, breadth, tract, spread, span

verge (vuhrj) *n.* the border or limit; threshold Synonyms: boundary, brink, margin thens mutter charms when I was in **extremity**; but now I prayed indeed, pleading **steadfastly** and sanely, face to face with the darkness of God. Strange night! Strangest in this, that so soon as dawn had come, I, who had talked with God, crept out of the house like a rat leaving its hiding place—a creature scarcely larger, an inferior animal, a thing that for any passing whim of our masters might be hunted and killed. Perhaps they also prayed confidently to God. Surely, if we have learned nothing else, this war has taught us pity—pity for those witless souls that suffer our **dominion**.

The morning was bright and fine, and the eastern sky glowed pink, and was fretted with little golden clouds. In the road that runs from the top of Putney Hill to Wimbledon was a number of poor **vestiges** of the panic **torrent** that must have poured Londonward on the Sunday night after the fighting began. There was a little two-wheeled cart **inscribed** with the name of Thomas Lobb, Greengrocer, New Malden, with a smashed wheel and an abandoned tin trunk; there was a straw hat trampled into the now hardened mud, and at the top of West Hill a lot of blood-stained glass about the overturned water trough. My movements were **languid**, my plans of the **vaguest**. I had an idea of going to Leatherhead, though I knew that there I had the poorest chance of finding my wife. Certainly, unless death had overtaken them suddenly, my cousins and she would have fled thence; but it seemed to me I might find or learn there whither the Surrey people had fled. I knew I wanted to find my wife, that my heart ached for her and the world of men, but I had no clear idea how the finding might be done. I was also sharply aware now of my intense loneliness. From the corner I went, under cover of a thicket of trees and bushes, to the edge of Wimbledon Common, stretching wide and far.

That dark **expanse** was lit in patches by yellow gorse and broom; there was no red weed to be seen, and as I prowled, hesitating, on the **verge** of the open, the sun

vitality (vie <u>taa</u> lih tee) *n.*   energy; liveliness   Synonyms: ardor, animation, vigor, pulse

stout (stawt) *adj.*   1. characterized by bravery and firmness of purpose   Synonyms: intrepid, steadfast, resolved, determined   2. sturdy; well-built   Synonyms: brawny, hardy, substantial, stalwart, robust

resolve (ree <u>zahlv</u>) *n.*   strength of commitment and purpose   Synonyms: determination, earnestness, steadfastness, will rose, flooding it all with light and **vitality**. I came upon a busy swarm of little frogs in a swampy place among the trees. I stopped to look at them, drawing a lesson from their **stout resolve** to live. And presently, turning suddenly, with an odd feeling of being watched, I beheld something crouching amid a clump of bushes. I stood regarding this. I made a step towards it, and it rose up and became a man armed with a cutlass. I approached him slowly. He stood silent and motionless, regarding me.

As I drew nearer I perceived he was dressed in clothes as dusty and filthy as my own; he looked, indeed, as though he had been dragged through a culvert. Nearer, I distinguished the green slime of ditches mixing with the pale drab of dried clay and shiny, coaly patches. His black hair fell over his eyes, and his face was dark and dirty and sunken, so that at first I did not recognise him. There was a red cut across the lower part of his face.

"Stop!" he cried, when I was within ten yards of him, and I stopped. His voice was hoarse. "Where do you come from?" he said.

I thought, surveying him.

"I come from Mortlake," I said. "I was buried near the pit the Martians made about their cylinder. I have worked my way out and escaped."

"There is no food about here," he said. "This is my country. All this hill down to the river, and back to Clapham, and up to the edge of the common. There is only food for one. Which way are you going?"

I answered slowly.

"I don't know," I said. "I have been buried in the ruins of a house thirteen or fourteen days. I don't know what has happened."

He looked at me doubtfully, then started, and looked with a changed expression.

"I've no wish to stop about here," said I. "I think I shall go to Leatherhead, for my wife was there."

He shot out a pointing finger.

CHAPTER 7—THE MAN ON PUTNEY HILL

"It is you," said he; "the man from Woking. And you weren't killed at Weybridge?"

I recognised him at the same moment.

"You are the artilleryman who came into my garden."

"Good luck!" he said. "We are lucky ones! Fancy *you*!" He put out a hand, and I took it. "I crawled up a drain," he said. "But they didn't kill everyone. And after they went away I got off towards Walton across the fields. But— It's not sixteen days altogether—and your hair is grey." He looked over his shoulder suddenly. "Only a rook," he said. "One gets to know that birds have shadows these days. This is a bit open. Let us crawl under those bushes and talk."

"Have you seen any Martians?" I said. "Since I crawled out—"

"They've gone away across London," he said. "I guess they've got a bigger camp there. Of a night, all over there, Hampstead way, the sky is alive with their lights. It's like a great city, and in the glare you can just see them moving. By daylight you can't. But nearer—I haven't seen them—" (he counted on his fingers) "five days. Then I saw a couple across Hammersmith way carrying something big. And the night before last"—he stopped and spoke impressively—"it was just a matter of lights, but it was something up in the air. I believe they've built a flying-machine, and are learning to fly."

I stopped, on hands and knees, for we had come to the bushes.

"Fly!"

"Yes," he said, "fly."

I went on into a little bower, and sat down.

"It is all over with humanity," I said. "If they can do that they will simply go round the world."

He nodded.

"They will. But— It will relieve things over here a bit. And besides—" He looked at me. "Aren't you satisfied it *is* up with humanity? I am. We're down; we're beat."

conviction (kuhn <u>vihk</u> shuhn) *n.* a belief firmly held
 Synonyms: certitude, opinion, partiality, predilection

vain (vayn) *adj.* ineffective in achieving a desired
 purpose Synonyms: unsuccessful, fruitless, worthless,
 futile

countervail (kown tuhr <u>vayl</u>) *v.* **-ing, -ed** to exert equal
 and opposite force upon; to offset Synonyms: coun-
 teract, abrogate, annul, cancel out, neutralize

I stared. Strange as it may seem, I had not arrived at this fact—a fact perfectly obvious so soon as he spoke. I had still held a vague hope; rather, I had kept a lifelong habit of mind. He repeated his words, "We're beat." They carried absolute **conviction**.

"It's all over," he said. "They've lost *one*—just *one*. And they've made their footing good and crippled the greatest power in the world. They've walked over us. The death of that one at Weybridge was an accident. And these are only pioneers. They kept on coming. These green stars—I've seen none these five or six days, but I've no doubt they're falling somewhere every night. Nothing's to be done. We're under! We're beat!"

I made him no answer. I sat staring before me, trying in **vain** to devise some **countervailing** thought.

"This isn't a war," said the artilleryman. "It never was a war, any more than there's war between man and ants."

Suddenly I recalled the night in the observatory.

"After the tenth shot they fired no more—at least, until the first cylinder came."

"How do you know?" said the artilleryman. I explained. He thought. "Something wrong with the gun," he said. "But what if there is? They'll get it right again. And even if there's a delay, how can it alter the end? It's just men and ants. There's the ants builds their cities, live their lives, have wars, revolutions, until the men want them out of the way, and then they go out of the way. That's what we are now—just ants. Only—"

"Yes," I said.

"We're eatable ants."

We sat looking at each other.

"And what will they do with us?" I said.

"That's what I've been thinking," he said; "that's what I've been thinking. After Weybridge I went south—thinking. I saw what was up. Most of the people were hard at it squealing and exciting themselves. But I'm not so fond of squealing. I've been in sight of death once

ornamental (ohr nuh <u>mehn</u> tuhl) *adj.*   for purposes of decoration or embellishment   Synonyms: adorning, furbishing, garnishing, ornate

assent (uh <u>sehnt</u>) *v.* **-ing, -ed**   to agree to   Synonyms: concur, accede, accept, comply, acquiesce or twice; I'm not an **ornamental** soldier, and at the best and worst, death—it's just death. And it's the man that keeps on thinking comes through. I saw everyone tracking away south. Says I, 'Food won't last this way,' and I turned right back. I went for the Martians like a sparrow goes for man. All round"—he waved a hand to the horizon—"they're starving in heaps, bolting, treading on each other. . . ."

He saw my face, and halted awkwardly.

"No doubt lots who had money have gone away to France," he said. He seemed to hesitate whether to apologise, met my eyes, and went on: "There's food all about here. Canned things in shops; wines, spirits, mineral waters; and the water mains and drains are empty. Well, I was telling you what I was thinking. 'Here's intelligent things,' I said, 'and it seems they want us for food. First, they'll smash us up—ships, machines, guns, cities, all the order and organisation. All that will go. If we were the size of ants we might pull through. But we're not. It's all too bulky to stop. That's the first certainty.' Eh?"

I assented.

"It is; I've thought it out. Very well, then—next; at present we're caught as we're wanted. A Martian has only to go a few miles to get a crowd on the run. And I saw one, one day, out by Wandsworth, picking houses to pieces and routing among the wreckage. But they won't keep on doing that. So soon as they've settled all our guns and ships, and smashed our railways, and done all the things they are doing over there, they will begin catching us systematic, picking the best and storing us in cages and things. That's what they will start doing in a bit. Lord! They haven't begun on us yet. Don't you see that?"

"Not begun!" I exclaimed.

"Not begun. All that's happened so far is through our not having the sense to keep quiet—worrying them with guns and such foolery. And losing our heads, and rushing off in crowds to where there wasn't any more safety

than where we were. They don't want to bother us yet. They're making their things—making all the things they couldn't bring with them, getting things ready for the rest of their people. Very likely that's why the cylinders have stopped for a bit, for fear of hitting those who are here. And instead of our rushing about blind, on the howl, or getting dynamite on the chance of busting them up, we've got to fix ourselves up according to the new state of affairs. That's how I figure it out. It isn't quite according to what a man wants for his species, but it's about what the facts point to. And that's the principle I acted upon. Cities, nations, civilisation, progress—it's all over. That game's up. We're beat."

"But if that is so, what is there to live for?"

The artilleryman looked at me for a moment.

"There won't be any more blessed concerts for a million years or so; there won't be any Royal Academy of Arts, and no nice little feeds at restaurants. If it's amusement you're after, I reckon the game is up. If you've got any drawing-room manners or a dislike to eating peas with a knife or dropping aitches, you'd better chuck 'em away. They ain't no further use."

"You mean—"

"I mean that men like me are going on living—for the sake of the breed. I tell you, I'm grim set on living. And if I'm not mistaken, you'll show what insides *you've* got, too, before long. We aren't going to be exterminated. And I don't mean to be caught either, and tamed and fattened and bred like a thundering ox. Ugh! Fancy those brown creepers!"

"You don't mean to say—"

"I do. I'm going on, under their feet. I've got it planned; I've thought it out. We men are beat. We don't know enough. We've got to learn before we've got a chance. And we've got to live and keep independent while we learn. See! That's what has to be done."

stir (stuhr) *v.* **-ing, -ed**   to animate; to bring about an emotional response   Synonyms: inspire, rouse, incite, provoke, inflame

profoundly (proh <u>fownd</u> lee) *adv.*   with great insight or depth of feeling   Synonyms: deeply, acutely, movingly, intensely

resolution (reh zuh loo shuhn) *n.*   1. firmness and fixity of purpose   Synonyms: dauntlessness, courage, tenacity, purposefulness   2. a course of action firmly decided upon

I stared, astonished, and **stirred profoundly** by the man's **resolution.**

"Great God!" cried I. "But you are a man indeed!" And suddenly I gripped his hand.

"Eh!" he said, with his eyes shining. "I've thought it out, eh?"

"Go on," I said.

"Well, those who mean to escape their catching must get ready. I'm getting ready. Mind you, it isn't all of us that are made for wild beasts; and that's what it's got to be. That's why I watched you. I had my doubts. You're slender. I didn't know that it was you, you see, or just how you'd been buried. All these—the sort of people that lived in these houses, and all those damn little clerks that used to live down that way—they'd be no good. They haven't any spirit in them—no proud dreams and no proud lusts; and a man who hasn't one or the other— Lord! What is he but funk and precautions? They just used to skedaddle off to work—I've seen hundreds of 'em, bit of breakfast in hand, running wild and shining to catch their little season-ticket train, for fear they'd get dismissed if they didn't; working at businesses they were afraid to take the trouble to understand; skedaddling back for fear they wouldn't be in time for dinner; keeping indoors after dinner for fear of the back streets, and sleeping with the wives they married, not because they wanted them, but because they had a bit of money that would make for safety in their one little miserable skedaddle through the world. Lives insured and a bit invested for fear of accidents. And on Sundays—fear of the hereafter. As if hell was built for rabbits! Well, the Martians will just be a godsend to these. Nice roomy cages, fattening food, careful breeding, no worry. After a week or so chasing about the fields and lands on empty stomachs, they'll come and be caught cheerful. They'll be quite glad after a bit. They'll wonder what people did before there were Martians to take care of them. And

sombre or **somber** (<u>sahm</u> buhr) *adj.* marked by darkness, gloominess, or melancholy Synonyms: dispiriting, doleful, drab, lugubrious, obscure, funereal

gratification (graa tih fih <u>kay</u> shuhn) *n.* the act or condition of being satisfied greatly Synonyms: regalement, fulfillment, relish

sentiment (<u>sehn</u> tih mehnt) *n.* a particular thought or attitude, based especially upon emotion Synonyms: inclination, partiality, predilection, tendency

pious (<u>pie</u> uhs) *adj.* earnest and reverent with respect to religious observant Synonyms: devoted, religious, sanctimonious, clerical

piety (<u>pie</u> ih tee) *n.* the act or state of being devout; religiousness Synonyms: devotion, ardor, piousness, reverence, veneration

succumb (suh <u>kuhm</u>) *v.* -ing, -ed to give in or over to a superior force Synonyms: accede, surrender, capitulate, buckle the bar loafers, and mashers, and singers—I can imagine them. I can imagine them," he said, with a sort of **sombre gratification**. "There'll be any amount of **sentiment** and religion loose among them. There's hundreds of things I saw with my eyes that I've only begun to see clearly these last few days. There's lots will take things as they are—fat and stupid; and lots will be worried by a sort of feeling that it's all wrong, and that they ought to be doing something. Now whenever things are so that a lot of people feel they ought to be doing something, the weak, and those who go weak with a lot of complicated thinking, always make for a sort of do-nothing religion, very **pious** and superior, and submit to persecution and the will of the Lord. Very likely you've seen the same thing. It's energy in a gale of funk, and turned clean inside out. These cages will be full of psalms and hymns and **piety**. And those of a less simple sort will work in a bit of—what is it?—eroticism."

He paused.

"Very likely these Martians will make pets of some of them; train them to do tricks—who knows?—get sentimental over the pet boy who grew up and had to be killed. And some, maybe, they will train to hunt us."

"No," I cried, "that's impossible! No human being—"

"What's the good of going on with such lies?" said the artilleryman. "There's men who'd do it cheerful. What nonsense to pretend there isn't!"

And I **succumbed** to his conviction.

"If they come after me," he said; "Lord, if they come after me!" and subsided into a grim meditation.

I sat contemplating these things. I could find nothing to bring against this man's reasoning. In the days before the invasion no one would have questioned my intellectual superiority to his—I, a professed and recognised writer on philosophical themes, and he, a common soldier; and yet he had already formulated a situation that I had scarcely realised.

presently (<u>preh</u> zehnt lee) *adv.*   current usage: very soon   archaic: immediately

degenerate (dee <u>jehn</u> uh rayt) *v.* **-ing, -ed**   to deteriorate   Synonyms: corrupt, decay, deprave, vitiate

lackadaisical (lahk ih <u>day</u> zih kuhl) *adj.*   without liveliness, interest, or energy; dispirited   Synonyms: languid, bathetic, languorous, listless, indolent, inert

cumbersome (<u>kuhm</u> buhr suhm) *adj.*   awkward and difficult to manage or bear   Synonyms: burdensome, cumbrous, unwieldy, ponderous, oppressive

taint (taynt) *v.* **-ing, -ed**   to corrupt or infect; to compromise the purity of   Synonyms: contaminate, smear, shame, infect, disgrace

"What are you doing?" I said **presently**. "What plans have you made?"

He hesitated.

"Well, it's like this," he said. "What have we to do? We have to invent a sort of life where men can live and breed, and be sufficiently secure to bring the children up. Yes—wait a bit, and I'll make it clearer what I think ought to be done. The tame ones will go like all tame beasts; in a few generations they'll be big, beautiful, rich-blooded, stupid—rubbish! The risk is that we who keep wild will go savage—**degenerate** into a sort of big, savage rat. . . . You see, how I mean to live is underground. I've been thinking about the drains. Of course those who don't know drains think horrible things; but under this London are miles and miles—hundreds of miles—and a few days rain and London empty will leave them sweet and clean. The main drains are big enough and airy enough for anyone. Then there's cellars, vaults, stores, from which bolting passages may be made to the drains. And the railway tunnels and subways. Eh? You begin to see? And we form a band—able-bodied, clean-minded men. We're not going to pick up any rubbish that drifts in. Weaklings go out again."

"As you meant me to go?"

"Well—I parleyed, didn't I?"

"We won't quarrel about that. Go on."

"Those who stop obey orders. Able-bodied, clean-minded women we want also—mothers and teachers. No **lackadaisical** ladies—no blasted rolling eyes. We can't have any weak or silly. Life is real again, and the useless and **cumbersome** and mischievous have to die. They ought to die. They ought to be willing to die. It's a sort of disloyalty, after all, to live and **taint** the race. And they can't be happy. Moreover, dying's none so dreadful; it's the funking makes it bad. And in all those places we shall gather. Our district will be London. And we may even be able to keep a watch, and run about in the open when the Martians keep away. Play cricket, perhaps.

vermin (<u>vuhr</u> mihn) *n.*   individuals or creatures considered repulsive or offensive   Synonyms: riffraff, rabble

That's how we shall save the race. Eh? It's a possible thing? But saving the race is nothing in itself. As I say, that's only being rats. It's saving our knowledge and adding to it is the thing. There men like you come in. There's books, there's models. We must make great safe places down deep, and get all the books we can; not novels and poetry swipes, but ideas, science books. That's where men like you come in. We must go to the British Museum and pick all those books through. Especially we must keep up our science—learn more. We must watch these Martians. Some of us must go as spies. When it's all working, perhaps I will. Get caught, I mean. And the great thing is, we must leave the Martians alone. We mustn't even steal. If we get in their way, we clear out. We must show them we mean no harm. Yes, I know. But they're intelligent things, and they won't hunt us down if they have all they want, and think we're just harmless **vermin**."

The artilleryman paused and laid a brown hand upon my arm.

"After all, it may not be so much we may have to learn before—Just imagine this: four or five of their fighting machines suddenly starting off—Heat-Rays right and left, and not a Martian in 'em. Not a Martian in 'em, but men—men who have learned the way how. It may be in my time, even—those men. Fancy having one of them lovely things, with its Heat-Ray wide and free! Fancy having it in control! What would it matter if you smashed to smithereens at the end of the run, after a bust like that? I reckon the Martians'll open their beautiful eyes! Can't you see them, man? Can't you see them hurrying, hurrying—puffing and blowing and hooting to their other mechanical affairs? Something out of gear in every case. And swish, bang, rattle, swish! Just as they are fumbling over it, *swish* comes the Heat-Ray, and, behold! man has come back to his own."

For a while the imaginative daring of the artilleryman, and the tone of assurance and courage he

practicability (prahk tihk uh <u>bihl</u> ih tee) *n.*   employability to a specific end; particular usefulness
Synonyms: feasibility, utility, viability, workability

susceptible (suh sehpt ih buhl) *adj.*   likely to be influenced or affected; particularly sensitive   Synonyms: disposed, movable, responsive, receptive

apprehension (aa pree <u>hehn</u> shuhn) *n.*   a feeling of uneasiness or dread concerning the future   Synonyms: alarm, disquiet, foreboding, trepidation, misgiving

inkling (<u>ihn</u> klihng) *n.*   a subtle suggestion or hint
Synonyms: innuendo, intimation, clue, telltale

speculate (speh kyoo layt) *v.*   to make an assertion in the absence of conclusive evidence   Synonyms: conjecture, hypothesize

CHAPTER 7—THE MAN ON PUTNEY HILL

assumed, completely dominated my mind. I believed unhesitatingly both in his forecast of human destiny and in the **practicability** of his astonishing scheme, and the reader who thinks me **susceptible** and foolish must contrast his position, reading steadily with all his thoughts about his subject, and mine, crouching fearfully in the bushes and listening, distracted by **apprehension.** We talked in this manner through the early morning time, and later crept out of the bushes, and, after scanning the sky for Martians, hurried precipitately to the house on Putney Hill where he had made his lair. It was the coal cellar of the place, and when I saw the work he had spent a week upon—it was a burrow scarcely ten yards long, which he designed to reach to the main drain on Putney Hill—I had my first **inkling** of the gulf between his dreams and his powers. Such a hole I could have dug in a day. But I believed in him sufficiently to work with him all that morning until past midday at his digging. We had a garden barrow and shot the earth we removed against the kitchen range. We refreshed ourselves with a tin of mock-turtle soup and wine from the neighbouring pantry. I found a curious relief from the aching strangeness of the world in this steady labour. As we worked, I turned his project over in my mind, and <u>presently</u> objections and doubts began to arise; but I worked there all the morning, so glad was I to find myself with a purpose again. After working an hour I began to **speculate** on the distance one had to go before the cloaca was reached, the chances we had of missing it altogether. My immediate trouble was why we should dig this long tunnel, when it was possible to get into the drain at once down one of the manholes, and work back to the house. It seemed to me, too, that the house was inconveniently chosen, and required a needless length of tunnel. And just as I was beginning to face these things, the artilleryman stopped digging, and looked at me.

reconnoiter or **reconnoiter** (ree kuh <u>noy</u> tuhr) *v.* **-ing, -ed**   to gather preliminary information, especially for military purposes   Synonyms: canvass, appraise, assay, survey

dispose (dihs <u>pohz</u>) *v.* **-ing, -ed**   to transfer possession of; to throw away or cast off   Synonyms: bestow, discard, jettison, relinquish, unload

venture (<u>vehn</u> chuhr) *n.*   an undertaking, often involving significant risk   Synonyms: gamble, enterprise, endeavor, investment, speculation

gaunt (gawnt) *adj.*   exceedingly thin   Synonyms: emaciated, haggard, attenuated, cadaverous

propagation (prah puh <u>gay</u> shuhn) *n.*   the act of increasing in number or spreading into a greater area   Synonyms: reproduction, dissemination, promulgation

"We're working well," he said. He put down his spade. "Let us knock off a bit" he said. "I think it's time we **reconnoitred** from the roof of the house."

I was for going on, and after a little hesitation he resumed his spade; and then suddenly I was struck by a thought. I stopped, and so did he at once.

"Why were you walking about the common," I said, "instead of being here?"

"Taking the air," he said. "I was coming back. It's safer by night."

"But the work?"

"Oh, one can't always work," he said, and in a flash I saw the man plain. He hesitated, holding his spade. "We ought to reconnoitre now," he said, "because if any come near they may hear the spades and drop upon us unawares."

I was no longer **disposed** to object. We went together to the roof and stood on a ladder peeping out of the roof door. No Martians were to be seen, and we **ventured** out on the tiles, and slipped down under shelter of the parapet.

From this position a shrubbery hid the greater portion of Putney, but we could see the river below, a bubbly mass of red weed, and the low parts of Lambeth flooded and red. The red creeper swarmed up the trees about the old palace, and their branches stretched **gaunt** and dead, and set with shrivelled leaves, from amid its clusters. It was strange how entirely dependent both these things were upon flowing water for their **propagation**. About us neither had gained a footing; laburnums, pink mays, snowballs, and trees of arbor-vitae, rose out of laurels and hydrangeas, green and brilliant into the sunlight. Beyond Kensington dense smoke was rising, and that and a blue haze hid the northward hills.

The artilleryman began to tell me of the sort of people who still remained in London.

grotesque (groh <u>tehsk</u>) *adj.*   severely distorted or hideous in appearance   Synonyms: deformed, bizarre, outlandish, aberrant, malformed

grandiose (graan dee <u>ohs</u>) *adj.*   great in scope, purpose, or intention   Synonyms: ambitious, stately, magnificent, majestic, highfalutin

dispose (dihs <u>pohz</u>) *v.* **-ing, -ed**   to transfer possession of; to throw away or cast off   Synonyms: bestow, discard, jettison, relinquish, unload

loath (lohth) *adj.*   marked by an unwillingness to undertake a particular task   Synonyms: averse, disinclined, opposed, hesitant

incline (<u>ihn</u> klien) *v.* **-ing, -ed**   to hold a particular preference or opinion   Synonyms: favor, bias, prefer, predispose

CHAPTER 7—THE MAN ON PUTNEY HILL

"One night last week," he said, "some fools got the electric light in order, and there was all Regent Street and the Circus ablaze, crowded with painted and ragged drunkards, men and women, dancing and shouting till dawn. A man who was there told me. And as the day came they became aware of a fighting-machine standing near by the Langham and looking down at them. Heaven knows how long he had been there. It must have given some of them a nasty turn. He came down the road towards them, and picked up nearly a hundred too drunk or frightened to run away."

Grotesque gleam of a time no history will ever fully describe!

From that, in answer to my questions, he came round to his **grandiose** plans again. He grew enthusiastic. He talked so eloquently of the possibility of capturing a fighting-machine that I more than half believed in him again. But now that I was beginning to understand something of his quality, I could divine the stress he laid on doing nothing precipitately. And I noted that now there was no question that he personally was to capture and fight the great machine.

After a time we went down to the cellar. Neither of us seemed **disposed** to resume digging, and when he suggested a meal, I was nothing **loath.** He became suddenly very generous, and when we had eaten he went away and returned with some excellent cigars. We lit these, and his optimism glowed. He was **inclined** to regard my coming as a great occasion.

"There's some champagne in the cellar," he said.

"We can dig better on this Thames-side burgundy," said I.

"No," said he; "I am host today. Champagne! Great God! We've a heavy enough task before us! Let us take a rest and gather strength while we may. Look at these blistered hands!"

pursuant (puhr soo ehnt) *adj.*   in accordance with

grotesque (groh <u>tehsk</u>) *adj.*   severely distorted or hideous in appearance   Synonyms: deformed, bizarre, outlandish, aberrant, malformed

appall (uh <u>paal</u>) *v.* **-ing, -ed**   to fill with disgust, revulsion, or dismay   Synonyms: horrify, consternate, disconcert, terrify, unnerve, daunt

degradation (deh greh <u>day</u> shuhn) *n.*   the act of debasing or causing shame; the act of deteriorating   Synonyms: defamation, disgrace, debasement, humiliation

interminable (ihn <u>tuhr</u> mihn uh buhl) *adj.*   without or seemingly without end   Synonyms: infinite, boring, incessant, eternal, perpetual

kinetic (kihn <u>eh</u> tihk) *adj.*   relating to motion; energetic   Synonyms: animated, lively, spirited

dormant (<u>dohr</u> mihnt) *adj.*   in an inactive state but still possessed with latent capability   Synonyms: abeyant, hibernating, suspended, potential

CHAPTER 7—THE MAN ON PUTNEY HILL

And **pursuant** to this idea of a holiday, he insisted upon playing cards after we had eaten. He taught me euchre, and after dividing London between us, I taking the northern side and he the southern, we played for parish points. **Grotesque** and foolish as this will seem to the sober reader, it is absolutely true, and what is more remarkable, I found the card game and several others we played extremely interesting.

Strange mind of man! that, with our species upon the edge of extermination or **appalling degradation**, with no clear prospect before us but the chance of a horrible death, we could sit following the chance of this painted pasteboard, and playing the "joker" with vivid delight. Afterwards he taught me poker, and I beat him at three tough chess games. When dark came we decided to take the risk, and lit a lamp.

After an **interminable** string of games, we supped, and the artilleryman finished the champagne. We went on smoking the cigars. He was no longer the energetic regenerator of his species I had encountered in the morning. He was still optimistic, but it was a less **kinetic**, a more thoughtful optimism. I remember he wound up with my health, proposed in a speech of small variety and considerable intermittence. I took a cigar, and went upstairs to look at the lights of which he had spoken that blazed so greenly along the Highgate hills.

At first I stared unintelligently across the London valley. The northern hills were shrouded in darkness; the fires near Kensington glowed redly, and now and then an orange-red tongue of flame flashed up and vanished in the deep blue night. All the rest of London was black. Then, nearer, I perceived a strange light, a pale, violet-purple fluorescent glow, quivering under the night breeze. For a space I could not understand it, and then I knew that it must be the red weed from which this faint irradiation proceeded. With that realisation my **dormant** sense of wonder, my sense of the proportion of things, awoke

grotesque (groh <u>tehsk</u>) *adj.* severely distorted or hideous in appearance   Synonyms: deformed, bizarre, outlandish, aberrant, malformed

revulsion (ree <u>vuhl</u> zhuhn) *n.* a strong and sudden feeling of disgust   Synonyms: abhorrence, repulsion, detestation, abomination, repulsion

remorse (ree mohrs) *n.* suffering inflicted by ethical regret   Synonyms: guilt, rue, contrition

gluttony (<u>gluh</u> tuh nee) *n.* eating or drinking to great excess   Synonyms: voracity again. I glanced from that to Mars, red and clear, glowing high in the west, and then gazed long and earnestly at the darkness of Hampstead and Highgate.

I remained a very long time upon the roof, wondering at the **grotesque** changes of the day. I recalled my mental states from the midnight prayer to the foolish card-playing. I had a violent **revulsion** of feeling. I remember I flung away the cigar with a certain wasteful symbolism. My folly came to me with glaring exaggeration. I seemed a traitor to my wife and to my kind; I was filled with **remorse**. I resolved to leave this strange undisciplined dreamer of great things to his drink and **gluttony**, and to go on into London. There, it seemed to me, I had the best chance of learning what the Martians and my fellowmen were doing. I was still upon the roof when the late moon rose.

tumultuous (tuh <u>muhlt</u> yoo uhs) *adj.*   characterized by confusion and disorder   Synonyms: clamorous, agitated, raucous, turbulent

presently (<u>preh</u> zehnt lee) *adv.*   current usage: very soon archaic: immediately

DEAD LONDON

After I had parted from the artilleryman, I went down the hill, and by the High Street across the bridge to Fulham. The red weed was **tumultuous** at that time, and nearly choked the bridge roadway; but its fronds were already whitened in patches by the spreading disease that **presently** removed it so swiftly.

At the corner of the lane that runs to Putney Bridge station I found a man lying. He was as black as a sweep with the black dust, alive, but helplessly and speechlessly drunk. I could get nothing from him but curses and furious lunges at my head. I think I should have stayed by him but for the brutal expression of his face.

There was black dust along the roadway from the bridge onwards, and it grew thicker in Fulham. The streets were horribly quiet. I got food—sour, hard, and mouldy, but quite eatable—in a baker's shop here. Some way towards Walham Green the streets became clear of powder, and I passed a white terrace of houses on fire; the noise of the burning was an absolute relief. Going on towards Brompton, the streets were quiet again.

Here I came once more upon the black powder in the streets and upon dead bodies. I saw altogether about a

profound (proh <u>fownd</u>) *adj.*   deep in feeling; insightful
Synonyms: deep, intellectual, recondite, reflective, sagacious

derelict (<u>deh</u> ruh lihkt) *adj.*   worn out; abandoned
Synonyms: dilapidated, desolate, forsaken, neglected

dozen in the length of the Fulham Road. They had been dead many days, so that I hurried quickly past them. The black powder covered them over, and softened their outlines. One or two had been disturbed by dogs.

Where there was no black powder, it was curiously like a Sunday in the City, with the closed shops, the houses locked up and the blinds drawn, the desertion, and the stillness. In some places plunderers had been at work, but rarely at other than the provision and wine shops. A jeweller's window had been broken open in one place, but apparently the thief had been disturbed, and a number of gold chains and a watch lay scattered on the pavement. I did not trouble to touch them. Farther on was a tattered woman in a heap on a doorstep; the hand that hung over her knee was gashed and bled down her rusty brown dress, and a smashed magnum of champagne formed a pool across the pavement. She seemed asleep, but she was dead.

The farther I penetrated into London, the **profounder** grew the stillness. But it was not so much the stillness of death—it was the stillness of suspense, of expectation. At any time the destruction that had already singed the northwestern borders of the metropolis, and had annihilated Ealing and Kilburn, might strike among these houses and leave them smoking ruins. It was a city condemned and **derelict**. . . .

In South Kensington the streets were clear of dead and of black powder. It was near South Kensington that I first heard the howling. It crept almost imperceptibly upon my senses. It was a sobbing alternation of two notes, "Ulla, ulla, ulla, ulla," keeping on perpetually. When I passed streets that ran northward it grew in volume, and houses and buildings seemed to deaden and cut it off again. It came in a full tide down Exhibition Road. I stopped, staring towards Kensington Gardens, wondering at this strange, remote wailing. It was as if that mighty desert of houses had found a voice for its fear and solitude.

desolate (<u>deh</u> suh liht) *adj*.   uninhabited; unfit for habitation   Synonyms: barren, unfrequented, vacant, waste

intolerably (ihn <u>tah</u> luhr uh blee) *adv*.   in a manner impossible to bear or accept   Synonyms: insufferably, excrutiatingly, unbearably, unacceptably, unendurably

sodden (<u>sah</u> dihn) *adj*.   soaked through   Synonyms: saturated, drenched, waterlogged

ominous (ah mihn uhs) *adj*.   indicative of a threat or an impending misfortune   Synonyms: menacing, threatening, baleful, sinister, inauspicious

infinite (<u>ihn</u> fihn iht) *adj*.   limitless in time or quantity   Synonyms: endless, perpetual, interminable

CHAPTER 8—DEAD LONDON

"Ulla, ulla, ulla, ulla," wailed that superhuman note—great waves of sound sweeping down the broad, sunlit roadway, between the tall buildings on each side. I turned northwards, marvelling, towards the iron gates of Hyde Park. I had half a mind to break into the Natural History Museum and find my way up to the summits of the towers, in order to see across the park. But I decided to keep to the ground, where quick hiding was possible, and so went on up the Exhibition Road. All the large mansions on each side of the road were empty and still, and my footsteps echoed against the sides of the houses. At the top, near the park gate, I came upon a strange sight—a bus overturned, and the skeleton of a horse picked clean. I puzzled over this for a time, and then went on to the bridge over the Serpentine. The voice grew stronger and stronger, though I could see nothing above the housetops on the north side of the park, save a haze of smoke to the northwest.

"Ulla, ulla, ulla, ulla," cried the voice, coming, as it seemed to me, from the district about Regent's Park. The **desolating** cry worked upon my mind. The mood that had sustained me passed. The wailing took possession of me. I found I was intensely weary, footsore, and now again hungry and thirsty.

It was already past noon. Why was I wandering alone in this city of the dead? Why was I alone when all London was lying in state, and in its black shroud? I felt **intolerably** lonely. My mind ran on old friends that I had forgotten for years. I thought of the poisons in the chemists' shops, of the liquors the wine merchants stored; I recalled the two **sodden** creatures of despair, who so far as I knew, shared the city with myself. . . .

I came into Oxford Street by the Marble Arch, and here again were black powder and several bodies, and an evil, **ominous** smell from the gratings of the cellars of some of the houses. I grew very thirsty after the heat of my long walk. With **infinite** trouble I managed to break

dismal (<u>dihz</u> muhl) *adj.* bringing about despair; exceedingly poor in quality   Synonyms: disheartening, inauspicious, tedious, depressing, lugubrious

monotonous (muh <u>nah</u> tuh nuhs) *adj.* tiresomely lacking in variety; unchanging in tone   Synonyms: banausic, tedious, repetitive, recurrent, pedestrian

clamber (<u>klahm</u> buhr) *v.* -ing, -ed   to climb or crawl with difficulty and awkwardness   Synonyms: scramble, wriggle, jostle, scurry into a public-house and get food and drink. I was weary after eating, and went into the parlour behind the bar, and slept on a black horsehair sofa I found there.

I awoke to find that **dismal** howling still in my ears, "Ulla, ulla, ulla, ulla." It was now dusk, and after I had routed out some biscuits and a cheese in the bar—there was a meat safe, but it contained nothing but maggots—I wandered on through the silent residential squares to Baker Street—Portman Square is the only one I can name—and so came out at last upon Regent's Park. And as I emerged from the top of Baker Street, I saw far away over the trees in the clearness of the sunset the hood of the Martian giant from which this howling proceeded. I was not terrified. I came upon him as if it were a matter of course. I watched him for some time, but he did not move. He appeared to be standing and yelling, for no reason that I could discover.

I tried to formulate a plan of action. That perpetual sound of "Ulla, ulla, ulla, ulla," confused my mind. Perhaps I was too tired to be very fearful. Certainly I was more curious to know the reason of this **monotonous** crying than afraid. I turned back away from the park and struck into Park Road, intending to skirt the park, went along under the shelter of the terraces, and got a view of this stationary, howling Martian from the direction of St. John's Wood. A couple of hundred yards out of Baker Street I heard a yelping chorus, and saw, first a dog with a piece of putrescent red meat in his jaws coming headlong towards me, and then a pack of starving mongrels in pursuit of him. He made a wide curve to avoid me, as though he feared I might prove a fresh competitor. As the yelping died away down the silent road, the wailing sound of "Ulla, ulla, ulla, ulla," reasserted itself.

I came upon the wrecked handling-machine halfway to St. John's Wood station. At first I thought a house had fallen across the road. It was only as I **clambered** among the ruins that I saw, with a start, this mechani-

clamber (<u>klahm</u> buhr) *v.* **-ing, -ed**   to climb or crawl with difficulty and awkwardness   Synonyms: scramble, wriggle, jostle, scurry

desolation (deh suh <u>lay</u> shuhn) *n.*   the state of being completely destroyed, forsaken, or abandoned   Synonyms: ruin, barrenness, extinction, dissolution

endurable (ihn <u>door</u> uh buhl) *adj.*   able to be borne or sustained   Synonyms: tolerable, bearable, sufferable, livable, supportable

gaunt (gawnt) *adj.*   exceedingly thin   Synonyms: emaciated, haggard, attenuated, cadaverous

temerity (tuh <u>meh</u> rih tee) *n.*   heedlessness of danger; recklessness   Synonyms: audacity, boldness, impudence, overconfidence, indiscretion cal Samson lying, with its tentacles bent and smashed and twisted, among the ruins it had made. The forepart was shattered. It seemed as if it had driven blindly straight at the house, and had been overwhelmed in its overthrow. It seemed to me then that this might have happened by a handling-machine escaping from the guidance of its Martian. I could not **clamber** among the ruins to see it, and the twilight was now so far advanced that the blood with which its seat was smeared, and the gnawed gristle of the Martian that the dogs had left, were invisible to me.

Wondering still more at all that I had seen, I pushed on towards Primrose Hill. Far away, through a gap in the trees, I saw a second Martian, as motionless as the first, standing in the park towards the Zoological Gardens, and silent. A little beyond the ruins about the smashed handling-machine I came upon the red weed again, and found the Regent's Canal, a spongy mass of dark-red vegetation.

As I crossed the bridge, the sound of "Ulla, ulla, ulla, ulla," ceased. It was, as it were, cut off. The silence came like a thunderclap.

The dusky houses about me stood faint and tall and dim; the trees towards the park were growing black. All about me the red weed clambered among the ruins, writhing to get above me in the dimness. Night, the mother of fear and mystery, was coming upon me. But while that voice sounded the solitude, the **desolation**, had been **endurable**; by virtue of it London had still seemed alive, and the sense of life about me had upheld me. Then suddenly a change, the passing of something—I knew not what—and then a stillness that could be felt. Nothing but this **gaunt** quiet.

London about me gazed at me spectrally. The windows in the white houses were like the eye sockets of skulls. About me my imagination found a thousand noiseless enemies moving. Terror seized me, a horror of my **temerity**. In front of me the road became pitchy black as though

contort (kuhn <u>tort</u>) *v.* **-ing, -ed**   to bend out of shape
Synonyms: distort, convolute, gnarl, misshape, warp

torrent (<u>toh</u> rehnt) *n.*   a great outpouring; a flood
Synonyms: flow, cascade, shower, spate

exultation (ehg zuhl <u>tay</u> shuhn) *n.*   a triumphant or
blissful state   Synonyms: celebration, elation, jubilation, revelling

lank *adj.*   long, thin, and often limp   Synonyms: gangling, gaunt, lean

rampart (<u>raam</u> pahrt) *n.*   a border built for defensive
purposes   Synonyms: embankment, bulwark, barri-
cade, stronghold

it was tarred, and I saw a **contorted** shape lying across the pathway. I could not bring myself to go on. I turned down St. John's Wood Road, and ran headlong from this unendurable stillness towards Kilburn. I hid from the night and the silence, until long after midnight, in a cabmen's shelter in Harrow Road. But before the dawn my courage returned, and while the stars were still in the sky I turned once more towards Regent's Park. I missed my way among the streets, and <u>presently</u> saw down a long avenue, in the half-light of the early dawn, the curve of Primrose Hill. On the summit, towering up to the fading stars, was a third Martian, erect and motionless like the others.

An insane resolve possessed me. I would die and end it. And I would save myself even the trouble of killing myself. I marched on recklessly towards this Titan, and then, as I drew nearer and the light grew, I saw that a multitude of black birds was circling and clustering about the hood. At that my heart gave a bound, and I began running along the road.

I hurried through the red weed that choked St. Edmund's Terrace (I waded breast-high across a **torrent** of water that was rushing down from the waterworks towards the Albert Road), and emerged upon the grass before the rising of the sun. Great mounds had been heaped about the crest of the hill, making a huge redoubt of it—it was the final and largest place the Martians had made—and from behind these heaps there rose a thin smoke against the sky. Against the sky line an eager dog ran and disappeared. The thought that had flashed into my mind grew real, grew credible. I felt no fear, only a wild, trembling **exultation**, as I ran up the hill towards the motionless monster. Out of the hood hung **lank** shreds of brown, at which the hungry birds pecked and tore.

In another moment I had scrambled up the earthen **rampart** and stood upon its crest, and the interior of the redoubt was below me. A mighty space it was, with gigantic machines here and there within it, huge mounds of

succumb (suh <u>kuhm</u>) *v.* **-ing, -ed**   to give in or over to a
   superior force   Synonyms: accede, surrender, capitulate,
   buckle

irrevocably (ih <u>reh</u> vuk kuh blee) *adv.*   in a manner
   impossible to reverse or retract   Synonyms: irreversibly,
   permanently, inexorably

inevitable (ihn <u>eh</u> viht uh buhl) *adj.*   impossible to avoid;
   certain to occur   Synonyms: destined, inescapable,
   obligatory, ordained

material and strange shelter places. And scattered about it, some in their overturned war-machines, some in the now rigid handling-machines, and a dozen of them stark and silent and laid in a row, were the Martians—*dead!*—slain by the putrefactive and disease bacteria against which their systems were unprepared; slain as the red weed was being slain; slain, after all man's devices had failed, by the humblest things that God, in his wisdom, has put upon this earth.

For so it had come about, as indeed I and many men might have foreseen had not terror and disaster blinded our minds. These germs of disease have taken toll of humanity since the beginning of things—taken toll of our prehuman ancestors since life began here. But by virtue of this natural selection of our kind we have developed resisting power; to no germs do we **succumb** without a struggle, and to many—those that cause putrefaction in dead matter, for instance—our living frames are altogether immune. But there are no bacteria in Mars, and directly these invaders arrived, directly they drank and fed, our microscopic allies began to work their overthrow. Already when I watched them they were **irrevocably** doomed, dying and rotting even as they went to and fro. It was **inevitable**. By the toll of a billion deaths man has bought his birthright of the earth, and it is his against all comers; it would still be his were the Martians ten times as mighty as they are. For neither do men live nor die in vain.

Here and there they were scattered, nearly fifty altogether, in that great gulf they had made, overtaken by a death that must have seemed to them as incomprehensible as any death could be. To me also at that time this death was incomprehensible. All I knew was that these things that had been alive and so terrible to men were dead. For a moment I believed that the destruction of Sennacherib had been repeated, that God had repented, that the Angel of Death had slain them in the night.

multitude (<u>muhl</u> tih tood) *n.*   a great quantity
   Synonyms: drove, horde, host, mass, throng

perpetually (puhr <u>peht</u> choo uh lee) *adv.*   without end
   or seeming to be without end   Synonyms: interminably,
   continually, everlastingly

sombre or **somber** (<u>sahm</u> buhr) *adj.*   marked by
   darkness, gloominess, or melancholy   Synonyms:
   dispiriting, doleful, drab, lugubrious, obscure, funereal

CHAPTER 8—DEAD LONDON

I stood staring into the pit, and my heart lightened gloriously, even as the rising sun struck the world to fire about me with his rays. The pit was still in darkness; the mighty engines, so great and wonderful in their power and complexity, so unearthly in their tortuous forms, rose weird and vague and strange out of the shadows towards the light. A **multitude** of dogs, I could hear, fought over the bodies that lay darkly in the depth of the pit, far below me. Across the pit on its farther lip, flat and vast and strange, lay the great flying-machine with which they had been experimenting upon our denser atmosphere when decay and death arrested them. Death had come not a day too soon. At the sound of a cawing overhead I looked up at the huge fighting-machine that would fight no more for ever, at the tattered red shreds of flesh that dripped down upon the overturned seats on the summit of Primrose Hill.

I turned and looked down the slope of the hill to where, enhaloed now in birds, stood those other two Martians that I had seen overnight, just as death had overtaken them. The one had died, even as it had been crying to its companions; perhaps it was the last to die, and its voice had gone on **perpetually** until the force of its machinery was exhausted. They glittered now, harmless tripod towers of shining metal, in the brightness of the rising sun.

All about the pit, and saved as by a miracle from everlasting destruction, stretched the great Mother of Cities. Those who have only seen London veiled in her **sombre** robes of smoke can scarcely imagine the naked clearness and beauty of the silent wilderness of houses.

Eastward, over the blackened ruins of the Albert Terrace and the splintered spire of the church, the sun blazed dazzling in a clear sky, and here and there some facet in the great wilderness of roofs caught the light and glared with a white intensity.

Northward were Kilburn and Hampsted, blue and crowded with houses; westward the great city was

multitudinous (muhl tih <u>tood</u> ih nuhs) *adj.*   existing
  in great quantity; consisting of numerous individuals
  Synonyms: abounding, abundant, profuse, myriad,
  multifarious, teeming

vacant (<u>vay</u> kihnt) *adj.*   without energy and focus;
  apathetic   Synonyms: empty, listless, lifeless

dimmed; and southward, beyond the Martians, the green waves of Regent's Park, the Langham Hotel, the dome of the Albert Hall, the Imperial Institute, and the giant mansions of the Brompton Road came out clear and little in the sunrise, the jagged ruins of Westminster rising hazily beyond. Far away and blue were the Surrey hills, and the towers of the Crystal Palace glittered like two silver rods. The dome of St. Paul's was dark against the sunrise, and injured, I saw for the first time, by a huge gaping cavity on its western side.

And as I looked at this wide expanse of houses and factories and churches, silent and abandoned; as I thought of the **multitudinous** hopes and efforts, the innumerable hosts of lives that had gone to build this human reef, and of the swift and ruthless destruction that had hung over it all; when I realised that the shadow had been rolled back, and that men might still live in the streets, and this dear vast dead city of mine be once more alive and powerful, I felt a wave of emotion that was near akin to tears.

The torment was over. Even that day the healing would begin. The survivors of the people scattered over the country—leaderless, lawless, foodless, like sheep without a shepherd—the thousands who had fled by sea, would begin to return; the pulse of life, growing stronger and stronger, would beat again in the empty streets and pour across the **vacant** squares. Whatever destruction was done, the hand of the destroyer was stayed. All the gaunt wrecks, the blackened skeletons of houses that stared so dismally at the sunlit grass of the hill, would presently be echoing with the hammers of the restorers and ringing with the tapping of their trowels. At the thought I extended my hands towards the sky and began thanking God. In a year, thought I—in a year. . .

With overwhelming force came the thought of myself, of my wife, and the old life of hope and tender helpfulness that had ceased for ever.

summit (suh miht) *n.*   the apex; the highest point or
   level   Synonyms: acme, apogee, culmination, climax

apprehension (aa pree <u>hehn</u> shuhn) *n.*   a feeling of
   uneasiness or dread concerning the future   Synonyms:
   alarm, disquiet, foreboding, trepidation, misgiving

illumination (ih loom ih <u>nay</u> shun) *n.*   the act of filling
   with light, clarity, or understanding   Synonyms: light,
   radiance, brilliance, enlightenment

CHAPTER NINE

WRECKAGE

And now comes the strangest thing in my story. Yet, perhaps, it is not altogether strange. I remember, clearly and coldly and vividly, all that I did that day until the time that I stood weeping and praising God upon the **summit** of Primrose Hill. And then I forget.

Of the next three days I know nothing. I have learned since that, so far from my being the first discoverer of the Martian overthrow, several such wanderers as myself had already discovered this on the previous night. One man—the first—had gone to St. Martin's-le-Grand, and, while I sheltered in the cabmen's hut, had contrived to telegraph to Paris. Thence the joyful news had flashed all over the world; a thousand cities, chilled by ghastly **apprehensions**, suddenly flashed into frantic **illuminations**; they knew of it in Dublin, Edinburgh, Manchester, Birmingham, at the time when I stood upon the verge of the pit. Already men, weeping with joy, as I have heard, shouting and staying their work to shake hands and shout, were making up trains, even as near as Crewe, to descend upon London. The church bells that had ceased a fortnight since suddenly caught the news, until all England was bell-ringing. Men on cycles, lean-faced, unkempt, scorched

gaunt (gawnt) *adj.* exceedingly thin Synonyms: emaciated, haggard, attenuated, cadaverous

demented (dih <u>mehn</u> tehd) *adj.* insane Synonyms: lunatic, mad, crazy, deranged

provocation (prah vuh <u>kay</u> shuhn) *n.* the act or instance of inciting to action, especially through negative means Synonyms: inducement, proviking, stimulus, taunt, harassment

wantonness (<u>wahn</u> tuhn nehs) *n.* the state of lacking restraint or chastity; immorality Synonyms: abandon, intemperance, impulsiveness, unrestraint

dissuade (dihs <u>wayd</u>) *v.* **-ing, -ed** to convince against a certain course of action Synonyms: deter, derail, disincline, exhort, remonstrate

CHAPTER 9—WRECKAGE

along every country lane shouting of unhoped deliverance, shouting to **gaunt**, staring figures of despair. And for the food! Across the Channel, across the Irish Sea, across the Atlantic, corn, bread, and meat were tearing to our relief. All the shipping in the world seemed going Londonward in those days. But of all this I have no memory. I drifted—a **demented** man. I found myself in a house of kindly people, who had found me on the third day wandering, weeping, and raving through the streets of St. John's Wood. They have told me since that I was singing some insane doggerel about "The Last Man Left Alive! Hurrah! The Last Man Left Alive!" Troubled as they were with their own affairs, these people, whose name, much as I would like to express my gratitude to them, I may not even give here, nevertheless cumbered themselves with me, sheltered me, and protected me from myself. Apparently they had learned something of my story from me during the days of my lapse.

Very gently, when my mind was assured again, did they break to me what they had learned of the fate of Leatherhead. Two days after I was imprisoned it had been destroyed, with every soul in it, by a Martian. He had swept it out of existence, as it seemed, without any **provocation**, as a boy might crush an ant hill, in the mere **wantonness** of power.

I was a lonely man, and they were very kind to me. I was a lonely man and a sad one, and they bore with me. I remained with them four days after my recovery. All that time I felt a vague, a growing craving to look once more on whatever remained of the little life that seemed so happy and bright in my past. It was a mere hopeless desire to feast upon my misery. They **dissuaded** me. They did all they could to divert me from this morbidity. But at last I could resist the impulse no longer, and, promising faithfully to return to them, and parting, as I will confess, from these four-day friends with tears, I went out again

melancholy (<u>mehl</u> uhn kah lee) *adj.*   markedly sad and despairing   Synonyms: despondent, funereal, lachrymose, somber

exultation (ehg zuhl <u>tay</u> shuhn) *n.*   a triumphant or blissful state   Synonyms: celebration, elation, jubilation, revelling

haggard (<u>haa</u> guhrd) *adj.*   worn and wearied in appearance   Synonyms: ashen, pallid, exhausted, fatigued

grotesque (groh <u>tehsk</u>) *adj.*   severely distorted or hideous in appearance   Synonyms: deformed, bizarre, outlandish, aberrant, malformed

flaunt (flawnt) *v.* **-ing, -ed**   to put on shameless display   Synonyms: show off, advertise, broadcast, vaunt

transfix (traanz <u>fihks</u>) *v.* **-ing, -ed**   to engross so completely as to render motionless   Synonyms: captivate, mesmerize, hypnotize, spellbind

placard (<u>plaa</u> kuhrd) *n.*   a small sign or notice for public display of information   Synonyms: notice, ad, display, poster into the streets that had lately been so dark and strange and empty.

Already they were busy with returning people; in places even there were shops open, and I saw a drinking fountain running water.

I remember how mockingly bright the day seemed as I went back on my **melancholy** pilgrimage to the little house at Woking, how busy the streets and vivid the moving life about me. So many people were abroad everywhere, busied in a thousand activities, that it seemed incredible that any great proportion of the population could have been slain. But then I noticed how yellow were the skins of the people I met, how shaggy the hair of the men, how large and bright their eyes, and that every other man still wore his dirty rags. Their faces seemed all with one of two expressions—a leaping **exultation** and energy or a grim resolution. Save for the expression of the faces, London seemed a city of tramps. The vestries were indiscriminately distributing bread sent us by the French government. The ribs of the few horses showed dismally. **Haggard** special constables with white badges stood at the corners of every street. I saw little of the mischief wrought by the Martians until I reached Wellington Street, and there I saw the red weed clambering over the buttresses of Waterloo Bridge.

At the corner of the bridge, too, I saw one of the common contrasts of that **grotesque** time—a sheet of paper **flaunting** against a thicket of the red weed, **transfixed** by a stick that kept it in place. It was the **placard** of the first newspaper to resume publication—the *Daily Mail*. I bought a copy for a blackened shilling I found in my pocket. Most of it was in blank, but the solitary compositor who did the thing had amused himself by making a grotesque scheme of advertisement stereo on the back page. The matter he printed was emotional; the news organisation had not as yet found its way back. I learned nothing fresh except that already in one week the examination of the Martian mechanisms had yielded astonishing

terminus (<u>tuhr</u> mihn uhs) *n.*   the end point, especially in reference to a transportation system

gaunt (gawnt) *adj.*   exceedingly thin   Synonyms: emaciated, haggard, attenuated, cadaverous results. Among other things, the article assured me what I did not believe at the time, that the "Secret of Flying" was discovered. At Waterloo I found the free trains that were taking people to their homes. The first rush was already over. There were few people in the train, and I was in no mood for casual conversation. I got a compartment to myself, and sat with folded arms, looking greyly at the sunlit devastation that flowed past the windows. And just outside the **terminus** the train jolted over temporary rails, and on either side of the railway the houses were blackened ruins. To Clapham Junction the face of London was grimy with powder of the Black Smoke, in spite of two days of thunderstorms and rain, and at Clapham Junction the line had been wrecked again; there were hundreds of out-of-work clerks and shopmen working side by side with the customary navvies, and we were jolted over a hasty relaying.

All down the line from there the aspect of the country was **gaunt** and unfamiliar; Wimbledon particularly had suffered. Walton, by virtue of its unburned pine woods, seemed the least hurt of any place along the line. The Wandle, the Mole, every little stream, was a heaped mass of red weed, in appearance between butcher's meat and pickled cabbage. The Surrey pine woods were too dry, however, for the festoons of the red climber. Beyond Wimbledon, within sight of the line, in certain nursery grounds, were the heaped masses of earth about the sixth cylinder. A number of people were standing about it, and some sappers were busy in the midst of it. Over it flaunted a Union Jack, flapping cheerfully in the morning breeze. The nursery grounds were everywhere crimson with the weed, a wide expanse of livid colour cut with purple shadows, and very painful to the eye. One's gaze went with infinite relief from the scorched greys and sullen reds of the foreground to the blue-green softness of the eastward hills.

381

vestige (<u>veh</u> stihj) *n.*   a visible trace of that which is no longer present, especially in the case of an obsolete part, organ, or system   Synonyms: sign, token, trace, residue, remnant

catastrophe (kaa <u>taa</u> struh fee) *n.*   an incident that results in overwhelming loss, often occurring suddenly Synonyms: debacle, fiasco, calamity, devastation, cataclysm

CHAPTER 9—WRECKAGE

The line on the London side of Woking station was still undergoing repair, so I descended at Byfleet station and took the road to Maybury, past the place where I and the artilleryman had talked to the <u>hussars</u>, and on by the spot where the Martian had appeared to me in the thunderstorm. Here, moved by curiosity, I turned aside to find, among a tangle of red fronds, the warped and broken dog cart with the whitened bones of the horse scattered and gnawed. For a time I stood regarding these **vestiges**. . . .

Then I returned through the pine wood, neck-high with red weed here and there, to find the landlord of the Spotted Dog had already found burial, and so came home past the College Arms. A man standing at an open cottage door greeted me by name as I passed.

I looked at my house with a quick flash of hope that faded immediately. The door had been forced; it was unfast and was opening slowly as I approached.

It slammed again. The curtains of my study fluttered out of the open window from which I and the artilleryman had watched the dawn. No one had closed it since. The smashed bushes were just as I had left them nearly four weeks ago. I stumbled into the hall, and the house felt empty. The stair carpet was ruffled and discoloured where I had crouched, soaked to the skin from the thunderstorm the night of the **catastrophe**. Our muddy footsteps I saw still went up the stairs.

I followed them to my study, and found lying on my writing-table still, with the selenite paper weight upon it, the sheet of work I had left on the afternoon of the opening of the cylinder. For a space I stood reading over my abandoned arguments. It was a paper on the probable development of Moral Ideas with the development of the civilising process; and the last sentence was the opening of a prophecy: "In about two hundred years," I had written, "we may expect—" The sentence ended abruptly. I remembered my inability to fix my mind that morning, scarcely a month gone by, and how I had broken off to

desolate (<u>deh</u> suh liht) *adj.* uninhabited; unfit for habitation Synonyms: barren, unfrequented, vacant, waste get my *Daily Chronicle* from the newsboy. I remembered how I went down to the garden gate as he came along, and how I had listened to his odd story of "Men from Mars."

I came down and went into the dining room. There were the mutton and the bread, both far gone now in decay, and a beer bottle overturned, just as I and the artilleryman had left them. My home was **desolate**. I perceived the folly of the faint hope I had cherished so long. And then a strange thing occurred. "It is no use," said a voice. "The house is deserted. No one has been here these ten days. Do not stay here to torment yourself. No one escaped but you."

I was startled. Had I spoken my thought aloud? I turned, and the French window was open behind me. I made a step to it, and stood looking out.

And there, amazed and afraid, even as I stood amazed and afraid, were my cousin and my wife—my wife white and tearless. She gave a faint cry.

"I came," she said. "I knew—knew—"

She put her hand to her throat—swayed. I made a step forward, and caught her in my arms.

speculative (<u>spehk</u> yoo lah tihv) *adj.*   based upon
  conjecture   Synonyms: conjectural, theoretical, hypothetical, notional

physiology (fihz ee <u>ah</u> luh jee) *n.*   the study of living
  organisms and their interrelated parts

perpetrate (<u>puhr</u> pih trayt) *v.* **-ing, -ed**   to carry out a
  particular act   Synonyms: commit, effect, execute

CHAPTER TEN

THE EPILOGUE

I cannot but regret, now that I am concluding my story, how little I am able to contribute to the discussion of the many debatable questions which are still unsettled. In one respect I shall certainly provoke criticism. My particular province is **speculative** philosophy. My knowledge of comparative **physiology** is confined to a book or two, but it seems to me that Carver's suggestions as to the reason of the rapid death of the Martians is so probable as to be regarded almost as a proven conclusion. I have assumed that in the body of my narrative.

At any rate, in all the bodies of the Martians that were examined after the war, no bacteria except those already known as terrestrial species were found. That they did not bury any of their dead, and the reckless slaughter they **perpetrated**, point also to an entire ignorance of the putrefactive process. But probable as this seems, it is by no means a proven conclusion.

Neither is the composition of the Black Smoke known, which the Martians used with such deadly effect, and the generator of the Heat-Rays remains a puzzle. The terrible disasters at the Ealing and South Kensington laboratories have disinclined analysts for further investigations upon

constituent (kuhn <u>stihch</u> oo ihnt) *n.* a part of a greater whole Synonyms: element, component

physiology (fihz ee <u>ah</u> luh jee) *n.* the study of living organisms and their interrelated parts

CHAPTER 10—THE EPILOGUE

the latter. Spectrum analysis of the black powder points unmistakably to the presence of an unknown element with a brilliant group of three lines in the green, and it is possible that it combines with argon to form a compound which acts at once with deadly effect upon some **constituent** in the blood. But such unproven speculations will scarcely be of interest to the general reader, to whom this story is addressed. None of the brown scum that drifted down the Thames after the destruction of Shepperton was examined at the time, and now none is forthcoming.

The results of an anatomical examination of the Martians, so far as the prowling dogs had left such an examination possible, I have already given. But everyone is familiar with the magnificent and almost complete specimen in spirits at the Natural History Museum, and the countless drawings that have been made from it; and beyond that the interest of their **physiology** and structure is purely scientific.

A question of graver and universal interest is the possibility of another attack from the Martians. I do not think that nearly enough attention is being given to this aspect of the matter. At present the planet Mars is in conjunction, but with every return to opposition I, for one, anticipate a renewal of their adventure. In any case, we should be prepared. It seems to me that it should be possible to define the position of the gun from which the shots are discharged, to keep a sustained watch upon this part of the planet, and to anticipate the arrival of the next attack.

In that case the cylinder might be destroyed with dynamite or artillery before it was sufficiently cool for the Martians to emerge, or they might be butchered by means of guns so soon as the screw opened. It seems to me that they have lost a vast advantage in the failure of their first surprise. Possibly they see it in the same light.

Lessing has advanced excellent reasons for supposing that the Martians have actually succeeded in effecting

THE WAR OF THE WORLDS

luminous (<u>loo</u> mihn uhs) *adj.* 1. emitting light; glowing Synonyms: brilliant, lustrous, incandescent, refulgent 2. intelligent and easily understood Synonyms: lucid, perspicacious, comprehensible

sinuous (<u>sihn</u> yoo uhs) *adj.* consisting of many twists and turns; winding Synonyms: circuitous, meandering, anfractuous, tortuous

simultaneously (sie muhl <u>tay</u> nee uhs lee) *adv.* at the same time Synonyms: concurrently, synchronically

serene (suh <u>reen</u>) *adj.* calm in the face of disturbance or difficulty Synonyms: unruffled, composed, self-possessed

decadence (<u>deh</u> kuh dehns) *n.* a state of decline or moral deterioration Synonyms: degradation, dissolution, debasement, degeneracy

scrutiny (<u>scroo</u> tih nee) *n.* close and careful examination, observation, or study Synonyms: analysis, inquiry, perlustration, inspection

apprehension (aa pree <u>hehn</u> shuhn) *n.* a feeling of uneasiness or dread concerning the future Synonyms: alarm, disquiet, foreboding, trepidation, misgiving

persuasion (puhr <u>sway</u> zhuhn) *n.* a belief firmly held; a conviction Synonyms: certitude, opinion, partiality, predilection

minute (mie <u>noot</u>) *adj.* especially small, barely noticeable Synonyms: miniscule, tiny, diminutive, infinitesimal

390

a landing on the planet Venus. Seven months ago now, Venus and Mars were in alignment with the sun; that is to say, Mars was in opposition from the point of view of an observer on Venus. Subsequently a peculiar **luminous** and **sinuous** marking appeared on the unillumined half of the inner planet, and almost **simultaneously** a faint dark mark of a similar sinuous character was detected upon a photograph of the Martian disk. One needs to see the drawings of these appearances in order to appreciate fully their remarkable resemblance in character.

At any rate, whether we expect another invasion or not, our views of the human future must be greatly modified by these events. We have learned now that we cannot regard this planet as being fenced in and a secure abiding place for Man; we can never anticipate the unseen good or evil that may come upon us suddenly out of space. It may be that in the larger design of the universe this invasion from Mars is not without its ultimate benefit for men; it has robbed us of that **serene** confidence in the future which is the most fruitful source of **decadence**, the gifts to human science it has brought are enormous, and it has done much to promote the conception of the commonweal of mankind. It may be that across the immensity of space the Martians have watched the fate of these pioneers of theirs and learned their lesson, and that on the planet Venus they have found a securer settlement. Be that as it may, for many years yet there will certainly be no relaxation of the eager **scrutiny** of the Martian disk, and those fiery darts of the sky, the shooting stars, will bring with them as they fall an unavoidable **apprehension** to all the sons of men.

The broadening of men's views that has resulted can scarcely be exaggerated. Before the cylinder fell there was a general **persuasion** that through all the deep of space no life existed beyond the petty surface of our **minute** sphere. Now we see further. If the Martians can reach Venus, there is no reason to suppose that the thing is impossible

conjure (<u>kahn</u> joor) *v.* **-ing, -ed**   to summon or affect as if by magic   Synonyms: entrance, invoke, raise, rouse

inanimate (ihn <u>ann</u> ih miht) *adj.*   1. lacking in energy or activity   Synonyms: dull, inert, inactive, quiescent   2. nonliving   Synonyms: barren, defunct

writhe (rieth) *v.* **-ing, -ed**   to twist and contort, especially when caused by pain or struggle   Synonyms: distort, thrash, wriggle

desolate (<u>deh</u> suh liht) *adj.*   uninhabited; unfit for habitation   Synonyms: barren, unfrequented, vacant, waste

vague (vayg) *adj.*   without definite shape, form, or expression   Synonyms: ambiguous, hazy, nebulous, indefinite, tenebrous

contort (kuhn <u>tort</u>) *v.* **-ing, -ed**   to bend out of shape   Synonyms: distort, convolute, gnarl, misshape, warp

multitude (<u>muhl</u> tih tood) *n.*   a great quantity   Synonyms: drove, horde, host, mass, throng for men, and when the slow cooling of the sun makes this earth uninhabitable, as at last it must do, it may be that the thread of life that has begun here will have streamed out and caught our sister planet within its toils.

Dim and wonderful is the vision I have **conjured** up in my mind of life spreading slowly from this little seed bed of the solar system throughout the **inanimate** vastness of sidereal space. But that is a remote dream. It may be, on the other hand, that the destruction of the Martians is only a reprieve. To them, and not to us, perhaps, is the future ordained.

I must confess the stress and danger of the time have left an abiding sense of doubt and insecurity in my mind. I sit in my study writing by lamplight, and suddenly I see again the healing valley below set with **writhing** flames, and feel the house behind and about me empty and **desolate**. I go out into the Byfleet Road, and vehicles pass me, a butcher boy in a cart, a cabful of visitors, a workman on a bicycle, children going to school, and suddenly they become **vague** and unreal, and I hurry again with the artilleryman through the hot, brooding silence. Of a night I see the black powder darkening the silent streets, and the **contorted** bodies shrouded in that layer; they rise upon me tattered and dog-bitten. They gibber and grow fiercer, paler, uglier, mad distortions of humanity at last, and I wake, cold and wretched, in the darkness of the night.

I go to London and see the busy **multitudes** in Fleet Street and the Strand, and it comes across my mind that they are but the ghosts of the past, haunting the streets that I have seen silent and wretched, going to and fro, phantasms in a dead city, the mockery of life in a galvanised body. And strange, too, it is to stand on Primrose Hill, as I did but a day before writing this last chapter, to see the great province of houses, dim and blue through the haze of the smoke and mist, vanishing at last into the vague lower sky, to see the people walking to and fro among the flower beds on the hill, to see the sight-seers

tumult (<u>tuh</u> muhlt) *n.* commotion, disturbance, and noise, as of a crowd uproar, clamor, row Synonyms: agitation, bedlam, about the Martian machine that stands there still, to hear the **tumult** of playing children, and to recall the time when I saw it all bright and clear-cut, hard and silent, under the dawn of that last great day. . . .

And strangest of all is it to hold my wife's hand again, and to think that I have counted her, and that she has counted me, among the dead.

GLOSSARY

afterglow (aaf tuhr gloh) *n.*
a lingering sense, especially of light, energy, or pleasantness

alight (uh liet) *v.* -ing, -ed
to come to rest, especially after a flight

battery (baa tuh ree) *n.*
an artillery unit

bolt (bohlt) *v.* -ing, -ed
to run away; flee

bulwark (buhl wuhrk) *n.*
a rampart; a raised wall or embankment used for purposes of defense

cannonade (kaa nuh nayd) *n.*
a period of heavy, continuous gunfire

chaise (chays) *n.*
a light, horse-drawn carriage

collier (kah lee uhr) *n.*
a coal miner

cope (kohp) *n.*
a long cloak

copse (kahps) *n.*
a cluster of small trees

cordon (kor duhn) *n.*
a line of personnel or vehicles that encloses and guards a particular area   Synonyms: perimeter

cowl (kaawl) *n.*
a hood or other garment used to cover the head

cumulus (kyoo myoo lihs) *adj.*
a type of cloud characterized by roundness and fluffiness

darkling (dahr klihng) *adj.*
in darkness or indistinctness

eddy (eh dee) *n.*
a movement contrary to the prevailing direction

ejaculate (ee jaak yoo layt) *v.* **-ing, -ed**
to speak suddenly and forcefully Synonyms: exclaim,
  bellow, squawk, vociferate

en masse (ahn mahs) *adv.*
as a single group; all together

erethism (ihr ee thihz uhm) *n.*
a pronounced and atypical sensitivity to stimulation

estuary (eh schoo eh ree) *n.*
the point at which a river meets the sea

flaunt (flowt) *v.* **-ing, -ed**
to display in open disregard of a rule or law

forthwith (fohrth wihth) *adv.*
without delay; immediately

fungoid (fuhn goyd) *adj.*
pertaining to or resembling a fungus

gloaming (gloh mihng) *n.*
dusk; twilight

gride (gried) *v.* **-ing, -ed**
to cut with a harsh, grating sound

hamstring (haam strihng) *v.*
to render completely ineffective

GLOSSARY

hansom (haan suhm) *n.*
a horse-drawn covered carriage, in which the driver is
  positioned above and behind the passengers

headlong (hehd long) *adj.*
headfirst; in a rash or bold manner

heliograph (hee lee oh graaf) *n.*
a device consisting of a surface that transmits messages
  by reflecting sunlight

hither and thither (hih thuhr, thih thuhr) *adj.*
here and there

hussar (huh saar) *n.*
a member of the cavalry

in vain *idiom*
unsuccessfully; without achievement of the desired outcome

kopje (kahp jeh) *n.*
a small hill or embankment

lord v. -ing, -ed
to dominate; to treat as though a servant

Maxim (maaks ihm) *n.*
a type of automatic machine gun used extensively during
  World War I

meteor (mee tee ohr) *n.*
the bright streak of light left in the sky after an object
  disintegrates in the Earth's atmosphere

overtake (oh vuhr tayk) *v.*
to catch up with a pass while traveling in the same direction

parabolic (paa ruh bohl ihk) *adj.*
taking the form or shape of a parabola; U-shaped

parapet (paa ruh peht) *n.*
a protective railing or embankment Synonyms: bulwark,
  bastion, barrier, safeguard

paroxysm (paa rahk sihz uhm) *n.*
a sudden and energetic occurrence

portmanteau (pohrt maan toh) *n.*
a large briefcase or suitcase that opens into separate
  compartments

presently (preh zehnt lee) *adv.*
current usage: very soon
  archaic: immediately

privet (prih veht) *n.*
a type of shrub, often used for hedges

promenader (prah muh nay duhr) *n.*
one on a leisurely walk, especially for purposes of social
  display

pugilistic (pyoo jih lih stihk) *adj.*
related to boxing

pursuant (puhr soo ehnt) *adj.*
in accordance with

sally (saa lee) *n.*
a sudden rushing or leaping forth

smoulder or **smolder** (smohl duhr) *v.* **-ing, -ed**
burning slowly and without flame

sovereign (sah vrihn) *n.*
a coin formerly in use in Great Britain

squadron (skwah druhn) *n.*
an armored military unit

stile (stiel)
a crossing, usually steps or stairs, over a fence or wall

tally (tah lee) *v.* **-ing, -ied**
to be equivalent; to agree

termini (tuhr mee nee) *n.*
the convergence of the end points of a number of railway lines on a single station

tidings (tie dihngz) *n.*
items of news or information

tocsin (tahk sihn) *n.*
an alarm or warning; an instrument used to sound an alarm

tramp (traamp) *n.*
a vagabond

ululation (oo loo lay shuhn) *n.*
a loud wail or cry

wayfarer (way fay ruhr) *n.*
one traveling on foot

wayside (way sied) *n.*
the side of a road or passage

weal (weel) *n.*
a raised area, especially a bruise

whither (wih thuhr) *adv.*
to what position, place, or condition

wont (wahnt) *adj.*
likely; used to

INDEX

INDEX

THE WAR OF THE WORLDS

INDEX